SERPENT BOX

A NOVEL

SERPENT BOX

VINCENT LOUIS CARRELLA

HARPER ● PERENNIAL

NEW YORK ● LONDON ● TORONTO ● SYDNEY ● NEW DELHI ● AUCKLAND

HARPER  PERENNIAL

P.S.™ is a trademark of HarperCollins Publishers.

FIRST EDITION

Designed by Mary Austin Speaker

Library of Congress Cataloging-in-Publication Data is available upon request.

ISBN 978-0-06-112626-0

08 09 10 11 12 ID/RRD 10 9 8 7 6 5 4 3 2 1

For Beverly

But now thus saith the Lord that created thee, O Jacob, and he that formed thee, Fear not: for I have redeemed thee, I have called thee by thy name; thou art mine.

ISAIAH 43:1

CONTENTS

SERPENT BOX

PREFACE: SNAKE CHILD

They tell stories about a boy who was born right here on this mountain, a child of the hollows, a child of the mists. His daddy was a snake preacher who had the eyes of a reptile himself, and his momma was a simple wife. They lived over in Leatherwood, where the Sequatchie River runs into the Tennessee. This was in 1936, the same year the Sequatchie flooded, and not so long ago.

They said he was a gift left by the storm and called him the son of the rain. He could wash a soul clean with just one tear from that big eye he had, and oh, could that big eye see—right through to a man's heart. That boy could find the good in anybody, and there were some who said he was a right gift from God. But they didn't start saying that until much later. In the beginning, he was beaten and he was scorned.

The story they tell about his coming speaks of a lightning-cursed birth in a hanging tree. They say he came in on a whirlwind, born feetfirst in a tornado inside that old Tyborn oak where the wolf dogs found him in the woods, guarded by black serpents in a tree-hole manger and branded by God with a thunderbolt tattoo. He was a prophet, they say, baptized by blood and protected by rain, a Holy Ghost baby who tamed his first snake two days out of the womb. And the wonders he did do. That boy could talk to Jesus and see the walking spirits of those who passed. His dreams foretold the future and his visions came straight from God. And he could tame serpents, Lord, could he tame them, and drink poison. He could pull cancer out of a body without drawing a drop of blood. And some claim he could raise the dead.

Snake child, they called him, son of adder, boy of asps, those solitary creatures whom the Lord Himself hath scorned. He had himself a blessing and a curse, doomed by stars and marked by planets, to go lightly with fear, to be admired only at safe distance for the way he moved and the way he shone, and surely his true self would never be known nor understood. But he feared not, that boy, for though the devil himself rode at his shoulder the one true God, Jesus, and the Holy Ghost thrived in his heart and showed him great answers with small signs and humble leavings. He paid this world close attention. He ignored not a single grain of sand. His gift was greater than most can bear, to see such small things, being so close to the ground as he was, and endowed with senses finely tuned to the tiniest movement and changes in heat. The pain of the world, the pain of man, that's what he felt inside him. In the end, he bore it hard. Mountain people are prone to much exaggeration, but I know this much is true: Jacob Flint was a true holiness child who did his greatest deeds in ways and places people never did see. I know he was real, for that boy was my brother and he gave me my life.

DJL

Daniel Jacob Lee

BOOK I

The Tyborn Tree

1

TOAD

It is still that part of the morning before the mist rises, in the time of ocher and amber and blue light that glows at the edges of things. Golden comes the sun through the ground clouds like a Bible picture.

Jacob Flint, a boy of nine summers, a boy of oddly shaped bones, whose large left eye seems to swirl in the socket of a head that, at a distance, appears to have been carved from a rough potato. It has that same organic, subterranean quality that earned him such names as Spud and Toad and Newt and Hog. There is no end to what he resembles from the very earth from which he sprang.

He stands alone now against a sycamore tree that is as small and crooked as himself, in the far corner of the play yard at the Toe Heel School in Leatherwood, watching the mist swirl above the ankles of the other boys, whose recent scorn has cast him again to the outskirts of the field. Here, the boys pay him no mind. They fight playfully among themselves over a handmade ball and thus pay him no mind. For the moment, he is invisible.

The ball is made of a rich brown hide stuffed with straw and sewn together with sinew. It wobbles in the air and careens off their fingertips. It flies off in his direction, vanishing beneath the mist and rolling unseen to his feet. They turn. Suddenly he is no longer the invisible boy.

He was at one moment part of the tree, part of the mist. Jacob Flint, part of the earth, part of the stone. A shard of ancient rock. A crude thing hammered out with the slow and deliberate chipping motion of a human hand. The jagged son of dust and chert. And now the eyes of the boys are upon him. They watch to see what he will do, if he will stand or if he will run. But they're not the only ones poised there waiting, watching, to see what he might do—his sister is in the tire swing, spinning slow, holding the rope in both hands and leaning up over the top of the tire to see if her little brother will stand or run.

Magdalena Flint can lick them all together if need be, she can swoop in like a hawk and save him the way she's done, and done, and the way she wants to do now. It's been hard for her to keep her oath to him, to keep her distance, to let him fend for himself. A man must fend for himself. But he will not have her protect him anymore. Tomorrow he will be a boy of ten summers, and perhaps, soon, a man of one. If what his daddy says is true, that manhood is not something you do, but something that is done to you, it could happen. So maybe it will come. It could come anytime. Ten is so close. It could come. It could come now if he stands and does not run. A man must fend.

The boys watch him. Jacob stoops down to pick up the ball. He pulls it out of the mist and holds it up to the light as if it was something he had discovered in a nest, and he holds it up for them to see in a gesture meant to claim it as his own. One of the boys steps forward. He is not the biggest of the bunch but he is by far the worst.

The Toad done got it, he says. Give it here, Toad.

They call him this a lot now. Because of his eye. He has not grown into his big eye as some have promised, and of all the names that are not his own this is the name that's stuck. It is not the worst thing he is called, only the most physically descriptive, the most relevant, and thus the most painful. You cannot run from what is true.

Jacob holds the ball. The hide is smooth beyond the stitching, and worn clean, and cracked in places, and it's cool and smooth like a good baseball glove, like the pocket of an old and trusted mitt. It feels good just to hold it.

I said give it, Toad, says the boy. The worst boy. Jude Acheson, with those Chinese eyes of his, and that flat pig nose, and all them square little goat teeth that bit Jacob once to the bone, the scar still there on his finger that holds the ball that feels so nice to hold. The other boys mumble and look to see what he will do. The tire swing is empty and spinning fast. Jude Acheson reaches down into the mist to pick up a walnut-sized stone.

Toad don't learn, he says. Do he?

Go get him, Jude.

Squish the Toad.

Jacob waits, too. He waits to see what he himself might do. His mind tells him to stand and fight, but his body wants to run. Why should this time be any different?

Toad, you got two seconds to find yourself some smarts.

Why not now? Jacob thinks. Why can't it happen now?

The stone comes at him like it was shot from a gun. It makes an audible pop when it strikes him in the head, just above his eye. Jacob drops to his knees. He sees stars. But he does not falter. He puts his fingers to his head and feels a small trickle of blood. He does not drop the ball. Jude Acheson stoops down for another stone.

You want it again, Toad? I can hit that big eye of yours. I been practicing for that.

Go get him, Jude.

Squish the Toad.

Kill the Toad.

I ain't gonna, Jude says. Let the Toad come to me. Come or run, Toad.

Jacob's head rings. Come or run, come or run. Purple stars, white hot specks that dance and swirl like gnats around his face, his whole head. He wants to fight, but he wants to fight a fight, not bring the fight. To move from safety, to close ground, to cover that ground, it might as well be a thousand miles and onto their ground. It is too much of a leap and his mind surrenders to his body that decision which to his body was never a decision at all. The body still suffers the pain that the mind has long since learned to ignore. The body turns and runs. Magdalena stands to face the boys.

Jacob runs into the woods, and who watches but the trees— his old and trusted bystanders calmly stoic at silent witness. Wahoos and willows. Birch trees like bones. Those white shafts alive amidst the wood gloom, their tiny leaves descending slow, swirling like the first flakes of winter quiet that speak of recent dead and the time of the dead, when all things must fall and wait, fall and wait. All things have their time. Seeds beget trees and boys beget men and trees beget boys, so what is the boy but a son of a seed if what they tell is true? He will go if ever he could find it. He will go the way he has planned, in the night, in the dark. He will go to the tree where he was born. He will bring with him a guardian serpent that winds and tightens and protects from harm. He will go and he will know. But now he runs. Again he is running. He's learned to run fast on his bad leg. He had to learn that skill or he would not have made it this far. Ten years tomorrow. Ten years tonight. At the stroke of midnight he adds a digit to himself. He doubles. He expands.

Two numbers define the boy, one and zero, zero and one. A code, a codex, an equation he's yet to cipher.

What did they say about me, Momma?

You know what they said.

Tell me again.

You were a miracle from thunder, you are the son of the rain, the way you came, the way you was born, too early in that place, with Daddy gone on his dream journey to his own mountain where he heard the Lord say you was coming. He said I had in me something wonderful that simply could not wait any longer to be born.

And what else?

The old woman, she said that you had the magic all right, that you got the spirit.

How'd she know?

She felt my belly. She said I was the acorn and you was the oak.

What else?

Baxter Dawes called you the prince of serpents, and Sylus, who you know killed a man just for looking at him, called you little Jesus.

I saved him, he said I did.

That's right. You had a light in you, like a firefly.

Like a lightning bug.

My lightning bug.

He runs and he runs, through the trees, through the woods, until the woods run out and the ground slopes up and the trees give way to mountain grasses taller than him so he cannot see beyond or above and he can no longer run. He paddles through the grasses, wading through tall weeds and wild sunflowers, parting the drooping heliotropes with swimming motions of his free hand, the mitt-brown ball held aloft like a prize. He cannot see the ground. Stumbling blindly through the mist, following the scent of wood smoke and carrion, the distant calls of gathering crows, he's lost among the switchgrass until he comes upon the beaten trail of his most recent tangent. He recrosses his own path and searches for a break, or some kind of landmark, moving toward a small gap on a narrow, broken track in the reeds, where he comes upon a sleeping deer who springs from her bed in a bounding leap that confounds him. He watches her tail flash and disappear into a meadow. He can feel the urgent pump, pump, pump of his heart.

He follows the deer's trail to a clearing on the mountainside, a great expanse of open meadow ringed with chinquapin and buckeye and a lone tree looming almost black against the sky. The Tyborn tree. A giant. The father of his dreams and visions, the reaper of stolen souls, the king of oaks. He knows this place. He's been here before, in a womb, in a dream, in a thousand dreams.

He approaches with caution, making his way past the branches that hang to the ground, and he sees something there, in the tree, above his head, a thing that sways limp and makes strange sounds. It stiffens him and his belly goes hot like death come a-knocking. It is a man. It was a man. A man hanging in the tree. There is the gentle creaking of a rope. He can smell it, a carrion smell, the cooling embers of a bonfire scraped together out of crate wood and mossy boughs. In the distance, the persistent cawing of gathering crows.

His head spins. His legs wobble, and, stricken with a sudden weakness, he falls to his knees. His fingers splay, on the trampled ground, that powdery earth that forms over time in places where crowds gather, where he can see the impressions made by the feet of men, children, and dogs. The breeze blows down from the north and rattles the dry leaves of the tree, moving the suspended corpse. It's a warm breeze that carries with it a pungent scent, luring hordes of blowflies that shroud the blackened figure in a ghostly curtain that ripples and hums, the droning of thousands of tiny wings. He breathes through his mouth to stanch the smell and manages to stand. He steps over the remains of charred wooden pallets. Protruding nails snag at his cuffs. He stands below the hanging man, in the remnants of the fire that still smolders. He watches him sway, trying to see who he is, but he cannot recognize the face, nor can he discern any distinguishable feature on the body. The hands have been severed, the offending axe buried in a nearby stump, its handle caked with pine resin and cocked toward the sky. The man's feet are missing and between his legs is an angry black wound with the flesh peeling off in thin, translucent layers like the wrappings of a nest constructed by paper wasps. If it were not for the smell and the flies he would swear this was just some window dummy torched by boys and strung up as a joke. He wishes it was, but wishing alone is not a powerful enough invocation to ward off such a terror, and he covers his eyes with the palms of his hands.

He does not breathe. He recites the Lord's Prayer in his head. But he cannot shut out the sound of the bones that rattle and clack in the branches, or the flies moaning like ghosts, and the body itself that crackles and ticks as it cools. The branch that holds the nameless man bobs slowly and the rope creaks like a ship as the body spins ever so slightly on an axis of blood-stained hemp. He can hear the chatter of the crows, which are closer and numerous, their clucks and caws a strange Nordic tongue.

He can see the man's teeth. He sees his tongue. He cannot believe that this is a man. It must be a dream, a manifestation of some darkness, or sin, or perhaps a vision of something yet to pass, yet he has the ball he stole from Jude Acheson in his hand. The ball is real. He can feel that, and the dull ache above his eye where the stone hit him less than an hour before.

On the man's back is a mass of sores and slashes. He's been burned from the feet to the waist, as if he was standing in fire. A denim shirt hangs from his shoulders in bloody tendrils like the hair of a rag doll, torn to pieces by a whip. One sleeve of the shirt is intact. The cuff is buttoned around a wrist cauterized by flame, and at the elbow, there's a homemade patch cut from a quilt and sewn with care and precision to cover a hole in the shirt. Somewhere he's seen this quilt, the pattern, he recognizes the needlework—the wiggle-stitch of Rebecca Flint, his own mother's signature stitch. The shirt is his father's. Was his father's. Who is this man? How can this be? He swoons.

I'll take no charity from you, the man says. I can work, Mrs. Flint, I surely can. I can dig holes and ditches and mines and wells. I can dig like a miner 'cause that's what I was 'fore I lost my own sweet Mercy and my boy Kish. My daddy was a real slave and I fought in a real war and I have here in my belly real German lead. I won't take no shirt lessen I work for it.

The name of the man is Cornelius Loop. Old Corny, the Leatherwood drunk. Jacob sees his face, his grin, his eyes big as boiled eggs. He remembers his smell, all fumey and sour, the essence of corn whiskey and leather. His long, thin, shaky fingers, his yellow nails drumming the bottom of a rusted coffee tin punctured with buckshot holes that he holds and shakes for pennies, old red paint and flecks of rust. For a penny he shows the boys the swollen belly scar that was his souvenir from the Krauts, that spun him like a top at Mailly-Maillet, and tells them terrible lies and disconnected truths of the great battles he fought in the first great war, where he killed men so close that he could see the color fade from their eyes like the spots off a dying perch. Old Corny. The way he gums down the little corn cakes Jacob gives him from his lunch pail, how he's always touching the smooth scar beneath his ragged shirt. An old shirt falling apart. A shirt in sinful tatters.

A tree can't sin, boy. A tree's just a tree. A tree don't do evil like a man does evil. It don't have no malice to it. It don't think no thoughts and it don't read no Bibles. And it ain't got no eyes to see, nor trade for what's done against the name of God. Jacob Flint, you are named after a man of tremendous faith, but you don't know what it means to live with such devotion.

He lived at the fishing hole, spending his days in the cool shade of a crude shack with a bamboo pole he waved like a dowser's wand above the still water to show how the line of the old rock wall dips under. He showed him the secret places. He showed him the forest of stumps where old lunkers and big black bass plump as dog pups lived in the crawdad hole.

Don't tell a soul. This is my place.

He always whispered when he was near the water.

That tree is your place now. You take it back from them, it's yours, but you got to share it with Bat Owens, and Walter Pike, and Clive Tiny Essler, and the Denton boy, who was fourteen when they lynched his mamma right up there beside him, which I seen when I was a boy no taller than you. And the others whose names you'll find inside. You'll see. But don't you be afraid 'cause it's your time now, and that's a place you got to go, Jacob Flint. Pay no mind to them boys. There's many shades of eyes you can't see till you look real close, and when you do, it's like the leaves of autumn and it never ends.

Cornelius Loop's face appears to him, forming itself slow, rising up from darkness and becoming known, like a turtle come up from the soft brown mud in the crawdad hole. He can see it, the two faces together, the one wrecked and the one whole, and the flesh becomes blood and the dead man becomes a live man and the stars fall, the white gnats that swirl up and turn other colors and dance around his head while his ears ring. He doesn't even feel himself fall. He hears a voice now that's not Cornelius Loop but some other.

It is I, be not afraid.

He sees himself as if in a dream.

2

DARK WAKINGS

I reach out in the darkness. I stretch my hand up and feel along the shelf for the flashlight. I turn on the switch so I can see the snakes. There's a hook-latch on the Bible room door that Daddy thinks is too high for me to reach, but it don't matter now because I float up, light as air, and I get in.

The Bible room is also the serpent room, and inside it's as cool as a cave, and dark too, with Bibles stacked all over the floors and on the wall. There are hundreds of Bibles that Daddy got before I was born. The gold letters on their spines sparkle in the beam of my light. Some are very old and written in Latin or Greek. Some are soldiers' Bibles, and there are ones that belonged to Indians too. Lots have family names and dates that mark when their souls passed into this world and back out again to the other, and Daddy says they're whole histories of generations dead and gone.

In the corner I can see the serpent boxes stacked like egg crates. They're all hand-carved with pictures and inscriptions and such. They're made of dark wood with lots of grain to it and hinged lids that open like the wings of a butterfly. Of course I go to the biggest box, for the biggest snake, which was Herodias until Baxter brought that new one in. She's as big as they come and loaded up with poison. Wicked as unwashed sin and real thick around the middle, like a husk of corn. She's as long as I am tall. I lift the box slow and easy and pass like a shadow through the back door and out under a moon bright as the sun itself, with the ground all blue and the trunks of the trees glowing under a billion other suns.

I keep to the dark places under the eaves of the house and out of the light of the moon. I drop below the rise near the root-cellar door and slip the snake into a gunnysack I hid, and then I glide over the ground on the balls of my feet, smooth as a cat. I run through the woods like a deer. My shadow pops up in odd places. In clearings and on trees, I float over the ferns, and flow over logs like a watery version of myself, seeping up the mountain against the very way things flow.

I jump right over the deadfall and into that old grove of birch. I can run all night. I can run. I run until I see a boulder that looks like an old ship. Just follow the bowline. And there's a thick patch of shrubs that I must pass through to get to Moss Creek. I find a hole of pure blackness under the big moon and I crawl inside like a snake and there's all kinds of beetles and big hairy spiders inside. And then I stumble over a thing that I know is not of this living world, so I turn on my light to see. It's a dead man, with his skin all brown and dry like paper and shrunken over his bones. His mouth's open and I can see his teeth and his hollow eyes looking up in sad terror at this world. But I'm not afraid.

I come out of the brambles, and the ground below me is soft and damp. I'm in a meadow with tall grass so fine and silver that it looks like it's covered in snow. In the meadow is a great big tree, all fat in the middle and twisted, with long branches that scrape the ground like the knuckles on a giant's hand. The snake goes stiff in the bag and I take it out to give it to the long branches. And I say, Thou could have no power against me except it were given thee from above. And it seems to hear me. I reach out and touch it, and I can feel the life in it, I can feel sadness and the pain. It knows me. And I calm it with my hand like it was a horse, and I speak to it.

Behold my hands, reach hither thy hand, be not faithless, believe.

Then I find the hole where Momma hid and I go inside. It's quiet. I can't hear anything outside, but I do hear a sound that comes from the tree itself. It's like a whoosh, it's like the ocean you hear inside a shell. I hear the sea. The tree knows that it's a place I want to go.

I loosen the sack cord and put my hands inside. I wrap my fingers around Herodias and hold her. From my toes to my ears I can feel that current of bliss and joy my daddy talks about when the spirit comes. The snake coils around my arm and slides up my shoulder. It tightens around my neck. I stare at its shiny black eyes, and it slides right into my mouth and down into my belly, where I can feel it like the whole of my guts gone loose. I fall on my face down into the dirt in the hollow of the tree where I was born.

Magdalena finds him lying beneath the tree, beneath the dead man himself, whose identity she already knows, since she was standing at the pickle barrel in Shuck's Mercantile when they came to take him away the day before. It was the Achesons of course, led by Jude's father, Clyde, so she knew right away what Old Corny's fate would be, and she knew that Jacob would have to be told. But she hoped to tell him herself when the time was right, before he went on his journey to the tree where she knew Old Corny would be waiting in a state of utter desecration.

As soon as he ran off into the woods she knew where

he'd go, even if he didn't know it himself. She felt it inside her just like that time she felt the big hail coming, and the whirlwind that came behind it out of a crazy yellow sky, and right down to the Croners' place, where it killed them all in their beds, sucking the house and the barn and the livestock up into a vortex that turned three generations of toil and blood into a cloud of splinters and dust. Sometimes she just knows.

She can see that he's breathing and, other than the cut over his eye, unhurt. Above him hangs a man who recognized in her brother a *like* soul, a blessed traveler, and a certain shine. To see him like this would have been a great shock, and she has seen what such a shock can do. He's had such episodes before. In times of great stress he's slipped into what they call his dark wakings, where he appears to be asleep yet his eyes don't close, they move back and forth like they do when he's dreaming and the only thing that can wake him is cold water. He's still holding the leather ball in his hand.

She pulls him out from under the tree and onto the soft grass beyond. She draws water from the creek in her cupped hands and drips it onto his head until he rouses. He blinks several times before the spark of recognition returns to his eyes.

Maggie, he says. I saw the tree.

I know, Jacob.

I saw a man in it, a dead man. Cornelius Loop was dead in that tree yonder.

It is so.

I was hoping it wasn't real.

I'm afraid it was. I saw them take him away.

Why would they do that? He doesn't bother anyone.

Something about chickens. They been going missing of late, and Surree Dern says she seen him do it. She came with them and said so. Pointed right at him and everything.

That woman's a known liar.

It's not like a lie ever stopped them before.

Jacob sits up and his eyes roll back for a moment. Magdalena takes his hands and holds them. She pats them the way one might do in the cold to get the blood flowing. Jacob sees that hers are dirty and scabbed. Her dress is torn at the hem.

What happened back at the school yard?

Nothing. I saw to it that justice was done.

You broke your promise.

I promised not to save you.

You've got to let me do things on my own.

You had your chance, she says. Come on now. Let's leave this place.

They cross the creek and bushwhack through the shrubs, avoiding the deadfall, and find the trail home. Two miles downhill, a slow go and both of them are tired and sore. Magdalena's knees are scraped and bruised.

So you've seen, she says.

What?

You know what.

Maybe I do.

You know.

I didn't see what I came for.

You shouldn't have gone.

I'm going back.

You aren't.

You know I am.

She looks at his eyes and sees that it's true.

Yes, she says.

Will you still help me?

All my chores for a week.

A deal's a deal.

And you owe me the same if ever I need it.

Of course.

They walk in single file, with Jacob behind swatting at tall weeds with the end of a stick. Their shadows have gone long, and Jacob's stretches out with legs like a carnival tall man.

Will he still be there tonight? he asks.

Where else would he be?

Won't someone cut him down and bury him?

They usually wait till they fall down on their own. Then someone will bury him.

That was the worst thing I ever saw.

You shouldn't a seen it. A boy like you.

Will they bury him?

There's a place for them. A secret cemetery.

You been there?

I found it, yes.

I want to see it.

Not today.

Did you lick Jude? he asks.

He won't be back to school for a few days, I reckon.

And the others?

Smart enough to stand back and watch.

Why, Maggie? Why'd you do that?

You'd do the same for me.

I wouldn't.

You just say that 'cause you can't. But you don't know. You don't know what you'd do if they was wrongin' someone of your own. If they hurt someone. You don't know what it's like to have to stand back all the time while things are going on around you that you can't help. Always being told it ain't your place, always being told you're just a girl and to mind yourself.

She stops on the trail and turns to him.

I'm just not that way, she says. I'm not like Momma at all, like they say. I'm like Daddy. I'm more like Daddy than you. I got to do things. I can't hold myself back.

Who says I don't know what it's like to do nothing? Jacob says. Who says I don't know what it's like? I know. More than you can imagine.

I'm sorry. Of course you do.

Anyway, he says, I thank you for it.

You're welcome. Is that his ball?

It wasn't right to take it.

It isn't right to hit folks with rocks, neither.

Still. An eye for an eye, and another and another. Then what? You ever think of that?

Go on, then, give it back to him. See if I care.

They can see the house now, small and bright on the hill below. They see smoke rising up from the chimney and the grass blowing sideways in waves that make the hills turn myriad shades of green.

So you're going back, then? she says.

I said I was.

You say lots of things.

You know which ones are true and which ones aren't.

Yes.

You knew where I'd be.

Before you even ran.

How did you know?

Same way as you know that you got to go back. It comes from inside me.

I don't know anything.

You know you got to go back to the Tyborn tree.

I want to be inside of it, at midnight, when I turn ten.

What do you think will happen?

I don't know. I just want to be there.

What if he's still there?

It can't be worse than it was today. Before I saw that, I was nothing, I was sleeping, I was like an ant crawling on the ground. I heard about it, of course. I knew what they did up there. I don't know if I'll ever be the same as I was before.

It'll be dark.

Well, I have a light.

It'll be worse than it was today. Maybe I should come too.

Don't you dare follow me. This is a thing I have to do. Alone.

3

NO BETTER CLOCK THAN A CHILD

Charles Flint stares through the screens in the Bible room out to the low hills beyond the house where the road cuts through and rises to meet the woods beyond. His children come out of those woods. They descend slowly, and he wonders what makes them stop when they do, and what they're saying that requires a halt to say it. It's well past the time when they should have been home, and they're coming from the wrong direction. They're not on the road itself, but on the hill, on a tangent whose line, if he followed it, would lead straight to the tree, where Jacob's been forbidden to go. He is well aware of the date and the promises he's made on the eves of all his other birthdays since he first heard the story of his peculiar coming.

I'll take you when you're ready.

I am ready.

When you're older.

How much older?

When you hit the double digits.

Now is that time. Jacob won't wait for permission, and

Charles knows that the boy's planning to go, most likely tonight. He found a bag hidden by the root-cellar door, and a gunnysack with some food inside and some candles. He won't stop him because he cannot. He's always been the kind of boy who, once he's got something in his head, can never let it go till it's worked itself out. He's the kind of boy who's got to touch and feel things for himself. He touched fire once just to see if it was really hot. He touched dogs until one finally bit. He cut himself open with a knife to see if those blue roots in his arms were really tubes that carried blood. He has been bitten, he has been burned. Pain does not deter his son, nor does fear—which seems to fuel him as much as wonder itself. Both must be fed and quenched and conquered. He knows that Jacob fears the Tyborn tree, he knows that he wonders at it. There is only one thing left for him to do. Go. And Charles will let him.

They come in quietly through the back door. The kitchen is empty. They turn to each other, and Magdalena gestures with her chin toward the back of the house where she knows he has been watching them and where he's waiting still. She kisses his cheek and goes to her room. Jacob washes his hands and drinks two tall glasses of water. The absence of his momma in the kitchen at this hour is a mystery. There's nothing on the stove, and by now there should be. He goes to the Bible room and finds his father reading one of the larger Bibles.

Daddy, he says.

Hello, Jacob, he says. He does not look up from the Bible.

Can I ask you something?

You can ask me something.

What do they mean when they say a man's got to do what a man's got to do?

Charles places his finger on the page to mark his place, and he looks up at the boy and notices the welt above his eye.

It means, he says, that sometimes a man has to listen to what's inside of himself, and act upon what he hears.

Is it also true that a boy's got to do what a boy's got to do?

Charles closes the Bible and lays it on the shelf behind him.

The use of the word *man* is simply a matter of convenience. A person, any person, comes to certain points in his life when his path becomes so clear, or so limited, that there is but one course of action between him and some greater truth.

When will I be a man?

Well, such a thing is not measured by a particular point in time. Manhood is not measured by a moment, but by an accumulation of moments.

Jacob fiddles with a button on his coat. He's looking at the serpent boxes stacked along the wall, one on top of the other. The snakes are quiet because the room is cool.

How was school today? Charles asks.

Jacob does not hear the question. He's transfixed by the serpent boxes. There are twelve today. Sometimes there are as many as twenty. His father's not just a snake handler, he's also a snake dealer. Sometimes folks from other holiness churches come with money or things to trade. A man brought a scorpion one time, and they've traded snakes for chickens, dogs, and cows.

Which is the worst? Jacob asks.

The worst what? Didn't you hear me? I asked how was school?

School was fine. Which is the worst snake, the most dangerous?

It's hard to say. They're all dangerous. They're all wild. That one there on the bottom, Baxter calls him Lazarus. Swears he played dead like a possum and will do it when it's scared.

Jacob stares at the bottom box. It's made of dark wood and has carvings on the sides he can't make out. He tilts his head to see.

You ever see a man hung dead in a tree? he says.

Charles was not ready for the question. He knows such a question was inevitable, but it catches him off guard.

Where were you today? he says.

Someplace I never been before.

What did you see?

It was Cornelius. At first I couldn't tell, but then I knew.

Oh, Jacob. I hoped you'd never have to see such a thing. Of course I knew about it, everyone knows. Your momma's sick over it, she's been in her room since she heard. She took a shine to that old drunk.

He spoke to me, Jacob says.

I know. He was your friend.

No. He spoke to me today. Inside me. I heard him.

You're a sensitive boy. I know you hear things, voices. You get that from me, from my side.

Maybe I'm not so sensitive, Jacob says. Maybe everyone else just ain't sensitive enough.

That's the truth of it, Charles says. The world's gone blind to the ways of Cain.

The ways of us all, Jacob says. How could He do it? How could He make us that way?

Charles takes him by the shoulders and holds him there. He still looks so young. The boy's eyes are at once ancient and new. They're as piercing as any two eyes he's seen, and they seem to see what others cannot. There are so many things about his son he doesn't understand.

We are far from His perfection, Charles says. It's fear that makes us that way, it's doubt. Never fear, Jacob. Never lose faith that He will provide answers. Now go on and wash up. Your face is dirty, and that cut on your head needs some iodine. Get ready for dinner. I'm fixing it tonight, and you know what that means. Burnt meat.

I'm not hungry, Jacob says. And I'm real tired. If you don't mind I'll just go to my room.

A thing like that's not easy for a boy to see.

Is it easy for a man?

No. But the first time's the toughest. I've seen a grown man go into a shock.

What's that?

A state of numbness, like sleep.

Do you dream?

I don't know. Maybe.

All right, then. Good night, Daddy.

Good night, Jacob.

He watches him go and listens to him on the stairs, the weight of the boy on the wood, and he follows the sound of the creaking floorboards as he goes to his room. He's growing, he's bigger, and then there's the sound of the door as it shuts and the gentle click of the lock. Before you know it he's almost a man, and where does the time go? The Lord made no better clock than the child, and none more bitter. Oh, what beautiful clocks they are.

4

TREE TALK

There is no sleep for the boy who will be ten. There is only darkness and waiting in the darkness and listening to the sounds that an old house makes as it cools and settles and yields itself to a night that is but one in hundreds of thousands, for the house has stood in one form or another since before the war between the states. But the boy knows nothing of this, nor does he know that it too will soon mark a milestone in its own life. One hundred years the house has stood, and as Jacob rises and passes through, it is not silent, despite his efforts to map out the weak floorboards and all the creaks. The house seems to rise itself, to awake to his passing, and its wooden voice greets him on the stairs and in the hall and on the threshold where he stands before the Bible room door.

Twelve boxes. Twelve snakes. Jacob can see them there in the dark through the screen door; which is secured by the hook-latch he cannot reach—a vestige of caution from when he was smaller and more likely to wander into places he didn't belong. Places he was forbidden to go. Places, his daddy said, where he might die. Will he die at the tree? Not by the tree. The tree won't kill him—but will it protect him? Will Jesus? Will the Holy Ghost? All the holiness people say so. They say he glows with the aura of divine protection, and the miracle that is the spirit of the Lord covers his body like a second skin and flows through his veins in the blood of his heart. If they only knew that he cried at night. If they only knew that on those nights, when he dreams of the tree, he cries out for his momma and wets his bed. Not on this night. Never again. Ten is a magic number, for God gave us ten fingers to count with and ten toes to run and ten years to grow into our own. The old woman says, if you can live to ten you can live to a hundred, because by ten, everything you need to know you've already learned. How to wonder, how to fall, how to rise again. How to laugh and how to cry and how to find joy in the small things that don't seem to matter to the grown-up world of women and men. You find your true spirit by searching for it, by asking for it, by wanting it. Now is the time to test his spirit, to test his faith. Now is the moment to see if what they say is true and if what they say is what he is, then the snake will not harm him.

He'd take all the serpents with him if he could carry them, though he's never even touched one, never handled a snake in all his life because his daddy says he's not ready, that he's not strong enough in his spirit or belief. He's still too young, he says, and though he knows the Bible better than most grown men, and seems to understand the deeper meanings behind the words, he lacks the maturity required to invoke the powers they promise. But his daddy is wrong, and tomorrow he will know, they all will. If what the old woman says is true, he has nothing to fear but the fear. A man must fend.

Twelve boxes. There they sit. It's not late yet, but they're all in bed and the house is quiet. The serpents know he's come for them. They hear the footstool as he drops it at the door, making much more noise than he planned. The snakes stir.

Before he even raises the hook-latch, before he sneaks in, and just before he flicks on the flashlight, they already know which one he comes to take, for they all move in their boxes except the one. Jacob hears them rattle and scratch. Heavy serpent bodies. Thump, thump, thump. The hollow clunk of snake flesh on wood. He removes each box from the pile and stacks them again beside the bottom crate where Lazarus lies quiet as the dead.

The box is constructed from what his daddy calls a tropical hardwood. Mahogany. It's heavy and hard to lift, hard to hold, and the serpent is playing possum now; which is a comfort at that moment when he must prop the box on his knee in order to pull open the screen door to leave the Bible room.

In the parlor where the floorboards creak beneath him, despite his caution, despite his plans, he is less than silent as he passes before the staircase. The floor moans loud, and he turns to see a beam of light at the bottom of the bedroom door where his parents are not yet asleep. He moves to the hall, where the door latch clacks and the hinges squeal, and finally, out onto the porch, where he stumbles and almost drops the box. He's breathing heavy. The sky is clear and the moon is as bright as it was in his dream, so when he steps out into the yard he casts a long black shadow that Charles Flint sees from the window above the porch. He steps back so the boy won't notice him, and the boy does not. Jacob does not look back. Charles watches from behind a curtain. It is the last time he will see him as a boy. He will come back something different. Young still, but not a child.

On the rise below the house the old woman waits in her shawl with her pipe lit and the warm bowl in her hand, the same tiny hand that held the serpent up to Jacob's mouth when he was but two days old. Ninety-odd summers now, Gertie Bates has stood silent witness to the endless flow of celestial bodies above this place on earth, nights filled with passing suns en route to some flaming death in some nameless future, where all this means no more than a single flake of snow that fell here a thousand years before she was born. She raises the pipe to her lips and puffs on it. She stares up at the house and sees a shadow move.

Magdalena sees the shadow. It breaks the blue light of the moon below her bedroom window and drifts across the yard. The window is cool against her face and on the tips of her fingers. She drags them through the fog that her breath creates on the glass and she makes five parallel lines. The shadow moves between those lines, and there's a moment when she's not sure it's him and then there's a moment when she is. She sees him as he squats down near the root-cellar door and pulls something out of the weeds. A sack. He opens it and prepares it for its cargo. He moves the serpent box into position, arranging it just so, as if all this had been scripted. He waits. Maybe he's praying, but she cannot see his mouth. He's on his way, then, she thinks. When he returns in the morning he will have eclipsed her in his spirit.

He runs his hands along the sides of the serpent box. It is a container fashioned with great love and devotion by the snake hunter Baxter Dawes, who makes each box unique to the serpent it's designed for, each with its own personality, like the snakes themselves, who he claims to know as well as people know their dogs. There are words carved on the sides of the box and his fingers trace the letters. He can feel each bite of the tiny chisel. He reads the words in the dark like a blind boy reads braille.

Go ye into all the world. . . . Preach the gospel to every creature. . . . He that believeth shall be saved, he that believeth not shall be damned. . . . These signs shall follow them that believe. . . .

He runs his hands up the sides and to the top, where he finds the latch and opens it. The snake does not move. He opens one half of the lid. The snake still does not move. He slips the mouth of the sack around the opening of the box. No movement. When he tilts it, the snake slides neatly into the bag. He ties it off with a buckskin cord and hides the box in the weeds.

The old woman sings to herself in the dark and rocks gently on the balls of her feet. Jacob can smell her pipe smoke long before he catches sight of her. In the glow of the moon she appears like a statue made of glass, small and precious, still as stone, with a dull shine to her skin and a strange nimbus of light about her head that is the diffusion of moonbeams in her wispy, unkempt hair. She has her corncob pipe in her mouth and something in her hand, a bone or a stick, which she holds out and passes to him without so much as a word as he walks by. He takes it. It's not a bone but a scroll of some kind, a scroll of leather rolled up and tied with a string. He looks into her eyes for a moment and sees two tiny lights there, two tiny moons.

Go with God, Jacob Flint, she says. Go like smoke.

When he gets to the end of the road he turns to wave, but she's gone. He turns off into the woods.

It's much darker than he had imagined, even under the moon, which he sees sporadically and only in glades opened by fallen trees. In such places there's enough light to read by, and he stops to examine the leather scroll. It's a map. It shows the house where he lives and the old woman's cabin just below, with the road that runs by both and then the little path that leads into the woods. On the map the path is a broken black line drawn with the pointed end of a burnt stick that winds its way up the far side of the mountain for two good miles or more, and she's got various markers drawn alongside to help him find his way.

The prayer pine, the deadfall, ship rock, Moss Creek. It's a good thing he's seen these places in the light of day. But it's a good thing he's got the map.

He's in now what she calls the dark of the wood, a grove of ancient poplar where her own father came for the timbers that compose her little house. Harp Spring is the first marker on the map and he stops there for a drink. The snake lies still in the bag in his lap. He listens to the sound of the water in the spring for a while and moves on up the high rocky grade that the old woman calls the Steep.

It's a long climb. He makes his way along a ridgeline, over loose gravel and crumbling scree. He slips often and bloodies his free hand on the uphill side of the ridge. It's hard to imagine a pregnant woman doing this, but his momma had always been sure-footed and strong, and in those days had walked the five miles into town and back with relative ease. She liked to boast that on the day she gave birth to Magdalena she'd been working like a mule in the fields. Of course, it was different with him. He came into this world unexpectedly, before his time, which is what both the old woman and Baxter Dawes have been saying to him for as long as he can remember.

Jacob Flint, you were born out of time.

He climbs. Slow, steady, low to the ground like an ape, with his hair in his eyes and a rhythm in his head played slow and steady by heart and blood. He's almost at the crest of the ridge and above him he sees a wide swath of stars. He rounds a bend, and the trail levels out and opens up into a grassy box canyon blocked by a wall of toppled trees. The deadfall—a tangled mass of boulders and uprooted trunks with root-balls upturned and poking out like giant claws, the whole mess as big as a house and blocking his way up the mountain, an obstacle that didn't exist ten years ago. His momma could not have passed such a threshold. Had Jacob decided to wait one more day to enter the world, he might have been born in this very spot instead of in the tree, for the same storm that forced her to take shelter in that unlikely place washed out a hillside that flowed down through the canyon like the earth itself become animate and unleashed. And here it stopped and became itself again, with all its pieces mixed up and turned over so that man might see the fragile underpinnings of it all and be warned.

There seems to be no path through it, so he climbs, one-handed, and it is perilous. The gaps between the trees are deep and dark. A false step here would cast him down into the snarled clot of jagged branches and broken stones. He's thankful for the rough bark of the oaks that are part of this natural creation, for they give him a toehold and a grip. At the top of the deadfall he can see where the path forks below. To the left lies a beaten trail that leads into Leatherwood. It is the path he came up on earlier in the day without even realizing where he was going. To the right is the trail to the tree. He slides down on his behind, crossing from trunk to trunk crabwise, with his sack over his shoulder like some bindle stiff, alone and lost at the edge of the world. He moves on.

To his left there's a sheer granite face close enough to the trail for him to run his hand along its cool, damp flank. The wall flattens and rises to meet the grade. The trail doubles back in a tight loop, with a huge boulder perched above it that looks like a demasted galleon. Ship rock, the next landmark on the map. He stops and pulls out the light and unrolls the leather scroll. Beneath this spot she has written something.

Rest here.

He opens one of his wax-paper parcels and eats a sandwich. Dry ham, stale bread. The snake has not moved in the bag, and he worries that it might be dead. This thought consumes him. A dead snake will be of no use to the tree, though he's not sure what the tree will do with a living one. But he cannot come empty-handed. He must come bearing a gift, and bringing the tree a dead snake would be like bringing his mother a bunch of dead flowers. He reaches down and grabs hold of the burlap where it bulges, and the snake tenses and stiffens. It lives. He must be close now. The tree, the time, the snake. He feels it all. He moves on.

Farther up the trail he comes upon the prayer pine, which in the dark looks more manlike than he remembers, and terrifying, like something about to pounce. There's an Indian legend about a man who was a fierce killer, a fallen Cherokee warrior who became an outcast and a rogue in these mountains, living for years among the animals and preying on his own kind, stalking them, terrifying them for his banishment, which he came to believe to be part of a prophecy in which he was a small but crucial component. They called him Dead Bear because that's what he was to them, dead, whilst before he was Great Bear, like the stars in the night sky, now fallen and lost with nothing but his animal half left to fuel his anger and his pride. They could never catch him, and he lived for years on this mountain in fear of no man, for it was told that no man could kill him. And it was true—no man could. But there was a boy, whose name was Tomogi, Tree Planter, and for reasons as mysterious as this tale itself, that boy came looking for Dead Bear and found him sleeping on the rock where Jacob now stands and slew him just as he woke with a flint knife created for that one purpose. It was said that the boy was born for this one task alone, and that upon its completion he cast himself from the cliff onto the rocks below. The tree that the whites call the prayer pine is supposed to be Dead Bear himself, who was redeemed and transformed, in a moment of startling recognition, for the boy was his own grandson.

It was the old woman who first told him this story, but Baxter Dawes told it a different way. He said the boy did not die, that he did not hurl himself off the cliff, but that he ran off and lived a solitary life in the woods, planting a new tree for every man that his grandfather had slain, and tending to each one with great care until the day he died. Baxter called him Tree Keeper and had it on good authority that it was he who had planted the very oak in which Jacob was born, on the spot where Dead Bear slaughtered a woman and her child, and if that were true, then he too would play some part in the strange prophecy of Dead Bear. Yet he would not say what that part might be.

The prayer pine is the last true landmark on the map that has a name. Beyond it lies a grove of stark white birch trees that glow beneath the moon. Just before this grove the trail forks again, with the longer but easier passage to the left that the lynch mobs sometimes use to bring the condemned to the tree. To the right is a more direct but difficult path. It is the path his momma chose, probably because of the inviting calm of the birch grove, where spikenard root will sometimes grow, for that was what she came for on that day, an herb to ease her pain. He passes through the white trees with the small leaves falling in the moon glow so quiet that he can hear them blowing and rustling on the ground. The serpent is still as stone in his sack, and this worries him. Perhaps it will rouse itself in the tree. Perhaps if he warms it, for it is cool here in the heights and his breath comes out blue and does not rise. He sees the dark wall of dreaded brambles and he hears the low whisper of cold water over stones, the sound of Moss Creek beyond, like the faint sound of bells. He walks along the bramble wall and searches for the tunnel through which, the map says, he must crawl. In his mind is the fresh vision of the dead Cornelius Loop and the corpse he discovered in his dark waking. He is close now. He feels the presence of the tree the way you feel a thing in the dark that's watching you, the way you just know that there's someone there, and the serpent, perhaps sensing this, moves suddenly in the sack. He feels the head of the creature trying to nose its way out. He stops and puts down the bag. He checks the knot to see if it will hold. Then he sees the critter hole that the old woman marked on the map. He ducks into it without thinking, without giving his mind a chance to fear what might lie inside. He crawls through the dark with the back end of the tin flashlight in his teeth and the bag slung over his shoulder. He breathes hard through his nose, and spit runs from the corners of his mouth. It's almost time. He's close to the moment when he'll be ten. The moon, when he saw it last, was near that point in the sky that he had measured with his outstretched hands every night for the past week. Eight palms up and then he extends his thumb like the hand of clock. That's midnight in early June. The possibility of missing that moment drives him on through the dark tunnel.

He emerges into a great meadow, just as he saw it in his dark waking—a grassy blue Eden bisected by a creek with its bone-cold water, which he cups into his hands and drinks until he's full. He crosses through the water. There are sounds of small life here—field crickets and click bugs and myriad frogs. Tiny bats wheeling up with their mouse cries and an owl someplace close that speaks secrets to Orion as he rises with his sword above the tree—which is as he remembers from his dreams, a living presence with a sense of age, a being like an ancient man who exudes a great strength in his bearing and in his eyes, where the life force flows, condensed and true, through all things but shows itself in but a few of the mortal, rare as ghosts but real just the same, so you know it when you feel it and come alive and alight and shiver at the realness that is the perpetual moment that was never born and never dies. He is home.

He draws nearer, and the serpent becomes agitated, winding, unwinding, aware and suddenly alive and afraid. Its tail responds to that same sense of power that Jacob feels. It rattles fast and then stops. Now that he's close he can see beneath the low-hanging branches where nothing hangs but the bones that were there before. There is no man, no corpse. Cornelius Loop is gone and he's greatly relieved, but how could this have happened? Who could have taken him down so soon? Some say there are panthers here still, roaming these hills, but he doubts such an animal could climb so high out on such a narrow branch and sever a rope with its teeth. No matter now. It is gone and he does not have to see it again.

All sound is muffled beneath the drooping branches and the dense canopy above, as if a curtain had fallen. There is only the gentle clack of bones. He reaches out to touch the trunk.

A tree is just a tree, he says.

He runs his hand around the trunk and goes behind to where it bends and twists. It is in the twist that he finds the gaping hole. He ducks inside to the smell of wet moss and old fires. The air is cooler within the great oak and it is quiet. He can no longer hear the crickets or the owl or the creek. But he can hear other sounds, faint at first, but growing louder. He hears a sound that comes from inside the tree itself. It's a gentle roar, like the sound of waves crashing on a beach. And then he hears what sounds like moaning. The ground below him gives off heat that he feels in his knees. And he hears the snake, rattling inside the sack.

He finds the flashlight in his coat pocket and sweeps the beam in front of him so he can see the inside of the tree hollow. There are spider webs and bearded mosses and words scrawled upon the smooth parts where the bark has receded. Names are carved here, and dates, and epitaphs scratched by mourners long ago. He reads them aloud.

Elias Simms, glory now in the presence of his God. William Watts, we pray for redemption. Thief-tree, bleed for Bill Hughes, stolen from us too young at 24. Horace Biggs—innocent, by God. Forgive them, Lord, for what they done.

He shuts his eyes and calms himself with long slow breaths, the way he's seen his daddy do a hundred times before. Breathe, breathe, then a slow, almost imperceptible movement of his neck, his shoulders. He summons something from within that seems to rise from the very root of himself, electric, old, running in waves down through his bowels and across all outside surfaces, his skin reacting with pulsing flushes and all the tiny hairs on his body raised up like blades of fine grass that he can feel as if blowing in a gentle breeze. It is right and it is time.

How do you talk to a tree? Not with words, no, not with voices. Trees are not horses, and sounds that come from the mouths of man do not mollify nor convey, from kind to kind, from heart to heart, from one thing of God to another across the divide of that first sin, where he who passed or she who plucked bears no witness to these first creatures—tree and man, boy and tree, where the one is cast from the land of Eden and the other tries of wont to warn without the gift of word, across time and forever where the trees do talk like they're talking now, with voices low as whispers in a wind storm, that strange yet familiar language he feels so deep within himself that he cannot distinguish it from himself for it is himself, and boy and tree are one.

And other voices come. Not of the tree but trapped within, cries of anguish, cries of crows, the dread tincture of blood calls and throats passing pain to places that mouths of teeth and tongue together pronounce in screams that come from the nether regions where souls are born and burnt, burnt and born, the sorrowful moans of all the dead to which this tree is but an unwilling host. He hears them, the unleashed voices of the black men pleading for Jesus, who will not come nor save them from that same cruel fate that washed a much younger world of sin.

Jacob opens his eyes and looks up at the inside of the tree, but he does not see darkness, and he no longer sees the words scratched there in the bark. He sees instead a host of images. He sees people, black people, the spirits of the departed dead. He sees ghosts above, and men gathered round the tree, white men holding torches, shotguns, bottles of whisky. There are women and children too, also watching, staring up into the flickering branches of the tree where gaunt corpses hang from ropes like rotten fruit and the ghosts swirl round and round. The onlookers are chanting and swaying, and suddenly he is above them, reaching up toward the swirling ghosts, the spinning stars and swirling himself. He hovers above them and rises into the night sky, ascending through a veil of shimmering white mist, which falls apart like pipe smoke into cloudlike clumps that coalesce into a ring of dark faces with glowing eye whites and teeth of pearl. He sees their lips moving, and there is a low chorus of old Negro spirituals, and behind those old songs he hears a voice.

It is I. Be not afraid.

Then, the images vanish. Jacob gasps for air. He looks up at the inside of the tree and sees nothing that should not be there. Then he looks down between his legs at the gunnysack. There's no motion in the bag, no sound. He unties the buckskin cord and puts his hands inside. The skin of the reptile is cool, its body firm. He wraps his fingers around its flanks and the snake contracts and quivers. It's strong and thick around the middle but he manages to lift it. He takes it out of the sack and holds it up to the tree.

Not water nor sun, he says, but from this earth, through my hands, to you.

Suddenly he feels overwhelmed with a radiant energy. From his toes on up to the ends of each hair on his head he can feel a current of blissful heat, a jolt of warmth and joy, and he knows now that he is safe from harm. He lifts the rattlesnake. It coils around his arm and slides up his shoulder and behind his neck. It coils around him, but he is not afraid because the Holy Spirit is with him. The Holy Spirit, which manifests itself with a strong surge of soul fire and inner peace, has risen up from a place deep inside.

He is in complete darkness now, complete silence, and he is calm. The snake constricts around his neck. He can hear it hiss and stiffen, and then comes the furious rattle that comes before a strike. It tightens around him and stretches out to face him, and for a moment he stares into the serpent's face. The flashlight lies at his feet and there is just enough light to see into its shiny black eyes and the dark workings of the mindless things that roam timeless toward heat.

It strikes him in the face like a pistol shot, and Jacob falls backward. The snake does not let go. Its head shakes, its fangs pump, and for a moment they are one thing, united, as they were before the notion of time. Then he reels and sways, and falls facedown into the dirt in the hollow of the tree where he was born.

BOOK II

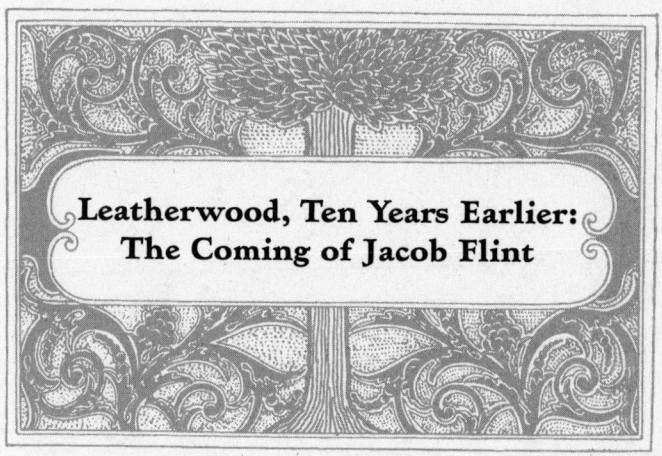

Leatherwood, Ten Years Earlier: The Coming of Jacob Flint

1

THE FLINTS

Charles Flint watches his wife soak her feet in a steel tub by candlelight. She's leaning back on the bed with her hands spread behind her and her swollen abdomen glowing a golden shade of yellow and appearing almost translucent. She's looking down at the floor. The dome of her belly is shiny and wet with some kind of ointment the old woman rubbed on her, and it glistens in the flickering light. He thinks he sees it move. He goes to her and puts his hand there over the womb. Her skin is slick and warm. She won't look up at him— as hard as he might stare, she will not meet his gaze. She moves her feet in the water and it laps against the sides of the tub. He can hear her breathing, and the water dripping off her legs, the wall behind her bathed in the throbbing light of a single flame, with the lath crumbling and a score of tiny round holes above her that the old woman will not let him repair. When he looks down at Rebecca, her eyes are wet and fixed upon him.

It's just for a little while, he says. A week. Maybe two.

She blinks at him twice and puts her hands upon her knees. Her hair is brown and wet. It is parted in the middle and it hangs down behind her back, past her shoulders. He wonders if the boy will have her eyes. They're so narrow and dark. He can't imagine where she got them because her father and mother don't have eyes like that at all. He puts his hands on the sides of her face and traces the contours of her forehead with his thumbs. Her eyes close. She has such clean white skin and her forehead is high and broad. She has that stern look about her that he's seen in old photographs of pioneers. She's plain and pretty and strong. She wears the blue-checkered dress her mother gave her, with a lace collar that lies flat at the base of her neck. She is just twenty-two.

What about Magdalena? she says.

Charles squats and puts his hands on top of hers, but she pulls hers back and looks away from him, gazing up at the crumbling wall behind her.

She's up at the big house, he says.

Rebecca looks at him and squints. Charles sees the tiny lines that appear on her forehead when she's scared.

I need her, she says.

No, you don't. You need quiet and you need rest, and the old woman will be here with you and you can't ask for anyone better.

I need my daughter, Charles.

You have your son.

I don't have him yet.

He's there. You talk to him.

He tries to kiss her, but she turns her face away. He takes hold of her chin and kisses her anyway. He kisses her cheek and stands.

I can't sleep anymore, he says. I can't sleep and I can't think. Every time I close my eyes, I see that mountain and I see that tree and I know that God's telling me something. It's a message, Rebecca, and I got to go.

Rebecca stands and her dress falls down over her belly. The fabric is so threadbare and worn that Charles can see right through to the outline of her flesh behind.

You do what you have to, she says. But I can't sleep either, Charles, and I can't think with all this pain. I got my own message here inside my head that won't go away, whether my eyes are open or closed, and I dream too, I dream of things that scare me and I don't have a good feeling about this one, Charles, I don't.

He puts his hands on her shoulders and squeezes them and they look each other in the eye and for one moment they are together again, they are of one mind, and everything is fine.

This child will survive, he says. I saw it in my dream.

I don't think so, Charles.

It will, he says. In my dreams and vision I see it. I've seen it a hundred times the same.

She sees in his eyes that he believes what he says, and it makes her believe it too. His eyes are big and dark. They shine in daylight and nighttime both, and she's rarely seen them closed. Even when she wakes at night and looks over at him, they're open, for he lies awake praying most of the time and wakes before she does. He never seems to sleep. His eyes have never lied to her, so he can always sway her, the way he sways all people who stare into his clear black eyes.

She steps from the tub and water drips from her feet as she crosses the small cabin. Charles watches the trail of shiny footprints on the wooden floor. She reaches into a sack and takes out a folded quilt and brings it to him. The quilt is all white and embroidered with their names, and the date of their wedding. It was a gift from the old woman. She took it from their bed so she'd have something to comfort her during her stay in the cabin.

You take this, she says.

I can't.

I won't have you sleeping on the ground.

The Lord will provide for me.

You take this, Charles. You hear me?

He takes the quilt and kisses her hand and walks backward to the door.

Rest now, he says. She'll be back soon with your dinner. I have to make a train.

He opens the door, and the candle flame blows in the wind that rushes in, and on the walls the shadows all dance and he blows her a kiss and he leaves. He closes the door and the shadows stop moving.

The rattlesnakes feel him coming long before he opens the sunporch door. They stir in their boxes and grow rigid. Their tails begin to shake all together and the sound of it rises to a loud hiss that makes his belly feel like a cold, heavy stone. He calls the sunporch the Bible room. This is where he keeps them, the Bibles and the snakes, and he often comes here to pray and talk to Jesus, especially at night. He lifts the hook-latch and pushes open the screen door, and it squeals on rusted hinges. He steps inside and walks to the portable pulpit and stands at the open Bible there, surrounded by all manner of wooden crates and boxes filled with lethal snakes. The boxes are decorated with quotes from the scriptures and images of serpents. They're long but not tall, with lids made from wire and screen that open on butterfly hinges. The boxes are stacked three and four high, and there are several of these stacks. He has to run a live trapline for all the rats he needs to feed them, but the rat supply is running low, and now he's thinking of breeding rabbits or letting some of the snakes go free.

At the center of the room stands the portable pulpit that he brings out with him to preach the gospel of Mark. Beneath the pulpit is the largest of the serpent boxes and the biggest of the snakes. It's a timber rattler more than six feet long that Baxter Dawes brought in only two days before and which has yet to be fed or handled by a man. Baxter told him that he found it beneath one of the wrecked cars that washed downriver and got buried up over its wheels in mud. He said it was the meanest snake he ever saw. It took hold of the Judaspole with its mouth and latched on to the handle so tight he had to pry it open with a screwdriver, leaving some of its teeth stuck into the wood. The snake killed one of his dogs, and Baxter had brought it to Charles so that it could be subdued by the Holy Spirit and broken by the power of God. Baxter Dawes is a snake hunter, but not a snake killer. Snakes are the one animal he will not harm.

Charles Flint believes in signs. He believes that God speaks to men with more than words, and that if you look real close you can see things that will tell you where to go and what to do. He believes in dreams and visions and the spirits of the unrestful dead. He believes in weather portents and in happenstance. Most of all he believes that the manifestation of God's will lies in the actions and behavior of animals. He's always on the lookout for omens, in the form of beasts that fly and walk and crawl. Animals are God's messengers. He relies upon them for guidance, direction, and reassurance. They do not lead him astray.

He lifts the portable pulpit from the serpent box beneath and lays it on the floor. He looks inside at the coiled rattler, who is quiet and still. The other snakes have settled now, and Charles prays in the new silence, working the tumblers of the brass lock with his fingers until it opens with a soft click. He puts the padlock down and raises the hasp, all the while whispering the name of Jesus and waiting for the rush of heat and wave of joy that starts in his toes and rises up through him, prickling the hair on his neck, making him smile. It's the feeling that marks the arrival of the Holy Ghost. When he clears his mind and prays to God, and breathes deep and holds Jesus in his heart, this feeling, which he calls the anointment of the Spirit, sweeps over him like a sudden fever and gives him the powers promised by the Bible—the power to preach, the power to heal, the power to confront deadly things and not be harmed by them. He feels that feeling now. It envelops him. Now that the Spirit has come to him he closes his eyes and opens the serpent box and lays his hands upon the body of the big snake. The flesh beneath its skin moves, but the serpent does not. It tightens itself and pushes its head farther into the corner of its makeshift lair.

He pulls on the snake and drags him into the open space below the raised lid. The snake tightens itself again, its head buried within its coils. Charles lifts this ball of snake from the box, no longer whispering Jesus, but speaking his name aloud. The other snakes all stir in their boxes and start up again their chorus of rattling tails. He holds the snake above his head and opens his eyes. He sees its tongue flashing, but it does not look alarmed. Of all the snakes in the Bible room, this one alone is quiet, and when Charles speaks, it cocks its head as if listening to his words.

Lord, I ask thee for affirmation, he says.

The Bible room is dark and the other snakes are making noise. Outside he hears no sound. There's no thunder, no wind, and he can see nothing that is strange except the coiled rattle-snake itself, which is getting heavy in his hands but shows no fear or concern. Charles thinks it might be cold. The Bible room is cooler than the rest of the house and this keeps the snakes docile, but still, it should be more aggressive than this, more active. He thinks that perhaps this is the sign, this snake so calm and tame. He's not seen such behavior from a wild snake before, not from a snake this large and old, and Baxter Dawes is never wrong, he knows his snakes. He claims to have been one in another time and place altogether.

He lowers the snake back into the box, pushes it inside, and closes the lid. He locks it up and puts it back under the pulpit and prays for a moment over the open Bible. He thanks Jesus for keeping him safe and for providing the old woman to look after his wife and child, and he takes up his quilt and leaves the Bible room, putting the hook-latch back on the door.

He stands on the rise outside the house and looks down at the light glowing in the window of the cabin below. He thinks he sees a shadow, but it's only the branch of a tree moving in the wind. He starts down the road on foot and turns up his collar against the breeze and walks into the cold. He thinks about the railroad and all the trains that are moving somewhere now, he thinks about the long freights running hard at night, and the men that are on them looking for work or new lives or easy scores, men without homes but not without hope. He wonders how they all felt when they left the places of their birth and their families. He wonders if they felt like he does now, if they felt they might never come back.

2

WAITING FOR THE BOY

Rebecca lies on the old woman's little bed in the cabin with her face turned to the wall and her knees pulled close to her belly. The old woman stands at the stove pulling apart a chicken. The candle sputters and the cabin walls throb gold and black. Rebecca turns suddenly and sits up. The old woman watches her sway and then vomit into the steel bucket on the floor. She brings her a swatch of cloth and helps wipe her mouth before giving her a sip of water.

Not too much, she says.

She sweeps the hair from Rebecca's eyes and feels her forehead with the back of her wrist. Then she presses down on the flat spot below her belly. Rebecca moans and sucks in air. The old woman looks into her eyes and doesn't like what she sees. She shakes her head and feels for her pulse. Rebecca holds her breath. The old woman smells like chicken and tobacco. She can feel her bony fingers on her wrist and marvels at the strength in her hands.

Rest now, the old woman says. I'll bring you some broth.

Tomorrow I'll go up the mountain and fetch you something for the pain.

Rebecca lies back and closes her eyes. Inside she feels the baby moving, she can feel the sharp jabs of its feet. Her bladder is full and the pressure on it from lying down is too great for her to bear.

I have to pee, she says.

The cabin has no running water, but there's an outhouse in back near the tree line. The old woman takes her by the arm to help her out of bed.

I can manage, Rebecca says, and the old woman lets go.

Rebecca goes to a high shelf near the door and takes down a kerosene lantern and lights it with a wooden match she finds there. When the mantle glows white hot, she turns down the flame and wraps herself in a shawl. The night air is crisp, and she takes several deep breaths before walking down to the little outhouse with a crescent moon cut into the door.

She manages a trickle and not much more, and when she's through, she stands outside under the open sky, taking in the vast array of stars. She turns off the lantern and waits in the dark for her eyes to adjust and the shape of the world to form itself out of the blackness. After a few minutes she sees the sharp outline of the trees and the features of the ground. She sees stones and clumps of weeds and yellow-star grass whose flowers appear purple under the moon. She looks up at the night sky, spinning slowly herself, and the stars turn and blur. She stops turning, but the stars continue to spin. This gives her the sensation that she's falling slowly, like a leaf floating to the bottom of a lake. She puts her hands on her belly and rubs herself and smiles. She talks to the child in her womb.

You just wait, she says. Wait till you can see the stars.

With her one hand pressed to her belly she walks back up to the cabin with the window glowing gold, and she sees the old woman pass by with something in her hands. A moment later she passes back in the other direction. She thinks about Charles hiking up to the railroad grade all alone in the dark with no light and no idea where he's going, and climbs the stairs and opens the door to the cabin. The old woman is sitting by the bedside. She's holding a bowl with a spoon in it. Her eyes are closed and her mouth is open. But she's not asleep. She's moaning some kind of spiritual and tapping the spoon on the side of the bowl in time with the slow rhythm of the song. Her foot is tapping too. When she sees Rebecca standing in the doorway, she puts the bowl on the table, turns down the bed, and removes from beneath the blankets a cast-iron pan filled with hot coals.

Rebecca lies awake in the old woman's bed. The baby moves inside her. It's a good bed, an old bed, but it's not her bed, and she's not used to sleeping alone. She likes to press herself into Charles at night, and with him away she finds that she cannot sleep. The baby is a night child, like his father. Always awake. He's restless like his father is, and when he grows up she knows he won't stay here for long. She can feel that like she can feel that he's a boy. She can read this child.

She whispers to him now. She tells him to be still and go to sleep. But he won't listen. She feels like he's spinning inside of her belly. Her feet tingle and her hands are numb. The old woman snores on a cot over by the stove, and this keeps her up too. She knows she will not sleep again until after the child is born. She reaches out to touch the wall and fingers a hole there that's as smooth and clean as a rifle bore.

3

JOURNEY ON A TRAIN

Charles sticks out his hand from the midst of his sleep. He feels the cold steel flank of the boxcar wall and the vibrations channeled through it from the iron wheels below, and he comes out of his dream to the smell of cut lumber and wet straw. He sits up with a pain in his back in a dark place where his breath turns to blue vapor in the light of a gibbous moon. He listens to the sounds of drunken men in the throes of troubled sleep. There are moans and wet snores and somewhere in the dark an empty whiskey bottle begins to roll as the train lurches to a near stop and then begins its slow climb into the hills of north Georgia. He emerges from the warm folds of his wedding quilt, and stands. He stretches his arms and steps over the man sleeping next to him, and over several other men, and goes to the open door of the boxcar to pee. The air outside is cold and damp and his fingers numb quickly on the iron handle of the door. He cranes his neck out to watch the line of boxcars climbing up out of the valley, where Tennessee lies dark and sleeping and where, until yesterday, he has never strayed from before.

The trackside is lined with jack pines and red spruce. They look flat as postcard pictures in the light of the glowing moon, and smell of wet moss and new rain. He holds his hand out and spreads his fingers in the wind and sees veins that are not his own, tendons newly formed—the hand of a healer who has yet to truly heal.

He turns around and stands for a moment to regard the sleeping men there on the floor of the boxcar, transients all, their black forms huddled in the straw, curled up for warmth and holding themselves against the mountain cold with their knees tucked into each other's backs and their arms around each other's necks. In this moment, among these huddled strangers in the light of a fat Georgia moon, he suddenly realizes that his child will come early and before he returns home. But it's too late now to turn back, and all such destinies are preordained. Both he and the child are on journeys that each must make alone. For that is what his visions told him. All he can do now is pray for the woman who will bear this burden. In his visions, her future remains mysterious.

From his coat pocket he pulls a hand-worn travel Bible bound in stippled pig's hide. Within its tattered pages lies the photograph of Rebecca in her Sunday dress, taken with her eyes half-closed and frowning. It's the same way she looked on the morning he saw her for the first time, standing on her father's porch so many years ago. He touches her face with his thumb, and though it's only a paper likeness he can feel her warmth radiating back at him. Soon, now, she will bear his son. He steps over the sleeping men, careful not to fall over in the swaying boxcar, his feet searching for placement in the few clear spaces where no hand or foot lies waiting to topple him. When he gets to the back of the car, he finds that someone has claimed his warm nest in the straw.

A man lies curled upon his wedding quilt, snoring like the rest of them, and nursing a bottle of clear liquor. When Charles kneels beside him, his eyes water and he gags. The man smells like a stockyard. His beard is speckled with flakes of dried vomit and between his legs there's a dark, wet stain. Even in this pale light Charles can see the lice that crawl about him like tiny men at some urgent task to which their drunken host is oblivious. He pushes at the man's leg with the toe of his boot, but there is no reaction, and there is no response when he kicks him in the thigh. He gags again at the stench of the drunk's soiled trousers, and when he tugs at the man's sleeve, the fabric tears away like damp paper.

The train continues to climb, now at a steeper angle. He can still hear the snoring of the men, but the light from the moon disappears as the door slides closed with a loud clack that makes his heart jump. The man shifts in his sleep. Charles is no stranger to violence, but the man is heavy and tall and in his boot he carries a bone-handled dagger tucked into a leather sheath. The handle of the knife is carved from the antler of a stag and inscribed with the initials S.K. He can see a glint of steel at the hilt where it has eased up from the sheath.

Charles moves his right hand with the slow deliberation of a man used to hunting reptiles. Each breath from the sleeping man draws his fingers closer and he studies the veins that run jagged across his knuckles like exposed roots of a toppled tree. The big man snores and the train climbs steeper. Charles can almost touch the knife now. A man woken drunk by a stranger in the night is prone to lash out before reason, and he knows that he stands a better chance with his words then with his hands. His fingers rest now on the cool handle of the dagger, and there's a moment when his thoughts turn curiously to the knife itself and the stories it might tell if it could speak. In that instant he's aware of more than death. For the dagger is older than the man who carries it, and it speaks to him in bloody pictures that flash through his mind like a zoetrope show.

He pulls the knife from its sheath in one quick motion

that is not fast enough to escape the reflexes of this old cheater of death, whose hand has grown strong from years of clutching onto to the sides of fast-moving trains. The man grabs hold of his hand and twists his wrist, rolling Charles onto his back. The man straddles his chest and Charles stares into his face as the man begins to push the dagger down toward his throat. He's smiling and Charles can smell his awful breath. His skin is creased and black with dust.

Slit my throat in my sleep, the man says.

Charles pushes back on the knife, but it's all he can do to keep it away from his face and the old man begins to grunt and huff.

Mister, you got it wrong, Charles says.

No, my friend, you did. Of all these here fellers, you chose the worst one to rob.

The train rocks then, from side to side, and this unbalances the old man, giving Charles leverage enough to throw him against the side of the boxcar. They struggle in silence, with only the sound of the big man's heavy breathing and his grunts above the clacking train wheels and the snores of the drunken men. The strength of the man is amazing and relentless, and soon the cold blade of the bone-dagger is flat against the neck of Charles Flint. There are four hands wrapped around the knife handle, two dirty and two clean. Their veins bulge up from beneath their skin like swollen green rivers as they twist and push.

That's my quilt, Charles says. That was my bed.

But the big man only smiles and leans on the knife as the train picks up speed and begins to level itself as it crests a peak. Charles begins to pray.

Lord, I ask thee for strength, he says.

The Lord can't help you now, mister. It's best you just relax and die.

Brother, Charles says, I'm no killer, but I ain't no die'r neither.

I'm the killer, the man says. I am the killer.

The knuckles of the man feel rough like tree bark against his skin. There's too much power in them, too much rage, and the knife cuts slow. He can feel the blood seep down behind his neck and he sees the whites of the old man's eyes. The train moves faster as the floor beneath him dips back the other way. Charles hears the whiskey bottle start to roll again, and he hears the old man groan. The boxcar's door slides back open with a bang and the car is flooded with moon glow that he mistakes for holy light.

Don't take me, Lord, he says. Not yet.

The man hesitates for a long moment. He stares into the coal-black eyes of Charles Flint and sees that they are not like the eyes of other men. They are all dark, and do not blink, and they glow with a curious light that comes from within, like an animal staring back from the woods—eye shine. Blue-black like the sheen off a lump of coal. His pupils are wet and fixed, not in death, but in life, and they speak without words. They speak of things left behind but not forgotten. In these eyes there are boyhood dreams and lost fathers and great deeds left undone. He can see the moon swimming there and a promise of redemption and his eyes look not at him, but past him, like the gaze of the suffering Christ from some oil painting on a cathedral wall.

Who are you? The man says and he eases his grip on the dagger.

I am but a messenger of God, Charles says, and you are my first disciple.

4

SERPENT DREAMS
AND SPIKENARD ROOT

The old woman dozes in the rocker and dreams about a snub-nosed snake moving through the fallen leaves. It's a brown snake with a long thin stripe down its back the color of butter. The snake is moving faster than any snake could ever go, and she can hear the leaves rustle under its belly and see its flashing tongue. In the dream she's above the snake but not above the trees. She follows it through the woods like a bird, though she can hardly keep up, this snake is so lithe and quick. It knows where it's going and it flows around the trunks of the trees and spills down into gullies and runs through crevices in the rock like a tiny muddy stream set loose from its banks. The brown snake is on the hunt for something she cannot guess at, and is now moving toward her house. Her dream self swoops low to follow it, this mysterious strain of serpent running down the ridge and over the path and around the outside of the cabin and on back to the little house with the crescent moon cut into the door. It vanishes beneath the outhouse, and she hears a woman scream. She passes through the door herself, she flies in through the moon hole, and Rebecca is there too, sitting, heavy with child. She hears a sound like rushing steam. Rebecca raises her legs and parts them. She braces herself and her waters flow out. The child is coming. There's a head crowning, but it's not the head of a baby. She sees instead the blunt nose of a reptile, the same one she followed in, with a butter-yellow stripe down its back. She shouts and wakes to the sound of the teakettle shooting out a vent of steam.

The kettle shakes on the stove, and the old woman takes it off, her hands still shaking. She pours out a cup of catnip tea for Rebecca and lets it steep there with a saucer on top and turns to look over at the bed. She sees her sleeping there, with her face turned to the wall. The old woman's face is hot and she sits back on the rocker. She feels in her pockets for the corncob pipe and a match. She finds the pipe and lights it, then sits back and smokes. It steadies her and she closes her eyes and she thinks about all the babies she's delivered in her time, and all the women she's gone to see, riding out alone on horseback, sometimes at night or in the driving snow with nothing but her little herb bag and her tobacco pouch and pipe. She'd be out for days in some dark hollow where the doctors never go. In all her years on the mountain she's never lost a child and only had one mother die, and she's never taken a single dollar for the work that she does. It's her gift and she considers it the work of God. They pay her sometimes with live fowl and pumpkins or a jug of molasses, and they make her corn bread and give the girl babies Gertrude for a middle name.

She's never been wrong about the sex of a child or the day that it would come, and she can always feel how it will be with a woman, she can feel how the birth will go. In her dreams she always sees this, she sees the babies come, but this one's not like the others. Rebecca's womb is dark. She cannot see it. The birth dream for this child has yet to come, and though she knows that it's a boy, she thinks there's something wrong, because she sees strange things in her dreams of late. She sees night birds and reptiles, jagged teeth and wild dogs. She thinks now that she is wrong about this child. It will come early, perhaps while Charles is away, and she needs to take proper precautions and prepare for a long and difficult birth.

So she does the things she's always done, the way her momma taught her. The mountain way. She hangs an empty hornet's nest from the rafters outside the door. She makes catnip tea and red alder broth. She grinds bark from an apple tree. She cuts diapers from old bed linens and brings the axe in from the woodpile and lays it point upward under the bed as an added measure to stem the pain of the birth—an old superstition that's never failed her yet. The last thing she does is stuff two silver coins into the mattress, coins passed down from her momma that she's brought to almost every birth she's handled. Two pennies with Indian heads, stolen from a church box by her older sister, Bess. This is a secret she's never revealed. The one time she didn't bring the church-box pennies, the poor woman bled out and died.

Rebecca wakes with the old woman's hands beneath the mattress and she turns over and sees her kneeling by the bed. She's wincing, the old woman is, and Rebecca can see she's in pain. Rebecca sits up and feels pain of her own. She feels it in her back, and she has to take a deep breath before she swings her legs over the side of the bed. She stares at the old woman.

What's wrong? she says

The old woman shakes her head from side to side and waves her off with her hand. She wobbles a little and sways, and Rebecca has to grab her wrist to keep her from falling over.

C'mon now, she says. Let's get you in bed.

The old woman tries to stand but she can't do it, so Rebecca helps her to her feet. She pulls her bony arm over her shoulder and lifts her from the floor. She's so light and frail, she could carry her in her arms like a child. She turns to lay her down in the bed, but the old woman stops her.

Put me in the chair, the old woman says. I'll never get up outta that bed.

Rebecca lays her in the rocker and puts her feet up on a wooden crate. Her head swims as she does it. Before her eyes she sees colored specks of light that swirl and pop like fireflies.

I don't feel so good myself, she says.

The old woman puts her hand on Rebecca's and runs her fingers up her arm. She grabs her by the elbow and pulls her close.

You're gonna be fine, she says. But we're not ready for that child.

The old woman closes her eyes and breathes deeply. Rebecca sees her hands shaking and hears a wheezing sound in her throat. The old woman tries to raise her head. She strains to lift her neck from the back of the chair and squeezes Rebecca's elbow.

I'm gonna give you some apple-bark tea, she says. That should give us more time. Later on I'll go up the mountain for the spikenard. This ain't gonna be like Magdalena. That girl came out like a pie from the oven. This one's early and he won't be smooth.

Rebecca stands and takes the old woman's hand from her elbow and gives it a slight squeeze. She walks across the room to the door and opens it. The outside air is cool and smells sweet. A band of sun streams inside and illuminates the dark room, and the dust motes sparkle in the slanted ray of early light. It's a fine day and the trees are full of hopping sparrows and blackbirds.

I'll go, Rebecca says. I can fetch it myself.

The old woman opens her eyes and looks at Rebecca standing there near the door. She doesn't think that the child's head has dropped. There's still time. Perhaps a few days.

It's too far, she says.

I want to go, Rebecca says. I need to get out. I need to stretch my legs. All this laying around has got me cramped, that's all. The air will be good for me, and it's only a couple miles. I'll go if you show me how to get there.

The old woman grasps the arms of the rocker. Rebecca can see the backs of her hands, she can see the shadows of her bones and what the years of mountain living has done to them. She thinks about all the fruit they've canned and the pies they've baked and the babies they've pulled into the light. She knows that hers will be the last one because the old woman is too weak to travel anymore and too tired for all the work that's in it. Roads are better now and doctors have trucks. Except for Mary Albert, the old woman is the last in her line of the old-time granny women.

The old woman leans forward as if to try and stand, and then falls back on the chair. She exhales and sighs.

You remember that tea I gave you when you had Magdalena? That bitter tea?

I do, Rebecca says. The thought of the tea brings her back to the smell of rotting greens and the flavor of charred wood.

I couldn't have done it without that tea.

That's the spikenard.

It had an awful taste.

Powerful medicine is what it is.

Where can I find it?

Up on Moss Creek, there's a place where it still grows.

Rebecca shuts her eyes and tries to remember the creek. The last time she was there she couldn't have been more than eleven or twelve years old. It was the day her own mother died. They were out catching pollywogs and it was hot. The kind of day that made your head ache and your ears ring, where the click bugs made such a racket in the trees that is was hard to hear yourself think. She stood barefoot in the creek bed, the sun shining through the mason jar. She could see right through the skin of the tadpoles. She could see everything inside. When Jeb Albert came running up and told her, she dropped the pollywogs onto the rocks and cut her foot on a piece of the broken glass. It was so long ago. She forgot the way to Moss Creek. She wonders if there'll be any pollywogs.

How do I get there? She says.

The old woman cranes her neck around, looking for something in the room, something she cannot find. Then she tilts her head back and her lips start moving and her finger waves in the air. Then she smiles.

Bring me something to write with and I'll draw you a map.

5

A DISCIPLE

At daybreak the train rolls at a slow and even pace and the sun streams in through the open boxcar door. Rancid mist rises from the bodies of the sleeping men snoring in the hay. Charles Flint stands above the bearded man, rubbing at the cut on his neck and watching him sleep, as he had done throughout the night. The air inside the boxcar is sour with the smell of road-weary men and dirty feet and leather blackened by wood smoke and sweat. In the morning light he can see the face of his former adversary growing younger and younger as the shadows ebb away. He is not as old as he had appeared in the night. He thinks he might be about forty-five. His long silver hair and flowing beard made him look older in the dark, but in the soft light of daybreak he looks like a young and wild Moses. His feet are bare and speckled with soot, and his mismatched boots droop beside his gangly legs like withered stalks of corn. The bone-handled dagger lies sheathed and hiding, below his wedding quilt, which is now infested with all manner of crawling parasites and stained with the effluence of this once-lost man.

Charles wakes him with droplets of cool water sprinkled from a tin canteen. The water drips down his face in shining rivulets that glisten like tears, washing away layers of ash and grime and leaving behind narrow streaks of tanned skin. The man sits bolt upright, wide-eyed and confused, grappling for the dagger but feeling only his knobby anklebone where the knife should be. He reaches up to feel the liquid on his face.

What's that? he says.

It's water. Drink some and put your boots on. We're getting off the train.

The man regards the canteen with suspicion but tilts it back and drinks from it while looking at Charles and remembering the events of the night. He slides his boots on and places his dagger inside the shorter of the two, which happens to be the left one. And then he stands, a full head taller than Charles. He looks down at him, and for a moment Charles fears the man may have forgotten their truce, and their long talk about truth and lies in this life, and how there's always hope of redemption from even the greatest of sins, of which this man is recently guilty and running from still. But then he smiles a mouth of crooked teeth and puts on his hat and scratches his beard. Charles motions to him with his head and steps toward the boxcar door.

Where we goin'? the man says.

To a place called Slaughter Mountain.

That don't sound too good.

There's a church up there run by twin brothers. They do something there we both need to see.

I seen plenty of churches.

Not like this one. Now we best be jumping while the train is slow.

They hit the trackside gravel and roll together like a couple of bear cubs. They dust themselves off and stand watching the train pass them by and vanish into the trees around a bend in the tracks.

Charles turns to regard his new companion. By the light of day he sees that this man has spent many nights in boxcars, truck beds, and places more forsaken. His skin appears almost blue-gray where it can be seen through the soot, and his fingernails are long and clawlike. He wears about him rags of sackcloth and remnants of wool sewn together in the patchwork fashion of a wandering tinker, and all about his head swarm tiny black flies.

He could not have picked a more suitable companion and was destined to find one such as this—the Lord told him so. In his dream, he showed him a man more wretched then he'd ever seen, a man of great strength in both body and heart. This man would forsake his wanderings and rebuke his sins once anointed with the Holy Spirit, and that day would come when the twin brothers performed miracles from the Bible by consuming poison right out of jars offered up by strangers.

But first he has to claim this man, and to claim him he must clean him, and find him new clothes, for he stinks most horrible and cannot be looked upon by any but the most faithful without true loathing and black fear.

The two men turn from the railroad tracks and walk into the woods, and Charles holds out his hand. The man takes it in his own and holds it there for a moment before remembering what to do, then shakes it with vigor.

My name's Sylus Knox, he says.

I know, says Charles. You told me last night.

I don't remember too good. I don't remember much of last night.

We'll work on that. My name is Charles Flint.

Sylus Knox nods and together they walk off into the woods.

6

A SON

The storm comes upon her as she kneels in the cool shade beside Moss Creek, where the old woman said the remedy herbs still grow and the hill people still live in crate-board shacks nestled in dark hollows.

The air grows cold as a cave, and she hears the distant growl of thunder as the leaves all around her begin to shudder. By the time she sees the first flash of lightning it's too late. There's a foot pushing up from within, or an elbow, she can't decide which. It's hard to stand with all that weight up front, and when she does, she feels dizzy and her legs wobble. So she sits and splashes cold water on her face and closes her eyes and remembers seeing the blue guinea hog this morning carrying a stick in its mouth, a sure sign of big rain coming. She never believed it until now.

The birds stop their chatter and the trees suddenly lose their shadows under the darkening clouds. The child moves and her stomach tightens. When Magdalena was born, she could not read the signs. Now they are clear. It takes one child to know another, and this one speaks to her from the womb with wild gestures and pain. It is time.

Rebecca takes a deep breath and raises herself up to a squat. She looks all around her to find answers among the trees, but only the clouds talk back. They crash together in the distance and the sky flashes pale blue and two red-bellied snakes crawl by in tandem, like animals in search of the ark itself. She leaves the basket by the side of the creek with the old woman's map and the bundle of sweet flag and retraces her steps, following her own trail of flattened grass until the sky opens and lets loose a torrent of water so thick that the ground disappears and her vision is obscured by drops of flying rain. She is moving as fast as she can, then slips on the mud, falls to the ground, and slides several yards on her back. It takes her a while to gather the strength to stand again, and when she does she sees no sign of anything familiar or safe; she sees nothing at all. Her hand reaches out in the rain and feels tree bark, slick as hide, the water running through her outstretched fingers and down her wrist, where it cools the skin there and makes her shiver. The baby kicks so hard inside her that she falls to her knees in the mud and her dress clings to her soaking thighs like wallpaper and forms a pool there where the rain gathers.

She breathes and water drips into her mouth and between her legs, where there now flows water of a different kind, a warm rush like urine. It streams down her legs and drips from her heels, and there's still light enough to see that the liquid runs pink.

Rebecca can hear the smack of the raindrops on the leaves overhead and the low rumble of thunder, and as she counts off the seconds before the next flash of lightning, she feels the first contraction of her impending labor. In the flash of light that follows, she sees the gaping hollow of the Tyborn tree where the old woman once told her runaway slaves had been hanged before the great war and where, to this day, they still lynch men for unspeakable crimes that are only sometimes true. She runs for the tree, holding her belly with both hands, racing out in that dark space between thunderclaps, and entering it through a slit in the trunk—a narrow opening whose vulvic folds are blackened by fire. She sits on the bare earth inside with her knees as close to her belly as they can get and her feet braced against the sides of the tree.

The air inside the ancient oak smells like wood smoke and earthworms. Outside she can hear the rain. She lifts the hem of her dress, parts her legs as wide as they can go in that small space, and waits for a lightning flash so she might see something of herself below—a sign of the baby's arrival. Rain drips in through some crack far above her and it spatters on her knee-cap and she sticks out her tongue and drinks three big drops that taste like barley water. The thunder rolls over her like the voice of God and shakes the tree and the ground below her, and she cries out her husband's name.

Charles, she says. Charles Flint, I need you now.

She cranes her neck forward and looks down at herself but cannot see beyond the mound of pale skin. Her belly becomes luminous and blue in the lightning flash that follows. She cannot see blood as she fears, but she can see the inner walls of the tree all around her and the strange words carved there by mourners long ago as she braces herself for a contraction. She can feel it build. With her hands behind her and her bare knees pressed against the opening that leads out into the dark world beyond, it rolls through her, and she cries out and moans.

She closes her eyes and presses her legs against the tree itself, waiting for the next contraction while the wind sweeps over the mountain and branches crack and break all around outside. By now they'll be out looking for her, but her scent will be washed away, and no man can track in a storm such as this; not even Baxter Dawes, though he's a full-blood Chero-kee mountain man and known all over Tennessee for finding lost men in these hills. She prays for him to find her. She prays for herself, and she prays for Charles, and most of all she prays for her son.

When the next wave hits her, she pushes at the earth with her heels and builds up a small mound of dirt at her feet that gives her some leverage and keeps the groundwater from flowing into the hollow of the tree. The next contraction comes faster and catches her off guard. She digs into the earth with her fingers, squeezing the rich soil in her palms, and she feels something below the ground, with the tips of her fingers, buried there. She clenches the thing, and feels it in the dark. It's a small and brittle bundle wrapped in what feels like beads. She waits for the contraction to pass as the rain falls even harder and the drops from the top of the tree fall faster onto her kneecap. The water runs down her legs.

She pulls the bundle from the dirt and holds it up to what little light shines in through the opening of the tree. She can see that it's a small clutch of dried flowers wrapped in what looks like a string of tiny pearls. When the thunder cracks overhead she does not have to wait long for the flash that shows her it's a necklace, with a crucifix of ebony, gilded with a tarnished silver Christ figure whose features are so finely crafted that in the brief instant of luminance from the sky, she can see a tiny crown of thorns.

The rain falls so heavy that water streams in through the opening of the tree. The slow drip from above becomes a steady stream. The water soaks her legs and washes away the blood that is released with a large contraction that squeezes her, tears her, makes her bite into her tongue. She clenches the necklace tight in her fist and pushes through the thunder. She can feel the head crown. It passes out between her legs as a bolt of lightning strikes the tree and shoots down the trunk, emerging at the opening like a latticework of Saint Elmo's fire and scorching both her ankles at the sharp bones above her heels. But this pain she does not feel until much later, because at this moment the boy pushes his way out into the world with a will all his own and she catches him in her hands and holds him to her chest. She sees that his eyes are open and aglow. He does not cry. He gasps and gazes at the dark space around him, a space that is neither womb nor world but some transitory place between the two. It is a cold place, whose blackened walls glisten with a new kind of fluid, less viscous and less warm.

Rebecca sucks at his nose and clears it with her mouth and she drapes the necklace around his head before bringing him to suck, which he does right off. She can hear the thunder rumbling again, not close by, and the space between the flashes grows wider as she passes the afterbirth with the water dripping onto her, her legs lying flat against the ground and stuck outside the opening of the tree. She closes her eyes, and tastes blood, and as she nurses the boy she prays aloud and holds him as close as she can. She is shivering now and can feel the tingle of the burns on her feet.

She lies there for a long while, listening to the slackening rain and the suck of the child. She drifts in and out of sleep. When she wakes there appears in the opening of the tree the black silhouette of a large animal. She hears a snuffling sound and a scratching, and beyond the hole she can see the loping shadows of many four-legged creatures whose paws smack at the mud and grapple there for purchase. In the opening of the tree, backlit by a flash of blue light, she sees something with a great head and ears that hang low below its jowls. She can hear the panting of the animal and feel its hot breath on her leg, and she turns cold at the sensation of its muzzle on her flesh. She cries out as it howls. She withdraws her legs into the folds of the tree hollow and holds the baby against her bosom as the animal begins to bay a long, sad note that triggers more howling from the woods beyond. It's Spider, Baxter Dawes' prize coonhound.

She hears the hounds gathered around the tree, yapping

and whining. She hears the voices of men. The yellow beam of a flashlight cuts through the darkness of the tree hollow and blinds her. Baxter Dawes squats and peers inside. He's holding a rifle on her at first but lowers the barrel when he sees what the dogs have discovered.

Lord, he says. She's in there with the child.

Rebecca shivers and holds her hand up to the light.

7

A FISHER

A cold mist rises from the grass in the cool morning air and the tree trunks glisten with dew. Charles Flint rolls over and sees light from above. Golden bands of sun slant through the leaves. The mist thins as it enters the warm beams and rises faster. It gives him hope after a night troubled by strange dreams. He remembers seeing dark-skinned men hanging from scraggly limbs, horses on the run, a fire. The cut on his neck opened up sometime in the night, and he did not sleep at all after that. A man can't shake the fear of waking to the sight of his own fingers slick with blood.

Sylus watches him wash the wound. The bleeding has stopped, but the gash still throbs. Charles lies on his side, his head propped on his elbow, and he lets water drip from the mouth of the canteen. It runs down his neck and pools on the ground. The wound looks clean. Charles tears off a strip of cotton from his shirt. He wraps it around his neck and tucks it down under his collar. They start out without a meal or a word.

They head into the woods on empty bellies. Sylus leads the way through the brush, sniffing the air and turning his head to hear things that Charles cannot. He stoops to examine impressions in the ground and eat plants that he finds, offering Charles leaves and mushroom caps to eat. Charles declines them. Sylus stuffs them into his mouth and spits out the dirt. After a while he stops and listens to a tree. He puts his ear to the trunk, grasps it with both hands, and smiles.

Bees, he says.

He mounts the tree like a cat and climbs up twenty feet or more. The woods are quiet and Charles hears branches snapping above and a yelp of pain. When Sylus comes back to the ground his mouth is glistening with what appears to be sap. He holds out a hunk of honeycomb that sparkles in the light and writhes with white larval bees still wriggling in their tiny chambers. Charles takes part of the comb and bites into it, savoring the sweetness of the fresh honey. He chews it slowly. He lets it drip from the corners of his mouth and closes his eyes, remembering his childhood raids on the bee boxes of Leatherwood. When he opens them again Sylus is gone, and he follows the sound of popping branches to a clearing with a small pond and a stream.

He finds him near a pool of still water fed by a spring that can be heard but not seen. He's smiling and pointing down at several black shadows floating just below the surface and he gestures with his arms like a man casting for fish. Charles nods and smiles. He sits on a log and removes his shoes. He soaks his feet while Sylus cuts down a sapling of green chestnut that he fashions into a pole, then produces from within his rags a ball of light twine and a bent hook. He holds this up to Charles and smiles. He unbends it and rigs up the pole, then begins to turn over logs and stones for bait. After a while he comes up with a spotted salamander that he hooks and throws into the pool. The creature struggles on the surface of the water for a moment and then sinks. Within seconds the tip of the chestnut pole dips and breaks the surface of the water. Sylus lets out some of his twine and steps out into the pool, keeping his pole low and even with the surface. Before long he swings the pole to the side and pulls up a large bass, which he scales and cleans with the same dagger that he had pressed against Charles' throat. He builds a fire, and they both sit back on the log eating and watching it burn.

When they finish eating Charles wades out to refill the canteen. The air is warm and still, and the surface of the water is alive with pond-skippers and tadpoles. From beyond the trees, at the far end of the pool, he sees a boy carrying a bucket and a pole. He's wearing a wide-brimmed hat made of straw. The boy eyes them for a minute and Sylus waves. The boy waves back and puts down his bucket.

Charles watches the boy wade out to his knees. Sylus dozes and snores. The boy works some sort of jig on the surface of the pond with quick jerks of his wrists. He skips it over the deep part of the hole, and the water ripples. The sun breaks through the trees then, reflecting onto the underside of the overhanging leaves. The boy stands powder white under its rays. For a moment Charles watches the boy fish. It's that special time of the morning when the sun is the dominant object in the world and all things beneath it come alive. The trees and the grass glow. Leaves flicker like flames. The secret language of birdcalls drowns out all thought. In these times there is perfection in pine needles and in fiddleheads and in stones. It is a fleeting thing, these moments of grace, when all things living are joined. Time stalls, and the lifeless parts of the world speak to men. It is in these moments when a man knows he was never alone. The crackle of a single leaf is a message from God. A dragonfly is an angel. Prophets speak from the throats of barking toads.

Charles returns to the bank and finds a place to lie down. He props his head on his folded coat and lets his eyelids droop. Somewhere in the reeds along the edge of the little pond he can hear a red-winged blackbird and it is a sound that fills him with joy. The boy dips his pole down and waits. The line is slack and wet. It glows in the sunlight like a spider's web dripping with dew. The bottom of the pond glows and the gravel sparkles. Charles can see the shadows of tree branches on the sand beneath the water. He can hear the boy humming to himself, the way children do.

When he was a boy, he'd go off alone, fishing for a particular largemouth bass the old-timers nicknamed Abbadon after a dark angel from the book of Revelation. He was what they called a lunker—a big fish too smart to be landed, hooked many times but never caught. They'd talk about him around Shuck's stove in the wintertime and each man had a story about him. Fights with Abbadon lasted for hours and would always end with a split pole and a favorite lure lost. They said he'd jump up out of the water six feet in the air and twist like a polecat. Some said he ate ducklings and chipmunks and that he could move from one fishing hole to another like a ghost. Charles loved those tales. He swore that he'd be the one to bring Abbadon into Shuck's. He played that scene out in his mind a hundred times. The old-timers would just sit there slack-jawed and fall off their stools. They'd pat him on the back, buy him a beer, and mount that fish up on the wall under the big twelve-point buck and proclaim him the best fisherman there ever was. His daddy told him Abbadon was just a myth spun by drunks with too much time on their hands, but Charles believed, he believed in the old fish. He'd pray to Jesus for him. He prayed for one chance to hook him, just one clean fight. He wanted that fish more than he wanted anything in the world. But when that day finally came, when he saw him up close, he changed his mind.

He remembers it being a day much like this one. He's twelve years old and it's bright, sunny, hot—not at all a good day to fish. He's standing in the water with a bass in his hand, its jaw pinched tight between his index finger and thumb. It's a small fish, maybe a pound at most. He brings him over to a flat rock and cuts off its head with a quick stroke of his knife. He cuts open its belly and removes the stomach and cuts that open too, because what's inside will tell a man what the fish are feeding on and thus what type of bait to use. In this one he finds three dark lumps with claws and hard shells. He pokes at them with his knife. They're shiny and half-digested, but he can still see their black eyes.

Crawdads, he says.

He cleans his little fish with water from his canteen, wraps it in brown waxed paper, and stows it out of the sun. He baits his hook with a crawdad, throws it back into the water, and rests under the shade of a hemlock tree with the line wrapped round his big toe. There's a mass of submerged willow roots where the big ones hide and he watches the water there for fish sign and he waits.

It's hot and the heat wilts all the trout lilies. The water is clear and still, like hardened resin. The overhanging branches clack with newly hatched harvest flies, whose larval husks can be found by the hundreds stuck to the bark of every tree, poised there with their backs split open and their front legs held up in a manner that resembles men in prayer.

Charles hums to himself and notices a boy standing waist deep in the water near the willow roots. He sits up and squints to see if he is really there. The boy is shirtless and his skin is so white that he looks like a ghost.

Hey, Charles says. What are you doing out there?

The boy reaches below the surface of the water so that his chin dips, and his arms disappear entirely. He makes small motions with his submerged hands that send ripples out across the surface of the fishing hole. The water laps at Charles' feet.

The hair of the boy is black and long. He is very thin. Charles can see his ribs and the bones of his face. He's never seen him before. He knows all the boys in town, but this one must be from far away because everybody from these parts knows that you don't walk into the water when folks are fishing. The hole is tainted now, the fish are all spooked. Charles pulls in his line.

Hey, boy, this ain't no swimmin' hole, he says.

He props his pole against a tree, watching the boy move his hands below the water. He cannot tell what he's doing, but by the way he moves, he might be grabbing at a large stone on the bottom. He pulls his hands out of the water and holds up a big black thing, shiny like a rock, but it's no rock, it's a fish. Cradled there in the arms of the boy is a big largemouth bass, just lying there, his gills pumping, his tail fin flapping slow. The boy walks to the shore and he offers the fish to Charles.

How'd you do that? he says.

The boy is small and his eyes are shiny and big.

You asked for him, the boy says.

Charles steps up and touches the fish. Its mouth is scarred from hooks and trailing bits of broken line. He can see claw marks on its flanks—gouges from birds and raccoons. And it is gigantic—it must weigh more than fifteen pounds.

Abbadon, Charles says.

The boy holds the fish and stares at him. Water drips off his arms and Charles can see gooseflesh rise up on his skin.

Here he is, the boy says.

The fish is big and old and beautiful. The slits on the side of his head open to reveal pink feathered gills. He's stippled black and yellow, and bright green like the moss that grows on the bottom of an old canoe. His eye is as big and bright as a new dime. For a moment he looks more like a painting than a thing alive. But the radiance fades. The color drains from the fish. His gills flatten. His eye clouds.

The boy gestures for him to take the fish. He holds it out to him but Charles does not take it. He stares into the eyes of the boy.

Are you from around here? Charles says.

No. I'm not from Leatherwood.

He looks at the eyes of the boy, and he sees in them a power that cannot be named. He trembles and his belly grows hot. He looks down at the fish in his hands. It's dead. Its gills no longer move and the slick coating of slime on its scales has dried and turned dull. Charles is dizzy. His head spins. The boy looks at him, unblinking, and tries again to give him the fish, but Charles will not take it. So the boy lays it on the ground at his feet.

He steps toward Charles and takes his left arm in his long narrow fingers and holds it up to look at it, as if there were something there that he was hoping to see. He touches the tips of his fingers with his tongue and lays them on Charles' left elbow. His fingers sting like snake teeth and the pain shoots up his arm as far as his shoulder. When the boy releases his grip, the pain stops. He steps back and lifts the fish from the ground and stands there with it in his arms.

The boy steps into the creek, lowers the stiffened body into the water, washes it, and speaks to it in a low voice. The fish swishes its tail and the boy pushes it back into the water. As it swims away, the boy says nothing. He turns and walks back out to the willow roots where Charles first saw him. He wades around the bend behind the hanging branches and vanishes from the fishing hole as silently as he came.

This is what Charles remembers as he watches the boy in the straw hat fish, as he listens to Sylus snore and the fire burn down to crackling embers. He remembers that day—the day he came to believe in God.

8

HOLY GHOST CHILD

When Rebecca wakes, her vision is blurry and the whole room swims as if she's staring up from the bottom of a lake. The old woman stands at the foot of her bed, in the gray pall of morning, looking more tiny and frail than she remembers. With her eyes closed and her lips moving, she wraps Rebecca's feet in a compress soaked in potato whites and the boiled ooze of chestnut leaves. The burns cool and her ankles cease to throb.

The baby sleeps by her bedside in a wicker bassinet, and when she lifts her head to see him better, the old woman pinches her ankles to keep her still.

He's all right, she says.

The old woman removes the compress and blows on each ankle at the spot where the lightning came out and she applies to them both a light coating of linseed oil. When she's through, she lays a palm over Rebecca's eyes. Her hand has an unnatural warmth to it and it smells of flax. Rebecca can feel the calluses on her fingers as she rubs the healing oil over her lids.

It'll draw the fire right out, she says.

The old woman wears upon her head a white kerchief made from thick homespun cloth, turned up at the sides and cocked back behind her ears. She's got on two pairs of boy's trousers, one on top of the other, both too short, yet cuffed up above her sagging ankle socks and pocked all over with small round holes from falling bits of hot tobacco.

Her sweater was once the color of rose petals. Now it's a moth-eaten thing, all stained and faded, and too small in the sleeves. Upon her breast she's pinned an old brass key that tingles against the safety pin as she bends to lift the baby. He makes a noise and she shushes him. She lays him at Rebecca's side.

Rebecca cradles the child in her arms and runs her palm over his head. He has an ample amount of dark hair that grows in clumps but doesn't cover his entire scalp. His head looks strange and misshapen. It seems slightly larger than it should be, and warped like a small squash. When he stretches out his arms she can see that one is shorter than the other. But his grip is firm and a warm current flows through his fingers, not unlike the old woman's touch, only stronger, hotter.

It was the lightning that did that to him, the old woman says. She sits down on a ladder-back chair that jiggles and creaks. She strikes a wooden match on the side of her shoe and lights her pipe.

He's got the power of that lightning and the strength of that old tree, she says.

Rebecca closes her eyes and brings the boy up to take her breast. Her milk has yet to come, but the baby sucks all the same, and the old woman says that he still gets nourishment from the clear liquid that comes out of her. She listens to the smack of his lips on her breast and the low squeak of the old woman's chair. She can smell her rich tobacco. The old woman's eyes narrow at the smoke rising up into her face. She clasps the pipe between her teeth and fiddles with her key.

Some say it's bad luck just to look at that tree, she says.

He'll be all right, Rebecca says.

I expect he will. Because that boy's got more God in him than a crate full of Bibles, and I should know. I birthed over a hundred.

Rebecca stares up at the bare posts of the coatrack near the door. She looks over at the picture hanging above it. It's the Sacred Heart of Christ. She watches the eyes of Jesus, and the eyes of Jesus watch her back.

Yes, she says. He is blessed and so am I. Though I do wish Charles would come home.

He will, the old woman says. When he's done with the Lord's business.

On the back of the door hangs the small basket woven from white oak splits that Rebecca took up the mountain to carry back the herbs. The old woman made it for her as a present for the baby. She wonders how it got back on its peg.

He'd a-gone up there himself, Rebecca says. He'd a-gone up there and this never would've happened.

Hush now. God's purpose is His own. That boy was born where and when He wanted him to be. That old tree's been part of so much death, I guess He figured it was time for it to be redeemed. And it was. A tree can't take a life but it can give it.

The baby finishes sucking and drops off to sleep. Rebecca's nipple pops out of his mouth and glistens there in the light of the oil lamp. She wipes herself and covers her breast.

You ever known a person to get struck like that? Rebecca says.

The old woman puffs at her pipe and blows out a smoke ring that hangs in the air. It wobbles and squashes and falls apart.

I do, the old woman says. Berthie Coy. Killed her right dead. Folks said she had no eyes left and her toes turned black as embers before they crumbled off like dust.

Good Lord.

Rebecca, what you got was a sign. He don't want you to forget it was him led you to that tree. Gave you that there beaded cross too, to scare off the fear and give you strength of faith.

The necklace.

All sorts of things buried up there under that tree. Not all of them good. They made themselves a little cemetery behind it, the Negroes did. I seen bones there poking up out of the ground.

Rebecca looks over at the wall closest to the bed, where the necklace hangs on a nail. Its shadow quivers in the light of the oil lamp.

Whose was it, do you suppose?

Most likely belonged to somebody's momma, somebody that got hanged.

Doesn't seem right I should take it, Rebecca says, and she lifts her hand and touches the necklace with her finger. It's like stealing flowers off a grave, she says.

The old woman sucks on her pipe and smoke curls from the corner of her mouth. The cross on the beaded chain sways a bit because the house has drafts that let in the wind, and this makes the lamp flame flicker too. The shadows shudder and the walls themselves look alive.

You take what the Lord gives you. Such gifts you can't return.

Rebecca watches the cross move like a pendulum on the nail. She watches its shadow and listens to the breeze and the sound of the trees against the side of the house. She hears a noise beneath her that is not caused by the wind or leaves scraping on wood. It sounds like scratching. The old woman hears it too. She puts down her pipe and kneels on the floor. She cocks her head and listens. There's a thumping sound and a low rattle from beneath the bed. The old woman crawls under and begins talking in a low, soothing voice. It sounds like a chant or a song, but there is no music in it, no rhythm. Rebecca can't make out what she's saying.

The old woman stands and pulls a long wooden box from beneath the bed that measures eight inches high and twenty inches wide. Its top is covered in chicken wire and it has a hinged lid that she opens with slow and deliberate care. Rebecca knows just what it is. All the while the old woman chants her strange song and shakes her head from side to side. It looks like her eyes are closed, but they're not. They're rolled back in her head, and her wrinkled lids flutter as she crosses herself several times and holds her fingers outstretched before her. She clasps her hands together in prayer. Rebecca hears the word *Jesus* spoken over and over, and she can hear the tree outside scratching at the shingles on the roof. The old woman reaches into the box and grabs hold of something, an object of great fragility or great danger, for her movement is slow and cautious. She brings it up out of the box with the reverence and fear of someone handling dynamite. It is what Rebecca feared, a thick black snake.

The snake moves in her hands and wraps itself around her wrists. Its head pops up and stands erect and it bobs. Its head bounces slowly, hypnotically. Rebecca can see its eyes shining like carpet tacks, and she can see its flicking tongue. She holds her child tight as the old woman comes close, within striking distance, and when the tail of the snake rattles, the boy opens his eyes.

They watch each other, the snake and the child. They seem to be measuring each other. The old woman watches too, no longer chanting aloud, but mouthing the words to some prayer. Her eyes gleam as she waits, watching, watching, looking for a sign. The snake seems to sense a danger coming from the baby, for it grows rigid and its tail becomes a blur. The sound of its rattle fills the room and drowns out the wind as the oil lamp brightens. The snake opens its mouth then, and shows its fangs, bobbing and hissing as it feigns a strike. The old woman speaks to it, with a voice far too great for one of her stature.

The spirit is among us, she says. He's here, in the room, he's in the boy.

She brings the snake closer to the bed, closer to the child, whose eyes are fixed upon it. Rebecca pulls the baby back and tries to cover him but the old woman grabs her wrist and squeezes it hard.

Keep still, the old woman says. He don't need you to protect him. He's got the Holy Ghost, by God he does.

She pulls Rebecca's wrist, throws back the blanket covering the baby, and brings the snake near. The skin of the child is red, and his face is still swollen. His mouth is open, his tongue is out and probing. He's looking to suck. His tiny fingers open and close, clenching into fists and unclenching. He's inches from the snake, which is still and quiet now, close enough for the child to grab. The snake senses the warm little body there before it, and its instinct tells it not to move but to wait. The old woman holds it out just a bit farther until its head lies on the baby, the pale skin of its lower jaw rests against his belly flesh. It flicks its tongue. Rebecca closes her eyes. The snake's head rises. The old woman moves it close to the boy's face and her eyes widen. There is no sound at all, no rattle and no wind. The child's arms move and the snake turns. The old woman closes her eyes and it strikes her, two quick bites on her shoulder. The old woman smiles and laughs at the thing. She shakes her head from side to side like a dog bit by bees. She spits three times off to the side and throws the snake to the floor with force enough to kill the thing.

Too much for it, she says. Too much spirit in that child.

The baby cries out and Rebecca soothes him. She brings him up close to her. The old woman finishes a prayer and pulls back her sweater to see her wound, which she rubs with her fingertips. She steps over the snake and comes to the side of the bed and lays her hand on the child's back.

Born with it, she says. Her eyes sparkle. Her hands tremble. Born with the Holy Ghost inside him, the vessel of the Lord is that boy. That snake didn't know which way to run. Every instinct he got told him to strike, told him to fear. But he couldn't bite that child. He could not.

She picks up the snake, walks over to the stove, and drops it into a pot. Rebecca nurses the boy. The old woman sits back down in her chair and taps the bowl of her pipe on one of its arms, then lights it again. The smoke curls up and she waves it out of her eyes and closes them. She begins to pray.

9

THE CROSS FARM

shadow passes over Charles and blocks the glaring sun. When he opens his eyes there is a moment of panic because he does not recognize the gray face before him. But the fear passes as quickly as it came. The sound of a blackbird reminds him he is still lying near the pond. Sylus Knox bends over him, his beard stained with white flakes of fish.

I reckon we best be moving, Sylus says.

Charles raises himself up on his elbows and sees the boy still fishing at the opposite end of the pool.

Hold on, he says.

He walks over to him, stepping softly heel to toe, careful not to spook the hole with sound or shadow. When he gets near the bank where the boy left his pail, he sees that he has a stringer of pumpkinseeds tethered to a branch and floating in the shallows.

Hey, he says. You live close to here?

The boy raises a finger to his lips and motions with his chin to a dark shape in the water. His little jig moves in short jerks and then stops. The dark shape below the surface lunges, hits the jig, and runs for deeper water. The boy sets the hook fast but does nothing. He lets the fish tire before pulling it in. It's a trout almost a foot long. He holds it by its gills and comes to shore, grinning.

I live less than a mile up that trail, he says.

Charles nods. That's a fine-looking fish. It wags its tail fin slow and glimmers in the sun.

My name's Charles Flint, he says. I'm a man of God in desperate need of a bath and a shave. Might I get one at your place?

You look clean to me.

I am clean, son. The bath is for that man over there. I just saved him from a life of sin.

The boy looks out across the water at Sylus Knox who sits scratching himself on a log. He looks back at Charles, straight into his eyes, and he squints for a moment. He has a lean and bony face, this boy. His cheekbones are high and visible below his pale skin. His eyes are set deep within his face. They're kind and soulful. One of them is blue, and the other as brown as a chestnut.

Momma never turns strangers away, mister. Get whatever you all is carrying and follow me.

With Sylus downwind behind them, they pass through thick brush and animal trails so narrow that they have to get down on their knees and crawl. The boy whistles the whole way. He tells them his name is Tobias Cross, and that's all he says until they break through a stand of trees above a small farm dominated by a large green barn and surrounded by newly plowed fields. They stand outside a split-rail fence that wraps itself around the whole place.

There's home, the boy says.

He hops the fence and heads down to the house. Charles does the same. But Sylus pauses at the rail. He has the look of some animal forced out of the darkness by hunger. Charles turns and motions with his hand, but Slylus shakes his head at him.

It's all right, Sylus.

There's a woman down there.

I expect.

I ain't seen one in a while.

Well, they haven't changed much.

I know it.

Well?

I ain't fit to be looked upon by a woman.

Charles smiles and nods. He reaches into his coat pocket for his Bible. He opens the book with great care and lays his finger on a passage, and he reads from it.

When he was come down from the mountain, great multitudes followed him. And behold, there came a leper and worshipped him, saying, Lord, if thou wilt, thou canst make me clean. And Jesus put forth his hand, and touched him, saying, I will: Be thou clean.

He holds out his hand to him.

These folks are Christians, Sylus. Now take my hand and get over this fence. Before this day is done you'll be a new man entirely.

Sylus runs his fingers through his beard and reaches back to feel his hair. It's been years since he's seen his face in a mirror. He takes a deep breath and reaches out for Charles' hand. He helps him over the fence and they walk down the hill to the Cross farm.

The house is painted the same color as the barn—green like the head of a mallard duck, with white trim and a fine garden beside it. It's a two-story place with white-framed windows and a wraparound porch and all manner of fowl pecking at the ground outside. An old dog besieged by flies raises his head from the dust as they approach and then drops it back to the ground and rolls onto his side. Several cats lie on the wooden steps in all aspects of repose, and a woman working a handmade broom turns from her chore and stares out at the two men, then turns back to her sweeping as if expecting them.

Tobias, she says, do you notice if there are any pies sittin' in that window?

She does not turn from her sweeping. The boy drops his head. He looks down at his stringer of fish, then looks back at the two men behind him.

No, he says.

No, you don't notice, or no, there are no pies?

There are no pies, Ma.

There are no pies, she says.

She continues her sweeping, raising up a cloud of dust and shooing the sleeping cats from the stairs in the process.

Then you'll have to explain to these two gentleman why they won't be eating any of my sweet rhubarb pie with their lunch today.

The boy shuffles his feet in the dirt and looks up at Charles, who's holding his hat in one hand and his Bible in the other.

She bakes the best pies you ever ate, says Tobias.

The woman stops her sweeping and turns, stepping down out of the shade of the porch and into the hot morning sun. She raises her hand to her brow, shading her eyes, and regards the two strangers standing in her yard. She is a handsome woman and she is tall. Her hair is somewhere between blonde and red, and she has it tied back away from her face. Charles notices that she is freckled, and this makes her look younger than she is. Sylus stares down at his shoes.

I'm Nettie Cross, she says, and turns to the boy. Tobias is supposed to be sweeping this porch, not fishing the day away.

The boy avoids her glance and looks back at the two men. Sylus gives him a wink.

I expect you'll be wanting lunch, and I'll give it to you

after you split that pile of wood there and stack it against the side of the house. My husband will be back shortly, and you can speak with him about a place for the night, if that's what you came for.

The woman hands her son the broom and turns to the house, but then stops and turns back. She looks over at Sylus, as if noticing for the first time his poor physical condition, then she turns to Charles.

You two travel together?

We do.

How'd that come to be?

We saved each other's lives.

The woman smiles. She sees that Charles is holding a Bible. She also sees that his eyes are clear and sharp. They do more than stare or gaze; they unravel that which they behold.

What's he? About six foot? she says.

I'd say a couple more inches than that.

I have something he can wear. I won't have him in my house like that.

We thank you.

Don't thank me, you'll be earnin' it. Soon as you're done, I'll pour him a bath out back and get him some scissors and a razor. God loves all men the same, but a clean heart starts with a clean body.

Amen to that.

Nettie goes inside. Charles slaps Sylus on the shoulder and a little puff of dust wafts up from his coat.

We're gonna have to burn this, Charles says. And shave off all your hair.

10

THE PROMISED CHILD

Mornings are always cold on the mountain, and the air in the cabin is cool. A mean draft blows through it sometimes, and this makes the candle flame lean sideways. Rebecca can see the baby's breath in the weak light that flickers on the wall. She can see her own breath too. The two of them are alone together in the quiet hour before dawn, and he is alive in her arms, the boy child that Charles promised her long before they fell in love. She remembers the day he told her, on that long walk they took down to the stream, with his hands clasped round his Bible and hers wrapped in her shawl. Her daddy walked behind them with his fiddle and the dogs.

The child does not cry much, and this worries her. He hardly makes a sound at all and he doesn't sleep like new babies mostly do. He lies wakeful and restless, watching her, his eyes moving in his head. They are blue-gray, his eyes, and his lashes are long. He stares up at Rebecca and follows the movements of her hands as she braids her hair. She tries to get him to smile but he won't, so serious is this child. He makes no sound. Even when he's hungry he won't cry.

She talks to him during the day and whispers to him at night. She tells him all her secrets and the few things she knows about the world. She tells him about the birth and death of mountains and where rivers come from, and she describes the very nature of rain and snow. She names for him all the animals she can think of and talks about the wonders of the weather and the magic of trees. She reads to him from the Bible, and he listens to her, his eyes never once leaving hers. They grow larger when she speaks to him, and they shine when she hums, which she does when she feeds him. He eats well and does not fuss at her breast the way Magdalena did. She sings him nursery songs, old hymns and music from the hills, the fiddle music her daddy played. This is what makes him smile for the first time, the folk songs from her girlhood.

And they make her smile too, these songs from her youth, they sound to her like home. She remembers her father tuning the fiddle by the light of the fire, rubbing rosin on the bow, and how he'd play for her in the evening times while she cleared the supper plates and tell her stories about mountain witches and strange things in the woods. He told her one day a man would come and take her away, a good-looking man with clear skin and clear eyes and a way with words that would charm her right out of the hollow and off the mountain for good. She would protest his predictions and smother him with kisses, and the tingle of his beard stubble and the smell of his hair tonic would linger on long into the night as she lay restless and dreaming of the piercing-eyed stranger who'd take her away from the only place she ever knew.

On the day Charles did come to take her, he was far from a stranger. She remembered her father's prophecy when he looked into her eyes and asked her to marry him. But she knew it was true the moment she saw him, on that rainy Sunday when he first came to the house. He was just a young preacher then, no more than nineteen. Charles wasn't like any other backwoods preacher. He was more like a regular man, not the kind of person Rebecca was used to seeing preach the gospel. He wasn't a man who'd shout hellfire and damnation and jump all around like his legs were full of lightning. He'd talk for hours with the Bible closed in his lap. He talked about Jesus the man, and the anointment of the Holy Spirit and how true believers could wield the power of God.

When they were alone, walking together on the path in the woods, he spoke to her about his visions and his hope for his own church on a mountain. He told her about the family he would raise and the son he planned on rearing who was destined to become a symbol of the living God. He said he saw it all in his dreams. He would teach this boy and guide him and name him Jacob for the faith he would have—for Paul said that God loved Jacob and not Esau, and that he was the living proof of his sovereign grace to man.

He came to the house each Sunday with his Bible and a snake box he carved himself from wood. He kept an old cottonmouth inside that box, a snake named after a demon out of Revelation. He called the snake Abbadon, and it was a pitiful thing. It had a severed tail that he told folks he bit off with his own teeth, but the truth was he caught it in a spring-loaded trap when he was a boy. That snake had been tame so long he'd hardly even hiss. He'd take it out sometimes when reading from the book of Mark. This is how he spread his name. Charles Flint, the preacher with a snake in a box. He told people he carved it from the coffin wood of Lester Poles—a killer they hanged, buried, and dug up to hang again. He claimed Lester's soul was in that snake, that the spirits of all evil men dwell in serpents after they die. It got to where people would stop him in the road just to see that box. That's when he let the cottonmouth go. And she remembers that day too. They were in a meadow beneath a tree, alone for perhaps the first time.

Rebecca, he said. I've been a damn fool.

No, she said. You're no fool.

My pride has got the better of me.

If it had, you wouldn't be talking like this now.

Still, I should never have made up those stories. I never dug up no grave and this snake is a lie.

Not anymore, she said.

People don't want to listen. They just want a show, a story.

Then give them that, but make it the truth.

I've got no truth to tell.

Then find it. You'll find it.

He looked at her then, and it was the first time they both knew what each was thinking, and it was that they'd be married and raise a family and live out their lives with each other and for each other. They kissed. They touched each other. They became one in heart and mind.

You'll bear me a son, he said. And I will take up serpents again one day.

Then he released the old cottonmouth and buried the box in the unmarked grave of Lester Poles, in a secret place beneath the Tyborn tree.

This is the story she whispers to the baby in the dark. She tells him so that he knows how he began, that he was more than just a prophecy—he was promise. The telling of the story reassures her that it's true. She whispers his name to him. She gazes into his eyes in stunned wonder at his true existence.

Jacob, she says. You're finally here, and your daddy will be proud.

She pulls her breast from the child's mouth. The nipple's all gummed down flat and shiny. He's got big plans for you, she says. But I know. You're gonna be your own man. She wipes his chin and puts him over her knee to burp him. She thumps on his back with her fingers and walks around the tiny cabin, bouncing him and humming. The sun has yet to rise, but she can see the sky turning light through the window. The old woman comes up the wooden stairs in her husband's shoes. She walks with the heavy steps of the old. Rebecca can hear her breathing hard and the sound of the bucket as she puts it down. The handle bangs against the side of the pail.

That'll be the milk, she says, and the door opens. The old woman slides the bucket inside and some of the milk spills. They stare at each other for a moment, and the old woman shuts the door with her foot. She scratches at her head and then looks down at her fingernails.

I seen him last night, she says. He's reached his destination, at the foot of his dream mountain.

Rebecca lays the baby down in the bassinet and sits on the bed.

Who?

Your husband is who.

You saw Charles?

An Indian mountain, she says. That's where he's going. Old place, south of here. I saw it in my dream as sure as I see you now. An old mountain, where many died in a war before the white man came, and I saw a big old snake with an eye on the back of its head. A snake like I've never seen before.

Rebecca gets up. It's brighter outside and there's more for her to see out the window. She can just make out the shapes of trees. On the hillside a pair of deer feed and everything looks strange. In the first moments of dawn it's all the same color and it looks like there's no shape to the world.

What's it mean? she says.

It is what it is. A big ole snake with funny eyes is all.

When's he coming home?

The old woman hefts the bucket up onto the table and scratches herself on the inside of her thigh. She shakes her head at Rebecca.

He'll be home when he's home, she says. If I knew more I'd say it, and if I see anything else I'll be sure to tell you.

The old woman pours out a cup of milk from the bucket and brings it to her. She stands there and watches her drink. The milk is sweet and thick. It runs down her neck. The old woman smiles as Rebecca tips the cup to swallow it all.

That's good, she says. You need strength. If I had me some chewin' plug I'd give that to you too. You know how good it is for baby's milk. But I don't have any, so you'll have to wait till somebody goes into Shuck's to get some.

Rebecca climbs back in bed where it's warm.

11

UNBENDING

Charles stands bare-chested and breathing hard in the hot noon sun. His back is slick and coated with wood chips and sawdust. He's done the work of two men while Sylus soaked himself clean and cut his beard. All about him lie splits of chopped wood. He leans against the handle of the axe and watches Nettie Cross cut the man's hair as he sits on a crate not far from the woodpile.

In his time, Charles has seen many men transformed. He's witnessed spiritual rebirth, complete redemption, the unbending of souls. He's watched in awe the Holy Spirit enter a man, purify his heart, and temper his body to withstand snake venom, searing flame, and the consumption of deadly poisons in miraculous displays of divine love and boundless faith. Yet he marvels at the complete metamorphosis of Sylus Knox.

He is lean, his jaw is sharp, his face is long and almost handsome. His skin is pink like the belly of a dog. Charles notices for the first time that his eyes are large and sad. But they sparkle now, in front of the hand mirror that he holds. His head is shaved nearly bald.

Be thou clean, Charles says.

Be clean yourself, Sylus says. I can smell you from here.

Nettie smiles too. She's measuring a cuff on a pair of trousers and holds a straight pin between her lips. But when she looks up from her work her smile disappears, and they all turn to watch a sputtering truck pull down the hill.

That'll be John, she says. And I forgot all about his lunch.

She gathers her thread and scissors and rushes inside, holding her skirts up from the ground with one hand and looking up at the truck as it pulls into the yard.

It's an older-model flatbed Dodge. Both its doors squeal as two tired-looking men climb out. One is a big black man with skin so dark that it appears featureless as a shadow. The other is a white man with broad shoulders bred to farmwork. He walks over to the woodpile with a limp, removing a dusty hat and wiping his brow with his sleeve. He stands for a moment, regarding the two strangers. One is shirtless and holding his axe. The other is wearing his old clothes and sitting comfortably on a stool surrounded by clumps of thick hair. He turns to the black man and shakes his head.

Crawford, he says, when you finally build yourself that house of yours, you build it as far from them train tracks as you can. A man never knows what he'll find waitin' for him when he gets home otherwise.

The black man smiles a mouthful of polished teeth and shakes his head.

I believe I'll take that advice, Mr. Cross.

I'm John Cross, this here's my hired man, Crawford Bughes.

Charles wipes his hands on his pants and looks over at Sylus, who stands and puts on a shirt. Charles steps out of the woodpile and faces John Cross.

Pleased to meet you, Mr. Cross. I'm Charles Flint and this here's Sylus Knox.

Cross spits to the side and wipes his mouth with the back of his hand.

We're just passing through, Charles says. We're on our way up to Slaughter Mountain, where we hear there's a church of true believers. We're men of God.

Charles extends his hand, but Cross does not take it. He stares into the eyes of the man holding his axe and does not break away from his gaze. He sees no fear in the eyes of Charles and he sees no lie. What he does see he cannot explain, and it makes him uneasy, for he does something that he has never done before, and that is to turn away from another man's stare. He looks up at Sylus and walks to him.

Men of God, you say?

Sylus stares at the man, rubbing his fresh-shaved chin.

He's the man of God, I'm just a follower.

Cross looks him straight in the eye.

You come to join them snake people?

Sylus looks over at Charles and points at him.

I didn't come to see nobody. He did, he says.

Them Bowsky boys have themselves some kind of racket up there, Cross says. Folks come from all over to watch them dance with snakes and drink poison. I went up there once to have a look. It's a regular three-ring circus.

Charles steps over and hands him the axe.

We thank you for the use of your axe and the other hospitalities. Your wife has been most kind. If you'd be good enough to let us stay here for the night, I'd appreciate it. We'll be gone first thing in the morning.

Cross takes the axe and examines the blade. He looks up at Charles and shakes his head. Then he looks over at Crawford Bughes.

Crawford, you ever get around to moving that pile of stones up there on the north slope?

Crawford smiles. No, Mr. Cross, he says. I sure haven't.

I'll tell you what, Mr. Flint, you move them stones for me and you men can stay on here till the morning. I'll set you up in the barn there. It's clean and warm, and I guess nicer than most places you've slept.

Charles nods and looks over at Sylus. He grins at him and winks.

We thank you, he says. We'll move them stones for you, and do whatever else you folks need.

Well, I'll think on it, Cross says. But first I need to eat. Crawford here will show you what needs to be done.

A large mound of heavy stones lies at the edge of a field. They're all coated with dark mud that's dried and rubbed off on the hands, arms, and clothing of Charles and Sylus. The rock pile is almost as tall as a man now. There're only a dozen or so stones left to be moved but they no longer stack them neatly on top of the pile. They drop them at the edge now, ignoring the art of placing them so that the mound grows evenly and domed, like a barrow.

They walk slow and breathe heavy, wiping sweat from their foreheads with the backs of their arms. Sylus is shaking, and he squats for a moment with his hand on his lower back. He shuts his eyes and waves Charles on.

I'll catch up, he says.

Charles pulls him by the arm.

You stop now and you'll stiffen up. You'll never be able to stand, he says.

I know it.

There's only a few left.

That was as good a lunch as I've had in a long time, Sylus says. But I'm not sure it was worth even this, and neither is a bed made of hay.

Hard work is good for the soul, Sylus.

They walk together and stoop to lift two more stones,

fifty pounds each or more. They wobble over to the pile with heavy steps, Sylus all spraddle-legged and bent. He's straining so hard under the weight of the stone that his eyes are clenched shut. His jaw is tight, his lips pulled back in a sneer that reveals what's left of his back teeth. He drops the stone and falls to his knees, panting.

Charles carries his stone to the pile and drops it there. The air is still, and before him he can see the fields drop away toward the farm. They're freshly plowed and rippling with waves of heat. The only sound he can hear are the harvest flies in the trees, all clicking and buzzing together. His ears ring and his head aches. He turns to Sylus and sees him on his knees. He goes to him and puts his hand on his shoulder. Sylus coughs and spits.

I'm done, he says.

Charles pats his back and looks him in the eye where he can see defeat, surrender, submission to habits long ingrained. He's a man retreating into himself because he's got nothing left to believe in. A faithless man is more than a danger to himself—he's a danger to the world.

You ain't done, he says. You're just beginning. He pulls him up by the arm, lifting his full weight from the ground, because the man's legs will no longer work. He holds him by the shoulders, holds him against his own will to drop. He tries to look him in the eyes, but Sylus turns away. Charles takes him by the chin like a child, forcing him to look into his eyes.

Do you believe in the Lord? he says.

I need me a drink.

You want a drink, but you don't need it.

I can't do this.

I was told that you can.

Told by who?

You know who.

Damn you, Charles Flint, he says and he pulls his arm away. You don't know nothing about me or what I've seen or what I've done. I killed a man. More than one. Them others came at me first, so I don't lose sleep over them, but the last one was no more than a boy, and I gut-stabbed him just for looking at me 'cause I was drunk and feeling mean at the time. A boy just trying to be a man was all he was. I was drunk like I'm always drunk, except now, and Lord knows I want to be. I'm no good to the core, and whiskey runs in my veins, whiskey and evil. I can't lift them stones, I can't come with you to your mountain, and I sure as hell can't change.

He turns away and holds his palms over his eyes.

You're gonna carry that stone, Charles says. You're gonna carry it up to the top of that pile, you hear me? You're gonna carry it up there, not with your own strength, but with God's.

I can't do it, Sylus says. I'm all burned up, inside and out.

I'm telling you that you can, Charles says. He places his palm on his shoulder.

Feel my hand, Sylus, feel how it burns.

Sylus squirms under the touch of his hand. His eyes open wide, and he looks back at Charles with confusion and fear. His hand is hot.

That's not me, Sylus. I'm what you call a conduit. I just pass it on.

You got something in you, that's for sure. I seen it in your eyes.

Charles moves his hand down his shoulder and arm. He grabs his hand and squeezes it.

You have to believe in something, Sylus, something outside yourself. If you can't believe, you can't live. You don't understand that now, and you may not be ready for the Lord quite yet, but you will be. For now, believe in me. You can carry that stone up to the pile because I said you can. You came this far with me. I wouldn't steer you wrong now.

Sylus looks down at the farm, far away. He sees the long rolling furrows stretch out over the fields. He sees dark lines and light lines, bending and curving, a thousand fresh ridges of turned earth and the heat rising off them in little waves. He can hear insects in the trees and the sound of his own deep breaths.

He stoops down and wraps his fingers around the stone. He sucks in air and lifts, pushing up with his feet and thighs. He hefts the stone up to his waist and then to his chest and waddles with it over to the pile. He tries to climb it, but can't get a good foothold and drops the stone on the edge. It knocks against another and makes a hollow noise, a deep, satisfying clunk.

That's as far I can go, he says. He falls down on his behind, shuts his eyes, and breathes.

Charles goes to him and touches his arm.

You just did what you swore you could not do, and that's a fine start. I'll get these last few and we'll go down and get us cleaned up. Tomorrow's Sunday, and we want to get an early start if we're gonna make Slaughter Mountain by church time.

As Charles goes about hefting the remaining stones, Sylus shuts his eyes and watches the red and orange specks that the sunlight makes behind his closed lids.

12

FIRE AND FROST

The old woman has the baby in her lap and her pipe in her mouth. The chair squeaks as she rocks in it and the room is filled with smoke. The baby is asleep with his arms up over his head. His hands are balled into tight little fists. There's a pot on the stove with something thick inside that bubbles and pops from time to time. It smells like a tomato stew. The old woman stares across the room at the wall behind Rebecca. Her eyes are glazed. She sits so still that she looks like a wax figure. Only the wisps of pipe smoke that stream from the side of her mouth indicate she's alive and breathing at all.

Rebecca's legs feel swollen and they ache. The air inside the cabin is stale from the smoke and the smell of the stew. The windows are steamed up, but outside the sun is shining. She goes to the window and rubs away the moisture with the palm of her hand.

It's a nice day, she says.

The old woman rocks slowly and puffs on her pipe.

But it's cool, Rebecca says. It looks like it might be cool.

The old woman takes the pipe out of her mouth. She's still not looking at Rebecca, she's looking at the wall behind her. She wipes her lips with the back of her hand.

Why don't you go on out and take a walk, she says.

Can I?

Just don't go too far. You're still weak and you might start to bleedin'.

Rebecca smiles and opens the door. The sun is warm on her face and there's a breeze blowing and on it she smells the flowers and the grass. She steps down onto the bottom step, which is warm. She can smell the dry wood. She lifts her dress and sits there in the sunlight, closing her eyes, feeling the heat of it on her skin. The harvest flies are all singing in the trees.

She knows she's not supposed to go too far, but she feels compelled to see Magdalena and finds herself walking up the dirt path toward the house. There's pain down inside her where the baby had been, but she keeps walking. The path is dusty and her toes are brown from kicking through the dirt. She sees a crow sitting in an apple tree on the hill. The bird doesn't make a sound, but its head moves, watching her pass. It's a big bird with shiny black eyes. When it cocks its head she sees a dark blue sheen on its neck. She walks up the path, around the hill, and keeps on walking until she's standing on the grass near the porch in front of the house. She hears Magdalena yelling inside.

The screen door slams open and Magdalena runs out holding a big wooden spoon in her hand and smiling with the rapturous glee of a child who knows she's got the best of a grown-up. Mary Albert is trailing behind her in her apron. She's a big woman with flushed cheeks who normally wears her hair up in a bun, though now it's unloosed and in disarray, showing streaks of black among the mostly silver strands. She had once been the old woman's apprentice until they had a falling-out over a woman's death. They haven't spoken in years. These days she's the only woman still birthing babies the old way, but now she's out of breath and out of patience. Magdalena runs behind the porch swing laughing, and Mary looks like she's had all she can take from the three-year-old. The girl runs from behind the swing and out onto the grass, where she falls on her face. Mary Albert comes after her but stops short when she sees Rebecca standing barefoot, her housedress soaked in breast milk, her face all pale and moist and red.

Rebecca, Mary says. You look like you was raised right up from the grave.

Rebecca nods and manages to smile a bit. The little girl stands and drops the spoon.

Momma, she says, and she runs to her. She throws her arms around her bare legs. Mary takes her by the hand and pulls her away.

You leave your momma alone now, she's don't need you hanging on her.

It's all right, Mary.

You should be in bed, Mary says. You should be in bed nine days after a baby come.

That's just superstition.

Nine days, Rebecca. Don't blame Mary Albert if something happens to you or that boy.

Mary grabs Magdalena to keep her away from Rebecca. The girl screams and struggles to get away, but Mary holds her back.

You go on now. Go look after your baby, she says.

He's fine, Mary.

He's not fine. He's not fine at all. I seen him. I seen his big eye and that warped head of his. I seen the scar on his back too.

That boy's marked, and it's no wonder why when you're out there birthin' him in the Tyborn tree of all places. What were you thinking?

Rebecca tries to hold back the tears, but they just stream out on their own, all down her cheeks, a flood of tears. She kneels in the grass and covers her eyes with her hands. Magdalena tries to go to her, but Mary holds her back. Rebecca reaches out and they touch hands, but Mary pulls the girl away.

You should be in bed, she says. Before you start bleedin' like the last time.

You know that wasn't my fault, Rebecca says. That baby came too soon.

Just like this one. A beautiful child that baby was.

Babies die, Mary, Rebecca says.

A face like an angel that one had.

He's with the old woman, he'll be all right for a few minutes.

That old woman's half blind and too feeble to care for 'em proper, Mary says. She was the best there was in her day, but that time is long gone. Lord knows she taught me well, but you already lost one boy child and this might be the last chance you got. If it was me, I wouldn't leave him for one second. That child would never leave my arms.

Magdalena reaches out for Rebecca, but Mary won't let her go. Rebecca grabs for her and falls hard, and she feels a pain inside her like a bad cramp. She can feel moisture seeping down her thigh. She's bleeding. This is how it started the last time. It took two days before it stopped, and the old woman said she almost didn't come through. When she woke from her fever they told her the baby had passed on. She never got to hold that child while he was alive.

She presses her legs together and wipes her hair out of her face.

He's not yours, Mary, she says. And for your information

his face is fine. It's as beautiful as any child, and if the Lord takes him it'll be because he needs him. But he won't. He won't take this child, not this one.

Magdalena breaks free from Mary's grip and embraces Rebecca, and smoothes down her mother's hair. She glares up at Mary and the woman squints back at her.

You should never have gone up on that mountain, she says. That old woman's a damn fool for lettin' you out of the house. And to have him in that tree, of all places. He'd be better off if he did pass on with that hanging over his head. You're still young.

Rebecca stands and wipes her face. She's bleeding worse now, and her legs are shaking. But she will not let this insult pass.

I won't have you talk like that, she says. It's all done now, Mary, we live with what there is. Jacob came to us the way He wanted him to come, and he'll grow up to be a fine man. You best not treat him any different, or ever say such a thing again. You hear me? Ever. And before you go on shootin' your mouth off to folks down at Shuck's, remember this: Jesus himself was born in a stable, John the Baptist in the wilderness. The only thing over Jacob's head is what you hang there yourself, so you hold your tongue and give him a chance.

Mary bends down and picks up the spoon.

So you went ahead and gave him the name, she says.

Of course I did. Like I should have done the last one.

That name's for a boy that lives.

He does live, and he'll keep on living, and I won't bury a nameless child again. This boy was born Jacob Flint and he'll die Jacob Flint, be it today, tomorrow, or in a hundred years.

Rebecca teeters and blinks. She shakes her head and drops to her knees again.

I'm bleeding now, she says. I think you better take Magdalena because I'm gonna faint.

Magdalena runs to Mary. Rebecca feels down at the blood between her legs and looks up at both of them. She opens her mouth and tries to speak, but nothing comes out.

Lord, Mary says. I'll go get the old woman.

She leaves Magdalena by her side and runs down to the cabin. Rebecca lies on the soft grass and closes her eyes. Magdalena holds her hand and rubs her arm.

Momma, she says. I'll help you, Momma. I know the words. Son and father, holy ghost, out goes fire, in comes frost.

13

THE ROAD TO HOLY MOUNTAIN

From his place in the straw Charles can see swallows wheeling in the rafters as the first amber beams of morning stream in through the slats of the barn. In those slanted rays of early light dust motes rise and fall like snowflakes. They sparkle. They swirl. All through the night he lay with his eyes open, looking out at the stars through the small window above him, watching the exodus of the bats. He read from his Bible under the light of a kerosene camp lantern and prayed for Rebecca and the child newly born.

He watches the eaves of the barn above him now, and the mud-daubed nests of the swallows. He sees the little dome-shaped caves of dried earth and clay, packed together bit by bit with tiny beaks and formed into hollow cocoons for the rearing of their young. Inside he can hear the nestlings. He sees their pink faces peering out from the holes when their mothers leave to hunt.

Sylus sleeps at his side with his arms clasped tight around his head to shield out the light. He's breathing loud and from time to time smacking his lips together, licking them. Below them livestock shuffle in the straw. The cows are all restless and spooked. Around their necks hang copper bells. They don't ring so much as they clank, and the noise makes him think of sunny hillsides and fields of windswept grass. Somewhere outside the barn, he can hear a horse blowing through its nose, and he lies staring up at the swallows, thinking about the boy. His boy. It is Sunday.

The hayloft grows warm and he dozes for a while. He dreams about a baby, stillborn and malformed, with a pinched and wrinkled face and a winding umbilicus coiling round it like a vine. He wakes panting to the sound of milk being squeezed into a steel pail. Someone is whistling and Sylus wheezes in his sleep. The ground below the hayloft is crawling with mewling cats. He sits up and dusts off his hat and smoothes back his hair. Then he climbs down the ladder and walks into the far stall, where Tobias is milking a brown cow. He clears his throat so as not to scare him.

Hey, he says.

Hey yourself, the boy says. Sleep all right up there?

Not so good.

Well, it ain't the Palace Hotel, that's for sure. But I always liked it. On warm nights I stay up there and watch the bats.

I did that myself. It's a fine spot, but I have some things on my mind and couldn't sleep.

Yeah. Momma said you was expecting a baby.

Not anymore. He's already come.

The boy switches his full milk pail for an empty one and looks up at Charles with narrow eyes. The cats are all around his feet now, rubbing up against his legs, trying to get at the milk pails.

How do you know he's come? the boy says.

Charles rubs his forehead and scratches his nose with his knuckle. He looks up at the roof and then down at the cats.

The Lord told me, he says.

The boy stops his milking and turns on his stool.

The Lord?

That's right.

He talks to you?

Not with words. He gives me feelings, he shows me signs in dreams.

You some kinda prophet?

No. Anybody can hear the Lord, if they know how to listen.

The boy stands and takes up his milk buckets and walks past him through the stall door. The cats follow. He puts the milk down on a small cart and wipes his hands on his trousers.

How do you do that? he says. Listen?

You have to open up your soul so your heart can sing out to him. You have to live a clean and simple life, and do right by others. You have to earn him.

That don't sound too hard, the boy says.

He stuffs his hands into his pockets and purses his lips. He pulls out a dollar bill from his overalls and unfolds it.

I earned this dollar for cleaning these stalls. Took me two days.

Well, it sounds easy, but it's not. If you come out to the revival with us, I'll show you what I mean.

Daddy would never let me go up there.

Well, minding your daddy's part of the bargain.

You all going up there today?

We are.

How you going to get there?

On the feet God gave us.

It's a long walk.

That's why we'll be getting on soon.

Maybe we could give you a ride into town. We go right by the road up the mountain.

We'd be obliged for that, but you done enough for us.

It's no bother. We're going to town anyhow.

We'll see.

C'mon in for breakfast and I'll ask.

The boy pulls the cart with the milk buckets out through the barn and into the bright light of the day beyond. He stops and puts his hand up to shield his eyes.

You coming?

I'm right behind you. Soon as I wake Sylus up there.

Charles hears the wheels of the wagon on the gravel. The cats are all licking at spilled milk on the ground. He watches the cats for a while and then something falls from the rafters above him, a swallow chick from a nest on the roof. It writhes on the ground all blind and featherless. He stoops down to see it closer, though he knows it can't be saved and cannot live. Its skin is bright pink and translucent, pulsing with blood and a tiny heart, and behind its closed lids the black orbits of its eyes swim in startled confusion. He touches the bird with his finger. It's warm and soft and it reacts to being touched by opening its mouth, expectant of a meal, but it is grabbed by a cat who trots away with the bird clasped in its jaws. Charles looks up at the nests, and down at the cats, some of whom are cleaning their paws with their tongues. He turns and climbs the ladder back up to the hayloft to wake Sylus.

It's far too loud in the truck bed for talking, so Charles and Sylus stare out at the receding countryside. They're holding onto the wooden rails to keep themselves from banging on the hard bed as they squat on their toes and bounce along with the action of the old truck. The road is cut deep with ruts and cratered all over with holes brimming with muddy water. The tires splash through these puddles with a great fanfare of brown spray and flying mud that chokes the treads and splatters all up under the wheel wells. The sun is hot on their backs and legs and the grass is thick and green around them. The trees are lush and wildflowers bloom everywhere, yet all they smell is gasoline and the remnants of a load of manure. The truck slides from time to time. It fishtails and rights itself, and the arms of John Cross work the wheel with fast, cranking motions, hand over fist one way and then back again the other. His right hand works the big Brody knob to avoid what holes he can and keep the truck on the road. Charles fixes his eyes on the horizon. He breathes deep and tries to keep steady, but his belly refuses to obey that logic. It yields to the swaying truck bed and the ripe smell of fuel, and he stands and vomits over the rail. He wipes a tendril of spit off his chin and Sylus pats him on the back and smiles.

Like a train, he says.

What?

I say, it's like riding the train.

Charles nods and holds his palm over his belly. He closes his eyes and the truck lurches over and sends him up against the rail. Sylus seizes him by the sleeve and pushes him back and then turns and raps on the window with his knuckles. He motions with his hand, and Nettie can see that Charles is ill, so they pull the truck over and step out. Nettie helps him out by the arm, and they sit him on the grass at the side of the road. She helps him drink water from a clear bottle that had one time held sweet syrup. Steam rises up from the cracks of the truck's hood and the engine ticks as it cools. John takes the opportunity to check the motor. He opens the hood and stands there looking inside. The boy picks mud from the tires with a sharp stick as Nettie holds Charles' hand.

Just close your eyes and breathe, she says.

Sylus joins John at the front of the truck, and together they discuss the merits of popping the radiator cap, each checking its temperature with his palm. The boy squats on his toes near a tire and Nettie turns to him.

You're going to church, Tobias, muddy or clean, she says. So don't you get any notions about getting out of it. Now get away from that truck.

The boy flicks one last piece of mud from the tire and goes to his father, whose sleeves are rolled back to his elbows. Charles tries to stand, but his legs wobble and he falls. Nettie takes him by the hand and squeezes it. With her thumb and forefinger she applies a gentle pressure to the area just above his thumb.

Close your eyes now, she says. Settle yourself. Breathe real slow, breathe all the air out of yourself before taking more back in.

With Nettie's hand upon his own, Charles begins to calm. He can feel a slight pressure in his hand. It tingles but soothes him. Nettie's soft fingertips relax him and make him feel warm. A strand of her hair goes loose and brushes against his arm.

Now you just think on good things, she says. Think about cool breezes and rustling leaves and the sound of faraway bells.

He hears the leaves in the trees as they rustle, and the distant call of songbirds. She squeezes harder with her fingers. The spot where she holds him grows warm and so does a spot inside his chest, where heat begins to well and spread. He's aware of the beating of his heart and the smell of her skin, and he hears her breathing now, at a pace matching his own. He opens his eyes and sees that hers are closed.

Thank you, he says. I believe I'm feeling better.

He stands, but she does not release his hand. For a moment she's kneeling and holding it. He slips his hand from hers and pulls it away. Sylus and John are bent over the motor and Tobias is standing on the bumper, peering in at the hot smoky engine. He looks up at his mother and then at Charles.

I believe God blessed you with the healing touch, Mrs. Cross, he says.

She stands and smoothes down her skirt and smiles at him.

That's just an old trick my granny taught me. There's a spot there in the hand that'll cure a dizzy spell. Nothing to it, really.

You have the touch, Mrs. Cross. The Lord speaks through you. I know, I can feel it.

Well, he speaks through all of us, Mr. Flint. It's love that heals, not God.

Charles puts on his hat and brushes off the back of his trousers.

Love is God's language, Mrs. Cross, and you speak it well. I wonder if you'd consider attending the revival with us this evening. With your husband and son, of course. The holiness church is not what it appears to be. These folks aren't outcasts, they're good people, they speak with the same language we're talking about.

Nettie sips from the bottle of water and offers it to him. He waves it off and she stops it up with a cork and holds it to the light. She swirls the bottle, and they both watch the water spin.

It's amazing to me, she says. Drinking lye. Have you done that, Mr. Flint?

Charles takes the bottle from her hand and turns it in his fingers. In the sunlight, the water glows pure silver and there are lots of tiny bubbles that rise and swirl.

No. But that's why I've come, to see it done.

It's a strange way of worship, she says. Drinking poison, fooling with snakes.

It sounds strange because in your mind you've only seen it as a spectacle, and not for what it is. The anointment of the Holy Spirit is a blessing, it's a state of mind, a feeling. Like love. You can't describe it to a person who's never felt it for themselves.

The hood of the truck comes down with a loud bang, but it won't close, and the boy climbs up on top to jump on it. John wipes his hands on a rag he keeps in his pocket and rolls down his sleeves. He stands with Sylus and the boy, watching them. Rebecca looks over and takes the bottle back from Charles.

I'll talk to John. Maybe we'll come, she says.

You do that. I don't try to convert folks. But there are people God speaks through. Sometimes they just need a little help hearing. People like Sylus over there, and people like you, and your son. You're one of us.

They climb back into the truck and it starts right up. John drives on down the road with more care and at a slower speed than he did before. Charles closes his eyes and dozes in the back, but he can hear them in the truck cab arguing. Sylus pulls his hat down over his eyes and snores.

The truck slows to a stop at a fork in the road two miles outside of Oglethorpe, Georgia. The engine runs and sputters and for a moment nobody moves. The grass all around them is high and buzzing with grasshoppers. The air is still. The trees aren't moving at all, but the clouds are scudding by like great white ships. They're white and silver, tinged with orange at their bottoms, stretched long and narrow, and they move slowly above them like an armada of ghosts. The boy hops out and walks to the back of the idling truck. He unhooks a latch and folds down the tailgate.

That road there'll take you right up to Slaughter Mountain, he says. It's about three miles, maybe.

The boy stands there with his hands in his pockets. Charles looks over at Sylus and they nod at each other. Charles can see Nettie and John sitting inside the truck, each looking out their own windows. He goes to the driver's side and tips his hat at them.

We thank you for your kindness. For the food. The roof. The ride.

He holds up his hand and John takes it. They shake hands.

We're happy to do it, he says.

If you come back our way, you're welcome to stop again, Nettie says.

John puts the truck in gear. The boy jumps in back. He waves at Charles and Charles waves back.

We just might do that, he says.

The truck pulls away, leaving them both coughing in the dust. Sylus shields his eyes from the sun, low now but still warm. He looks up to the mountain road and back at Charles. He wipes his mouth with his sleeve and spits.

We going? he says.

Charles watches the truck vanish up the road.

Give me a minute, he says. I want to remember this. I want to remember everything about this moment because this here's a crossroads for you and me both. I have a feeling that when we come back down this mountain, the world will be changed.

14

BLOODSTOPPING

The old woman stands by the side of the bed holding her Bible in her hands, whispering, swaying slowly, and Rebecca cannot hear her words. Her feet are raised up on pillows and her hands are down by her side. The bed beneath her is sticky and wet with her perspiration and her blood. Her head spins. She's weak and shivering. There's nobody else in the cabin, and she doesn't remember how she got there, whether she walked or was dragged, and she looks over and can't see the baby. The room smells like burning leather.

Where's my Jacob? she says.

The old woman turns and puts a finger to her lips, a wrinkled finger stained black with soot. She pulls the blanket back and raises Rebecca's nightgown over her belly and checks between her legs. She removes the old dressing, soaked in dark blood, and she places her fingers on her and smiles.

Baby's sleeping, she says. It's getting better, so lie still. Don't talk or move.

What's that smell?

Shush now. Don't you worry. It ain't the cabin afire.

Smells like a slaughterhouse.

I done burned your shoes, is all. Same thing as last time, but you was too sick to remember. Soot from a burnt shoe stops blood sure as anything. Now lie still.

I'm still bleedin'.

This one's worse than the last.

She opens the Bible, flips a few pages, and reads, her eyes locked on Rebecca's. She reads from Ezekiel.

Thou was cast out in the open field, to the loathing of thy person, in the day thou was born. And when I passed by thee, and saw thee polluted in thine own blood, I said unto thee, live, yea. I said unto thee, Live.

She turns, and walks to the window, holding the Bible up to the light. She mumbles to herself and Rebecca just lies there as the blood seeps out of her. She wonders if she'll ever rise to hold the child again. If she's going to die, she wants to hold him one last time.

The old woman opens the door and steps outside, the Bible still in her hand. She turns and watches Rebecca and waves her hand back and forth in the air like she was swatting flies.

Father, Son, Holy Ghost, she says. Out comes fire, in comes frost. Stop bleedin', stop bleedin', stop bleedin'. Stop.

The old woman makes good soup from marrow bones and vegetable skins, and it tastes fine, even from an old tin cup. It goes down smooth and hot and it gives Rebecca strength inside where she needs it. The baby's awake by her side and he stares up at her. He's almost smiling. The bed is dry and the dressings are gone. The old woman's washing the sheets outside in a bucket of lye.

Rebecca drains the whole cup of broth. She tilts it back for the last bit and drops the cup. The noise it makes when it hits the floor is the loudest sound she's heard since the thunder the day the child was born, and it startles him. He cries out and the old woman comes in breathing hard. She looks over at the bed and places her hand up to her heart.

I thought you fell out the bed, she says.

I just dropped the cup, is all. I'm sorry.

That's why they make 'em out of tin.

The old woman stoops down to get the cup and goes to the stove to refill it. She tastes the soup to see how hot is, and she likes the flavor of it so she drinks some from the dipper. She drinks several sips and smiles.

Now that's soup, she says.

She fills the cup and brings it over to Rebecca and helps her to sip it.

You need to stay here in this bed, she says. I don't know what I was thinking lettin' you go out. I'm getting old. I'm getting too old for this.

Where's Mary?

I went up and told her you was all right.

She ain't worried about me anyway, Rebecca says.

That woman don't like nobody. It ain't personal. You know she lost two of her own?

I didn't know that.

Well, she don't tell nobody. And I don't neither. Even Charles don't know.

Rebecca stops drinking and looks up at her. Her eyes are so old and red, they always look wet. The baby cries and Rebecca rocks him. She drinks from the cup again as the old woman holds the back of her head.

What were they? She says.

What were who?

Mary's babies. Were they boys or were they girls?

They were boys. They were both boys. After that her husband left her.

The old woman stands up slowly and her joints pop. She puts the cup away and goes outside to finish her washing. The door does not shut all the way, and Rebecca can see the daylight and hear the old woman washing. She hears the water sloshing in the tub. She holds her baby as close as she can and puts her cheek to the side of his face. His head is warm. Her first child, the boy that was born dead, would have been five years old by now, and it was true, he did have a beautiful face.

15

SLAUGHTER MOUNTAIN

The Slaughter Mountain church is too small for the hordes descending upon it on this night. They've come to see the King Cobra and the twin brothers drink their lye beneath a patched-up circus tent staked out in a field behind. The cars park along the side of the road for more than a mile downhill. People are walking up to the church, whole families, tired and poor, their eyes set upon the peak of the tent poking up out of the trees with a flag on top, hanging limp and tattered. Charles and Sylus join the procession of gaunt and ragged hill folk making their way up the dirt road and trailing behind them their emaciated dogs and their barefoot young ones all covered in scabs and dirt, with the Chinese eyes and flattened faces of incest children. There are granny women shuffling along in the dust and long-bearded geezers learning on twisted willow canes. Some are singing hymns together, their fingers joined in prayer, as they gather outside the Slaughter Mountain Holiness Church in Jesus' Name.

Charles leads Sylus through the large crowd of devotees, some reading from Bibles, others holding wooden snake boxes.

They pray aloud, holding hands with their eyes closed or rolled back in their heads, their lids fluttering. Near the steps, an old man is holding a bottle torch, running his hand back and forth above the flame. He steps aside to let them pass, his hand blackened by soot but not burned. Someone has posted a sign on the church door, a sign with a crudely rendered picture of a hooded snake, below which reads these words:

King Cobra
The World's Deadliest Serpent
Join us today to see this demon subdued by the
SPIRIT OF GOD
All Welcome—No Pictures

Sylus turns and looks out at the crowd, counting heads with his finger.

Five hundred, I figure, he says. What's that sign say?

You can't read?

Nope.

All you need to know is that we're in store for something big.

I knew that soon as I seen all them cars.

They make their way through the crowd, around the back of the church, to a large circus tent raised up on tall wooden poles and staked out with guy ropes. Charles peers up under the dome. It's patched up with red and blue swatches of discolored canvas and strips of tanned rawhide, all sewn together with thick black stitches that run up the sides of the tent. The chairs beneath it are already filled with worshippers, and people are taking up positions around the outside perimeter. Two men carry snake boxes up the aisle and lay them near the pulpit, another is lighting kerosene lanterns that hang from the tent poles. Sylus ducks his head to fit underneath.

Well? he says.

It's almost time, Charles says. You just watch and stay back.

Where you going?

Closer. I feel it coming on me.

Feel what coming on?

The Spirit is strong here tonight. You just wait.

Charles wades through the crowd, stepping on chairs and over folks bent in prayer. An older man stands at the pulpit, his eyes closed, his hands resting upon an open Bible. A reverend, maybe. A preacher. Charles sits down in front of him and opens his own Bible. The crowd hushes. There's commotion coming from the little church behind them. A low murmur, then voices raised together in song, moving closer, a procession of believers chanting the name of Jesus. A woman shouts out.

He's here. The Spirit is come.

Those seated beneath the tent stand, and Charles stands with them. All heads turn and the onlookers part. The crowd steps back to admit two men clad in white suits, bearing a large chest made of ebony. In all manner of dress and appearance the two men are the same. They are clean-shaven and their shoes are polished and their suits are bright and stainless. Their hair is slicked over identical bald spots that show pink through strands of greased black. They call them the God-loving twins, and they are small men with scarred hands, thick, twisted fingers distorted by nerve-wrecking venom. Their eyes shine like wet stones.

There are rope handles on each end of the chest and it hangs between them and they walk slow with it, hunched over, praying aloud. Their lips are moving, they're saying Jesus, Jesus, Jesus. They place the chest near the pulpit, so close to Charles that he could touch it if he chose. But he has no desire to. Not yet. It is old and black and carved with figures both strange and primeval. There are elongated men with spears, naked but for loincloths about their waists, and gravid women with pointed breasts and large protruding lips and the heads of wild beasts with long curving tusks and sharp fangs, and the wood shines like obsidian from hundreds of years of fondling worship in some dark godless jungle. He shudders then, not at the chest, but at the feeling inspired by it. The feeling that there is power in the room and opposing forces soon to be unleashed. In his bowels he feels a wave swell up, a rush of unbridled joy. The twins have brought the Spirit with them, and the crowd can feel it too. Several women have fainted, and men drop to their knees. The rattlesnakes can feel something in the air as well, for behind the pulpit there rises a sound like water spraying from a hose. The snakes shake their tails in unison, and the air is filled with gasps and cries of Jesus, Jesus, Jesus.

Dressed in vivid white, the twins flank the pulpit, their hands clasped at their waists, their heads bowed. The old reverend raises his hands, then lowers them, slow, gentle, quieting the onlookers but not the snakes. They can still be heard in their boxes, rattling and thumping their tails.

The man at the pulpit is older than the twins, and taller. He resembles them, his eyes, the shape of his nose, he is surely their father, the famous Earl Bowsky who started the holiness movment in these mountains in 1910. His eyes sparkle too, and when he speaks, all raise their heads to watch him.

We've a crowd tonight, brothers and sisters, yes we do, he says.

The onlookers all draw in. They stand several deep around the outside of the makeshift church, and now they step forward, a sea of faces, filled with reverence and wonder. The sun dips below the trees and the lanterns all flicker, casting long shadows on the roof of the tent and lighting the crowd with a pulsing glow, like a campfire, their faces half-golden and half-shadowed and the sky beyond a deep shade of cobalt pocked with early stars.

Why have you come here today? Earl Bowsky says. Why have you come? Ask yourselves that question now. To watch the crazy man hold the serpents? To see his brother drink the kitchen lye? There are no miracles here, you will not see miracles tonight, brothers and sisters. These acts we do are signs, signs of true believers. Are you believers? Do you believe in the resurrected Christ? If your brother bears witness to the walking Spirit, will you heed his vision? Will you give it credence? It was from the mouth of a whore that we heard the first word of the risen Jesus, and those that followed him did not believe, those close to him did not heed the word of the harlot Mary Magdalene, from whom Christ had cast out seven demons. Even they, the truest believers, would not believe that he woke from the tomb to walk among us. Do you? Ask yourselves, do I believe? If there is a doubt within you, if there is trepidation, if you feel the icy hand of skepticism scratching at your throat, then, people, we are here today to pull the hood of darkness from your eyes, we are here to open your hearts—not to test your faith, but to grow your love. We are here today bearing the signs of true followers. Not to entertain or bedazzle, not for profit or self-glorification. This may be a carnival tent above us, but this is no sideshow. Read your Bibles. Study the gospel of Mark. We take these extreme measures so as to break through the logic of man, to shatter his inborn doubt—to open the eyes of a creature who, by his very nature, must see in order to believe.

The old reverend takes a handkerchief from his shirt pocket and wipes his brow. He turns to the twins and then turns back to the crowd. The lanterns are burning brighter and are besieged by swarming moths. It is so quiet under the tent that Charles can hear their wings tapping at the glass.

Jesus told us we may hold serpents, Earl Bowsky says. And we hold serpents. Jesus told us that we may drink deadly elixirs, and we do, we drink poison out of the jar. He told us to lay our hands upon the sick and to heal them, and we do that, brothers and sisters, we have healed many of you. Jesus said that we, the true believers, will speak in the sacred tongue of the Holy Ghost, to affirm the living Jesus, and it is his glory that we recognize, not our own, and today, people, we have brought here to this holy mountain, a serpent as lethal and as vicious as there ever lived on God's green earth, and Ray Bowsky, my son, will hold this serpent, and Esau Bowsky, my son, will hold this serpent, and some among you may hold this serpent, those within whom the Spirit runs strong. But first, first, we will pray, and we will invite the Holy Ghost into our congregation, and into our hearts, and when he comes, I can feel him now, when he comes, we will be protected by a living fog of joy and love so powerful that the very fires of hell will be quenched by it, and Satan and his minions, in whatever form they manifest themselves, will hide and will run, and those who cannot run for lack of legs and feet will tremble and they will be cowed.

The old reverend drops his head, his chin resting on his chest, his eyes closed, and he grasps the Bible with both hands and lifts it from the lectern and bangs it back down with a great force that rings out like a pistol shot, and those up front all jump, and heads turn and eyes that were shut pop open. All is quiet under the tent, including the snakes, as he raises his arms up over his head and shakes them from side to side. His body sways and his fingers all wiggle and he shakes from his hands down to his feet as a shiver runs through him. He sucks in air and he gasps.

I feel the Spirit, he says. I feel it coming on.

He steps back and places a hand on each of the twins' shoulders and shakes them. They raise their arms up and step to the pulpit. Cries come from the back of the tent, random shrieks of joy and shouts of Jesus and Praise the Lord, and some folks sitting in chairs begin to stand and sway, and others standing fall to their knees or raise their arms, and from somewhere the music of a pedal organ can be heard as the Bowsky brothers remove their coats and roll up their sleeves in preparation for their acts of faith.

Bring it forth, says Ray Bowsky. Bring me your poisons. I feel it now, I feel the Lord inside me.

Charles can feel it too, he can feel his whole body, every nerve, ever hair, every part of him aflutter. He is seized by a wash of bliss, a warm tingle, that rains over him like the onset of a whiskey high. He stands as a big man with dark oily hair and narrow piglike eyes forces his way through the crowd holding a jar in his hands above his head. His skin is pink and his arms are swollen and his hands are small and fat. The pig-man places the jar on the pulpit, but not before holding it up to the crowd and showing all who can see the label printed with the likeness of Satan and the words written there in black: Red Devil Lye. The pig-man's eyes are sparkling and he smiles like an idiot. More of the crowd are on their feet now, and Ray Bowsky has his hands on the open Bible, and his brother behind him has his hands on his shoulders, and the pig-man with the lye opens the jar and lays it down in front of the Bible and disappears back into the crowd. Ray Bowsky puts his hands on the jar and turns his head to the sky.

Lord, I am your vessel, he says.

He raises the jar, but before he can get it up to his mouth, a young man steps from the crowd and stops him. He's a boy with red hair, eighteen or maybe twenty, skinny and tall and clad in overalls and barefoot in his brogans. He's wearing a plaid shirt with snap-pearl buttons down the front and there is terror in his eyes. He holds Ray Bowsky's wrists down, and they look each other in the eye. Between them is some vast and tragic history, alive but unspoken. The tent grows quiet but for the organ, whose player cannot see over the heads of the onlookers. All watch the pulpit to the sound of the organ.

The red-haired boy grabs the jar of lye and sniffs it. He dips his pinkie inside and brings it to his tongue and for a moment he begins to smile, but the smile soon fades. He releases the jar, his eyes open wide, and he begins to shudder himself, not with joy but with pain. His mouth starts to open and close in spasms, his tongue flicks in and out, and his head turns from side to side searching for a remedy to his agony. He drops to his knees and scoops up dirt and eats it, and he vomits and rolls, and not a person in attendance moves to help him. The boy is panting and coughing and rolling from side to side, and in his frenzy he rips the shirt from his body and stuffs it into his mouth as far as he can get it down. But this does not help stem the pain. His face turns bright red and his veins pop out of his neck and he stands and runs from the tent screaming, with the shirt hanging from his mouth and trailing behind. The old reverend steps up to the pulpit then, between the twins.

Someone see that boy gets a doctor, he says.

The lye jar sits at the edge of the lectern and the old reverend wipes the outside clean with his handkerchief and then steps back. Ray Bowsky starts to shake his head and bob, and the chanting starts up again. Esau Bowsky begins to shake as well, and he starts to talk, but the words that come from his mouth are not English or any known language of man. He speaks directly to his brother, as if he can understand. He's saying things that make no sense to Charles or to the crowd, but which seem to be clear orders to Ray Bowsky, who lifts the lye jar from the pulpit and brings it to his lips. He sips from it once, and then again, and he holds it out for all to see that the level of the poison has dropped. He hands the jar to his twin and watches him sip from it as well. They pass the thing back and forth until the jar is drained. Ray Bowsky holds it upside down for the crowd to see and they smile as the congregation chants.

Glory, Glory, Glory. Glory is the power of the Lord.

The twins step back and fold their hands in prayer. Their faces are flushed, tears run from their eyes, and they're shaking all over. They both drop to their knees and fall forward, their hands on the ground. They stay that way while the old reverend steps into the pulpit and raises his arms to bring the crowd back to him. He places his hands on the Bible and reads from it.

He that believeth and is baptized shall be saved, but he that believeth not shall be damned. And these signs shall follow them that believe. In my name shall they cast out devils, they shall speak with new tongues. They shall take up serpents, and if they drink any deadly thing, it shall not hurt them. They shall lay hands on the sick and they shall recover.

He looks up from his Bible as the organ plays, and those anointed with the Spirit raise their arms in praise of his words and shout.

Praise him. Praise him. Praise Jesus.

The reverend bends over and grabs onto the shoulders of the twins and lifts them bodily from the ground. He pulls them to their feet and embraces them both, and the three of them stand there, huddled and praying. The Bowsky brothers are sobbing, looking up toward the sky and thanking the Lord. The old reverend lifts his hand and signals to a man standing behind them who begins to bring out the serpent boxes.

The boxes are all handmade, crafted out of solid wood and brought from all over Georgia, South Carolina, and Tennessee. Some are simple pine boxes with hinged lids, others are ornately decorated, painted, stained, and carved with Bible verses, crosses, and serpent imagery. Each contains a poisonous reptile. There are copperheads and water moccasins, black cottonmouth snakes, big swamp massasaugas, timber rattlers, pygmies, diamondbacks—whatever folks could find. The boxes are brought to the front of the pulpit and placed on the ground, and their locks are removed. Every box is laid out except the large ebony chest, which sits on a table behind the pulpit, flanked by two tallow candles that sputter and spark. The twins roll their shirtsleeves above their elbows. They shake their arms. They close their eyes and stretch their necks. Their shoulders move up and down and they begin to shuffle their feet. The old reverend walks from snake box to snake box, opening lids and poking the snakes inside with a pointed stick. The crowd steps back and those sitting pull their chairs aside, creating an open space in front of the pulpit large enough to park a truck. Charles does not step back. He remains near the pulpit, his eyes closed, his feet moving in the same shuffling manner as the feet of the Bowsky twins a yard or so away from him. He neither sees the crowd move back nor hears the warnings offered by them. The old reverend waves his hand in front of his face and snaps his fingers, and Charles opens his eyes real slow and stares at him.

Mister, Earl Bowsky says, you stand now in a pit of live demons, wild and unfed. They will strike you, and they will kill you dead unless you're with us here under the Lord's protection.

Charles walks past the old reverend, bends down at the first box he sees and reaches inside with both hands. There are gasps from the crowd and the Bowsky twins open their eyes. Sylus steps through the onlookers and into the open space. The old reverend holds him and the crowd back with outstretched arms as Charles pulls out a knotted mass of snake, an orange and tan copperhead curled round his wrists and hissing at the people in the front row. He holds the snake up for all to see, tilts his head back, and lowers the snake to his lips. Its mouth touches his own and in that position he begins to sway. The snake does nothing. It hangs there above him, limp, subdued. The Bowsky twins come out from behind the pulpit as if summoned by this act, and they bend to the boxes and pull out snakes, two apiece, and the three men all pray aloud there, holding up the reptiles and spinning slowly with their arms raised in surrender to God. The old reverend steps up between the three snake handlers and raises his arms high and shouts.

They shall take up serpents and be not harmed, he says.

Sylus stands ten feet away from this spectacle, elbow to elbow with the chanting worshippers. He feels himself shaking now. There's a tingle in his head and he feels dizzy. But he can't tell if it's the Spirit that's come upon him or the lack of drink starting to take effect again. He feels the crowd behind him surge, and someone pushes him aside and steps up front to see. It's a boy, panting, with his hands on his knees, and Sylus recognizes him. It's Tobias Cross. He taps him on the shoulder and the boy turns.

What are you doing here, boy?

I've come to see, Tobias says.

Sylus kneels and takes him by the shoulder, but the boy is transfixed by the snake handlers and does not turn. Sylus speaks into his ear.

Your daddy and momma here with you?

I came by myself.

Do they know you're here?

I told them I went out hunting frogs.

Charles' copperhead has curled itself around his neck and he goes back to a different snake box and reaches in for another snake. The old reverend reads out of the Bible as the Bowsky twins repeat phrases from Mark, echoing random words from the verses like men shouting out from troubled sleep.

You feel it, Mr. Knox? the boy says. You feel God?

I feel something. But nothing like what's in those three.

I do, the boy says. I feel the Spirit inside of me.

Don't you get any ideas.

But Tobias does not hear him. He steps into the clear space before the pulpit. Sylus grabs his shirt to pull him back, but the boy twists out of his grasp and moves toward the boxes lying out on the ground. The old reverend does not see him, for he is reading from the Bible, and the Bowsky twins do not see him either because their eyes are closed. Charles is draped in serpents, his vision obscured by the Spirit, and by the snakes. Tobias stoops down at a small snake box stained black and inlaid with polished bone—the tiny ribs of a snake. On top is an inscription painted in gold.

Be not afraid, only believe.

Inside there lies a pygmy rattler coiled up tight at the back of the box. Tobias can no longer hear the chanting of the crowd, or the moaning organ, or the preaching of the old reverend. He hears only the rush of wind and the steady intake of his own breath. He can see his hands on the snake, hands that feel separate from himself. His fingers look familiar but feel thick, dumb, distant. His hands move, beyond his control, beyond his desire to control them. They reach for the little snake and lift it from the box, and Tobias feels the living muscle beneath its cool dry skin. He feels it stiffen and flex, and he can feel the power in it as he takes it up in his arms. He stands to face the crowd, who have become enraptured by the sight of this boy, consumed by the Spirit and subduing a serpent. There is not a soul left sitting in the entire crowd, and all are praying or singing, including Sylus himself, who cannot believe what he sees—the three men under the spell of God, and the boy too, infused with the same Spirit, calm as can be and smiling, as if what he holds in his arms is no deadly serpent but some pond turtle he caught with his own two hands.

A warmth spreads through Sylus's body, the warmth of kindness, a hot wave of joy and peace. It glows inside him, from his belly up to his ears, it brightens and burns like a steady flame. He can't help but move his hands and feet, he can't help but smile and shout the name of Jesus, because Jesus is in him. He receives the anointment of the Holy Spirit with tears and laughter both. He feels he can walk through fire if asked to do so. He feels, for the first time, alive.

The old reverend, seeing the child with the rattlesnake and Charles with the copperhead, and more than a dozen onlookers awash in the radiance of the living Spirit, brings out the African chest and sets it among the smaller snake boxes. He folds down the hasp at the front and springs up onto the chest, throwing his arms up to the sky.

Never have I seen the Spirit so strong, he says. We are blessed today, people, blessed with new pilgrims in whom God truly dwells.

He leaps from the chest and throws back the lid. The crowd steps back. The organ has stopped playing.

They say the bite of the cobra-king can knock an elephant down in mere seconds, Earl Bowsky says. They say he can spit his venom into the eyes of a lion, thus blinding him. But we have nothing to fear, for there is a wall of love here ten feet thick, a wall of love that neither fang nor poison can puncture or penetrate.

He jumps down from the chest and swings open the lid. The crowd gasps as the head appears, popping up from the inside of the ebony box and forming a hood, with a mouth on one side and a false eye on the other. It's a thick snake, longer than any of the rattlers and far more sinister. This snake sees and thinks, and it reads the eyes of man for weakness and resolve. It watches the faces of the crowd and turns toward its every movement. There is no more praying or shouting. The only sound that can be heard at all is moth wings fluttering against the lanterns, and the cobra itself, hissing like a cat.

The Bowsky twins peel the snakes from their arms and return them to their boxes. Charles unravels himself from his reptiles, and they all three face the cobra. The boy holds his rattler near the edge of the crowd, still taken by the Spirit and swaying slowly. Ray Bowsky steps to the chest and faces the new snake, and the snake faces him. They look into each other's eyes as the crowd whispers the name of Jesus. He reaches out for the cobra, and the big snake feigns a lunge and hisses. He pulls his hand away and steps back out of its range. The cobra stands taller in the box now, swaying from side to side, turning its head and flicking its tongue as Esau Bowsky approaches the chest and kneels there, within striking distance. He begins to pray. He peers into the black eyes of the snake, holds his hands up, and then spreads them apart, palms out, fingers splayed. The snake is confused by this gesture and turns its head from one side to the other, trying to follow the man's hands as he brings them slowly forward.

Have no fear, he says, in a low, even voice. I am here to save, not destroy. In the name of Jesus, have no fear.

But the snake is not fooled by this, nor lulled by words. He strikes out, biting the man on the face and retreating back into the ebony chest in one blinding motion that is a marvel of terror and speed. The crowd jumps back and there is screaming as Esau Bowsky falls over, his hands grasping at his face, his eyes wild and rolling, and there is a sound coming from the back of his throat, a terrible sound, a coughing hack that quiets the crowd. His brother rushes to his side and the old reverend kicks the chest closed, but Charles raises his arms and speaks.

People, he says. Panic only fans the poison and weakens the spirit. A bite is not death, he will be healed, that I promise you. Pray now, pray and I will show you that your faith has the power that was promised you by Jesus.

He goes to the chest and kneels to open it. The crowd rushes back, knocking over chairs and colliding with tent poles and guy wires and tripping over themselves and causing the lanterns to sway. Ray Bowsky cradles his brother's head in his arms and prays. The old reverend prays and the boy prays too, his snake now back in its box. Sylus stands alone at the outside edge of the clear space.

Charles opens the chest and does not step back. The cobra remains coiled inside.

First mistake is keeping him in here, he says. In this den made by heathen hands, this evil box adorned with the lewd carvings of a godless man. Reverend, I'll need an axe.

He kicks the chest and it rolls over, spilling the big cobra out onto the ground where it curls into a tight ball.

He's on hallowed ground, Charles says. No place to run. That's why we fashion our own boxes, and smother them with gospel. You take them from the darkness and bring them to the light and they will live by the rules of God. You people hear me now, this is not just a lesson for reptiles.

He turns to Sylus and stares at him hard, peeling him open, rendering him naked before God.

Only a serpent can live in a den of snakes, he says. But you come to my church, and I'll make a lamb out of you, and your black fleece will turn white, and you will hunger no more for flesh, but will sup upon the oats of forgiveness and sip from the cup of love.

The old reverend brings him a double-headed axe and stands back as Charles chops the chest to splinters, raining blow upon blow down into the dark wood and sending black chips up into the air. When he's through, he wipes his brow with his sleeve and hands the axe back to the old reverend, who looks upon it with awe and passes it around the crowd.

Charles approaches the snake with the same callous air he used to destroy its home. He does not pray, he does not use caution or whisper soothing words to it. He bends down and picks it from the ground like it was an old and beloved dog and lifts it up high above his head.

I am the everlasting light, the everlasting love. I died for you so that you might live forever in the glory of God. There is no darkness but that which you create by shutting out my light, and there is no evil, only the absence of love.

He hurls the cobra down to the ground with such force that it breaks the creature's neck and kills it. The crowd stands stunned. All eyes are upon him, not a jaw is closed, and the only sound that can be heard is the rasping breath of Esau Bowsky and the prayers of his brother Ray. Charles goes to them and lays his hand on Esau's face. He kisses him on the mouth and spits off to the side.

I want you all to take home with you tonight a piece of this broken box, he says. I want you to bring a splinter of this dark African wood back to your churches. Look upon these black shards when darkness falls and remember that the light of God does not seep. It comes crashing in.

He stands and holds the cobra by the neck. His face is red and sweaty.

Stand, Esau Bowsky, he says. Stand and take this serpent, whom you should have left where it was born.

And he does. Esau Bowsky rises to his feet and wipes the dust from his pants.

16

MÁDSTONE

The old woman dreams of owls, a whole flock of owls, awake and a-wing, the intent raptors diving toward fleeing prey. They appear first above her and then below, where she sees they are chasing a pack of sleek black dogs on the run at night. The dogs are loping through the cotton grass with their mouths agape and their tongues flapping, their backs shiny wet and bony, with the skin on the high ridges of their spines pulled taut around the bones and a streak of silver moonlight running from the crest of each flat skull down their backs to tails that stick out behind them sharp as swords.

The owls swoop in a unified mass, climbing straight up, diving back, looping, banking, back and over, all turning as one and wheeling like bats, so quietly that nothing can hear them, not even the sharp ears of the bounding, leaping dogs who seem not to perceive the night birds at all, for they are on some mad quest born of their own instinct and are a terrifying sight to behold. And she know they came for her.

• • •

Rebecca sits up in bed and watches the old woman sleeping in the rocking chair. Her hands dangle down over the arms. Her palms are turned up with her fingers spread wide and her neck hangs over the back of the chair. She looks dead. The room is quiet and she can hear the low hum of flies. The sun streams in through the window and she can see them flying in tight circles in the rays of light.

The old woman lashes out in her sleep. She swipes at the air before her, fending off some phantom from her dreams. She's breathing fast and turning her head from side to side now and she suddenly grabs hold of her arm, slapping at it hard, as if she was bit by a stinging insect. Then she sits bolt upright in the rocker, her eyes blinking and turning in their sockets.

The stone, she says. The madstone.

This startles Rebecca. She jumps and the baby startles too, and she pulls him up to her breast and strokes his head. The old woman stands and pats at her chest with her hand, feeling for the brass key. She finds it and holds it between her fingers. She unpins the key from her sweater and takes it over to the bed and bends down with great pain in her joints. She reaches under the bed, feeling for something. She's looking up at Rebecca with wild, frightened eyes before pulling out a small wooden box with a hinged lid and a small lock. The wood is blackened by age and dry as an old bone and it has tarnished brass cornices hammered out crudely by a man long dead. It's handmade and older than she, passed down to her by her father and only brought out in times of dire need. She calls it her potion box, but Rebecca has never seen what she keeps inside. It is her most precious possession.

She opens it with the key that hangs from her sweater. She rummages through the box and pulls out a small object, which she palms and holds close to her bosom. She clutches it in her clenched fist and mumbles some words meant for no ears but her own. Her eyes widen as she opens her hand and holds it out for Rebecca to see. It's a small rock the color of bone, porous, the size of a walnut. It's almost a perfect sphere. The old woman presses the strange object against her arm just below the shoulder. She holds it there for a moment, then releases her hand, and it stays there all by itself. It sticks to her.

Madstone, she says.

Rebecca has seen the madstone only one time before. But she's heard about it all her life. Years ago, when Charles was bit by a coral snake, it stuck on his arm too, and it stayed there three whole days. The old woman's madstone is legendary in Leatherwood and beyond. One time Baxter Dawes showed up in the dead of night and asked to take it to a girl out on the reservation. But the old woman wouldn't let him have it. She brought it up there herself and saved the Indian girl, whose leg was bit by a rabid dog. As far as Rebecca knew, she kept it inside her potion box, locked up with her amulets and other secret charms, and had never used it but those two times. Folks said a man once came all the way from England and offered to buy it for a thousand dollars in gold. But the old woman wouldn't sell, and Rebecca never could understand why. Charles told her that it was a rare and powerful thing, considered by many to be a miraculous all-purpose charm. The gallstone cut from the belly of an albino deer.

The old woman sits back in her rocker with the madstone stuck to her arm. Her eyes dart to the door.

Charles will be home soon, she says.

Rebecca stands and goes to the door and then turns back to put the baby down. The old woman shakes her head.

Soon don't mean now, she says. Could be a couple days. But he's coming.

What did you see? Rebecca says. In your dream?

The old woman puts her hand back up to the madstone and jiggles it. It doesn't budge. It just hangs there like it was glued on.

Nothin' that concerns you, she says. I just know he's headin' home.

She stands slowly, pushing herself up from the chair with great difficulty. She goes over to an icebox and takes out a pitcher of buttermilk. She pours some into a shallow pot and places it on the stove. Rebecca looks over at the baby sleeping on the bed and then back at the old woman's arm.

That ain't where the snake bit you, she says.

No, the old woman says. Wasn't a snake, it was a dog in my dream.

The old woman shakes the pot of foaming buttermilk and looks down at her arm.

You know how old I am?

Rebecca shakes her head.

I look old, don't I?

Rebecca says nothing. The old woman puts her hand to her face, then runs her fingers through her hair.

I look older than I am, but I'm still old, she says.

You look fine, Rebecca says.

The old woman points at the wall across the room, above the bed, where the lath has crumbled.

You see them holes?

Rebecca nods, looking over her shoulder at the holes in the wall.

Bullet holes, the old woman says. Springfield rifles.

Rebecca goes to the wall and runs her fingers over one of the holes there.

Up there on the ridge, the old woman says, where the big house stands today, they were shootin' at the blue-bellies, right here in this room. It was our boys shootin' down. They come in while we was eatin' breakfast. Bust out all the windows and took up there, and there.

She points at various spots in the room and Rebecca looks at each one, as if expecting to see soldiers crouched down behind their rifles. The old woman pulls out her pipe and stuffs her finger into the bowl, feeling for what tobacco might be left in it.

My momma and I laid there under the bed for two hours or more while they shot at each other, she says. Of course my daddy wasn't here, he was already dead, but we didn't know it at the time. He took a shot in the eye at Sharpsburg, God bless Zebediah Bates.

She taps her pipe on the stove and stirs the simmering buttermilk. She lights her pipe and a stream of smoke shoots out the side of her mouth.

That's how old I am, she says. I remember that war.

She checks on the madstone by flicking it with her finger. It's stuck fast.

One of them died right there on the bed, she says. The rest all jumped out the window and left him here bleedin'. Just left him to die. Of course that's not the same bed, but the wall there is still full of lead slugs. We used to dig 'em out with our knives when we was small.

She squints up at the wall and out at the room and she turns her head around to look at the inside of the cabin.

I was born in this very room, she says. And it is where I plan to die. My little house. My father built this house. Zebediah Bates came to Leatherwood in 1846 and built this cabin in the lee of yonder ridge, where it's protected well from wind and snow but not from gunfire raining down from above. They called him an Indian killer in his day, when such a name was a source of pride, because he fought with Davy Crockett against the Creeks. But the truth was, he loved Indians and only killed a few out of necessity.

She takes the pot of buttermilk from the stove and moves it off to the side to cool. She stares at the bed, watching something that is no longer there, except in her own mind.

He wasn't dead when they left him, she says. That soldier. He could still talk, and we sat with him. Momma gave him some broth. His name was Gabriel Snead and he come from a place called Cape Hudson in the great state of Maine.

Just then the madstone drops from the old woman's arm, and she smiles wide and picks it up off the floor. She hurries over to the stove and drops it into the pot of warm buttermilk.

He was a fisherman, she says. And he gave us a letter to post that he had in his pocket, had blood on the paper. He called me Bonny. Kept tellin' him my name's Gert, but he just called me Bonny anyhow, holding my hand the whole time until he died.

The old woman pulls the madstone from the buttermilk and holds it up to the light. She turns it over in her fingers, looking for something on its surface perhaps, some mark or sign. She brings it over to Rebecca and shows it to her.

Can you see what color it is? she says. I can't see nothing anymore.

Rebecca takes the madstone. It looks the same as it did when the old woman took it from the box.

It's white, she says.

Good, the old woman says. White is good. Green ain't good. This here stone come to me from Zebediah himself who got it from his daddy, who come over from Wales. It goes way back. The man who cut out this belly relic killed that stag with a spear. That's how the story goes.

The old woman puts the stone back into the little chest and locks it and then stuffs the box beneath the bed. She pins the key back to her sweater and sits down.

When our boys came down from the hill, she says, they took all our food, our chickens, the hog, all the blankets. They took Gabriel Snead's rifle and powder too. They turned his pockets out and took his money. And they took his shoes. That was the worst part of it. I didn't so much mind all the food being gone, or even old Kate, the hog. But that boy's shoes done broke me up. Momma and I buried him up there on Dogwood

Hill where you buried your first boy. Dragged him out and dug a hole. Just the two of us. A woman and a young girl all alone. We buried a barefoot man and mailed a letter home for him.

Rebecca never heard the old woman tell that story and she's never seen her cry. She tries to hide it, but her shoulders are shaking now, and Rebecca sees her wet, shining eyes. The old woman wipes her face with the sleeve of her sweater.

I don't know, she says. I still see them sometimes, that boy's feet. I see 'em in my sleep. I ain't afraid of nothing in my dreams neither. Not wolves or demons, nothin', and I've seen plenty of folks die. I seen men cut open, with their innards hanging loose. I've seen folks burned up so black you couldn't tell if they was man or woman. But that boy's feet, they just terrify me.

Rebecca sits down beside her and pats the old woman's knee.

I never knew there was another grave up there, she says. There's no marker.

I'll show you, the old woman says. We made him a wooden cross. But that's gone now. Rotted.

She goes to the window and looks up at the hill with the little dogwood tree on top.

That's where I'll be buried too. When my time comes. Right beside Gabriel Snead. You make sure now.

17

A RECKONING

When the boy went missing there was no cause for alarm until the sunlight faded and the darkness came. They sat in the truck outside the empty church with John Cross telling Nettie she worries too much because she was raised in a house full of girls and promising that Tobias would surely return on his own. And then they drove home.

Boys are just like dogs, John says. Lost out on a hunt, they'll come home when they're hungry, but not if you call them, and if you show them too much attention, they'll get soft and lose the fire that turns them into men.

He waits inside, reading his newspaper at the supper table while she sits out front on the porch steps under a yellow moon, holding her knees in her arms and watching the hilltop road for signs of Tobias's promised return.

The leaves are all rustling at the tops of the trees and the air grows cold. A couple of horned owls are calling to each other in the darkness behind the house. The moon is almost full, but it keeps fading out behind the rushing clouds, and she prays for the boy to get home before the rain. One of the cats rubs up against her legs, and she scratches at the base of its tail. She smells the moisture in the air and hears things inside the barn—the jangle of a cowbell, the soft whinny of a horse. The cat lifts its nose to catch a scent. It opens its mouth and bears its yellow teeth, sniffing at the air for sign.

The screen door creaks open and John steps out, holding her shawl. He wraps it around her shoulders and stands listening to the owls.

It's gonna come down, he says. Hard rain for sure. The owls never lie.

Nettie wraps herself in the shawl and shoos away the cat. She pats the step beside her with her hand. John sits beside her.

Can't you go out and look? she says.

He'll be along.

They clasp hands and stare out at the sky. There's a rumble from the clouds that starts off low and builds to a loud smack that makes the livestock jumpy. The chickens cluck in the barn.

You should've taken us, John, she says. Half the county was up there tonight. It wouldn't have done any harm to go and look.

We been through this, Nettie.

Yes, well, now I have to think about him all soaked and frozen.

The wind begins to blow through the yard now, and they see the trees all leaning over and the backs of the leaves. Then the moon vanishes behind the clouds and the yard darkens. They no longer see the hilltop road. The rain starts to fall on the rise, and they hear it moving through the fields. They can smell it too. John stands and steps out into the yard and looks up at the sky, his hair blowing and his eyes squinted against the wind.

The rain moves down the hill and into the yard now. They

hear the first clatter of it up on the roof. At first there's just a few scattered pings, and then a sudden rush of droplets beating down above them, and John ducks back under the cover of the porch. Rainwater rushes through the gutters. They both look up and follow the sound of it as it travels from the left side of the house to the right and then down and out onto the ground near the porch steps, where it all gushes out from a pipe.

It's only rain, he says.

I'm not afraid of him coming home in the rain, Nettie says. I'm afraid of him not coming home at all.

The yard in front of them is awash in mud, and the barn looks blurry and distant behind a curtain of falling water. The rain falls straight down in blowing sheets that sweep across the yard before them. Water drips from several spots above now, and the wind blows and sprays rain up under the porch. They step up closer to the door, where the boards are still dry.

He puts his arm around her shoulders and holds her close and then kisses her on the side of the head. There's a flash of lightning and then a loud crack in the sky and behind it a deep rumble of thunder. He turns to the door.

Where you going? she says.

To get my coat.

The screen door bangs closed behind him as the rain sprays up into Nettie's face, and for a moment there's just the sound of water falling into the mud, splatting against the side of the house, gurgling through the gutters and dripping from the eaves. She looks out at the barn and past it, out into the road, and she sees a man walking, holding his hat on with his hand. Then she sees another man and then, a boy. All three are moving slowly, dragging their feet in the mud. Their heads are bowed and their shoulders hunched against the cold. She turns to the house and yells for her husband and then yells for her son, but they can't hear through the din of the rain. She runs out into the storm, splashing barefoot through the yard and waving her arms over her head until they see her and wave back. John steps out onto the porch with his slicker half-buttoned and his hat in his hand. When he sees the three soaking travelers coming down the hill, he pulls off his coat and goes back into the house to fire up the stove. Nettie stands in the mud with the water dripping through her hair and her clothes all stuck to her skin. With all this rain in her eyes they won't ever know that she had been crying.

Charles stares in through the open door of the potbelly stove and watches the shimmering embers glow. He hears the wood pop and the suck of air in the flue. He sips his coffee with both hands wrapped around an enamel cup, naked beneath a soft quilt stuffed with goose feathers and scented lightly with mothballs. Sylus dozes beneath a blanket of his own. He has his feet crossed at the ankles, sticking out from the blanket and close to the stove. His toes are long and curved inward like cupped hands and they're all white from the cold. Charles stares at the fine blue veins that run across the tops of his feet, bearing the warm blood that will ease the stiffness that's in them.

Tobias sits close to the stove sipping cocoa. His mother's rubbing his shoulders and humming an old church song. She's got his feet soaking in a steel tub of warm water and a heavy quilt draped over his knees. John leans on the doorjamb, sipping coffee and watching the steam rise from their clothes, which are strung up on a line he rigged between the pantry and the curtain rod over the sink.

The boy's rubbing a broken shard of dark wood with the pad of his thumb and he has a gleam in his eye, like he just caught the biggest fish in a derby. Charles knows that he's bursting to tell them everything. But they have an agreement that he won't say a word unless asked.

We were hoping to get here before the storm broke, Charles says.

Nettie takes the cup from Tobias and brings it to the stove to refill it.

We thank you all the same, she says. For bringing him home.

Well, we planned on coming back through this way anyway.

I bet you did, John says.

He looks at Charles, and the two men stare at each other for a moment before Charles turns to the fire in the stove.

We were hoping we could do a bit more for you before we passed on through, he says.

I think you've done enough, John says.

Sylus opens his eyes just a little. Charles stands, wraps the blanket around his shoulders, and walks to the clothesline to feel his pants. They're still damp.

I take full responsibility for him running off, he says. We spoke about the revival and I asked him to come, but I hoped you'd bring him. I never thought he'd go on his own, and I don't approve of a boy who don't mind his father.

He looks over at Tobias with scolding eyes, and the boy looks down at his feet.

I apologize for my part in it, he says. I had no right to talk to him at all. For what it's worth, he behaved himself up there and he acted like a man.

Nettie brings more cocoa to her son. She pushes his chair closer to the stove and dips her fingers into the steel tub to check the temperature of the water. She's got three pots warming on the stove, and she takes one and pours hot water into the tub and then puts it back on to simmer. John walks to the stove himself and refills his cup with coffee and sips it only a few feet away from Charles, who looks small wrapped up in the overstuffed quilt.

Just what did you do up there, Mr. Flint? What was it that my boy had to run away to see?

A prayer meeting is all it was. Folks singing and reading from the Bible.

And those twins brought out the snakes, I imagine.

Yes, they did.

So it wasn't just folks singing and reading the Bible.

No. Not when you put it that way.

The true way.

I speak nothing but truth, Mr. Cross.

John puts his cup down and wipes his hands on his shirt. He takes a long deep breath and a good hard look at Charles, whose eyes are locked upon his own. Sylus uncrosses his ankles but otherwise does not move.

You filled my boy's head with crazy ideas and lured him up there to see the snake twins dance and carry on and Lord knows what—filled his head with that backwoods nonsense. All them serpent crazies, like some hillbilly medicine show. I seen 'em, up there jumping and howling like Indians. That ain't a civilized church, that ain't for us. A man's got a right to worship his own way, as long as it don't interfere with my way, or my family, and, mister, you crossed that line.

Tobias jumps up from his blankets, standing in the tub of water with the cup in one hand and the splintered wood from the African chest in the other.

Daddy, it wasn't like that, he says.

Don't add to your troubles, boy. You stay quiet.

Charles is still staring at John, and the two of them stand facing each other in silence. He hears the fire crackling in the stove and the heavy breathing of Sylus beside him. Steam rises from their clothes.

I am deeply sorry for the trouble I've caused, he says. When our clothes are dry, we'll leave.

John steps toward him and puts his coffee down.

You'll leave now, he says.

Nettie pulls the boy from the tub of water and steps between the two men.

John, she says. She puts her hand on his arm and he shakes it off.

They'll leave now, Nettie. I can't stand to look at them in our blankets, and I can't stand the way the boy looks at them either.

John, it's dark and it's cold, and he said he was sorry, and I believe he is. He didn't mean any harm.

I don't believe he is sorry, I think he's not telling us something. I think there's still something we don't know.

What you don't know, Charles says, is that the Holy Spirit runs strong in your boy. He glows with the light of God, and Jesus sits at his shoulder. He's a good boy, but he's better than good. He's good in ways you don't understand because your mind is closed to it. What you don't know is that your son is blessed, Mr. Cross, he's got hidden talents. Talents which, if properly nurtured, can be used to break through darkness, to spread joy and love and to heal. He can be a great man, a better man than his father, and that's what we all want for our sons, isn't it? For them to become better men than ourselves. Tobias can make a difference in this hard world, he can change people's lives for the better, he has within him the power to move souls toward the light, and I'd sure hate to see that power wasted. I'd sure hate for you to be that selfish.

Charles sees the hand coming, but he doesn't move, he takes it square on the jaw and staggers. He falls back, I believe he is standing and spills his coffee. He hears the cup rattle on the floor, and he hears the other chair, the one beneath Sylus, he can hear it tumble and crack. Before Sylus hits him, Charles calls out his name.

Sylus, he says. Don't you do it.

But Sylus Knox is a man who acts upon instinct, and instinct alone. He's already got both his arms wrapped around

John's neck. His blanket has fallen to the floor, and Nettie turns away in shame from his nakedness. The pallor of his skin is so white from the cold that he seems to radiate light in the darkness of the room. His legs are long and sinewy and his body is hairless and smooth, and as Charles bends to pick up the blanket he suddenly remembers a cadaver he saw floating by his canoe the day the Sequatchie flooded.

18

HOMECOMING

The trees brush up against the eaves and branches crack and fall upon the roof, along with acorns that pop and rattle in the eaves. The wind blows. Rebecca jumps every time she hears a sound—bird chatter and the shutters up on the big house, she rises at them all, expecting Charles. The old woman takes her by the arm and pulls her back to the bed each time.

I don't want you moving, she says. Sit now and be still.

The old woman stands at the stove holding Jacob Flint in one strong, practiced arm while pinching dried herbs into her pots with her other hand. She whispers to the boy, but Rebecca cannot hear what she's saying. The pots bubble. She taps their rims with the edge of her spoon. The wind blows, and the old woman begins to hum an old mountain song that wells up from the deep place where sorrows are born. It seems to come from the floor itself and all around her, rising from the earth in a slow and stirring wave resonant with both sadness and joy, that old feeling rendered new again by this harmonic moment of love, light, and loss. Rebecca shivers. And then there's a sound. Outside, a rattling metallic clatter, gears grinding far away. She stands and goes to the door. The old woman hears it too.

There he is, she says.

They both hear the muffled clump of doors and the whine of an engine in reverse. Rebecca shuts her eyes and listens to the boots on the stairs. The door swings open and Charles steps in. He stands there with a week's worth of beard and eyes red and wide with wonder.

The light that spills into the room is so bright that Rebecca and the old woman squint and shield their eyes from it. Charles drops his bundle and removes his hat. Rebecca points to the baby and Charles smiles.

Jacob?

Rebecca nods. The old woman offers him the baby, but he's beside himself with joy and just stares. He sees the tiny lips of the child, his red feet, his hands balled into fists. He looks at Rebecca with tears in his eyes and kneels by her side. He takes her hand.

You did it, he says. You had my son.

He kisses her as Sylus ducks inside. He stands behind them, holding his hat in his hands. He looks over at the old woman and the baby in her arms. It's been a long time since he's seen a baby. Charles stands and turns to him.

Rebecca, this here's a new friend of ours, he's going to stay with us for a while. His name's Sylus Knox.

Pleased to meet you, Mrs. Flint, Sylus says.

Likewise, Mr. Knox.

And this here's Gertie Bates, Charles says.

I'm happy to meet you, Mrs. Bates.

Well, I'd be happy if you was to bring me in some wood and fetch me some water, she says.

He nods, puts his hat on, and leaves them.

It's quiet in the cabin, and warm with the pots bubbling on the stove. The windows are fogged.

You were early again, Charles says. How'd it all go?

You picked a bad time to leave her, the old woman says.

I thought for sure I'd make it back. I'm sorry, but when you hear what happened, you'll understand why I had to go.

Whatever it is, Charles Flint, the old woman says, it don't compare to what this woman's been through. So forget about your own self and let me tell how it was this child came into the world.

The old woman licks her lips and swallows, and she tells him the story of the herbs and the mountain and the tree and the storm.

The mountain itself is a yarn spinner that spawns yarn spinners and there is no lack of magic or myth here in the hollows. A man who lives among hillfolk will have heard all stories ever told in one form or another and rarely will he be moved, like Charles Flint is moved, to tears and wordless wonder.

Jesus, he says. Sweet Jesus. Rebecca. Are you hurt? Is he hurt? I'm so sorry, I'm so sorry.

I'm burned, on my ankles. But otherwise I'm fine, she says.

She avoids looking into his eyes. Charles turns to the old woman.

What about the boy? he says.

He stares into her milky gray eyes and finds them cold and hard and dull.

Misshapen, she says. But marked for greatness. He's got Spirit inside him. Inside this child the Holy Ghost runs strong. He's fine. Just fine.

Show me, he says.

She holds the baby up in her arms and lets the blanket fall to the floor. It's difficult to see the disparity in his legs because they're small and somewhat curled, but it's there, he can see it, one is shorter than it should be, and his head is somewhat larger than that of a normal child. It appears slightly skewed. One time, when he was preaching out in the woods, a young mountain woman came to him to have her child healed. She passed him up through the crowd. When he unwrapped the blanket he saw his first encephalitis baby and it made him break down and cry. That child still comes to him in his dreams.

Oh, Lord, he says. Gertie, you tell me this boy's all right. Look me in the eye and say it.

You see for yourself, she says.

Can he see?

He ain't blind, Charles, the old woman says. He's fine, as far as I can tell. Stop worrying yourself. He's sharp and smart. I see it in him. Look, he's got a mark on his back.

She turns the boy around and shows him a small dark line on the small of his back, a jagged line about an inch long that looks like a thunderbolt—or a snake.

Charles Flint, he is what you asked for, she says. The snakes won't have any part of him. He's full of light, got the mark on him for sure, but it's the mark of God. This is a blessed child.

The old woman sits in her rocker and sticks her pipe in her mouth. Charles stands in the sunlight holding the child.

There's a fire burnin' inside that boy, the old woman says. He's the best I ever saw. You got what you was promised.

She takes the pipe from her mouth and her eyes gleam. Outside they can hear Sylus chopping wood. They hear the chuck and crack of the axe, and when the split wood falls from the block into the pile, it sounds like wooden chimes. The baby starts to cry, and Charles passes him back to the old woman.

I need some air, he says.

He still hears the baby as he walks to the woodpile. It's as loud a cry as any child. Jacob's lungs are strong, and that's all a preacher really needs is a good set of lungs and a pure heart to drive them. Even if he can't walk right or look a person straight in the eye, he'll still be able to speak, and that's God's greatest gift—speech, language, and the power to change lives with words.

Charles stands watching Sylus raise the axe and drop it. He listens to the measured breathing of the man swinging it. He walks around to the front of the woodpile and takes the axe from him. He says nothing. He pushes him off to the side, raises the axe, and lets it fall on top of the hunk of wood already balanced there, splitting it. He bends and lifts another from the pile and splits that one too. Sylus steps back and watches him.

I can do that, Sylus says.

Charles does not look up. He keeps splitting logs, faster now, sweat breaking out on his forehead. He rolls up his sleeves and lays into the next log and it explodes into splinters and the axe sticks fast into the stump. He has to use his foot to pull it out, pumping the handle and twisting the blade. It's a fine evening and the sky is clear. Sylus squats on his toes, barefoot in his shoes. His pants are too short, they ride up on his ankles and are tight at the knees.

Sylus, Charles says. Rebecca gave birth to my son in a big oak tree up on the mountain where they used to hang Negroes and sometimes still do.

Charles looks out at the trees around his house and he looks into Sylus's eyes.

That old tree's like a graveyard, he says. With roots fed by blood. There's bones lying on the ground. The old power doctors used to go up there for mandrake root. She had the baby in the tree, Sylus. Inside that tree.

Sylus puts his arm on his shoulder.

I don't know what to say, Charles. They both look fine.

No. You didn't see. The boy doesn't look right, Charles says. His eyes and his head don't look right and one of his legs is short. But the old woman says he burns with the holy light, and I can feel it in him too. Remember how it was on the mountain when the Spirit came upon us all? He feels like that. He feels like a holy mountain.

Sylus takes the axe from him and lays it on the stump.

Charles, he says. Let me tell you something that I know. Just be his father. Don't doom that boy like I doomed my own. I had me a son and a wife and a house, and I lost them with my foolishness and my pride. My boy, William. We called him Willie and all he ever wanted was to please me, and that's what got him killed. And I'm the one who killed him. Charles, I shot my own boy because I wasn't paying attention. Not just on that day, when we were hunting, but every day that led up to it. I told myself he'd never be more than half a man. I convinced myself he was a certain thing, a certain kind of person, and would never be anything more than a scared little boy. I was drinking, I was not a good man. And I killed my son.

Sylus, Charles says. I'm so sorry.

Don't be sorry, Sylus says. You're a better man than I ever was, but I can see it in your eyes the way I saw it in my own. Disappointment. Doubt. And that's poison. Let him find out who he is in his own way, in his own time, and everything will be fine. You do that, and we'll have both served our purpose here on this earth. If he's as blessed as you believe, then he's got everything he needs but you.

Sylus bends to pick up some wood. He stacks it into Charles' arms and then takes some for himself. They each carry an armload back to the cabin. They drop their wood beside the stove and Charles takes the child from the old woman's arms and cradles him close to his face so he can smell him and feel his skin. Jacob is warm and his skin glows, and in his eyes, eyes that have not yet become a color, Charles sees himself.

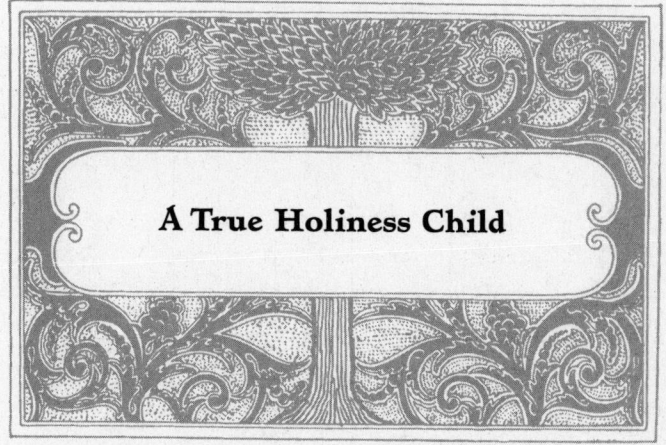

BOOK III

A True Holiness Child

In him was life;
and the life was
the light of men.

JOHN 1:4

1

THE SNAKE HUNTER

Jacob wakes to the sound of wind and rustling leaves. The air inside the tree hollow is cold and dank. It's still dark outside. He can see nothing of the place around him—there is only blackness and the sound of the peepers at the creek. He pats his coat pockets, feeling for the flashlight, and he finds it still there, sticky and coated with the crumbs of the pork biscuit he rolled over and squashed sometime during the night. He slides the switch over with his thumb and it will not light. He bangs it against his thigh until the beam flickers and steadies. He can see again. The first thing he's aware of is the gunnysack, crumpled and turned inside out near his feet. His head swims and his eyes roll back and he can feel an intense throbbing on his face. He remembers now where he is and what he's done. The snake is gone. His mind flashes to an image of his father standing in the Bible room counting snakes over and over and only coming up with eleven.

From the wound on his cheek there comes a heat that feels more like a sizzle than a burn. The fingers on his right hand are numb. But he's not worried about the venom. The old woman always said that the spirit ran stronger in him than her, and she has survived more bites than he could count. And his daddy has been struck several times. Just a year ago he was bitten by a water moccasin, and his arm blew up like a dead cat in the sun and oozed yellow pus. His skin, from his fingers up to his shoulder, turned the color of blackberry wine. He told Jacob that he survived because he kept the spirit in his heart and prayed all night and all day, with the whole congregation gathered round the house in the pouring rain, singing and praying while the old woman tended to the wound. She sucked out the poison and spat it into a little clay Indian pot and dabbed the wounds with kerosene-soaked rags.

His bite doesn't seem that bad. But he prays anyway. He prays for protection from the poison and he prays for strength and he prays that he will make it home before dawn. When his head clears he looks up, sweeping the flashlight beam in front of him. He can see the inside of the tree hollow in sharp detail, the words scrawled there by the hands of mourners long ago, and the names of the hanged, scrawled with unsteady hands on the inside of the tree. He wants to write everything down, but it's getting late and his momma will soon be preparing breakfast. His daddy sleeps late when he's not out on the road. If he hurries, he can make it back before he's dressed. But the snake is gone and his daddy will see and there will be questions. He needs another snake.

When Baxter Dawes looks at Jacob Flint, he sees himself as a child. They share a loneliness, the boy and the snake hunter, separated by forty years but joined by the unspoken bond of outcasts. They spend much time together in his tar-paper shack in the woods where the snake hunter teaches him to see beyond the surface of things, where he teaches him to listen and feel, where every green leaf is a wonder, where every wet stone is a prize, where man and boy and boy and man blur and fade and fuse and lose their distinctions, so that between them there passes only the pure word that was at the time of its creation, God. Before light there was the Word.

His shack sits perched upon high wooden stilts that keep it above flood level. Over the years the stilts have warped, so that the house now leans downstream. It's built of scrap wood and flotsam and sheets of rusted tin. Parts of old cars adorn the outer walls and sit propped up on posts as decorations—hubcaps and hood ornaments, tailgates and tires. Everywhere about the place are the remnants of trucks and automobiles marooned by the great flood that raged through this part of the Sequatchie on the night that Jacob was born. Baxter has built a row of kennels the same way as the house itself—out of scrap, and raised up on poles with wooden ramps that lead down from a narrow catwalk ten feet off the ground.

The dogs all begin to yap and whine long before they see Jacob come. He makes his way up a path that winds through the hulks of the rusted cars swept downriver after the flood. There's a dozen of them scattered around like toys, buried up over their running boards, some to their windows; some upside down. All lie in the very same places they were deposited the day the Sequatchie jumped its banks and washed out the Oakburg Bridge, and all the folks stuck on it. Fourteen people drowned on that day. Some of them were found draped high in the branches of the willow trees.

Jacob climbs the ramp that leads to the snake hunter's shack, but before he gets halfway up, Baxter appears at the door, bare-chested and gnawing on a bone. Jacob stops to watch him. He's a tall man. His body is sinewy and lean. His hair is wild but stiff and shiny as steel. The deep creases that run across his brow rise and fall as he chews, and his thick, silver eyebrows draw together and merge into one line of wiry hair that stretches from ear to ear. Baxter spits something out the side of his mouth, a tiny fleck of gristle he worked from his teeth with the tip of his tongue. He drops the bone at his feet and the dogs all whine to get at it. He squints down at Jacob as if he'd never seen him before.

Awful early for a visit, he says.

Baxter's skin is smooth and dark. There's no hair on it at all. Around his neck he wears a necklace of tiny bones. He's got strange black markings on his arms and belly that look like pictures drawn in charcoal and washed out by rain. Indian tattoos. That's what his daddy told him. Folks say Baxter Dawes was born in the woods, just like he was.

I need a snake, Jacob says.

Baxter pulls a buck knife out of a sheath hidden somewhere in his pants and picks at his teeth with the point of the blade. He's missing an incisor on the left side of his mouth and also several molars. He steps to the side, clearing the way for Jacob to climb up the ramp. He gestures with his hand for him to come up. Jacob does so and walks past him. He enters the house and sits on a crate near a large wooden spool once wrapped in telegraph wire that Baxter now uses for a table. Baxter does not sit. He takes two tin cups down off hooks above the stove and pours them both coffee. It's hot and strong and Jacob fumbles with the cup handle and drops it, spilling some of the coffee on his shirt and lap. He stands and wipes himself off and looks up at Baxter, who's not smiling. The shack is dark and Jacob sits mostly in shadow. Baxter notices the swelling in the boy's cheek where the snake bit.

Lemme see your face, he says.

He grabs Jacob's chin and inspects the puncture holes there. Baxter's fingers are rough and his nails are long and dirty. He has great strength in his fingers. Folks say he once ripped the head off a snapping turtle. Jacob believes it's true.

Fang marks, Baxter says. That's a rattlesnake bite. Big snake. When did this happen?

Few hours ago. Midnight.

Baxter draws near Jacob's face and sniffs at the wound.

You clean this?

No.

Baxter turns and removes a lantern from a hook near the door. He sets it on the table. Now he can see the boy's face and neck. He squints at him and puts his hand to Jacob's throat. He runs his fingers over the wound and looks deeply into Jacob's eyes. He pulls the lids down the way a man might do when deciding whether or not to buy a certain horse.

Look up, he says.

Jacob obeys. He rolls his eyes back and Baxter takes his hand, working his thumbs into the flesh around the snakebite, pushing hard, as if trying to squeeze out something.

That don't hurt?

No. It stings a little is all, and my fingers feel kinda funny.

Stings a little, huh? Baxter says.

Jacob nods and Baxter sips his coffee. He looks long and hard at the boy, studying him. The skin around the wound is not infected or discolored. But he can still smell the venom.

The snake that bit you was about four, five feet long, he says. It was a good clean bite. He stuck in there awhile too, plenty a time to work in the poison. It was Lazarus, wasn't it?

It was, Jacob says.

Baxter peers again at Jacob's wound. The boy tilts his head back to give him a better view. The snake hunter places his splayed hand over the bite mark, noting the distance between the upper and lower puncture holes.

Yup, Baxter says. It could only be Lazarus.

I took it from my daddy last night, and I lost it.

Baxter squints at the boy. He's never lied to him before and he has no reason to believe he's lying now, not from the look in his eyes, but if he is telling the truth, then the boy has survived a bite from the largest rattlesnake he's seen in years. This fact would not only prove the old woman was right—it would prove the boy's father was wrong. Jacob is indeed ready for the snakes and perhaps has more natural spirit than any of them has believed.

I need another, Jacob says.

Baxter smiles and scratches the back of his neck.

You can't fool him, he says.

Jacob's big eye starts to twitch, and he blinks several times to regain control of it. Baxter stares at him, his own eyes wide with wonder. The boy weighs less than a hundred pounds and the rattlesnake that bit him could have killed a cow. He's never seen so small a person take such a bite and survive.

Wait here, he says.

Baxter drinks the remainder of his coffee and vanishes into the darkness at the back of the shack. Jacob stares up at the walls, which are papered from floor to ceiling in pages torn from mail-order catalogs and old newsprint. He's reading about a big sale over at the Lynchburg Grocery when Baxter comes in holding a flour sack cinched up with a buckskin cord. He can see that there's something inside, twitching. Baxter drops the sack in front of him on the table and the bag moves, knocking the empty coffee cup to the ground.

Happy birthday, Baxter says.

Jacob smiles.

He's almost right, Baxter says. In color I mean. But your daddy will know the difference. But maybe by the time he gets to taking this snake out, he'll be so caught up in the rapture of the Spirit he won't remember how big he really was.

Jacob stands and places his hands on the sack. He can feel the serpent inside. It's large but not as large as Lazarus.

It don't matter, he says. I aim to tell him.

Baxter smiles and scratches at his hair, which is pushed up around his ears and flat on one side where it was squashed from sleeping. He takes Jacob's cup and swirls it. Coffee sloshes over the side.

That's the smart thing to do, he says. Your daddy ain't no fool.

Baxter drinks from the boy's cup.

Thank you, Jacob says. I got to be going. He turns to leave but Baxter holds him back.

Wait, he says. He removes the string of small bones from around his neck and places it over Jacob's head.

What's this for? He says.

It's for courage, he says. It was my father's. He give it to me after I was bit the first time. Said it was to remind me how close I came to death. It's a sign of being a man.

Jacob fondles the necklace, rolling the small bones between the tips of his fingers.

Thank you, he says. What are they?

Toes, Baxter says. And there's power in them, power to face danger, power to heal.

Jacob fondles the bones. They're old and brown as cocoa and they click together like beads.

But these were your daddy's.

I'll never have me no boy and you're as close as I got to a son. Now you best be getting on home.

Jacob goes to the door and Baxter follows him. He watches him walk down the wooden ramp, which bounces and creaks beneath their combined weight.

You look him right in the eye, Baxter says. Stand your ground.

I will, Jacob says. He raises his hand and waves, and the dogs all begin to bark in their kennels as Baxter watches him go. He squats on his heels and scratches the back of his neck as he sips the remainder of Jacob's coffee. He picks up the bone he dropped earlier and flings it over to the dog kennels where it lands on the catwalk. The dogs all howl and scratch at their cages. Jacob walks back into the woods. He hears them pawing at the wire trying to get at the bone.

2

BIRTHDAY GIFT

Jacob kneels in the tall grass beyond the house where he can see the serpent box partially covered by the ivy near the root-cellar doors. He didn't hide it as well as he thought and he sees the first rays of sunlight flare off the polished hasp. He looks up at the house and sees Magdalena's curtains are blowing out her open window. He wonders if she knows he's not in bed. He makes his way around back, keeping to the cover of the high grass and watching the house out of the corner of his eye. He runs out across the open ground, keeping himself low and holding the snake close to his body. He can feel it squirming against his belly, trying to nose its way up and out of the mouth of the sack. He ducks behind the hill, at the root-cellar door, and pulls the snake box out from the tangle of vines. He lays it on the ground and works on Baxter's knot. The cord is wound tight. Baxter must have got it wet. The snake is nervous and won't lie still and Jacob can't find its head, so he grabs the bottom of the sack and dumps it into the box before slamming the lid closed. He rolls up the sack and stuffs it under the vines and carries the snake box up the hill and around to the back of the house.

The back door is closer to the Bible room, but going in that way would require passing through the kitchen, so he goes instead to the front door and enters without making a sound. He stands in the hall, listening to the mantel clock ticking in the parlor. The house is unnaturally quiet and he can feel the beating of his heart. He moves on, wondering why he doesn't hear anybody in the kitchen.

On most days he can smell breakfast all the way up in his room—smoked bacon, biscuits, and, sometimes, baked apples. He smells nothing now but furniture polish, and the snake shit on his hands. He wonders if they've all gone out but can't imagine where they'd go. He walks through the hall, staying near the edges where the wall meets the floor, placing one foot in front of the other with great caution. He holds his breath as he rounds the corner and enters the dining room, where his father, mother, and sister sit silently at the long pine table they use for special meals and home services.

Charles sits in a ladder-back chair facing the door. His hands are folded atop the table. His mother and sister both peer down at the floor, as if praying. Rebecca gasps when she notices him, and Charles reaches out and squeezes her wrist. Magdalena does not move. She won't look at him.

A moth flutters against the window. Jacob hears the ticking mantel clock and the snake rustling inside the box. Magdalena stares down at her feet. She's banging her heels against the rung of the chair. He hears the clunk, clunk, clunk of her shoes. His father raises his right hand, lifting it slow, his palm facing outward, as if waving hello. But he's not waving. He stares at Jacob for a moment then slams his hand flat down on the tabletop with explosive force. The sound makes them all jump. Magdalena stops kicking the chair. The rattlesnake too ceases to thrash in the box, and all is quiet again except the moth. Jacob hears the gentle buzzing of its velvet wings against the screen.

Charles stands, his hands gripping the edge of the table. Jacob stares into his eyes. He steps forward, puts the serpent box on the table, and wipes his hands on his pants. His father's eyes narrow, and the corner of his mouth begins to twitch in the way it does when he's angry.

Take that thing off the table, he says.

Jacob places the box on the floor, and his lazy eye begins to roll back in his head. His tongue feels thick and his belly growls so loud that they all hear it. Charles steps away from the table and squats on his heels in front of the serpent box. He takes a quick look inside. Jacob does not blink. Charles sees the wound on his face and notices the necklace of small bones he now wears. He touches the snakebite with his fingers. When he told him Jacob wasn't ready for the serpents. He was wrong. He did not listen to the old woman, whose advice had never failed him. He didn't listen to Baxter Dawes or Sylus. He allowed the gossip to cloud his mind. He succumbed to vanity and shame for how Jacob was born. He held the boy back.

The eyes of his family are upon him now. They're waiting for an admonishment, for a sermon, for a punishment doled out with words. Charles can talk fast and think even faster. He has the wisdom of a man twice his age and what some call the great blessing of articulation. This is his gift and his weapon. He can outtalk anybody and outthink anybody and outstare anybody, and he knows the Bible so well that he can use it to back whatever point he chooses. With the written word of God behind him he is invincible. Yet now, he finds that he cannot speak at all.

I'm sorry, Daddy, Jacob says.

Charles shakes his head. He shuts his eyes and takes a long deep breath. Rebecca clears her throat. She senses something in Charles that she has not felt before.

Charles, she says. It's his birthday.

Charles turns to her and opens his eyes and Rebecca doesn't see anger there as she expects. Instead, she sees regret, pain.

I was wrong to deny you, he says. I've been a selfish man, a frightened man. I see that now. I'm the one who's sorry, and I'm ashamed.

He takes Jacob's hand and kisses it.

But let me tell you something about snakes, he says. Something I should have told you a long time ago. There's a proper time and place for serpent handling. There's a procedure to follow, a ritual, a way. We must earn and wait for the anointment to come. We must pray for it and build up to it, and any other way is like playing with a loaded gun, worse even. A serpent has guile and volition and the instinct to kill. I told myself you weren't ready for this life, and the truth was, I thought you'd never be. I hoped you'd never be. I realize now I was wrong, and there are things you must know.

He holds the boy by his shoulders.

Ours is a dangerous life, he says. We shoulder a great responsibility. The holiness churches are under a lot of scrutiny, a lot of suspicion. Folks want to shut us down. They don't believe we're a legitimate religion. They think it's all a trick, like a carnival show done in some dark tent with mirrors and fast-hand magic. If one person were to die of snakebite, or if some fool was to burn his gut out with drain cleaner, it could bring the law down on us and the churches could die out, all of them. If that happens, the hope and faith of thousands of believers would be forced to go underground. We'd have to hide our ways.

Jacob's eyes are red and wet from exhaustion, and now he's trying as hard as he can to hold back tears. He's been waiting for this for a long, long time. Charles pulls out the chair nearest him and sits. The moth has settled on the window screen.

I know why you did what you did, Charles says. I didn't

believe in you. I wasn't paying enough attention, and I take the blame. But, Jacob, though you may have the power and the skill to handle the serpents, you do not have the judgment for it. You didn't think. And above all things, a holiness man must think, because if he don't, he will die, and I don't want to lose you. I love you, and I don't want anything to happen.

Charles lays his hand on the boy's head and then leans over to kiss him there. Jacob feels the snakebite throbbing on his cheek. Rebecca goes to him, and takes him in her arms.

Jacob, she says. Are you all right? You look terrible. Where have you been?

I wanted to see it, Momma, he says. I had to see where I was born.

Is that where you went? she says. Up to the tree?

I sat inside, just like you did. I sat in there with the snake and I saw the names, and I saw the faces and I saw all the things that tree ever saw.

Charles squints at the boy.

Faces? he says.

Those men, he says. The colored men. It's true, Momma, what they say, it's all true what they did to those men, to that tree.

All right, now, she says. It's going to be all right. Let's get you fed and cleaned. I think your daddy has something for you.

Momma, he says. I just got what I wanted.

Well, then, how about breakfast? Anything you want.

Pancakes.

All right, pancakes it is.

Rebecca takes him into the kitchen and Magdalena follows them. Charles leans down for the serpent box, and as he lifts it, the snake inside strikes hard at the screen. The snake hisses at him and shows his fangs and Charles sees that it is not Lazarus inside the box but a new snake entirely. He'll have to have a word with Baxter Dawes.

3

A NIGHT VISITOR

The tree outside his window is a mossycup oak with wide limbs that stretch up to Jacob like gangplanks. He steps out onto one of them and comes down the tree with relative ease, sure-footed and nimble in the branches. He crosses the yard quickly and kneels in the bushes on the ridge. From here he can see the tiny window of the old woman's cabin. There's a candle flickering inside.

He finds the door ajar and enters without knocking. The cabin has a sour smell to it, and the tiny room is filled with a rank steam that makes him gag. The old woman stands near the stove with a spoon in her hand. Jacob's eyes water, and he winces at the smell in the air.

Don't you make that face, she says. This is for your snakebite. I want you to sit and breathe this air for the medicine that's in it.

Jacob sits in the rocker. He closes his eyes and breathes steam that smells of wet cigars.

You know I was bit? he says.

The old woman dips the spoon into the pot and pulls it up

filled with dark brown muck that hangs down like pond weeds, and steams and drips as she pokes it with her fingers. She drops the spoonful of muck into a square of cloth.

I knew you'd get bit before you even left, she says.

She pulls the corners of the cloth together and twists them, forming a little sack, and spins it in her fingers to make a poultice. Jacob opens his eyes.

How'd you know? he says.

She taps the spoon on the lid of the pot and ties off the poultice.

You take a snake to a place like that and he's gonna get antsy, she says. Snake knows danger when he feels it, he knows fear, and fear makes 'em bite. And there weren't nothing in that tree to bite but you.

She takes the poultice and dips it into the pot, leaving it there to steep. Then she reaches into a basket and pulls out a handful of yellow mullein flowers, which she picks off a long stem and lays at her side. She makes a little pile of the petals, pulls the sack out of the pot, and rolls the poultice in the petals so that they stick to the wet cloth. She binds it up with a dozen turns of light twine, spinning the sack in her fingers.

I saw things, he says. In the tree.

She looks up at him and studies his face for a moment. She puts a finger on the poultice to stop it from spinning.

The faces, she says. The tree Spirits.

She takes the poultice and brings it to him. She inspects the wound and pinches the skin between her fingers.

That hurt?

Jacob shakes his head and the old woman pulls his eyelids up with her thumbs and makes him swirl his eyes.

That's good, she says. She lays the poultice on the wound and presses out some of the liquid. It runs brown as tobacco juice down his face.

Those faces, she says, are the souls who perished in the

tree. And they don't show themselves to just anybody. You got to have something inside. Light. A boy like you, got the mark on him. They know you're favored by the Lord. They come to you like moths to a candle wick.

She holds the poultice to his face, shuts her eyes, and prays out loud for him.

Jesus, she says, heal this boy's wound, but leave him a scar to consider. Help him to be grateful and deserving. Protect him from evil and show him the way to the truth.

She wraps the poultice in bandages she tore from a bed-sheet and stands before him with her hands on her hips and her eyes wide. She looks at him and does not blink. Her once blue eyes are now milky gray, and something in them frightens him. He wants to turn away.

Your daddy don't understand yet, she says. He's got himself all confused. He don't see you for what you are, but it ain't his fault. He's just doing what a father needs to do to raise a boy. But he's afraid.

Jacob blinks and his eyes tear from staring so long. He rubs his cheeks with his good hand and drums his fingers on the arm of the chair.

What's he scared of?

Why, he's scared of you, boy, she says, and she smiles wide. Jacob can see all the gaps in her mouth where her teeth once were. Those that remain are small and brown. He doesn't like to look into the old woman's mouth.

Now, that snake poison just went right through you, she says. You don't even need that poultice, but take it on up to your room and hold it there for an hour or so, just to be safe. And you walk through the front door. Don't be climbing that tree. The good Lord Jesus can protect you from snakes, but if you fall out of that tree you're gonna get hurt.

The fresh cool air from outside is a welcome relief to him. Jacob shuts the door and the old woman listens to him on the stairs. She peeks through the curtain to make sure he's going up to the house, then she sits down on the rocker and lights her pipe.

* * *

He sees the girl, running, in her nightgown. She's scared, breathing fast and she's barefoot. Her soles are dirty. She stumbles in a thicket and scrapes her arm, and when she rises again, she leaves a swatch of her torn nightgown hanging from a black-thorn bush. He's seen this girl before. She used to go to the Toe Heel School when he was in the second grade. She's the Horton girl, whose mother died of the winter flu. Her name is Daisy Jane, and she runs with her hands outstretched before her, leaping over fallen trees, splashing through creeks and her nightgown is billowing behind her, glowing under the light of the moon. The trees all around her are black, and boulders loom up out of the shadows, stark and tombstone blue. She makes no sound running through the woods. She's been running for miles and has miles to go before she gets here, to his house. The last thing he sees is a swatch of faded pink fabric blowing like a tiny flag on a blackthorn branch.

Charles makes a habit of sitting up late in the Bible room. At this hour it's cooler than the root cellar. But the cast-iron flank of the potbelly stove is warm and heat ripples off the sides of it. From the inside of the stove he hears the rush of the flames. He feeds dried oak splits in through the hole in front, and they pop and they crackle. As the room warms, his breath can no longer be seen, and he begins to hear the snakes rousing in their boxes. Their heads scrape along the chicken wire, stretching out toward the warmth and the light at the back of the room.

As he reads aloud from his favorite Bible, his pigskin Bible, and the Holy Spirit wells up inside him. His toes start to tingle. He hears voices. He hears the apostles and the saints. He hears all the prophets and all the kings. He hears Habakkuk and Job, the rush of the ocean and a deluge of hail. There's a cacophony of voices, a sea of chants, and songs from beneath the stippled hide of the Bible, but there is one voice that he's never heard, the voice of Jesus.

He raises his head and looks out through the window screens, beyond the porch, and sees a flash of light through the trees. He sees a streak of white and puts the Bible down on the pulpit. He stands and looks out into the night, but sees nothing. He closes the stove door and turns down the lantern so the room goes almost dark. He hears the patter of bare feet on wood and rapping at the door. Someone's on the front porch.

The girl is small and panting hard. One of her nightgown straps hangs off her shoulder and she's bleeding from a cut on her arm. Her face is scratched and streaked with dried blood. She wipes the hair from her forehead and tries to catch her breath. She coughs and spits there on the porch but can't yet speak. Charles opens the door to let her inside. He sits her down and goes to the kitchen for a glass of water. When he returns she's at the bottom of the staircase peering up at Jacob, who is standing at the top of the stairs. The girl takes the water and gulps it down. She wipes her lips with the back of her wrist.

You got to come, she says. He's dying.

Charles looks up at Jacob, who's standing there fully dressed.

Who's dying, girl? Charles says.

My daddy. My daddy's dying up there. He can't breathe.

The girl's shivering and pale. Jacob comes down the stairs and stands behind her. He can see her flesh all raised up in tiny bumps. It looks like pigskin and he has the urge to touch it.

All right, now, Charles says. Take it easy.

Please, she says. He's gonna die.

Is there a doctor with him?

He don't want one. He asked for you. He asked for Charles Flint.

Who's your daddy, girl?

Poppa Hooch. My name's Daisy Jane.

She takes him by the hand and pulls him toward the door. Charles follows her and turns to Jacob, who's standing on the stairs.

Wake Sylus. Get my Bible and meet us out front.

The girl tugs on his father's arm. Jacob looks into his father's unblinking eyes and sees in them the moon, as clear and round as it sits in the sky. Jacob steps down and takes his coat off a hook on the wall.

I'm coming with you, he says.

4

POPPÁ HOOCH

Sylus is behind the wheel of the old lumber truck they use to haul logs up out of the woods, the big Ford with a wide wheelbase and good ground-clearance for the road into Owl Hollow where the Hortons live in what had been an abandoned hunting shack in the woods until Poppa Hooch claimed it as his own. The truck is cramped and Jacob sits on his father's lap. Daisy Jane sits between him and Sylus, with her legs straddled round the gearshift. They bounce around on terrible roads all the way up the mountain, with the tires slipping and spinning in mud that shoots up underneath in loud bursts that Jacob can feel on the soles of his feet. He's got them pressed against the hot transmission hump.

They drive through the night, until Orion appears low on the horizon, and the sky turns from gray to indigo, and they see a shimmering band of paler light below the foot of the constellation marking the imminent arrival of dawn. They stop at the base of a steep grade that banks off to the left and narrows into a footpath. The truck can go no farther. When Sylus shuts down the engine, they hear the chatter of hundreds of small birds. It's light enough now to see.

The woods are dense around them and the center of the road is waist high with weeds. Blackened oil drums and piles of scrap wood are strewn about, and a tall column of old tires rests beside the skeletal hulk of an abandoned truck raised up on blocks. It's an old Dodge with no doors. The engine's torn out, and nothing's inside but weeds and white adder's tongue growing up through the rusted frame.

The girl doesn't wait for them. She scampers up the steep trail, dropping down on all fours, using her hands to steady herself before vanishing over the rise. Sylus and Charles stare up at the hill.

Can you make that, Jacob? Charles says.

The boy nods. He sits on the running board of the truck removing his shoes and socks.

I can now, he says.

They follow the girl and climb a steep trail rising up over a hollow. Below them the tops of tall hemlocks poke high above a thick layer of white mist. They can see nothing beneath this fog, but above it the sky is brightening. They continue on down, passing through the mist layer, sliding and sometimes falling onto their behinds. Soon, they can see the floor of the hollow and, nestled in the brush, a tarpaper roof with a rusted tin smokestack poking up through the mist. There's a fire burning inside the shack, and they can smell burnt coffee amid the moist earth below, where the ferns grow thick and large as trees. The shack itself sits perched upon pilings that rise up from a carpet of these giant ferns.

Beneath the shack lies a trio of mangy hounds who neither bark nor raise their heads in response to the approaching strangers. Their gray flesh is stretched tight over their sunken bellies, and their bones show through like the ribs of small rotting ships. One of them is missing a foot. The dogs appear to be dead, until they get closer and see their ears twitching mechanically to ward off the flies, which buzz about the place in swirling swarms amid the stench of smoldering corn husks and dog shit. A ladder made from hemlock splits rests against a hole cut in the wall of the shack above them. Charles shakes the ladder to test its strength. He slides it back a bit and puts some weight on the bottom rung.

Used to be a hunting blind, he says. When there was still some bear back here.

You been here before? Sylus says.

When I was a boy I sat out a storm inside. There was only a shake roof then, and no stove. That was before Poppa Hooch lost his house to the bank.

The head of the girl pokes out from the hole above them and she makes a clucking noise with her mouth that sounds like the call sound of a squirrel. They look up at her and she waves them up.

Charles puts all his weight on the ladder and it creaks beneath him.

I'll go up first. Jacob, you come after me. Sylus will hold it steady and I'll pull you on through.

I can make it, Jacob says.

All right, then.

They climb up and through the hole in the wall of the shack, which is a lot bigger than it looks from outside or above. At first it's too dark to see much of anything, but they see that the shack is composed of two separate structures built on either side of a massive tree. They're connected by a covered footbridge made of rickety planks. A light flickers from the room in back, and when their eyes adjust to the relative darkness, they can see that the space is very small. It smells of mildew and rancid grease. In the back chamber Jacob hears the wet coughing of a large man. He hears him spit and swear as he crosses the bridge. He sees his father in the doorway, and he can see the girl now too. She stands in the corner of a room no bigger than a chicken coop. Her face is partly in shadow and it looks very grave. Jacob steps into the room and stumbles over a shoe. He falls facedown onto a floor covered in damp sawdust and finds himself inches from the feet of Daisy Jane. He lies there for a moment and hears the voice of a feverish, dying man.

What's that shuffling? the voice says. Who's there?

A boy, the girl says. He fell.

What boy?

Charles bends to help Jacob up, grabbing him by the back of the shirt.

My boy, he says.

I don't want no boy in here. I didn't ask you to bring no boy.

Jacob stands in the midst of this small room humming with blowflies, where he sees a huge, pale man lying facedown on a mattress raised off the floor on a platform perched atop four wooden crates. Poppa Hooch's arms and feet hang off the sides of his makeshift bed. His head is fleshy and bald, and he has large ears that droop at the tops. His chin hangs over the edge of the mattress, and below him, on the floor, lies a mason jar half full of what looks to Jacob like partially beaten eggs. Poppa Hooch lies uncovered and his drawers are filthy. He is almost naked and, like that of Baxter Dawes, his body is devoid of hair. He has great rolls of flesh at the base of his neck, at his waist, and on the inside of his thighs. These rolls shake in unison during his violent coughing spells, which conclude with him spitting a gob of mucus into his jar. His nose is large and red and pocked with tiny bumps and craters.

I don't want nobody else in here, he says. Bad enough you got to see me like this.

Charles steps closer. At the foot of the bed is a galvanized pail he uses as a chamberpot. He glances inside and turns his face away.

Take this out, Daisy, and stay in front until I call you.

The girl lifts the bucket and leaves. They hear her on the ladder and then the sound of the empty pail rolling somewhere outside.

Hooch, Charles says. This here's my boy Jacob.

The man raises his head and peers over at him. He squints at him and in his eyes is recognition.

The son of the nigger tree, he says.

Jacob looks over at Charles. Sylus once broke a man's nose for saying that to his face in Shuck's Mercantile on a crowded Saturday when the Acheson boys were at the checker table. The one who said it was young Luke, and as Sylus walked by him he thrust his elbow back into the boy's face, cutting himself open on his teeth.

Joel Peter Horton, Charles says. My Jacob isn't the son of a tree. He is my son, the son of Charles Flint, and a true holiness child, with more grace and goodness in his little finger than you've got in that whole forsaken body. If you want my help, you best not ever say that again. You hear me?

I apologize, Charles, Hooch says. A fevered mind knows not what it speaks.

Jacob's going to help me, Charles says. And he's going to try to help you.

Poppa Hooch is sweating and shivering, and when he breathes, a high whistling sound issues from his massive, wrinkled throat.

Come here, boy, he says. Let me see you.

Jacob steps close to the sick man. He smells very bad.

You know who I am? Hooch says.

Jacob shakes his head. He's never seen Poppa Hooch before. He would have remembered a man with such bright green eyes.

They call me Poppa Hooch. Come over here and look at me. Let me see if the Lord really does shine through those eyes like they sayin'.

Jacob stands near the bed. Below him is the horrible jar. But he does not look at it. He does not breathe. He looks instead into the eyes of the big, sick man, and at once he knows he is dying. His eyes are the color of fresh sweet peas, and deep lines radiate from their corners stretching out like fingers on the side of his swollen face.

Jacob sees in him a glimmer of light, and he takes him by the hand. He lifts his fingers and holds each one between his own, as if he had never before seen fingers, as if he were marveling at the wonder of them for the first time. Poppa Hooch takes a deep breath and moans. The boy's fingertips are hot and he feels something pass through them into his own as he lies back down with his face on the mattress. Jacob turns Poppa Hooch's hand so that his palm faces upward. He places his own hand on top and presses their two palms together.

I'm gonna die, Hooch says. They sent you here 'cause I'm gonna die.

Jacob smiles.

It's not for you to know the times or the seasons, he says, which the Father hath put in his power. But ye shall receive power in the form of the Holy Ghost and you shall be witness unto me.

Jacob does not know where these words came from, the Bible, yes, but he's never spoken them aloud before and does not remember having read them.

Charles turns to the doorway and gestures to Sylus, who's watching this with as much curiosity as Charles.

I never taught him that, Charles says.

What's he doing?

I don't know.

Is Hooch dying?

Charles looks back over his shoulder, where Poppa Hooch now appears to be asleep.

He's bad sick. But he's lived a bad life. A big smoker, he

was, and he's drank a whole lot of corn liquor. Had himself a still up here for awhile. He hasn't got much time left.

The sun has risen now, and it's burnt off most of the fog. The room is still dark, but they can see the walls and the floor. There's a tiny cot where the girl sleeps, and a stove that gives off little heat. In the corner, there's a crate of empty mason jars. Sylus bends down and picks up one of the jars. He opens it and sniffs.

I think he still has one someplace, he says.

Charles leans out the hole that serves as a door and shouts down at the girl.

Daisy Jane, I want you to take a ride with Sylus here to go and get us some things that we need to help your father.

She nods and Charles turns back to Sylus.

You go tell the old woman to send up some marrow soup, he says. Then have Rebecca give Daisy Jane a bath and something decent to wear. While she's doing that, you go into town and see the undertaker about a coffin, a big one. I'll pay for it. God only knows how we're gonna get him out of here.

Sylus nods and takes one more look at Jacob holding Poppa Hooch's hand.

What about the boy?

This will be good for him. Hooch will hold on until you get back, then you can take Jacob home. I'll stay up here and sit with him tonight. The soup is for me.

All right, he says. Sylus backs out the hole and climbs down the ladder. Charles goes back to the little room where Jacob is sitting on the edge of the bed. Poppa Hooch is on his back now, sleeping. Jacob is still holding the big man's hand. Charles motions for him to come into the other room and sits the boy down, wiping the hair from his eyes.

Jacob, he says, a man's body is a temple of the Holy Ghost. And to that temple we must be true. Sometimes the bad habits of a man's life can destroy that temple to such a degree that it cannot be repaired, no matter how much we love and pray. Now, Poppa Hooch is sick deep inside, and I'm going to tell you now that he will die. There are some things too far gone for us to heal.

He takes the boy by the hands and looks into his eyes and sees in them great hope and strength. He sees the look of a person set to do something bigger than he's ever done before, and it makes him proud. He feels a powerful love for his son, who is blessed with strong will and strong faith. He hates that he had to bring him here to see sorrow and despair and death for the first time. But if he truly wants to live the holiness life, he's got to see it sometime.

You know that old Dodge truck back there? Charles says. The one sitting out there in the weeds? That was a fine truck in its time. When Hooch bought that truck he was the envy of every man in town. Gave us all rides, and would carry whatever you asked him, free of charge. He drove that thing day and night, running fresh-cut timber in daylight, and bootleg whiskey after dark. Man can't run a truck that way and expect it to last too long. Gets to a point when no mechanic alive can keep it going. So there it sits, a home for wildflowers and snakes. That truck will never run again, Jacob, and I fear that Hooch has reached that point in his own life.

Jacob says nothing. He stares into his father's eyes, to see if he truly believes what he's saying. To see if he's testing him. They hear Poppa Hooch snoring in the next room, and Charles drops the boy's hands and takes out his pigskin travel Bible.

We'll sit here and pray for him, Jacob. We'll do the best we can. Because that's what we do. When Sylus comes back, we'll feed him some of the old woman's soup and make him as comfortable as he can be. But I want you to go home with Sylus. I'll stay here tonight and sit with Poppa Hooch. He'll pass on before morning.

No, Daddy, Jacob says. He won't.

Charles smiles.

Jacob, you're a good boy. I don't tell you that enough. You got a good heart inside you, but I've been close to death enough times to see it when it's coming. Poppa Hooch will never see the sun rise again.

Jacob takes the Bible from his father's hands and thumbs through the pages. It's heavy for a small book, and the pages are thick and gilded in gold.

Daddy, I hear Jesus talking.

I know you do, son. Sometimes I think I hear him too.

No, Daddy. I hear him talking now.

Jacob's eyes are narrow and steady as he looks up at the roof.

What does he tell you, son?

He tells me not to be afraid. He tells me, simply, to believe. And he tells me that if I stay here, Poppa Hooch won't die.

Charles stands and looks down at his son. He's small for a boy his age, yet his eyes are very big, and in them he can see that he believes what he says is true. Maybe he does hear Jesus. Maybe it's enough to simply believe that he can.

Who am I to argue with Jesus Christ? he says. You can stay if that's what you really want.

It doesn't matter what I want, Jacob says. He wants it.

Then you need to be prepared for a long, hard night. You see the way he is. He can't get up. He can't go to the outhouse. He can't clean or feed himself.

Jacob hands his father his Bible back.

I'll do those things, he says, and he'll see the sun again. I know he will.

Charles hands him back the Bible.

You'll need this. Take it. It was my daddy's and now it's yours.

They get up and go back inside to the little room to check on Poppa Hooch. Jacob takes one of the empty mason jars and brings it with him. He puts it on the floor below the bed and screws its lid onto the jar full of mucus and blood. He takes that jar to the window and drops it outside and it breaks open on a stone below. They can hear a hollow pop muffled by the ferns.

It is well past noon when Sylus gets back with Daisy Jane, who's wearing one of Magdalena's dresses. Her hair is clean and tied back with a bow. She has shoes on her feet and wool stockings. They brought back with them lemonade and pork sandwiches and several jars of the old woman's bone.

Daisy changes the bed linens while Charles and Jacob eat. Sylus holds Poppa Hooch up off the bed, the big man's arm draped around his neck. The girl cleans him with a special soap the old woman sent up for the purpose and then puts him back to bed, where he falls into a deep sleep. They leave him alone in the back room while Charles, Sylus, and Jacob climb down the ladder and stand together at the front of the shack.

It could get real bad, Charles says. If he gets to hollerin', then you back off. He might lash out and he's a big man. He could hurt you, Jacob.

I'll be all right, Jacob says.

I know you will.

If you want, I'll stay here with you, Sylus says.

Jacob shakes his head and looks at his father.

He needs to do this alone, Sylus, Charles says, and he takes the boy by the shoulders. You just remember all the things the old woman told you, and remember what I told you too. Speak the words of Jesus. Bring the Holy Ghost into this house. If you do that, then you've done all the work the Lord can ask. We'll come back with breakfast in the morning.

Jacob watches them walk up the trail and vanish into the ferns. He stands outside for a while listening to the woods and praying softly to the trees.

• • •

By midnight Poppa Hooch is fading away. He lies on his belly, gasping for breath and spitting up blood into the mason jar. Daisy Jane wipes his forehead with a cloth soaked in cool water and fans him with an old newspaper. Jacob sits on a crate with the Bible in his lap while Poppa Hooch groans and talks in his sleep. He calls out the names of his old friends and enemies alike. He pleads with his long-dead wife. He tells Daisy Jane that he loves her. He tells her he always loved her mother, and that he's sorry for the life she now lives. He tosses and turns on the bed, and the wooden platform creaks and splinters beneath him. He throws his arms out to the side and knocks over the bowl of water and flails at the girl, and she falls from the bed and cries. He pleads with them to leave, coughing violently, his eyes bulging from his head, begging them to let him die alone. Daisy Jane runs from the room. But Jacob does not move. He reads aloud to him from the gospel of Mark.

> And they came over unto the other side of the sea, into the country of the Gadarenes. And when Jesus was come out of the ship, immediately there met him out of the tombs a man with an unclean spirit.

Poppa Hooch raises himself up on his elbows and coughs so loud and with so much force that the bed breaks. The big man's mouth opens and a rasping sound issues forth. His face is swollen and violet. He spits off to the side, a great gob of lung muck that sounds like cake batter when it hits the floor.

Leave me, boy, he says. Let me die here. Just let me die.

Jacob does not hear him. He puts the Bible down and recites the rest of the passage from memory.

> And always night and day, the man was in the mountains, and in the tombs, crying and cutting himself with stones.

Poppa Hooch coughs and heaves. He grabs at his throat and kneels in the midst of the broken bed, hacking, coughing, trying to breathe. Jacob does not move.

But when he saw Jesus, the man ran to worship him.

Poppa Hooch holds out his arms and staggers like a man shot in the neck. Each cough shakes the room. There are terrible sounds coming from inside his throat.

And Jesus said unto him, come out of the man, thou unclean spirit. And asked him, what is thy name?

Poppa Hooch then drops to his knees as if trying to vomit. He places his hands on the floor and begins to crawl. A trickle of blood leaks from his mouth. Now Jacob rises, and he lays his hands on Poppa Hooch's head.

And the man answered, saying, My name is Legion: for we are many.

Poppa Hooch crawls, banging his fists on the floor, searching for the mason jar, his throat filled with the sound of gurgling blood.

And there was nigh unto the mountain, a great herd of swine feeding, and the devils besought him saying, send us into the swine.

Poppa Hooch grabs hold of the mason jar and brings it to his mouth and he opens his jaw wide and closes it, he does this over and over, like a rabid dog, until, from his throat, there issues a great crimson gob, big as an egg, that he vomits into the jar.

And the unclean spirits went out of him, and entered into the swine and the herd ran violently down a steep place into the sea, and were choked in the sea.

Poppa Hooch falls back onto the broken bed. He breathes hard and spits again. His whole head, from his neck on up to his bald scalp, is wet and red. He stares at the boy and begins to shake. He reaches out to him, his thick fingers stretching for Jacob. His eyes roll back and he falls to the floor with a great thud.

It is quiet in the shack at dawn. Jacob can hear the crickets outside, and the girl breathing in the other room. The candles have all melted down into soft white pools. Outside, the first birds flitter in the trees and he can hear them scratching on the roof. He can just begin to see the words in the Bible. There's light enough to read the chapter numbers and the names of the books. After they got Poppa Hooch back onto his broken bed, and the girl went down to sleep, he read all of Corinthians and a good part of Timothy before the candles died and it became too dark to read.

Jacob is not tired, but he is hungry. The big man has the blankets pulled up around his shoulders, and he sleeps on his side with his legs pulled up like child. Jacob cannot resist touching his ear. He takes it between his fingers, lightly, and feels the folds of it. Poppa Hooch grumbles and moves his head, and Jacob steps away. On the floor, at his feet, is the mason jar. He bends to pick it up. He holds it up to what light there is and looks at the thing inside, remembering the time Lucas Hyde brought the plucked eye of a cow to school. He brought it in a mason jar just like the one he's holding now. They all passed it around the school yard staring at that eye. The thing that Poppa Hooch spat out looks about the same, only darker. Jacob takes the jar and climbs down the ladder. He makes his way up out of the hollow, taking the same trail he walked before. He rises up from the mist, crests the ridge, and drops back down to where the road stops near the junk pile and the old truck. He finds himself a flat plank of wood with a sharp edge and sets the jar down in the weeds. Then he steps carefully into the remains of the old Dodge truck. He brushes away shards of glass and broken pop bottles and removes the heavy stones thrown through the windows. He clears a space between the adder's tongue, digs a hole in the black earth and buries the jar there. Years later, a magnificent scarlet oak would grow up through the windshield and doors and slowly tear the steel truck apart so that it no longer resembled anything made by the hand of man.

Charles climbs the ladder with Sylus behind him. The first thing he notices is the brightness of the shack and the missing boards on the south wall. The front room is flooded with sun and the girl is sweeping the floor. When she sees him, she turns and smiles and resumes her work more vigorously than before. He walks to the back room, where he finds Poppa Hooch sitting up in the bed eating the remainder of the bone soup with a wooden spoon. It's a shallow spoon with no lip on it and he can't get much in his mouth, so he tilts the soup jar and drinks from it. Jacob sits on a crate with his back to the door, sleeping now, with the Bible in his lap. Charles goes to the bed and looks Poppa Hooch in the eye.

Lord, Charles says. I swear you look better than I've seen you in years.

Sylus pokes his head inside and looks over at the bed and smiles.

Poppa Hooch puts down his soup and throws his legs over the side of the bed and stands. He has to stoop in the low room.

I never felt so good, he says. I don't even remember what happened last night.

Charles kneels in front of Jacob. He puts his hand on his

shoulder and looks back at the two men. He shakes him, and the boy rubs his eyes and drops the Bible. He peers around the room and scratches his head.

Hey, Daddy.

Hey, yourself. I don't know what you done, but he looks to me like a new man.

He's the same man.

Jacob stands and goes to the bed. Poppa Hooch holds out his big hand and squeezes the boy's.

I hope I'll see you again sometime, Jacob says. Maybe Daisy Jane will come back to school.

Jacob leaves the room and climbs down the ladder. Charles and Sylus stand staring at Poppa Hooch.

What do you make of that? Sylus says.

I don't know, Charles says. I've never seen the likes of it.

Poppa Hooch bends down to pick up the Bible that Jacob left behind. He turns it over in his hands and thumbs through the pages before handing it to Charles.

I been to yarb doctors. I've seen all manner of goomers and power healers too, Hooch says, but none of them can a hold a flame to that there son of yours. He's got the Jesus hands, and the Holy Ghost in his pocket.

I suspected he might have the touch, Charles says. But I never knew it for sure till now.

You take him out on the road, Charles Flint, and you'll make yourself a name and a fortune to boot. They'll come for miles to see that boy.

Whatever power we've got is a gift from the Lord above, Charles says. It's not about getting rich. It's about helping people find Jesus.

Well, you ain't gonna help nobody here, not in Leather-wood. They're all lost anyhow, lost and beyond redemption. If it's souls you want to save, then you best pack up and do your preachin' somewhere else.

. . .

Nobody speaks as they make the long drive home. Jacob sits between Charles and Sylus with his eyes closed, but he doesn't sleep. Every so often Charles looks down at the boy's fingers. He has his mother's hands but his fingers are from his side of the family—the fingernails and thumbs. Good hands and long, nimble fingers—serpent hands, with thick-jointed thumbs.

Charles had long wished to travel outside of Tennessee with the snakes. It was what he had been planning to do when the boy was older. He had always hoped for a father-and-son road ministry, with their own tent and a truck with the words FLINT MINISTRIES painted on the side. That dream faded when he first saw his misshapen son.

Maybe it was true what Poppa Hooch said, maybe they would come for miles to see such a child. The old woman would know for sure. Her dreams and predictions were often mysteries, but in the end, they were never wrong.

5

FATHER AND SON

Charles finds the old woman in her vegetable garden pulling out weeds on her hands and knees. She stops digging when she sees him and puts her hand up to shade her eyes. Charles squats beside her and she smiles. She puts her hand on his knee.

How'd he do up there? she says.

Poppa Hooch is a new man, Charles says. There's no sign of the sickness left in him. And it was all Jacob's doing.

The old woman leans back on her heels. Her fingernails are black and her hands are soiled up to her wrists from digging.

That boy's full of surprises, she says. When he puts his mind to somethin', he gets it done. There's no telling what he might do if you give him a chance.

The old woman's eyes sparkle in the morning sun. It's been a long time since he's seen her smile so shamelessly. She's taking pleasure in his unspoken affirmation of what she told him when Jacob was born. He smiles back at her and she pats him on the knee.

I'm thinking of going out on the road, Charles says. And taking Jacob with me.

Now that's wisdom, she says. You best pick the fruit while it's ripe or it'll go to rot.

She wipes the dust off her legs and slowly stands. Charles helps her to her feet. She takes his hand and holds it within her two withered palms.

Precarious lives we lead, Charles Flint, she says. And it all goes by so fast. If you're gonna go, then go soon. Leave this mountain. When I see you again, it'll be in a better place than this.

She turns from him and walks back to the cabin, singing something he can't recognize. She's much smaller now than she has ever been. She seems to have shrunk a full size since he saw her last. She's slower and less steady on her feet, and she must rest for a moment at the foot of the steps before she climbs dogs.

Watch out for dogs, she says. I don't know what it is, but I keep dreaming of dogs.

He watches her until she enters the cabin, and even after she shuts the door he can still hear her mumbling to herself inside.

Charles sits on the porch with Rebecca as the sunlight fades, watching the light turn her hair from brown to red. She knows what's happened with Poppa Hooch, and what he tells her is not at all a surprise.

It's time, Rebecca, he says. He's ready.

She nods and brushes the hair from her face. She doesn't look at him.

I suppose it don't matter what I think, she says.

He takes her hand and squeezes it. But she won't squeeze his back. Her fingers lie limp within his own.

I been waiting all my life for this, he says.

I know it, she says. That's why I won't tell you not to go.

You've seen now how strong the spirit runs in him. There's the snakebites, and what he did to Poppa Hooch. The signs don't get any clearer than that. You got nothing to worry about. We'll be back before you know it.

It's a mother's instinct to try to keep her children close, Charles. I can't help that. But he's not the only one I worry about.

We've been through this before.

Well, that was a long time ago. I guess I was a fool thinking you'd given it up for good.

Then we're both fools. Because I did too. But that boy, he restored my faith. And if he could do that for me, then Lord knows how many others are out there who might also be helped by him. We'll leave in a few days. We won't be gone too long.

That's what you said the last time.

I know. It couldn't be helped.

She turns to look at him. He hasn't shaved in days and his face is drawn and haggard. He looks older than he's ever looked before.

I suppose you want my blessing, she says.

I do.

Well, I won't give it to you.

He takes her hand. She always had good, strong hands. His momma told him he'd never have to worry about a woman whose strength lies in her hands. Strong hands, strong heart, she said. It makes it easier to leave, knowing she can take care of herself.

Rebecca, the Lord watches over the Flints, he says. It don't matter where we go. He was there with you that night up on your mountain and he was there with me on mine.

She takes him by the arms and pulls him close to her. She can smell him, and she can feel his warm skin through his clothes.

Send word back once in a while, she says. Let me know you're safe.

I will.

Don't push that boy too hard, Charles. Let him make his own choices. Right now he's doin' this for you.

They sit together and watch the sky burn down to a dark, rosy orange. The breeze picks up and the air cools. He kisses her softly on the mouth and she shivers. He can smell the lavender soap in her hair.

* * *

They drive the winding back roads of southern Tennessee, watching the sun rise, counting the roadside deer, and calling out the names of the stars. They watch reflections on the windscreen—a rising stream of clouds and shadows broken by sunlight in the patches of open road. The skies are deep blue in the daytime, the dusks glow like stained glass. Broad curtains of violet cirrus clouds stretch across the horizon, promising hot days to come. Time passes slow.

Jacob sits on a fruit crate so that he can better see the country before him. He props his feet on a lard bucket that sits on the floor of the old lumber Ford, and he rests his elbow on the open window. The truck constantly rattles as it bounces over tractor ruts and sinkholes. The roads are almost empty, and they travel miles between encounters with other human beings. The few people he does see walk stooped along the roadside carrying bundles of farm goods, or sit fanning themselves atop fence rails or stalled plows. He counts fence posts, and eats stolen apples and sips spring water from a brown clay jug.

They drive together eating the green apples and tossing the cores up over the roof of the truck where they gather on the rolled canvas army tent and on the tarp that covers the snake boxes in back. They brought only what they need to build the makeshift churches in the woods—a handsaw, two claw hammers, a hatchet, and an axe. They purchased a surplus military tent with a simple canopy that has a red cross painted on top. Charles extended the bottom of the cross with red paint so that it's no longer the symbol of an army field hospital but a symbol of their faith. They brought with them two Bibles, the one big Flint family Bible and the small pigskin travel Bible that is now Jacob's. They brought seven serpent boxes—six containing live snakes. They brought two warm blankets and the portable pulpit that Charles carried years back on his first excursions into the hills. They brought a jug for spring water, a fishing pole, and a clean white suit for Charles. They did not bring more than a few days' supply of food and a little money for gasoline. They have everything they need to hold a tent revival, yet Charles knows there is one thing left to do before the two of them can work together as a team. They must come to understand each other in ways they have never done before.

With their meager provisions they wander southeastern Tennessee, with no destination and no plan. They don't talk much as they drive. Jacob sits atop his crate, watching and listening, and everything he sees speaks to him like no words ever could. The images of his first journey away from home seem placed in his path for reasons meant for his eyes alone and it all passes by like a prophecy from some book whose author is fate and whose pictures paint themselves as they go along, unfurling before him like the stark and vivid scenery of dreams. Squeaky windmills loom above the roadside, their blades turning awkward and slow. He sees dark-windowed barns set deep within the woods, and slanted squatters' shacks built up on pilings in places where there are no rivers and no streams. Filthy hounds slink beneath the shade of low porches, and children coated with black dust stare out at him hollow-eyed and unblinking, their splayed fingers waving slow as memories. He sees rusted coal tipples and the hulks of abandoned trucks listing among stalks of broken corn. Everywhere are signs of good lives gone bad, and squandered fortunes and promises broken a long time ago.

Their truck tilts and bucks in the tractor ruts and is sometimes blocked altogether by crossing livestock and storm-toppled oaks. They make slow progress, but it doesn't matter. Their journey requires neither speed nor schedule, and they camp wherever they stop. They sleep in back of the truck, in fields and, whenever possible, near fast-moving streams where the water is rich with oxygen and insects, and fish for them to eat over the small campfires they make.

They stand in these streams at dusk, watching the surface of the water together, and this is how Charles breaks down the barrier between them. He shows Jacob how a stream moves, and where the water is deep and where it is shallow. He shows him the kinds of places the fish like to hide and how to work a fly in the current so that it drifts past the dark holes slowly, spinning like a trapped bug. He teaches him how to tease a fish with a fly, how to make him crazy for it, so when it bites, it bites hard and swallows it deep. He teaches him patience and timing through the art of fishing. And he teaches him trust. He holds the boy's hands on the pole and stands close behind him, nestling Jacob's head nestled in the crooks of his arms. They whisper to each other in the twilight, sharing the secrets of water and fish that only a father could know; and for the first time in his life Jacob feels like his son. Charles shows him to fish. He shows him how to build a fire. He shows him the best kinds of places to set up a camp and how to find shelter from the wind. They walk the creek beds at daybreak and study the impressions they find in the mud there, and Charles shows him the difference between the print of a possum and that of a raccoon. They eat roasted fish for supper and gaze into the fire at night. They read from their Bibles, and they begin to plan out how the revivals themselves will go.

Charles has a way of building anticipation in a small town. He knows how to stage an entrance, and how to walk and what to say to maximize the effect of his words. And they practice his plans together, over and over, around the campfires at night.

They read aloud from their Bibles, rehearsing their rhythm, polishing their tone. They work on timing and those nonverbal cues that make it seem as if the two are of one mind entirely. And they practice with the snakes. They handle them in front of the fire, becoming familiar with each serpent's temperament so that they can pick and choose based on the size and mood of each crowd. They study the snakes to the point where they can tell the difference between each one in the dark.

Charles is not the kind of preacher to throw up his tent and hold a revival unless he's sure the crowd will be large and willing to listen with an open mind. He doesn't want any trouble and he won't preach in a town if he's not invited. But he has a way of making people curious, a certain routine that often results in more than just an invitation. Sometimes it becomes a downright plea. He drives into some little town in the mountains, fills the truck's radiator with hose water, and lets it cool in the shade. He checks the tires and the engine, making sure that Jacob is visible to whomever passes by. He stands at the open hood of the truck, feigning concern for the engine while holding his Bible under his arm, waiting for someone to ask what's wrong. When they do, and they always do, he tells them that he's a messenger from God whose mission has stalled. He tells them that he's lost his way, that he's in search of a sign. He tells them that people have lost faith in Jesus, that they have forgotten the Holy Ghost, the almighty spirit of the Lord whom he bears with him, right there in the back of his truck. Then he reads from the book of Mark, waiting for that perfect moment to peel back the tarp to reveal the snake boxes. And this is how it begins. This is how the word spreads. They stare at Jacob and ask if he's blind, if he's dumb, if his wits are slow, and then Jacob surprises them with eloquent recitation from the gospels. At such times Charles instructs him only to speak directly from the Bible. When strangers come by, he is to remain silent until

Charles gives him the sign—a blink and a nod just as they're drawing the conclusion that the boy's a half-wit; and then the words begin to flow. Words of hope and beauty, strung together from both testaments, from many books and holy speakers spanning a vast expanse of time. This is something that people cannot forget.

Soon folks are talking about a man with a truckload of snakes and an idiot boy who speaks the words of God. The news travels faster than the old Ford itself, and people soon know who they are even before they get to the next town. They set up the tent in cornfields or school yards or sometimes in the woods. They cut down tent poles from local trees and cover the floor beneath the canopy with fresh hay. The crowds get bigger at each town and they no longer have to put up signs. People begin to follow them, attending several meetings in a row. After a few weeks of this routine, they earn both a reputation and a name. Some call them the Flint Family, or the Snake Boys, or sometimes simply the Father and the Son. When they pull into a town, folks gather round the truck window before they have time to fill the radiator. And when they ask what time the revival starts, Charles tells them: when the sun sets, always at the setting of the sun.

Nighttime is best time for fire and for snakes because torch-light is the most effective for creating a sense of an impending spiritual presence. Firelight has a wavering quality whose flickering shadows suggest the transitory nature of life itself, and when Jacob Flint comes down the aisle lit by the glow of those torches, the effect is startling. He appears from the darkness, hobbling, bearing a stick wrapped in rags that slowly drip flaming kerosene. He comes up the aisle with it ablaze and sputtering. They all whisper and gasp when they see his face in the strange orange light of that fire. He comes up the aisle and places the hand torch in a specially made receptacle behind the portable pulpit. Then he walks back down and vanishes into the night to wait for his cue.

Charles emerges soon after, holding his big family Bible between his hands. He comes out with his head bowed. When he gets to the pulpit, he looks up at the sky and addresses the stars. He prays to them. He raises his Bible above him in his outstretched hands, as if trying to get the book as close to heaven as possible. Then he takes three deep breaths and turns to the crowd.

You don't know me, he tells them. But you know the Lord and you know Jesus. Some of you believe, but some of you have your doubts, and I'm here to deliver proof. There is a manifestation of heaven here on this earth, a power from on high, a living spirit of love and joy that you can see, and feel, and harness for your protection. The Lord is here on earth, he dwells among us, and he has given us the means to believe.

He shows them all the cover of the Bible, holding it for them to see its golden letters and the big gilt cross on the front.

We won't be needing this tonight, he says.

He walks to the pulpit, sets the Bible down, and looks out at the crowd staring back at him. They are farmers and farmhands, their children and their wives. They gaze up at him with eyes wide and faces half-hidden in dancing shadow. Some have their Bibles perched open upon their knees with the pages glowing in the firelight and their hands placed there upon their favorite passages. The men sit sunken and dirty, their heads drooping, their shoulders hunched forward, holding their hats lightly in their fingers, not hiding the exhaustion from their hard day's work. There are babies sleeping in baskets and some draped over their mother's shoulders, fussing and being shushed. Shoeless children sit uneasy and distracted.

I see some of you brought your Bibles with you, Charles says. Well, you won't need your Bibles on this night. This night is about deeds, not words.

Those folks holding Bibles look at each other to see what to do. One woman puts her Bible away beneath her seat and a few others do the same. They look up at Charles and see a grim face with shining eyes. He scans their faces. Their eyes are tired but wide with expectation. They want to believe that something great will happen. They came not just to hear the words of God but to witness his power. Charles Flint knows this because he knows them. They are dusty and disheveled, but their hearts are clean and strong. They are bent and tired, and he stands tall and clean, backlit by fire in a suit that is phosphorescent in its brightness. His skin is pale too, and he's shaved and scrubbed clean. He does not look like he belongs to this place, or even to this earth. The congregation sits hunched there in the gloom, and he stands above them in a starched white suit, appearing to hover, appearing to glow. He raises his arms to the sky and lowers them slowly. Their heads follow the descent of his hands.

You know the Lord, he says. And you know Jesus. But you don't know the living spirit, the Holy Ghost who dwells among us and who is proof of God's love and devotion to us all. We're not alone, or abandoned, or forsaken. And I'm gonna prove it to you tonight. Yes, I am.

He looks up at them, then he closes his eyes and opens his mouth and mumbles words that sound strange to them. He speaks in foreign languages, in Hebrew and Aramaic and Greek—though he has never learned these tongues. His head begins to shake and his body starts to sway as the spirit of God manifests itself through him. The crowd watches him with great interest, and they sit up and stare as he begins to stomp his feet.

I'm bringin' the spirit down here to you, he says. You're gonna feel him inside you, and see what he can do, and through him I'll show you the power of clean living and true love.

He begins to shuffle in the dust. His hands shake and his

head bobs and his entire body is gripped in a quivering palsy. His eyes are pressed closed and the tips of his fingers dance on the balls of his thumbs. The crowd is so quiet that beyond the torchlight Jacob hears a chorus of spadefoot toads.

This power can protect you from the wicked, Charles says. It can shield you from sickness and sin, and when you leave here tonight, you will carry the spirit in your heart. You will bring him home.

He steps down the aisle, glancing at people, smiling at them.

You will carry him home, he says. And you'll remember the things that you see tonight, for they will remind you that we are not alone here on this earth, and that the Lord is watching us all the time, and that he loves us so much that he sent a Holy Ghost down from heaven to inspire and protect us. All it takes is a certain state of mind to overcome that which ails us, that which causes pain, and that state of mind is faith in the Lord. For with that faith, we can achieve great things.

He walks now to the rear of the gallery, and all heads turn to him. He can see the glimmering whites of their eyes flickering in the firelight.

I can read to you from Mark, he says. I can tell you about Jesus in the tomb and the two Marys and Salomé. I can tell you about the return of Christ. But you can read that for yourself. You didn't come here because you was lazy. You can read for yourself. Let's be honest with each other. You came here for proof, you came to see firsthand what faith can do. You came to witness miracles.

He returns to the pulpit and surveys the crowd. He turns and faces the rear of the tent and raises his arms. He lifts the little hand torch from the holder behind the pulpit and holds it above his head. Then he turns back to the crowd with his eyes closed and his mouth moving. He begins to speak, but the words he utters are not English or Latin or anything they've ever heard spoken before. But he is saying something with meaning, his language has significance, because as he speaks, their hearts fill with what can only be described as pure joy. The Holy Spirit speaks through him, and they can feel the fatigue lift from their bodies, they can feel the waning of despair. Charles Flint is speaking in tongues, and they understand this language instinctively. It bypasses their minds and speaks straight to their souls, and what it says is: Believe.

Charles Flint holds the torch in his clenched left fist. His right palm is open wide, his fingers are spread and lit yellow by the light of fires. His fingers are long and thin, and the crowd cannot believe what they are seeing as he lowers them into the crackling flame. He holds them there in the fire, and his palm blackens with soot. The flames are in direct contact with his pale fingers and they dance between them. He waves the torch from side to side beneath his hand and stares out at the crowd. He does not flinch. He does not cry out. His hand is steady. There is gasping from the back and people stand for a better look and Charles steps down from the pulpit to let them see. He allows them to touch his hand, to inspect the torch, all the while speaking in the rapturous language of the Holy Ghost. Then he suddenly stops speaking in the strange language and speaks to them with his own words.

A miracle, he says, is the Lord reaching out and acting upon us. A miracle is destiny undone. A miracle is not the impossible, or the illogical. A miracle is simply a change of his plan.

Several of the onlookers touch his hand. They rub away the soot and inspect his fingers. His skin is white and unmarred.

This is not a miracle, he says. The Lord is not extending his hand to me. I am extending my hand to the Lord. Do you see the difference? Do you understand?

He walks backward to the pulpit, holding the torch out with one hand and his blackened palm up to the stars. He looks down at the Bible and recites something from within, a verse they cannot hear.

The sky is full dark now and they can see on the horizon the glare of a single point of light. It's the steady glow of a rising Mars. They whisper among themselves, watching him. But he does not speak or move. There is a full minute of silence in which the crowd begins to wonder. Then Jacob comes. He marches up the aisle one step at a time, holding in his little arms the biggest of the serpent boxes, and the prettiest of them. The wood is varnished and shiny—it looks almost wet under the light of the torches. The serpent box is adorned with polished brass cornices and golden hinges and studded along its outer edges with brass upholstery tacks. He walks slow so they can read the words painted there in gold.

Trust in Jesus, Absorb the Living Spirit, Be Worthy, Let Go.

Jacob keeps his eyes on the ground while Charles dances at the pulpit, waving his arms above his head and fluttering his eyes. He taps his feet and sings the praises of Jesus while Jacob turns to the crowd. He lowers the snake box to the ground and stands looking up at them. He doesn't speak and he doesn't move. He lets them have a good look at himself. He lets the silence take hold and work its magic.

His head is big and his eyes are wild, both rolled back and all white with the lids above aflutter. His face pulses and his skin glows. They can see the moisture on his upper lip, which is raised slightly, his teeth showing in the darkness of his mouth—the oversized incisors of a preadolescent boy, gapped in the middle, protruding and wet as polished bone. To gaze upon Jacob Flint in the flickering light of the fire, with Charles standing above him in his radiant suit, his arms raised to the sky and still muttering the forgotten language of angels, exalts the onlookers. Their very limbs tingle, their hair stands on end, and they now see things unfold in the slow, vivid motion of an old and tragic dream.

Jacob lifts his arms and shakes his hands. He sways and prays to himself. He kicks the serpent box and the snake wakes inside. The air is filled with the sound of its rattle as he bends to unlatch the hasp. He prays aloud now as he gets down on his knees in front of the lid of the serpent box. He takes several deep breaths, but he does not open the lid.

No, he says. They are not ready. They do not believe.

He stands again and raises his arms, teetering from side to side. To those watching there appears to be something wrong. He cannot be well, this child. He's got the shakes, the quivers, his muscles begin to seize. Surely he will fall and flop around on the ground. But he does not. Instead, he begins to utter mysterious words. He raises his arms, and those close enough to him can see that his big left eye rolls in its orbit. They think he must be sick because his jaw spasms and his hands shake and his eyes are rolled so far back in his head. But to Charles, it is a signal. Jacob turns to his father and stops shaking.

Do you believe? Jacob says. Charles nods with his eyes closed.

I believe, son, I believe.

Do you feel him, Daddy?

I do, son, he's here, the spirit is here with us.

They then begin to talk back and forth the way they practiced in the campsites at the onset of their journey, Charles at the pulpit, Jacob below him in a trance. Charles becomes the medium, with Jacob transmitting the word of the Holy Ghost, passing messages between them as if the crowd wasn't there.

There are unbelievers among us, Jacob says.

Oh yes, son, there are many.

Can they be swayed, can they be saved?

Their salvation is at hand, Charles says.

Do they see the walking Jesus? He has risen. Do they believe?

They deny him, as his own brothers once did.

But we have faith in our hearts, Jacob says. In our hearts we know it's true.

Show us the light, son, show us the way.

Jacob looks up and out toward the horizon. The crowd follows his gaze.

I see a young man, dressed in flowing robes of white, he says

They cannot see, they are yet blind, Charles says.

The door to the sepulcher is open.

They don't see, they will not see.

The stone is rolled away.

Whom will they believe? Charles says.

She of the seven devils, Jacob says. Mary Magdalene.

But they will scorn her.

Jacob stretches up toward the sky and throws his hands in the air.

Without faith, he says, it is impossible to please the Lord. For he that cometh to God must believe that He is, and that He is a rewarder of them that seek Him.

Show them, son, show them, show them the power of faith.

Jacob bends to the serpent box with his eyes closed, and lifts the lid. He places his hands inside. The crowd steps back. He talks to the snake but does not yet reveal it. As he talks, he opens his eyes. His voice is soothing and he touches the snake with the tips of his fingers. He calms the reptile with words and light strokes of his hands. He puts his fingers around it and lifts it from its wooden lair. It is a big snake, black and thick, longer than the boy is tall. It's hard for him to hold, and he struggles with it. He pulls out the snake and raises his arms as high as they will go, and still it is not fully out of the box. It is a huge timber rattlesnake that they call Anathoth.

The head of the rattler is big and quick. Its long black body lies slack in the arms of the boy, and its head moves, sweeping back and forth before the crowd and flicking its tongue. Its mouth opens and its eyes shine as it coils itself around his arm. Jacob prays, and as his feet begin to move the snake lets out a hiss. Charles is praying with him and the crowd is praying now too. They can feel the current in the air, the night is alive with something that runs through them all, and the sight of the small boy and the snake makes it tactile and contagious. Some hold hands and sway. Others dance and close their eyes. Jacob walks among them, up and down the aisle. People are growing brave now. They're leaving their seats to follow him as he walks around the perimeter of the tent. Women are weeping with joy. Men are kneeling and praying aloud, their hands clasped and raised to God. Jacob leads the procession up the aisle to the pulpit. He stands below his father with the snake still rocking in his arms and rattling even faster. Charles raises his arms and lowers them to silence the chanting crowd.

Do you feel the spirit now? he says.

We do. We do, they all say. They're praising Jesus and chanting now.

Glory, glory, glory, they say.

Is this boy not blessed? Charles says.

He is. He is truly blessed, they say.

For if even he, Charles says, the most small and unlikely, can harness the spirit, then surely you can too. The cursed are the blessed, I tell you. The wretched are the strong. Do not see with your eyes. Feel with your heart. This boy, born as he was, mangled and malformed, amidst the thunder on the mountain, alone in the dark of the woods, this boy who appears to be blind, who seems not able to walk, was given the gift of the Holy Spirit. Touch him and you'll know. He burns, I tell you, he burns with the love of the Lord.

The crowd turns to Jacob, with the snake around his neck. His eyes are closed and his mouth is open and his body slowly sways. They come to touch him and the snake goes rigid and it ceases to shake its tail. They come to feel the boy's skin and quickly step away. Some lay their fingers on his arm with great caution, fearing that he might actually burn. The snake is wary of the people around him. It pulls back and bobs. But Jacob brings it around to the front of him. He brings its mouth close to his own. He stares into the black glass beads that are the eyes of the serpent. Nobody speaks or moves. The reptile is inches from his face now, and it rears back and rises up, sweeping slowly from side to side. Then it stops. The serpent, with its flattened head and coal-dark tongue, stares at him for a moment, then strikes him like a spear.

The onlookers grow suddenly quiet. The mouth of the serpent is locked onto the cheek of the boy, and it shakes itself from side to side, pulling at him, tugging on him, trying to withdraw the curved fangs stuck in his skin. Jacob steps back and swipes at the snake with his free hand, swatting at its head. The jaw of the reptile loosens and the fangs slip free. Jacob drops the snake and staggers. Nobody moves. Charles lowers his arms as his son raises his own. He puts his fingers up to the wound and shakes his head several times. He takes three short steps, one forward, one back, and then forward again. He totters and sways. He turns to look up at his father, his mouth wide open, his eyes wild with fear. The crowd is quiet, but the atmosphere beyond the tent is alive. He can hear the sputtering torches, the crackle of the flames. He can hear spadefoot toads and the sounds of insects in the trees. He hears these things clearly as his legs begin to wobble. His hands shake and his body becomes gripped in a sudden and violent paroxysm that throws him backward to the ground.

Somebody screams. People back away, and some start to run. Charles watches from the pulpit, unable to speak, unable to move. His mouth is open and his hands hover above his Bible. He feels the rush of air in his throat. Some are calling for a doctor and looking to him to see what he will do. But he does nothing.

He stares down at Jacob, still quivering in the dust with his eyes rolled back and his tongue lolling out. He's got a swelling bulge on his face that leaks a shiny liquid that runs clear as water.

The offending serpent lies coiled near the body of the boy. It raises itself up and its big tail stands erect. The tail quivers and begins to rattle. The head bobs again and then the tail blurs. The rattle startles the onlookers and they stumble back and turn to flee. They trip over crates, and their legs become ensnared in the guy wires that stake the tent to the ground.

Charles remains at the pulpit. He looks down to where the gallery had been seated and sees dropped Bibles, paper fans, and lost shoes. Jacob lies prone there among those things discarded by the panicked congregation. Every person has fled now, except one.

In the back stands a young man whose eyes are obscured in shadow. He has a narrow, bony face, the kind of face that becomes warped by the light of fires, with the skin pulled taught around the bones. He looks like Jesus risen from the tomb.

The man steps over the hay bales and the upturned fruit boxes and stands over the quivering body of the boy and over the coiled snake. He's lit now in a much stronger light that reveals his eyes and the bloodred color of his lips. He stares into the eyes of Charles Flint. The eyes of this stranger are gentle and moist. The snake hisses and rattles its tail, and the stranger raises a large knife that he brings down swiftly upon the serpent, cutting it neatly in two.

Charles Flint, he says. You don't recognize me.

The man kneels and takes hold of Jacob's head, cradling it in his arms.

Lord, he says. Save this boy. Cover him not with dark earth but white light. Bring him back to the light of your fire and let him again radiate and glow.

The man kisses the boy on the spot where the snake bit

him. He locks his lips to the wound and sucks. He sucks out as much venom as he can, spitting it off to the side. He repeats this many times. Charles does not move from his place in the pulpit. He stands watching this strange man ministering to his son, this man who has the look of a healer, the hands of a farmer, and the eyes of a boy he once knew.

6

GERTIE BATES

The black dogs come running. She sees first the green eye shine of doom, the bobbing lights of demons, dark set within those flat skulls open wide at their snouts with fangs of silver bone and a slaver. Lank bodies shiny with the wet of the dew, wide paws on crazy dog legs of pure speed and sinew. She sees the mud kick up behind them and hears the sound of air passing through mouths designed by God to seize and kill. The black dogs run quick and quiet, their legs loping smooth and easy on a slope of blowing pepper grass, the ground luminous with moonglow, and their shadows stretching out before them like pulsing black flames. Everything is moving slow.

She sees him now, as he lies dying in a bed of dank straw, and reaches out for him.

Jacob, she says. Take this old hand. And she wills the boy to reach for her across the dark divide, and he does, they touch hands in that null space where hearts are connected by hope, and by dreams such as this, and she can feel his burning fever and see his face now, bloated and large. His eyes are closed and his face is swollen red like a scalded man, and she sees Charles too, praying over him, offering his own life in trade for his son's. The boy's hand is hot. She feels needles in her fingertips and in her wrist and in her shoulder. She feels herself warming, and her limbs begin to swell. The snake venom is moving quickly, slithering, winding through the dark channels of her old bones.

Jacob's fever has broken now and she sees the whites of his eyes.

She pulls her hand back and rises from the bed in a cold sweat and watches the walls of the cabin throb. The skies outside are gray and the air in the little house is moist and cool. The windows are frosted over with tiny crystals of ice. She's panting and is startled by her visible breath, which leaves her mouth like a stream of pipe smoke and does not vanish in the cold air of the cabin. This cold air feels good on her hot skin, and she stands, and wobbles. Then she builds a fire in the stove.

She scuttles about the cabin on her gnarled, bare feet. She stares out the window, she stands at the stove. She places her palms over each of the bullet holes in the wall. The arm that touched the dream-Jacob is numb and swollen. She is in much pain. The poison is deep within her now. She does not have the strength to leave the house. She listens to the jingle of the old brass key pinned to her sweater. She holds the key and opens the cabin door to let more cool air inside.

She can no longer feel her feet. Her hair tingles and her vision grows dark. So she does the only thing she can do now—she warms a pot of soup. She stands at the window and watches the sky above the outhouse, with the crescent moon cut into the cracked wooden door, built by her father a hundred years ago. The paint has long since peeled away and shaggy green lichens cover its graying wood from foundation to rooftop. It looks like some portal from the nether regions of the inner earth that just sprang up from the ground. She wishes she could sit once more on the little bench inside and feel that familiar seat, the wood smooth as river stone. She thinks of the thousands of hours she's spent inside there as a girl, sometimes just to escape the cramped cabin by reading the walls, from which still hang the yellowed pages torn from the Sears catalog, pages she has memorized, pages she loves, pages whose promises have now faded, been discontinued, or fallen out of fashion altogether.

She goes to the soup pot and is warmed to a sweat by the stove. The light in the cabin is fading, and the pot swirls black. She can see the coals through the open burner. She steps back and trembles and turns her face to the peppered wall, where the old bullet holes are now pushing white smoke into the cold room. The wall is breathing, and she can hear a young man moan. She turns to the bed and sees him there.

Gabriel? She says.

His feet are sticking out from the blanket; and they are no longer bare. She is spared of that, his poor white feet. They're shod now in fine kid-skin boots that are oiled to a high sheen.

She goes to his bedside and reaches out with both her arms, and her legs buckle and she falls to the floor. She lies there, in the darkness and she can hear the sound of creaking wood and the wind whistling in the flue. These things have not changed in all this time, the sound of the rushing wind, the creak of the wood. The only thing that's different now is the smell. The air smells of gunpowder and dried blood.

She holds the brass key and can see now the congregation of black dogs standing on a bluff. Their snouts are raised high and their ears are flat against their skulls. The dogs sniff the wind. Their nostrils flare and the leader paws at the ground. The old woman takes the key from her chest. She holds it tight, squeezing it as hard as she can. It burns her but she does not let go. Her hand opens and it lies on her outstretched palm. A tiny swatch of pink wool hangs from the safety pin.

When she dies, it is a peaceful thing and free from any pain. She had always believed this, that dying was the same as falling asleep, like slipping back into a favorite dream, where the light is forever golden, as it is in the ebb of the day.

She kneels beside the bed. Gabriel's barefoot again. She rubs the soles of his feet with linseed oil and reads to him, from memory, the walls of the tiny house with the moon cut into the door.

Jacob wakes in an unfamiliar barn. It's dark out, and he hears the clatter of raindrops on the roof. The straw he lies upon is musty and damp, and water drips in from many places overhead. Droplets fall onto planks and into tin buckets. They ping off the tops of paint cans and solvent-filled jars.

His first sensation is that of biting cold. He's shivering and lying half-dressed in his bed of straw. He rises and sees his father curled in a horse blanket beside him. He's sleeping, with a Bible open before him and a lantern sputtering by his side. Jacob's head throbs. His face aches and his lips feel puffy. He brings his fingers to his cheek and feels puncture holes, freshly scabbed and tender. It is perhaps only a few hours before dawn.

He stands and moves a wooden box beneath the window so he can peer out at the rain. He sees a big farmhouse, and below the window the Ford truck, with the canvas tarp thrown carelessly over the bed. He wonders how he got to this place.

Charles lifts his head and sees a silhouette standing at the window, and what he thinks he sees is Jacob's ghost. He turns up the lantern and floods the hayloft with light. The shadow at the window does not disappear.

When they brought him here to the Cross farm, he barely had a pulse. His pupils were fixed, his skin cool. His face was puffed up to twice its size, and they were so sure he was going to die that they began the task of building him a coffin.

Now, his face looks normal; the swelling has all gone down. There are two small holes just above his jawbone on the right side of his mouth. A clear liquid oozes from this throbbing wound. Charles touches him there and brings the light close to inspect it.

* * *

Daddy, Jacob says. Charles shakes his head. He's groggy and this might still be a dream.

Daddy, where are we?

Charles squints at his son.

Jacob? How do you feel, son?

I'm fine, Daddy. I feel fine.

Charles stands and holds the lantern higher. Jacob blinks. A clear liquid oozes from his wound. Charles touches his face. He brings the light close and stares at the bite mark.

Lord, he says. It's a true miracle. He holds the boy's head in his hands. His eyes are clear and wide. Charles kisses him on the mouth, and Jacob wipes his lips with the back of his sleeve.

What did you do that for?

Charles smiles at him.

To make sure it's really you and that this ain't a dream. Don't you remember? I was so scared, Jacob. I couldn't even move. Tobias sucked what he could out of you, but it was too much, even for him. Too much poison. We brought you back here, to his father's house, and when we laid you down, you were this close to dead.

I feel fine, Jacob says. I remember parts of what happened, but not the bite. I remember holding the snake, and I remember my dream. The old woman came to me. She told me to hold her hand. She said to me, Take my hand, and I took it. She gave me peace. I never felt so happy.

Charles stands and smooths the boy's hair. He looks out the window and watches the rain. Above him he can hear the swallows.

That's a good dream, he says. Hold it inside you and never forget it. That old woman's hands have enough strength for us all.

Jacob lies back down in the straw, and Charles lies down too. They stare up at the rafters.

Where are we? Jacob says.

This is the boyhood home of Tobias Cross. I was right here in this very spot on the night you were born. He was about your age then; we had both just come back from Slaughter Mountain.

I never heard you tell that story, Daddy, Jacob says.

I was always scared you'd get ideas about runnin' off to handle snakes, Charles says. I was waiting for the right time to tell it. I guess that time has come.

John Cross did not have time to measure the boy, so he builds the coffin a little long. He fashions the planks from a piece of storm-blown cedar while Nettie boils bark, tearing strips from old bed linens to soak in a wahoo tea. It's an old custom that works wonders on a corpse, preserving the flesh and keeping it from putrefying.

John Cross works all night under an awning outside his woodshop. He's got the box built and now he's working on the lid. He cuts a tiny cross into the top with his chisel. The wood is still wet and it smells rich and clean. When the sun breaks through the clouds, wisps of steam rise up from the coffin as it begins to dry.

He was not asked to do this thing, and does not enjoy the task, though he loves to work with the adze and the saw. This is what folks do for each other where he comes from; they help make preparations for the dead.

The boy was hardly breathing when they came. He offered them a room with a bed. He urged Charles to bring him into the house, to give him a decent place to die. But Charles would not accept his offer of reconciliation. He told him that if a manger was good enough for the birth of Jesus Christ, it was fine for the death of Jacob Flint.

John Cross remembers a night like the one just past, when thoughts of this same chore entered his mind. But his son came home that night. He came home alive, but somehow changed.

Tobias did not speak with him for days, nor did he speak to his mother or visit his friends. After he came back from Slaughter Mountain, he spent much of his time in his room, reading the Bible and praying quietly to himself. It was weeks later, while loading grain at the feed store, that he overhead folks talking about a holy boy wielding a snake. That boy was his own son, and they spoke with great reverence and admiration for him, and he felt something stir inside him then that he had never felt before, but longed for from his own father. Pride. His son became a legend, along with a man named Charles Flint, who they say brought the spirit of God back to Slaughter Mountain and shattered an African cobra to pieces like a porcelain doll.

There was no turning the boy back after that night. No amount of persuasion could convince him that farming could be a good life. Tobias no longer talked about frogs or fishing, he spoke of God and the spirit, quoted scripture to them at the supper table, and admonished them for their lack of faith.

A few days later, a big sedan pulled up to the house. It was a long black car free of grime and rust and decorated on both sides with the face of Jesus. On the doors were words painted in gold—Slaughter Mountain Holiness Church in Jesus' Name, it said. The Bowsky twins climbed the porch steps and rapped on the door. They were dressed alike in clean white suits, smelling of hair tonic and bath salts. Despite their reputation for hollering, they were soft-spoken men who removed their hats and waited for Nettie to sit before taking chairs of their own. They refused lemonade and tobacco. Their eyes were dark and serious, for they had come that day to take his son.

He was gifted, they told him, a one-in-a-million child. He could do great things for great numbers of needy people, they said. They spoke to him of rare talents given to only a few men by God himself, and how such talents must be encouraged, fine-tuned, and used for the benefit of mankind. It was his duty, they told him, his own sacred purpose, to let Tobias come with them to live and be schooled. He had planted the seed, they said, and tended to the crop it had grown. Now that crop was ready for harvest. All things green must be cut, they told him, or they will wither. If not tended and pruned, they will grow wild, they said, and serve not the good of man, as God had ordained. They reminded him of the depression and falling crop prices and the thousands of folks on the dole. Tobias would be well taken care of, they told him. He would send money home. The farm was failing. John's back ached worse and worse each day. In truth, he did not wish this on his son, this faltering life of pain where the work piles up and the day never ends. Sending him off with the Bowsky brothers was the right thing to do.

So they packed him a small bag right then and walked him outside to say good-bye. Nettie kissed his head and he shook his son's hand. They promised to come see him at church and told him to behave. The Bowsky brothers helped him into the front seat of the shiny black car, and they drove back up to Slaughter Mountain.

7

TRINITY

The sun rises. Light streams in through the slats of the Cross barn and swallows swoop in and out of the window. On the straw below, Jacob sleeps soundly with his mouth open and his legs folded and his hands cupped together as if in prayer. He is alive. Charles sees the iridescent wings of the birds as they shoot through the rafters, flying fast and reckless in the tight spaces. They are a welcome sight to him, and so are their nests of brown mud. The order of the world. Small things in their living. Life above and life below and life unseen—the great surge of it all, the everlasting, manifest in the smallness of feathers and eggs. Miracles abound, and the boy is but one of the unexplained. He shuts his eyes and listens. Milk streaming into an empty steel pail. The flat jangle of a copper bell. The lowing cows.

He rises quietly and climbs down the ladder out of the hayloft. Outside the sky above the farmhouse is clear and still and cold. He warms his hands in his pockets, and walks to the milking stall, where Tobias kneels beside a cow, singing softly to himself. The cow turns to look at him and shakes her head so that the bell clatters. Tobias turns and squints.

Charles? he says.

The fever broke, Charles says. The swelling's gone and he's sleeping now. Tobias, he's alive.

Sweet Jesus, Tobias says. And he stands. He wipes his hands on his pants.

I am at a loss for words, Charles says.

It's a true miracle, says Tobias. And the Lord's will that I came, last night. It took the two of us to save him, your faith and mine.

A miracle did not save that boy, Charles says.

He was as good as gone, Charles. You know it.

I don't speculate as to the how or why of things.

I don't have to speculate, Tobias says. The Holy Spirit brought that boy back to life.

Be not rash with thy mouth, Tobias Cross. He was not dead.

Tobias bends and picks the milk pail from the stall. It's nearly full and the milk sloshes out onto the ground.

Charles, we haven't spoken in ten years. And I don't want us to get off on the wrong foot. If you don't want to talk about it, it's fine. I'm just happy he's alive, and happy you're here. I always hoped I'd see you again. In fact I prayed for it. You showed me the light that night on the mountain. You set me on the path and for that I'll always be grateful. When you're ready, come on in for breakfast. My daddy's out back of the house building a coffin for your boy. I better go tell him we don't need it any longer.

Jacob sees them both through a hole in the floor. He watches his father and he watches this other man who he has seen before. In his dreams, when the old woman came to take his hand, before she saved him, he saw a young man with an old face. Jacob was afraid of him. His skin was deeply creased and weathered, his head was too large for his body, and on his back, he had a tiny set of butterfly wings. He took hold of Jacob's wrist, and said to him, I am the amber light of fire, I am the glory of God, and he pulled him down. When the old woman came, the man flew off into a golden meadow ringed by trees. The man below the hayloft is the man from his dream, his vision, though his face is not old or creased and as far as he can tell, he bears no set of wings.

When he stands his head swims. He blinks, and stars swirl and pop before his eyes. There's a dull throb in his face and a swollen patch of tender skin there that aches at the touch. He peers out the little window and sees a farmhouse painted green like the head of a mallard duck. Chickens are kicking up dust in the yard. He can hear the gentle clank of a cowbell. He climbs down the rickety ladder and stands in the doorway of the milking stall. He sees his father with the man. He's young, but has old eyes, eyes that are large and deep. Like his father, he carries his power in his eyes. The look there is strong, as if he is prepared at any moment to order men to their deaths. His face is firm and there is much resolve in it. It is not a warm face, it's a face hardened by burdens and knowledge well beyond the man's physical age. They are two wheels along the same axis, this man and his father.

When he sees Jacob, he smiles and comes to him. He offers his outstretched hand.

Hello, Jacob. I'm Tobias Cross, he says.

Jacob looks into his eyes and he feels drawn to them. Tobias Cross has a long boyish face and a wide forehead, and his eyes burn with the telltale residue of glory. He is a man who has seen and felt things at their deepest levels. He radiates awe and joy.

When Tobias takes his hand, he feels a surge of heat, and the power of the boy's touch. And he winces.

I sure am happy to meet you, Tobias says.

I'm happy to meet you too, Jacob says.

Are you hungry? I bet you're hungry.

Jacob looks at his father, who is watching them with his hands in his pockets.

I'm half-starved, Jacob says.

That's the venom, Tobias says. You need to eat and get some strength back in you. Come on in and see my momma. She'd love to meet you. You're famous, the two of you. Do you know that? We heard of you long before you came down this way.

Fame is a fleeting thing, Charles says. Fame is a vanity, wet like an eel and impossible to hold onto.

Yes, Tobias says, but times have changed. The world has been through a terrible war. Folks have radios and the picture show now. They want to be entertained, they want to escape. We need to reach as many people as we can, Charles. And what you got here is a powerful thing. And when word gets out about what happened last night, this boy's gonna be a legend, and legends never die.

Charles reaches into his pocket and pulls out a small dark thing. He holds it in his palm. It's a shard of ebony from the broken African chest.

I put this in the mail to you, he says, six or seven years ago. I sent it down here to let you know I hadn't forgotten about you. But it came back, addressee unknown.

Tobias takes the fragment of wood and holds it up to the light. He rubs it with his thumb and turns it over in his fingers.

I did not want you to forget how we came to understand the glory of God, Charles says. The light of the Holy Ghost shone on us both that night.

Tobias turns the shard of wood over in his hand.

My daddy must've sent it back, he says. I had left home, and moved up to Slaughter Mountain with the Bowskys. They were good men, Esau and Ray, but I always hoped you'd come back and lead that church, Charles. We needed you.

You did all right for yourself, Tobias. You didn't need me. I always planned on coming back to Slaughter Mountain, but not until Jacob was ready.

I'd say he's ready, Tobias says. I'd say he's ready not just to see the Slaughter Mountain church, but to lead it.

They walk out into the yard, over to the little woodshop behind the house, where, beside an oak tree and in sight of an old tire swing, they see a short coffin atop a pair of sawhorses. Its lid leans against the side of the house. John Cross stands with his back to them, tapping a chisel with a ball-peen hammer. They stare at the coffin and John stops hammering and turns. He sees Jacob and he drops his hammer.

Lord, he says. That boy was at death's door not five hours ago.

I know it, Tobias says.

Your face, he says to Jacob, was swollen up something awful.

I don't remember anything, Jacob says.

Well, I'm happy to see you alive and well, young man, though I must say, this here's the finest box I ever built. Look how pretty it is. Now I have to tear it apart.

There's an angel carved on the lid of the coffin with a halo floating above its head formed by a serpent consuming its own tail, and Jacob's initials between the angel's wings, a beautifully carved *J* and an *F* inside a tiny heart whose outline John had yet to finish.

Jacob touches the face of the angel with the tips of his fingers, feeling the freshly carved wood, and Charles whistles a long note of admiration and shakes his head in wonder, the way men do when they see good horses or a night sky filled with stars.

You're a fine carpenter, he says.

He is, Tobias says. He builds all the coffins in these parts, takes great pride in them, don't you, Daddy?

It's bad luck to keep an unused coffin, John says.

Jacob walks around the perimeter of the coffin tracing the lip of the box with the tip of his finger. The air is rich with the smell of fresh cedar, and the shavings are soft under his feet. The wood, pink as a sunset, banded with thin streaks of amber and rose, is a wonderful thing to behold.

We should keep it, Jacob says. And use it in a revival.

He turns to Tobias.

We can fix hinges to the lid, he says. And carve it all over with scripture. And then, we'll get the biggest snake there is and keep him inside and we can bring it out on our shoulders and march out real slow.

Sounds like a sideshow, Charles says. It's too theatrical.

What if it is? Tobias says. Stage actors use props all the time. That's all it would be, just a prop. That cobra box you smashed that night was a dark and evil thing, an idol, like the Asherah poles of Baal, and you destroyed it for effect in order to make a point. That was nothing more than a prop and just as theatrical. Don't you see, Charles? What we have here is a resurrection of that box. Except this one was built to hold the body of a blessed child saved from death by faith and devotion. This box stands for what we preach. The story of how it came to be is the very foundation of our beliefs. In fact, don't think of it as a prop, because that word implies a falseness. This box is no prop, it's a tomb for a boy who came back, it's a vessel of faith and strength for a holiness man.

Charles is not unmoved by this appeal. The coffin would surely have a powerful effect, and it would be a great symbolic vehicle for the snakes. The box that he used to carry his first snake, the one he claimed was made from the coffin wood of Lester Poles, was a lie. This box is the truth.

He kicks at the sawdust and bends to pick up some of the shaved wood. He holds it to his nose and smells it. Then he tosses it into the air. He sees himself as a man of God, and as such, a man of God's will. Clearly, Jacob's gifts can no longer be denied or contained. It would be easier to hold back the tide. If he truly believes in the stories of Jesus, then his choice is clear. Faith implies risk, danger, and hardship. Did Jesus not enter the gates of Jerusalem on the back of a donkey? Did he not upturn the tables of the money changers? That was theater in its own right and the message was not lessened by it.

When's the next big revival you have planned, Tobias? he says.

Next revival's in ten days.

All right, then, Charles says. We'll need to get moving if we're gonna do this right. We need to get a message back home.

For what? Tobias says.

Well, I need to let Rebecca know we're all right. And if we truly want the biggest, meanest snake we can find, we need the best snake hunter in Tennessee. We need to send for Baxter Dawes.

8

BEAR HUNT

Baxter Dawes can smell game like a dog. He can smell wild pigs and snake scent and the musk of a deer rubbed off on the sharp edge of a stone. And he can smell the she-bear. He smells her in the Rooneys' chicken coop before dawn, he finds the doors torn from their hinges and cast aside all twisted and broken. He finds the hens disemboweled and lying in the bloody straw, their insides still steaming, and he picks up her trail outside the barn, where he follows her upwind into the woods before losing her scent at a creek so small and sporadic that it has no name. He crawls about on his hands and knees, flattening the saw grass at the edge of the water and confusing the already spooked dogs with his strange behavior.

The dogs circle him and whine. Spider scratches at the mud with his paw. Baxter waves them off with a swiping motion of his hand. With his face down low, near the ground, he moves slow, like a stalking dog himself, placing each hand down in turn, soft and easy in the dark mud near the creek bank, palm first, then fingers, quietly crawling, listening to the rushing gurgle of the stream and stopping only to examine the impressions made by the bear. The prints are partly filled with clear water. Bits of wet mud crumble down from its sides. She is very close. He moves away from the bank and finds a tuft of matted black fur hanging from a blackberry thorn. He pulls it off and sniffs at it and turns to show Sylus the fresh game sign. He gestures with his chin toward the berry thicket, and Sylus nods. He brings the rifle up to his chin and brushes his index finger over the trigger guard. Baxter signals to the dogs.

He brought all five out with him this time, because this is a bad bear who's been causing trouble for months, having come down off the mountain and acquiring a taste for barn-yard fowl. During the night, she killed eight hens and a good pointer dog named Rooney-Finn. The bounty has grown to a hundred dollars, plus what he can get for the hide, which is twenty dollars more.

He sends all the dogs back behind Sylus, except Spider, who's the only one who's ever seen combat with a rogue bear and knows enough to keep back and stay clear of the swiping paws. Spider stands poised and waiting, a paw raised in the air. His head is cocked toward his master. Baxter creeps slowly into the blackberries, his hands sunk wrist deep into the mud. The air is bone cold in the tiny canyon where the creek runs and the mist rises up all around them. There is no sound save the rushing of the creek. Sylus takes a half-step and a fat raindrop smacks against the barrel of the gun. He looks up at a smoke-gray sky and sees black clouds rolling up and under the higher grays as more drops begin to fall. The dogs are antsy. They step lightly in place and whine low as Spider's ears flatten. He grows rigid and his hackles stand up at the nape of his neck. Baxter moves into the brambles. He can hear the hammer of the rifle snap back and click as the she-bear comes. She bursts from the blackberries to Baxter's right, flanking the lead dog, her head low and charging straight at her like a boar. The first shot misses wide, and the bear bumps Sylus. He falls back and rolls on the ground. Baxter backs out of the thicket in time to see the bear knock Spider into the creek with a quick slap of her open paw and Sylus fumbling for the rifle in the deeper water near the reeds. The bear turns to face them, and now they've lost the gun.

Baxter once said that a man in the woods was about the purest thing there was in the world, and the closest he could come to knowing God. A man can never buy with money this thing that the Lord gave him for free, he said. That sense of awe and respect one derives from the trees and the earth and all things that dwell in between them. He told Jacob that poetry was all around him, in the grass and on the surface of the leaves, and that the Bible was full of good words designed to mimic what could never be written, but could sometimes be heard and always seen—the rising water, the falling rain, the rush of river and wind, the passage of cloud banks and great ruminant herds, buffalo and elk and the trailing packs of carnivores, both man and wild dog, wanderers all, in endless migration to the grasslands that feed them. He told him that magic is neither myth nor mystery but that which cannot be explained or understood—which is how the world was and should always be. There's magic in a caterpillar, he told him, and in an acorn and behind the stars. His ancestors had understood this. They worshipped the forest as some white men worship God. He had only come to know and love God through time spent in the woods and through his proximity to death, which he gained in the trenches of the first great war.

All his life he had lived in the woods, as his father had, and the fathers of his kind. He built his own cabin by hand. He cut his way through the trees and found a place that felt right, a clearing near a natural spring, far from any road or trail and removed from the sights and sound of men and machines. He saw that in the past, the nearby river had flooded, so he built the cabin on stilts, far above the high-water mark he found on nearby trees. He earned a little money selling the meat of game, but he earned his reputation tracking fugitives and lost men in the mountains and through harsh terrain. He raised his dogs for this purpose. He is full-blood Cherokee, a born tracker and woodsman, as was his father, who had hid in the hills during the Indian roundup of 1839, thus escaping the long march on the Trail of Tears. His name was Crowfoot Jack Dawes, and he took three wives, who were sisters, the youngest of which died during Baxter's own birth.

Crowfoot Jack was what they called a civilized Indian, who raised cattle and ran a farm. He was a scout with Davy Crockett, was wounded in the war between the states, and was an old man when Baxter was born. He died three days before the boy turned ten. He left all the children a little bit of money, and he left Baxter an old Indian knife with a handle carved from the horn of a buffalo.

Baxter spent his inheritance money on dogs. He raised hunting dogs and sold them and kept the best ones to track game. He left home at sixteen. He worked alone in the mountains, where he always felt at home, and for a long time he wandered, living outdoors, learning what he could by true experience on the land. He grew wise in what wilderness was left at the time, stalking the last panthers and the remaining lowland bears. He answered to no one and worshipped nothing but the forest around him, knowing little of Jesus and nothing of God until a great war broke out across the ocean and he left the mountains to hunt men in the forests of France.

He left Tennessee and saw his first ocean. He didn't get sick on the steamer like the other men, nor was he afraid to die. He kept with him the big buck knife with the buffalo horn handle, and he kept that blade sharp enough to shave. He was twenty-two years old when killed his first man in the Argonne-Meuse. He fought alongside other Indians, some of whom were

Cherokees from Oklahoma, and he fought with Alvin York, the hero from Tennessee. The trench fighting was very bad and there was much killing at close quarters with the bayonets. He often thanked his father for the Cherokee knife, which had saved him many times, and fit so well against the bone inside his boot.

He would remember what his father told him about the siege of Vicksburg and the war against the Creeks. In those stories his father's voice would get very quiet and he would not look at him, but off at the trees or the stars, and though he never once smiled in the telling of those tales, he could tell that those were the times when his father had felt most alive. He told him that war was in his blood and urged him to go if ever he could, and so he did. But he did not find it to his liking. It wasn't the killing he minded as much as the destruction of the earth and woods.

The French forest was much like the forest of his home in that it too was a sacred place where the trees grew tall enough to keep out much of the sun. The light that did shine through to the forest floor was a strange light that made him feel lucky and small, but the solitude and serenity of the Argonne had long been shattered by the time he went home. The trees had all been sheared off to waist-high stumps, with clublike limbs and splintered branches dotting the moonscape battlefield like splayed scarecrows. The forest had changed, but the light did not. It still looked strange and fractured in the ruins of the woods, and the barbed-wire obstacles were like denuded blackberries from which the Germans sprang, dark in the gun smoke and hunched, charging the line, the sunlight glinting off their helmet spires like lightning bugs.

Sylus Knox cannot find the gun. The stream runs fast and the water is icy cold. When he pulls his hands up out of the water they are red and numb. He shakes them and bangs them against his thighs and peers into the water for any glint of steel. But it's too muddy and too deep. The bear rears up on her hind legs and paws the air. Spider comes up limping from the reeds. The dog's head has a funny tilt to it. He stands there, wobbly, with blood in his eye and a torn ear hanging down against his neck.

Baxter pulls the old knife up from his boot. He backs away slow and crouches over like a man prepared to wrestle, the blade hanging just below his knee, loose in his hand. The other dogs snarl and yap. They try to circle the bear. She pivots in the mud. They come up close, the younger dogs do, and she catches one across the snout with a razor-sharp claw that spins the animal and smashes its head. The dog slinks away into the brush. Another jumps up from behind her and grabs onto the loose flesh at the nape of her neck. She tries to turn on him, but he's latched on tight, so she shakes. The dog clings on with its teeth and his body flails behind her, a sixty-pound dog. She backs away from the creek snarling and shaking her head. The other two dogs lean in close, with their weight on their front paws, and their teeth bared, and growling, while Sylus dips his head into the freezing water to look for the gun. Baxter yells at the dogs, calling them off, but they're not listening; they cannot hear—the smell of the bear is too strong. They are shaking with rage.

When he looks back over at the creek, Sylus is not there, but after a moment he comes up from beneath the water, dripping and panting, but empty-handed still. The two men stare at each other while the dogs force the bear back into the blackberries.

Get that gun, Sylus, Baxter says. Get in there and get that gun.

Sylus shakes his head and throws up his arms. His face is white with the cold.

It washed away, I think.

It's down there, Baxter says. It's too heavy to wash off.

Sylus goes back under. One of the dogs lunges for the bear, but she catches him in the belly with a deft thrust of her paw, and the dog falls back to the bank with its entrails hanging out blue and shiny in the mud. Now the bear drops down on all fours and feigns a charge at the lone dog before her. He slinks backward and she rolls over, crushing the one still clinging to her neck. Baxter can hear the muffled yelp of the dog as Sylus bursts from below the water with the rifle raised high.

Got it, he says. Dark water spills from the muzzle and he fumbles with the hammer. He shakes it before aiming and the gun will not shoot. The trigger is frozen with grit from the stream bed.

The bear backs deeper into the blackberries, but the brush is too dense for her to escape. She paws at the ground and snorts. Baxter sees white smoke jet from her nostrils like steam from a teakettle. Her nose is wet with blood. Sylus has come up onto the bank, bent over the gun, pounding on the stock with the butt of his palm. Spider crouches, bleeding still from his head but creeping forward. The bear waits and the other dog is unsure, now that he's alone. He growls and steps toward her, with his head close to the ground.

Get back, Teebo, Baxter says. Off.

The dog turns and looks at him, and the bear backs into the brush. Branches snap and the dog turns back and advances.

Ha, Teebo, git now, git out.

The bear shakes her head from side to side and steps as far into the brush as she can. Teebo sees that she won't come out, so she moves in. Sylus raises the gun and cocks the hammer, and Teebo leaps as he fires. The slug passes through both dog and bear, and he fires again as the bear turns. She stumbles into the thicket, falls, and dies there amid the blackberries and the dogs.

9

THE SLAUGHTER MOUNTAIN CHURCH

They leave the Cross farm behind them, all three riding together in the Ford, Jacob sitting between the two men, staring out the rear window and watching the cedar coffin bounce and jostle in the bed of the truck. They drive up into the same hills that Charles and the young Tobias had come out of that night in the pouring rain ten years ago. They sit in complete silence until they get to the turnoff that leads to Slaughter Mountain, where there's a new sign that's bigger than the old one, and fancier. It's painted with the name of the church in yellow and gold and bears the image of a coiled rattlesnake above a glowing cross.

They ride along the Slaughter Mountain road flanked on both sides by tall conifers that lean in above them and gradually give way to jack pines and large granite boulders. As the grade steepens, the truck slows, and Tobias tells them of his boyhood journey to this place the night after Charles and Sylus had left. He walked this road in the dark, but he wasn't afraid because he told himself he was in a holy place protected by God. He didn't know about the legends of Cherokee ghosts and the wandering sprits of slain Creeks. Scores had fallen here long before the white man came, their bones buried beneath a pile of stones and three hundred years of pine needles and fallen leaves. He didn't know this was why they called it Slaughter Mountain— until he saw them moving in the trees. They looked like smoke from scattered cook fires, he said, seeping up from the forest floor and taking form in the moonlight as crouching, half-naked men. They moved liked the creeping mist, advancing in silence toward the edge of the road, and stopping there. The longer he looked, the more he could see. They gathered by the side of the road and he saw their painted faces, their fingers curled around war hammers, their arrows rattling like bones in the buckskin quivers. They stood at the road's edge, those specters of a lost age, looking past him, waiting for something he could not see. Then they crossed. They passed through him, and he could smell their bodies and their deerhide clothes. They moved into the brush and vanished into the trees on the other side. And he never saw them again.

He ran the rest of the way up to the church and stopped at the doors and banged them with his fists until the twins answered, Esau with a lantern in his hand, Ray with a shotgun that he uncocked when he saw that it was only a little boy. They took him in and put him to bed, and the next morning they drove him straight home. He did not speak about his encounter on the mountain to them, or to anyone, but he was much affected and did not sleep that night for fear of those spirits returning. That was the same day that the Bowsky brothers spoke to his father in private. Less than an hour later, his father told him to pack his things.

The truck pulls up before the Slaughter Mountain church, which had been struck by lightning, burned to its foundation, and rebuilt even larger since Charles had seen it last. It is now twice the size as it was before. There's no longer a need for pitching a tent out back for the huge revivals that are now regular events. This new church has stained-glass windows and a sign carved out of wood over the front doors, and they even built a steeple with a bell inside. It's painted a shade of blue that matches the color of the sky on a bright, sunny day, and there's a cross on top of the steeple that looms above them as they sit there in the cab of the truck.

The top of Slaughter Mountain is a windswept bluff where weathered spires of granite poke up from the ground like broken teeth. Nestled between the boulders are ancient pines whose trunks conform to the shapes of the stones themselves. The wind blows all the time here. It rumbles and hums through the stone formations and moans in the steeple where they hear the harmonic ringing of the bronze bell above.

The sun is high. It rises up from behind the church, where the Bowsky brothers built their residence and where Tobias now lives alone. He opens the door of the truck and stands before his church.

Why don't you get your things? he says. I'll take you to your room.

They follow him around to the side of the church, through a door and back to a large room with a single window that overlooks the valley below. The room is paneled from floor to ceiling in fresh pine boards. The floor is all wood, save for a single carpet the color of wine. There are two beds. The walls are bare but for an oil portrait depicting Jesus hanging from the cross. The eyes in the portrait are painted open and the clouds above him are parted to emit a single band of light. The Lord's head is turned toward the heavens in anguish, this being just before, or just after, his final utterance to the Father above, and there is a great pathos in the image that permeates the room and affects all who look upon it—an unspeakable grief and a sense of the infinite life that lies beyond words and walls.

In the far corner stands a woodstove coated with a thick

layer of dust, and near this is a table with a washbasin on top and a mirror above. Tobias brings them an armload of wood and fresh linens and fills the washbasin with water. He lights a fire in the stove and makes up their beds while they go to the truck for the snake boxes. When they return, they find him standing before the two beds, staring transfixed at the wall above. Charles and Jacob arrange the serpent boxes on the floor.

It gets mighty cold in this room, Tobias says. At night, I mean. He goes to the wall and straightens the painting.

It's been a while since I've been in here, he says. You probably guessed it was their room.

What happened to them? Jacob says.

I don't suppose you heard, Tobias says.

I did, Charles says. Baxter Dawes told me. One week apart, I heard. Jacob was still too young to understand.

Well, I was too, Tobias says. I was just fourteen and not at all prepared for the things I had to do.

He walks to the window and opens it. The smell of pine floods the room.

Was it the snakes? Jacob says.

Esau died from snakebite, he says. Seven days later Ray died after drinking lye. And the thing was, they'd been bit before, many times, and had drunk poison with no ill effects. There were no signs of impending doom, and no iniquities that I had known, though Esau had predicted it. The week before it happened, he took me aside and said, Tobias, your time has come. He made me promise that the church would go on if anything should happen, and I made that promise, though I didn't truly understand why.

Tobias goes to the washbasin and looks into the mirror on the wall, his face so close to the glass that it fogs as he speaks.

With Ray, he says, it was quick, there was no time for good-bye. He dropped the lye chalice and fell like a stone. He had a terrible fit, and then he was gone.

Tobias dips his fingers into the washbasin and wipes his hands on his shirt. He opens a drawer in the table and pulls out an old black book.

Esau suffered longer, he says. I sat up with him all night. We both knew that it was over long before dawn. He said to me, This is all you'll ever need, Tobias, and he gave me this Bible, and then he died.

He holds a small Bible that's worn and scuffed, and there are slips of paper sticking out from the tops of the pages, marking passages and places from which the brothers once read.

They shared a dream, Tobias says. The two of them had the same dream, on the same night, the night before you came, Charles. In that dream they saw their own deaths; they knew just how they would die. They saw the holiness people, all of them, from the scattered mountain churches, a great multitude of believers, and they said that a child would lead them after they had gone.

He holds it in the sunlight and turns it over and brushes the dust off the cover.

They were wrong about me, Tobias says. I wasn't the boy they saw in their dream. You were, Jacob. You're the one.

He thumbs through the Bible and smiles. He offers it to Jacob.

You can't know that, Tobias, Charles says. It could've been anybody, or nobody at all.

Yes, but in the dream there was a tree, Tobias says. A great oak, as big as a house, with dead men hanging from its branches, and the tree was struck by a bolt of lightning, that split the trunk open so that the inside was filled with light, and out of the light came a boy who was not fair to look upon. These are their words. The boy they saw had a mark on him, a lightning bolt, and he bore within him the Holy Ghost.

Jacob takes the Bible and opens it. He turns to the title page and reads the inscription there.

From Earl James Bowsky to his sons, Esau and Ray, on
this day marking their first 21 years, October 8, 1899.

If they knew how they would die, Jacob says. How come
they let it happen?

That's a question I've asked myself a thousand times,
Tobias says. Destiny is a powerful thing, and they believed in
it. They believed that every moment of a man's life has significance. Everything has meaning. How he comes into the world
and how he passes through it. Each breath, each gesture, every
person we ever meet, all our tiny footsteps, all tallied, lead us
to a singular end, a death all our own, a death that will feed
someone, and make some other person strong.

The sun is low now, coming in through the window. It hits
Charles' face and makes him squint. He shields his eyes with
his hand.

Would you show us the inside of your church, Tobias?
he says.

I'd be happy to.

It's been too long, Charles says, since we've gone down
on our knees and given our thanks to the Lord inside a true
church.

Follow me, Tobias says, and we'll pray together.

10

A MESSAGE

It's impossible for them to haul out the carcass of the bear. Even field-dressed it's too heavy to drag through the thick woods, so Baxter skins the animal, and removes what he can sell—its heart, the front paws, and the gallbladder. All the dogs are dead but Spider, who whines beneath Sylus, who pins him down while Baxter sews up his severed ear. The other dogs lie on the ground together. Smoke curls out of Teebo's ear.

The woods are quiet. The men don't speak, and the birds are all gone. All they hear is the creek, the crackle of the fire, and the snapping of the branches fed to it by Baxter's bloodied hands. Sylus shivers in his wet britches. He lets the dog free and heaps armloads of pine needles and fallen limbs on the fire, building up a huge, all-consuming blaze suitable for the immolation of the skinned bear and the bodies of the dogs.

They roll the bear onto the pyre with a lever fashioned from a green sapling and a tree-trunk fulcrum. The carcass burns loud and furious. With its fur all gone and its paws chopped off it looks like a giant pig. They can smell the flesh cooking and it makes their bellies growl. They're tired and weak and haven't taken a meal in hours. They're bruised and bloodied and their hands still shake, and before them lies the bleak task of burning the dogs. Baxter lays them in one at a time, and says a few words for each one before they are consumed. Each dog has a story of its own, some unique aspect that sets it apart from the others, and he tells these stories to the fire itself with a heavy heart and great pride. He chants the old Cherokee funeral songs that his father taught him as a boy while Sylus watches the fire. Spider laps at his wounds and cleans his crude stitches with his wet paw. They sit and watch the dogs burn, with old Teebo the last to go in. Baxter holds him in his lap and smooths down his ears and he whispers to him and kisses the flat spot where his snout meets his eyes. The bullet that passed through him had killed the bear, but not the dog. His lungs were pierced and he was coughing blood, there was no chance for the animal. He put his gun barrel to his ear and watched the white part of his eye as he looked back at him the way he always did in the latter part of the evenings, on his lap before the stove when he'd stroke his head and coo to him. In his life he'd killed eighteen men that he knew of, but pulling the trigger on Teebo was the toughest death he ever took part in, and he knew it would be so, for it was the only time he ever killed a thing that he loved.

He walks into the woods so as to avoid having to watch him in the flames. Sylus hears him wailing an Indian song, a long plaintive wail that causes Spider to cock his head in the direction of that mournful sound.

They pull up outside Shuck's Mercantile late in the morning, and Sylus waits in the truck with Spider while Baxter takes the bearskin inside to claim the bounty. The regulars here don't like Indians, nor anyone with dark skin, who they lump together into the category of nigger. There's bad blood between Baxter and some of them, and quarrels that go back to the time of his father. He avoids the place if he can.

They see him come in with blood on his hands and face and the thick hide under his arm, and they stop their chatter as they watch him cross the floor. Somebody whistles a note of admiration, and the men begin to mutter among themselves. Baxter speaks not a word. Art Shuck stands at the counter watching him come. He's not a man to ask questions. He unfolds the hide and inspects it, fingering the bullet holes. He shakes his head and pays the bounty. He gives twenty dollars for the skin, though it's worth much more. But Baxter figures he'll make up the difference in Knoxville, where he knows a Chinaman who'll pay handsomely for the paws and the gall. He counts his money and turns to leave, but Shuck grabs him by the sleeve.

I almost forgot, he says.

He reaches behind him to a corkboard next to the telephone and takes down a slip of paper pinned there to the wall.

Message for you, he says.

He hands him the paper, which is folded in half. Baxter looks at it.

A message from who? he says.

Come this morning from Charles Flint, in Oglethorpe, Georgia.

Baxter opens the slip of paper and reads it to himself. The message reads:

Need you and Sylus on Slaughter Mountain soon as you can get here. Bring the biggest serpent you can find. Tell Rebecca we're okay. We'll be home soon. Tell the old woman she saved the boy. Jacob's alive and well.

Baxter folds the note and slips it into his pocket.

You going to Georgia? Art says.

Baxter ignores the question.

Tell Bill Rooney it was me who killed that bear, he says.

And it cost me a helluva lot more money than a hundred dollars. You tell him I lost four good dogs.

I'll tell him, Art says. But if you want to make some money, I got cargo needs a ride into Georgia. Pays a hundred dollars for the load.

No thanks, Artimus.

Hundred dollars buys an awful lot of dogs.

I won't run liquor for you.

All right, then. We'll see you around.

Baxter pushes himself through a group of men standing at the door and leaves. He hears them laughing as he gets into the truck where Sylus is dozing with Spider's head on his lap.

Get me home, Baxter, Sylus says. I got three days of sleep waiting for me and I don't want to disappoint that bed.

No time for sleep, Baxter says. Change your clothes and pack a bag. We're taking a trip.

Don't even joke with me. I couldn't pull my pants on if I tried.

Baxter reaches into his shirt pocket and hands him the slip of paper. Sylus's face falls. He rubs his eyes with his palms.

Georgia, he says. Goddamn, Baxter, don't he know I'm a wanted man?

We're all wanted by somebody, Sylus.

Not for murder.

Who was he?

A sonofabitch.

How long ago?

Ten years.

Have you made your peace with it?

I've always been at peace with it, Baxter. Some men just don't deserve the life they're given, and when such a man comes between me and my livelihood I will happily take that privilege away.

Your livelihood being?

Why, cheating at cards.

Baxter turns the engine over and the truck misfires. He does it again, and it rattles up to a hard idle. He puts it in gear and pulls out into the road.

Well, Sylus, he says. We'll just have lay low.

The house is too big and too quiet, and there are far too many rooms for one small woman and a girl. The silence is the worst part. Day after day of no voices and no footsteps and nothing to clean but the dust. And now they have the cabin to worry about. They haven't touched the old woman's things since the day she died.

It was Magdalena who found her, lying on the floor at the stove. A pot was still on the fire, but whatever was inside had long burned away. In the top half of the cabin hung a layer of stale, pallid smoke. The old woman was lying with her mouth open and her arms spread wide. In her hand she clutched a wooden spoon. Magdalena did not scream. She simply bent over, unpinned the old woman's brass key, and put it in her pocket.

Sylus carried Gertie Bates to the root cellar to keep cool, and left her there in the dark while he built a coffin and dug a hole at her chosen spot on the hill above the house. Rebecca washed her in the cool darkness of the root cellar and dressed her in the only good dress the old woman owned before covering her with white linen. They waited until dawn.

It was a rainy Sunday morning when they buried her on the hilltop, in the place where she and her mother had dug the grave for Gabriel Snead. They stood looking over her coffin and didn't know what to say. So Baxter sang her a funeral song, and Sylus read from the gospel of Luke. Rebecca didn't speak at all. Magdalena read a poem that she wrote for the occasion. Stepping up to the graveside and holding in her hands a clutch of golden daffodils, she said these words:

Flowers on a Sunday morning,
Beside a soldier's grave.
She left us without warning,
Though many she has saved.
She never had a true love,
A one to call her own,
A man named for an angel,
Come to take her home.

She released the daffodils into the grave the day before Baxter and Sylus went out after the rogue bear.

And it is that image that Baxter carries in his mind as the truck comes round the bend and stalls on the rise. He sees the yellow daffodils falling onto the coffin as the truck skids in the dust and grinds its gears. The sun flashes briefly off the windscreen and Magdalena, who is sitting on the porch swing, feels she has seen this happen before, in the exact same moment, in the exact same way. She knows that they bear tidings of her father and brother, and she knows where they're going, and that they'll be gone for a long time. She sits in the porch swing pulling the ribbons out of her hair and conjuring images from disconnected dreams—images of a mountain and a church and a cave filled with snakes.

Baxter and Sylus get out of the truck and she sees that both men are dirty and covered with blood. They wave to her but don't say hello. They move with the slow, painful motion of men besought with great fatigue and exchange a somewhat worried look between them. They are keeping something from her and she knows it.

Baxter doesn't stop to sit with her like he usually does. He goes straight inside without even wiping his boots. Sylus walks quickly to the shed behind the barn. Magdalena follows him.

She squats in the brush behind the shed and puts her eye

up to the slats. It's too dark to see, but she hears the hinges on the cedar box that holds her father's white revival suit. The scent of mothballs wafts out through the boards, strong enough to make her eyes water. She has to hold her nose for fear of sneezing, but knows for certain now that they are going to meet her father. That suit has one purpose, and one purpose only: to enhance the natural radiance of a man begot with the Spirit. The white suit is specially tailored for Charles and is used for those occasions when he seeks to renew what he calls the waning faith of the multitudes. If they are bringing that suit it must mean that something big is going to happen, something important, something she cannot miss.

Slaughter Mountain. She feels it in her heart. She's heard the story, and she's heard her father's promise to return one day to preach beneath the stars. And the image of the mountain that she's created in her mind sudddenly appears as if she were standing there at the foot of it.

Slaughter Mountain has always filled her with a peculiar sensation of excitement and fear. Her father never told her the story about his journey directly, but she's gathered enough through eavesdropping to have put most of the pieces together. She knows that this is her only chance to see it for real, and the thought both exhilarates and frightens her. But it's not the tales of Indian ghosts that scare her, or anything that had occurred on that mountain in the past. It is something else that she fears—something she cannot see in her dreams, though it's connected somehow to the wind up there on the mountain, and the stunted pines that grow so low to the ground. *That* she has seen. She has been to the top of that mountain in many a dream, and it's filled her with a sense of purpose and a sense of dread. She has a role to play in something yet to unfold there, so she must move quickly. She hasn't time to pack, or think, or take anything more than her shoes. She scurries back to the truck and crawls under a canvas tarp. She pulls her feet in just as Sylus returns and throws his rucksack on top of her.

Rebecca is baking when Baxter comes in through the door. He's so covered in dirt and mud that she gasps at the sight of him and drops her spoon. When she sees the look in his eyes, she knows he's heard from Charles.

He's fine, Baxter says. Just got word.

She's already turned back to her baking. She picks up her spoon and bangs it on the side of a bowl.

He asked me to come and tell you everything is fine.

That's kind of him, Rebecca says. Thank you, Baxter.

She pours batter into muffin tins and lays them aside.

Will you be staying for supper? she says.

No. But if you'll part with some of them corn muffins, it'll do for us just fine.

You're going to meet up with them, aren't you?

We'll be leaving directly.

Sylus is going with you.

He asked for us both.

She pops hot muffins out of a tin that had been cooling and begins to wrap them in a checkered napkin.

I see, she says. Will you be gone long?

A week at least. Maybe longer.

She ties the top of the napkin with white kitchen string and bites the end clean from the spool. She hands him the bundle and pours him a cup of coffee. He drinks it standing up.

Where are they?

In Georgia, he says.

He managed to find his way back to his mountain, didn't he?

I suppose he did.

Well, you tell him that everything back at the house is just fine. Except of course for the old woman. But I expect you'll be telling him about that.

I wish I didn't have to.

Rebecca turns to look at him. She wipes her hands on her apron and leaves the kitchen. Baxter sips his coffee and puts the cup down, and Rebecca returns, carrying a small wooden chest. It is the old woman's potion box.

Bring him this, she says. I don't know what's inside because I don't have the key. She kept the madstone in here, I know that. She must've hid that key, though I ain't never seen her without it.

Baxter shakes the box gently. There are many small things that rattle and clink inside.

I expect he'll find a way to open it, if he needs to.

He tucks the box under his arm, takes the bundle of muffins, and finishes the remainder of his coffee.

I'll make sure he sends word back, he says.

She smiles at him and pats him lightly on the arm.

I'm gonna leave Spider here with you, Baxter says. If that's all right. He's all cut up from a run-in with a bear, but he'll be good around the house. Just feed him table scraps.

A dog's a poor substitute for a man, Baxter, you tell my husband that.

I don't disagree with you, he says. But we'll all be home soon.

Baxter bites into a corn muffin and leaves her, and she finds herself wondering if they really will return. Never has Charles been so far away from her or been gone for so long. She knew the kind of man he was when he married her. She knew he had a purpose and a burning passion he could not suppress. That's what drew her to him, that passion, that desire to do the Lord's work and spread love and hope to other people. But now, after almost fifteen years of marriage, they have spent more time apart, and he has continued to test his faith by courting dangers of ever-increasing magnitudes. She feels like the wife of a man who continually goes off to war, like a soldier's wife, waiting, always waiting. Her emotions are always running haywire. Every time she hears an approaching vehicle, she must be prepared for his joyful arrival, or the news of his terrible death.

When Baxter Dawes gets back to the truck, Sylus is waiting with the engine running. Baxter puts it in gear and the wheels spin in the gravel before it lurches into motion. Rebecca watches them from the window. Spider barks and chases them down the road.

Sylus, Baxter says, there are places in these mountains that the white man don't know. Not because he hasn't seen them, but because he can't see them. I know places that haven't even been hunted for game, let alone snake, places where buck deer grow big as horses, with racks that have branches like winter trees.

We gonna get us a big snake, Sylus says.

Oh, yes, Baxter says. You just wait and see.

11

THE POISON JAR

The room, when he wakes, is cold and he sees his breath rise like a gray plume through a blue shaft of moonlight that cuts through the darkness and bisects the space between him and his daddy, who lies in the adjacent bed with his face to the wall. Jacob rises and dresses. He stares at his face in the mirror above the washbasin, an old mirror, mottled with wispy veins of charcoal and gray. His hair sticks up in odd places, and in the filtered moonglow his skin looks ancient and cracked.

His eyes move to the reflection of the Jesus painting. He sees it there above the two beds, reversed now in the mirror so that the centurion stands on the other side of Jesus, gesturing forward with his spear. Jacob's hand moves beneath his shirt. He runs his fingers over his bottom rib and presses in with his nails until he feels a dull ache. He leaves the room quietly and makes his way into the adjoining church.

There are tall windows in the far wall and moonlight shines through. It is not dark here. He can see the moon, high in the window behind the pulpit, and the shadows of the benches stretched across the aisle. He shivers, and the soles of his feet numb on the paving stones. He kneels in the aisle between the rows of benches, but he does not pray. He lets his arms hang down at his sides, resisting the urge to hug himself for warmth, and he listens. He's not concerned with the noises of the house or even the sounds outside it. He listens for a voice, not think-ing, not speaking, not imagining anything. He drains his mind of words and images. He forgets this place, and he forgets his name, and he forgets what it is to forget. He becomes nothing, and that's when the voice comes.

Behold, I have set before thee an open door, and no man can shut it; for thou hast strength.

Behind the pulpit there's a door in the back wall. The door leads to the chamber where Tobias keeps rabbits and torches, poison and snakes. It's a small door through which a grown man would have to crawl and its lock requires an old-fashioned key. But Jacob is not thinking about this. He's not thinking at all. He walks to the door and his first sensation is the cool lock in his hand. He tugs on it, pulling it three times, and when it clicks open, he's not surprised.

Inside the chamber boxes of serpents are stacked against the wall and there's a chicken-wire cage with rabbits asleep inside. It's warm here because it's insulated against the cold. He steps into the chamber and feels in the darkness for the matches that he knows are on a shelf at the back wall. He does not feel the strike of the match or smell the combusting sulphur, but he sees the flame, and the candle in the holder affixed to the wall. His hand goes straight for the wick. It sputters for a moment and threatens to go out, but when the soft wax at the center begins to melt a bit, the flame grows and the contents of the room take shape in a soft, orange light.

The light wakes the serpents and spooks the rabbits in the

cage. They scratch at the wire and the snakes all begin to stir. Their tails begin to tick. They're hungry, and they hiss. But he does not hear even this. The animals are not what he seeks. He sees now what it is that came to him in the night. There are poisons here. Mason jars filled with black powders and vials of viscous goo, narrow cobalt bottles with tiny bubbles suspended in the glass, vessels of white dust and brown granules, bloated solvent tins, corrosive acids with skeleton-head labels, their necks caked with dried foam and frozen drips of amber slag—an apothecary of deadly things. But his eyes sweep over them all. His hand reaches for a common drain cleaner. He takes down a jar of Red Devil Lye.

There's no need for anything other than this, his daddy told him. Folks know just what it is, and what it can do to the skin. They can bring their own if they have a mind to test a man. There's no mystery to the lye. It is simple, deadly, and quick. The Red Devil brand is especially good for the symbolism of it. The picture of Satan on the label is a reminder to them all of the struggle against temptation and the raging battle with sin.

This is all I ever use, his daddy told him, and all you'll ever need. There's no reason to get fancy with exotic poisons. All you need is lye. It is the truest and final test of a holiness man, for the rest of it they can say was dumb luck. A snake can be tamed, or be naturally docile. A sick man may mend on his own. They've all seen fire handling in carnivals, so they know that somewhere there's a trick. But the lye cannot be denied. The lye is truth. It can't be faked if it's done right. The greatest tool of our faith is the poison jar, his daddy said, and when it's time, it will call to you, not with words, but with light. For that's the voice of the Holy Ghost. He doesn't speak, he glows. Words are the devil's tools, he told him. The spirit speaks with shades of light. If you drink from the jar when there're words in your head, you'll surely die. This was the day that Charles had first allowed him to watch as he drank from the poison jar.

Tobias uses a crystal wineglass that he calls the poison chalice. He keeps it in a wooden box lined with blue felt on the shelf beside the candle. Jacob takes this box down and opens it. He holds it up to the light and spins the stem in his fingers, watching the candlelight sparkle on the facets of cut glass. He fills the vessel with water, which is kept for this purpose in an earthen Canopus jar in the corner of the room. He places the glass down on the shelf and unscrews the lid from the top of the lye. He doesn't know how much to use, but he's seen his father mix in two big spoonfuls. There's a spoon here used for this purpose that's bent and tarnished solid black. He dips it into the jar and drops the lye into the poison chalice. He does this three times and stirs the contents of the glass.

Swirling, swirling, the powder dissolves, but a light foam remains spinning on top. Then he hears a thunderous roar, his head is filled with whooshing sounds, and then a roar, as if he had just swum up from the bottom of a lake and burst through the surface into the light. He hears a rushing wind. And it *is* rushing wind, blowing through the slats of the church wall and making the candle flame lean sideways and split like a serpent's tongue. There's light too, filling the room, and the animals move with desperate confusion in their containers. The vials and jars rattle on the shelves as he drinks quickly, gulping and spilling it on his chin and shirt. He staggers and falls backward as the candle blows out. He waits in the darkened chamber to die.

At first there is no light. Death is nothing like he imagined. Everything around him has grown dark. But it's an incomplete darkness and somewhere from beyond the darkness he sees a wavering amber glow that flickers and then disappears. He feels pressure in his head. His ears ring. There's a sensation of sinking slow in deep water. His belly swells and sinks, and heat spreads from his center point, just below his navel. It feels like boiling whiskey running down his throat. But this sensation is a fleeting one. It soon passes, and there's a momentary flash of pain, and then darkness again, a deep gloom that lasts only for a moment, before splotches of color begin to emerge from the murk. Something's moving in the dark; the splotches turn slowly and throb. They're irregular shapes that are shiny with wetness, shaped like tree fungus, entrails, mushroom caps. He sees blobs of dirty gold and bilious yellow, mottled crimson and calf-liver brown—the colors of the womb. These things he sees are not flat shapes or flashes of light—they have volume, they are tactile, they float and turn. He is drawn to them, and they to him.

He feels that he's suspended in heavy liquid. There's a sound here that is muted, a gushing, bubbling, underwater sound. But it's too dense to be water, and all around him are the splotches, which now look like rotting meat, decayed fruit, organic things with sloughed flesh and puckered skin, swirling around him like the emerald matter stirred up from the bottom of a stagnant pond. There's a presence here that is beyond human, and his first instinct is to flee. He tries to kick, he tries to swim, but this place is not a place—there is no leverage here, no toehold, nothing to move through. He's filled with fear and wonder. The shapes speak without voices, telling him all things at once, everything there is to know. He's dying and he's being born. There's great pain and immense pleasure. He suddenly realizes that he's very, very small.

He wakes, and there is light again. It's soft light and the shapes he sees now are familiar to him. He sees straight lines and right angles and a regular symmetry to the world. He's back in the world. He's alive. He sees the bottles on the shelf, the candle in its holder, and the snake boxes along the wall.

These are things that were made by hands, but he sees them from a strange angle because he's lying on the floor like a dead man with his hands spread out. Hot wax from the candle is dripping into his palm. He closes his fingers around the soft wax and hears the rabbits gnawing. He sits up on his elbows and the floor of the chamber is twinkling like a sky full of stars. He sweeps his hand over them, grasping at the stars, and he feels a sudden rush of pain. There's blood on his fingers, and he knows now that he's alive. These are not heavenly bodies, they're shards of broken crystal from the chalice that shattered when he dropped it to the floor.

Charles wakes well after dawn. The room is so cold that he can't bring himself to leave the bed. He pokes his head up from the blankets and sees that Jacob's bed is empty. But he's not concerned. The boy's often the first to rise, sometimes taking long walks or reading by himself. So he lies back and enjoys the lazy feeling of one fresh out of a good dream.

Tobias also sleeps through the rising of the sun, which is an easy thing to do on a cloudy morning. But unlike Charles, he does not lie back in bed. He has guests in his home. He has coffee to make and eggs to collect, and he must make preparations for more arrivals.

The house is quiet. He goes to the room where Charles is lying and sees the open door. He shuts it quietly, walks down the hall, and enters the church. The first thing he notices is that the room is usually warm. The second is the open lock hanging from the snake chamber door and the light glowing from inside. He stoops down and pushes it open and sees the boy on his knees, with bleeding palms. The floor is dusted with broken glass. The chalice box is open, as is a jar of lye. On the ground near his feet is the tarnished silver spoon. He gasps, and the noise is so startling that Jacob jumps and the rabbits rush the wire at the back of their cage.

Jacob stands and wipes the blood on his pants. He's frightened by the look in Tobias's eyes.

I'm sorry, he says. I broke your chalice.

Jacob's shirt is wet and the whole front of it is eaten away with burn holes from the spilled lye. His skin is pale, but his eyes are steady, *both* of them. And they appear to glow. There's strength in them now. Tobias can feel it. He seems to have grown taller. He takes the boy's hands and holds them up to the candlelight, examining the cuts on his palms. He rubs them gently with the pads of his thumbs.

It doesn't look like there's any glass in there, he says. But we have to wash these hands.

I broke the chalice, Jacob says.

I know you did.

I'll pay for a new one.

It's all right, Jacob, Tobias says. He leads him out of the chamber by the hand.

I don't know what happened, Jacob says. I don't know how I got here. Only that I drank from the glass. I must've walked in my sleep.

Let's clean your hands, Tobias says.

The water runs clear and cold from the pump, and he makes Jacob hold his hands beneath it until they are numb. He checks them, and there's no glass beneath the skin.

It wasn't sleepwalking that led you there, Tobias says. It was the Holy Ghost come to you in Esau Bowsky's bed.

He holds the boy's hands between his own to warm them.

Let's get you inside, he says. You feel feverish, and we have to tell your daddy what happened. He must be wondering where you are.

What did happen?

You was baptized unto the Spirit, Jacob.

Jacob's stares up at the trees. Tobias shades his eyes with his hand. The sun has risen above the house, and the glare of it makes him wince. He takes Jacob by the arm and leads him inside.

They find Charles drinking coffee in the kitchen, and when Charles sees him he can tell right away that Jacob is somehow changed. There's a radiance to Jacob, a calm glow in his eyes.

The telltale signs of poison burns are on his shirt and trousers. His hair is tousled and out of place, his feet are bare. He looks as though he's just returned from a long spell in the wilderness.

Charles stands and goes to his son. He kneels at his feet and kisses both his palms. He smiles at him and embraces him, pulling him close and squeezing the breath out of him. The boy he tucked into bed the night before has risen a full holiness man.

12

THE STORY CAVE

When the truck finally stops, and there's no more lurching, bouncing, or sliding in the mud, Magdalena hears the doors creak open and the men step out to pee in the weeds at the side of the road. They're talking about a bear and a gun, and there's considerable disagreement over the two, and between the men themselves, who blame each other for the demise of Teebo, a dog who as a pup had once bit Magdalena on the nose. She remembers that bite and how her nose bled, as her head spins and her belly rolls. Her insides feel like they've been shuffled and put back in all the wrong places. She's got pain in her ribs, and her neck is so stiff that she can't move her head. Jolts of fire shoot up from her tortured back. They'd been driving for hours over the poorest roads in the state, climbing and falling and fishtailing through endless switchbacks. As they descended into Georgia the roads got worse. They pulled over as the sun began to dip behind the trees in the late part of the afternoon. Now it is cooler.

She throws back the canvas tarp and sits up in the bed of

the truck and sees the two men on opposite sides of the road, with their heads thrown back, arms akimbo. Sylus has his pants bunched around his ankles and he appears to be in a state of pure bliss with his eyes closed. She takes a few deep breaths, but it does her no good, the sky is swirling above her and the horizon teeters up and down like she's sitting in boat. She feels that sour juice at the back of her mouth that signals an imminent heave. She can stay hidden no longer. She leans over the side of the truck and vomits with great force onto the road. The men turn suddenly, in the midst of peeing. They yank up their trousers, and Sylus trips and tumbles backward into a patch of blackberry bushes that have just started to bloom. Baxter buckles his belt and tucks in his shirt.

Magdalena, he says. Get down outta there.

She vomits again, and Baxter steps back to avoid it. He turns around to give her privacy as she coughs and spits.

You got any water? she says.

Baxter runs his fingers through his hair. The canteen is on the seat up front, and he goes inside for it and holds it just out of her reach. She climbs with great difficulty over the wooden rail, and her legs can't support her when she lands, and she falls over and lies on the road. Baxter reaches down for her hand.

I know you didn't just happen to fall asleep back there, he says. He pulls her to her feet.

Please, Baxter, she says. I need some water.

I know you do. But you ain't gonna get it.

Sylus appears from behind the truck. He's rubbing his backside and cursing quietly.

Damn you, child, for spooking a man like that, he says. I was peeing on them blackberry blossoms and now the damn bush got its revenge.

Watch your mouth, Sylus, Baxter says.

It ain't my mouth what worries me, he says. It's my ass, all scratched to hell, and I'll be sitting on these itches the rest of the day.

You're just having a bad day all around, Baxter says.

That bear swiped that gun right out of my hand.

Oh, now you got her swiping it?

Just forget that nonsense, Sylus says. We got a new problem. How we going get her home?

Same way we got her here.

I'm sorry, Sylus, she says. I didn't mean to scare you. I didn't mean to show myself at all.

Sylus grumbles, pulls his trousers away from his skin, and walks bowlegged back to his side of the truck. Baxter unscrews the cap of the canteen and hands her the water, but as she grabs for it he pulls it away.

You probably think I won't drive you home, don't you? Thought maybe we'd gone too far to turn back?

I would have stayed hid if I could, she says. If it wasn't for them fumes coming up through there and choking me.

Well, the Lord does work in mysterious ways. Gave Sylus here the bladder of a mouse.

He gives her the canteen and she tips it back, swirling the water in her mouth and spitting it back out onto the ground. She does this again before swallowing, which she does too fast. She coughs and hands him back the canteen.

You can bring me back home if you want, Baxter Dawes, she says. But it'll be a big waste of time. I'll just leave again the second you're gone. I'll walk if I have to. I'll ride in a boxcar like Daddy did, but I'll get there. Jacob needs me, and I'm going to help him one way or another. There's nothing nobody can say or do to stop me.

Baxter stares at her. She looks just like her mother, with that same glare in her eye she gets when she's bent on getting something done. He takes a sip from the canteen and wipes his mouth. Sylus's face is cradled in the palms of his hands.

Your daddy'll have the final word on this, Baxter says. I'll take you up there, but you know as well as I do that getting there's only half of it. Staying's the hard part, and you better think of something smarter to say to your daddy than that.

She slides into the truck and sees the old woman's potion box on the seat. She looks at it and looks up at Baxter, but he doesn't look back. She puts it in her lap and sits between the two men. Baxter starts the truck and puts it in gear.

She's just gonna get in the way, Sylus says.

I don't know, Baxter says. She might come in handy where we're going.

Baxter grinds the gears and the truck bucks before it begins to roll. Magdalena stares out the window with the potion box in her lap. In her pocket she carries the madstone, and she rubs it with the ball of her thumb as they drive up into the hills.

For the first time in her life she sees flowers that she's never seen before and trees she cannot name. It smells different in Georgia, and the birds all sing new songs. The light in the low hills has a sacred quality to it, golden, glowing in the grasses, and the sky above them is a deeper shade of blue. To Baxter Dawes, these hills are holy places and the land speaks to him, the boulders call him by name and the tall grasses whisper. The ghosts of his ancestors roam here in the dark places, in the shadows, in the tree hollows and clusters of half-buried stones.

As they drive through this new country, Baxter tells them about the first time he came to this place.

My father came here, he says. He hid in these hills in the time of the great Indian roundup, wandering about for years. We came here together on horseback to hunt when I was just a boy. He could still ride and was strong as a man half his age. There were black wolves here then, and big mountain cats, and he showed me the places where our ancestors lived, their burial mounds and secret caves. He took me to where battles were fought and showed me the very spot where he lost his two toes. He was called Redfoot then, because of a burn he suffered as a boy, but after his toes were hacked off they called him Crowfoot. Crowfoot Jack. A legend he was. He slew the Creek warrior who cut off his toes, killed him with a flint axe, and he wore the bones of his own toes on a sinew cord tied round his neck. That's one of the things my father taught me, to make things part of yourself. To hold onto things that have meaning to you. To remember.

He taught me to remember everything. He showed me how to see. He made me study these hills, and keep them well in my dream place so that when I needed them again, they'd come back. He taught me that you can take a place with you when you leave it. You can own a place. If you find a stone that speaks to you, pick it up off the ground and hold it in your palm. Feel the fire in it. Take it with you. Such things will always bring you back to the places that you loved. I got a stone in my pocket right now that I found that summer when we lived alone together. We wandered these hills living on what we could catch or find, and he told me I'd come back to this place because our blood is here. Your blood will always call, he said, and when you come back, the bones of your brothers will rise up from the ground to greet you.

Baxter stops the truck as the grade steepens, and he sticks his head out the window to smell the air. He closes his eyes for a moment and breathes. Then he puts the truck back in gear and continues on.

There was a place I remember, he says. It's called White Hawk Rock. It's on a hill overlooking a hidden valley meadow, where arrowheads lie all over the ground. There was a terrible fight in that place and many died. He told me about the battle, and took me to the spots where he had knelt and hid, and where he had killed men. It was the best summer of my life, and my father's last on this earth.

One time we were sitting on top of White Hawk Rock. It was hot, and the air was thick with moisture. I remember there was a whip-poor-will perched on a stone, and we was watching it when there came upon us a fast-moving storm. The hail fell big as acorns from a black sky, and my father took hold of my hand and we ran. We took shelter in a cave whose mouth was so narrow that my father had to pass through it naked. It was in that cave that I came to understand my past and my future.

The truck slows as Baxter negotiates a series of deep holes in the road. Both Sylus and Magdalena stare at his glassy, far-away eyes.

There was food cached in that cave, he says, and plenty of dry wood, and there was a natural smoke hole somewhere in back of the cavern so that those hidden within could cook and keep warm without being found. It was an ancient sanctuary. We built our own fire inside, and as it grew, the power of it became apparent to me and I marveled at the size of the chamber. The bones of animals were lying all about the ground and there were pictures drawn with charcoal on the walls. There were pots for collecting water and old hides rolled up for men to sleep on. There were weapons and tools for making them and torches and everything a small band of braves might need to stay alive for days. My people must have spent a lot of time in that cave, for there were charcoal drawings on every wall, and on the ceiling too. There were images of every kind of animal and man. My own people were drawn there, as were the other local tribes, and the English, and every person the cave painters had ever seen. My father called it the story cave because the pictures told the history of our people from the days before the white man came to the time we were marched off to the Oklahoma territory on the Trail of Tears. Though some like my father stayed behind and hid in the hills. He hid in that very cave. He showed me where he marked off the days with a sharp, white stone.

. . .

They're deep in hill country now, where the meadows are lush and fragrant. The grass is tall, and big black grasshoppers fly up from the dust as if flung at them, smacking the windscreen and twanging against the grill of the truck.

We slept in the story cave, he says, beneath those stiff hides, and that night I woke to the sound of dripping water and faraway thunder. I couldn't sleep, I felt so excited, so alive. I lit a torch and went off to explore the cave on my own. I dropped through a hole I found and crawled on my belly for a while until I came to a small chamber that was warm and moist. In the center of the chamber was a hot spring that bubbled up into a pool. That place had a peculiar smell to it that I later learned was the musk of reptiles. And when I held my torch high, I saw them—a whole den of snakes, hundreds of them, lying one on top of another. They were curled into a deep crevice along one side of the wall. There were snakes of many types and sizes, some I'd never seen before or since. They all woke up in the brightness of my torch and started in, hissing and rattling. I got scared and dropped the torch in the water. Then I stumbled and fell. I fell right among those serpents. If my father had not woken I would have died there, for I was bitten several times on the hands and once on my face. One of the bites was very bad, and I laid up in the cave for days while my father gave me what medicine he could.

I survived those snakebites, and for that my father gave me his toe-bone necklace. It was his way of saying that I was a man. I never went back there since. But my father was right, I would come back, because that's where we're going now.

They turn off the road onto a narrow cart track. The truck shimmies, and the high weeds rustle beneath it as they enter the thick woods. Tree branches crack against the side of the truck and whip into the open windows. The truck bucks and sways. Baxter works the gearshift and wheel with all his strength, trying to keep them on the road, but the truck dips into a sinkhole filled with brown water as high as the wheel hubs, and stops, the engine hissing with steam venting out from under the hood. When Baxter shifts into reverse, the wheels just spin. He throws the door open and steps out into tall reeds and cattails. He's driven the front end of the truck into a small pond that had filled in the rains.

We'll have to walk from here, he says.

He goes to the back of the truck and Magdalena watches through the window as he lifts out two lanterns, a length of new rope, a burlap sack, two flashlights, and a heavy staff with a funny hook on the end that he calls the Judas pole. Sylus opens his door and steps out into the water. He takes one of the lanterns and the rope as Magdalena hops out her side. They follow Baxter into the brush.

It takes them less than an hour to climb to White Hawk Rock, and when they get to the top there's little light left. Sylus bends to catch his breath, his hands on his knees. Magdalena sits and removes a rock from her shoe. There's nothing here but stunted pines and half-buried stones.

Where are we? Sylus says.

Baxter does not answer. He gathers handfuls of dried pine needles and stuffs them into his coat and then lights the two lanterns before setting them on the ground. Then he stoops down at the base of an old pine tree whose gnarled roots grow around a large stone. He crawls behind it and drops the ropes through a hole. Then he motions for them to come. They can see a hole beneath the tree no wider than a truck tire. Sylus kneels and peers inside.

I'll go first, Baxter says. Send Maggie down when I call. Sylus, you come in after her. There's plenty of room down there. It's dry, and once we build a fire it'll be warm.

A gust of cool air rushes from the mouth of the cave. There's a blur of motion, and from the darkness there issues a thick swarm of bats. For several seconds they hear a whooshing sound as they come, and the air vibrates around them. Sylus falls back onto the ground and covers his eyes with his arms. Then it stops and it's quiet again. Sylus backs away as Baxter peers down inside.

You're gonna have to shoot me to get me down that hole, Sylus says.

Magdalena smiles and ties her hair back with a piece of waxed twine. She's known Sylus to run from his bed in the middle of the night if he sees a bat.

They go out to hunt when the sun sets, Baxter says. There's no need to worry. A big strong man like yourself should have no problem with it.

I don't like bats, Baxter, Sylus says.

You can stay out here if you want to, but it'll be cold and lonely. There's a fire pit inside, smoke vents out back, on the other side of the hill. There's pictures on the walls drawn by Indians and places for us to sleep more comfortable than the back of the truck. So you do what you want.

Baxter enters the hole feetfirst and Magdalena hands him a lantern. They can see the light for a while, but it soon vanishes, and for several minutes they see and hear nothing. The sky is now a dark shade of indigo, and they can see the first faint stars above them. The air has grown cold fast and Magdalena shivers without her coat. Sylus mutters something about bats. Then the light appears at the mouth of the hole, and Baxter's head comes up trailing cobwebs and streaked with soot.

It's all right, he says. I had to make sure there weren't any bears.

He holds his hand out for Magdalena. She takes it and ducks into the hole, leaving Sylus alone on the hilltop. After a minute they call to him, their voices distant and echoing. He swallows hard, puts one leg in the hole, crosses himself, and drops down inside.

At first it's a tight squeeze for the big man., but after a brief moment of panic when his shoulders get stuck, he climbs downward, hand over hand. His feet find holds in the rock wall cut out by stone axes long ago. He ducks through another opening and the cave opens up into the large chamber where Baxter and his father had spent those nights after he was bitten by the snakes.

As Baxter gathers wood for the fire, Magdalena holds the lantern up to see the walls, marveling at the drawings and pictures. Everywhere she looks there's something new to see. She turns in place with her mouth open wide, unable to contain her surprise at what she sees in the lantern's glow. There are countless faces staring back at her from the walls, slant-eyed men with long noses, whose cheeks are painted with streaks of red and ochre, and animals she recognizes and some she's never seen before—deer with great racks of antlers, and packs of slinking wolves, panthers, and bears taller than men, and great hunting falcons, and a whole menagerie of beasts long vanished from these parts that she's only read about in books.

Baxter lights the fire and it grows fast. It pops and crackles and spits out hot sparks when he drops the old pine needles on top. Within seconds the walls of the cave are aglow, and they can see it all around them, the artwork of a lost people.

What is this place? Sylus says.

I don't know exactly, Baxter says. We just called it the story cave. It was a hiding place for Indians, and a place for fathers and sons to come, but it goes back a long, long time. Who made these pictures we'll never know. But it's a strange and ancient place and the caves go back for miles.

He shows them his snakebite scars and the place on the wall where he and his father added their own part of the great story depictd there. They drew figures to represent themselves, one large and one small, both enclosed within a large serpent eating its own tail.

The place where I found the snakes is through a very

narrow cavern, Baxter says. The cave of the serpents. It's about a quarter mile through there. He points up at a crack in the high back wall.

That was a long time ago, and it was tight, even for me. But my father made it in and out again, so there must be a way. Sylus, you'd never get through, so I'll take the girl. But before we go, there are some things I want to show you.

The fire burns steady, and the vast extent of the chamber can now be fully seen. It's a much bigger room than it first appeared. The smoke drifts up and clings to the stone ceiling, then it flows back, gathers speed, and thins as it catches a back draft that pulls it through calcified formations hanging down like frozen tendrils of Spanish moss. The smoke separates and curls around these before it's sucked into another hole at the back of the chamber.

That's where we're going, Baxter says. We follow the smoke.

Baxter checks the flashlights and ties one end of the rope around a reinforced loop at the back of his pants. He tugs on the rope to ensure that it won't come loose and gives the girl the burlap sack and a flashlight of her own.

Don't turn that on unless I tell you, he says.

Then he picks up the long staff with the hook. The Judas pole is an old shovel handle sawed off and attached to a specially made iron hook. The top of the hook is shaped like a horseshoe. This is how he pins down a snake by the neck. On either side of the horseshoe is another blunt-nosed hook. This is how he pulls them out of tight places. The hooks are also strong enough to use as crowbars and can lift stones and chop apart rotted logs.

The shaft of the pole is worn smooth and black from years of handling, and words and numbers are carved into the length of the pole, on all sides, from the hooks to the tip of the handle. They're the words spoken by Jesus to his apostles, and by the apostles themselves, and angels, words from the books of John and Mark and Luke. Magdalena tilts her head to the side and tries to read them, but she can only manage to make out one before Baxter hands her the pole.

> The Holy Ghost shall come upon thee, and the power of
> the Highest shall overshadow thee.

These are Gabriel's words to the Virgin mother in Nazareth. Magdalena takes the Judas pole from Baxter Dawes and finishes the quote aloud.

> And that Holy thing which shall be born of thee shall be
> called the Son of God.

She takes the pole and holds it with two hands, surprised by how light it feels. Baxter points to the floor of the cave where there are scattered pieces of wood and broken tree branches lying about.

You see that one there, he says. With the white fungus on it? Pin that down with the hook.

Magdalena holds the pole out in front of her. She finds the balance point and sights down the shaft. She feigns a jab, then another, and then spears at the hunk of wood, snapping the branch in two.

Good, he says. That's all you need to do. You lean on the tip of the pole and keep the snake down until I say to let go. But I won't need you, so don't worry. Just follow me, keep quiet, and open the bag when I tell you.

He takes the pole from her and they walk to the back of the cave, following the stream of smoke above them to a rock shelf below a hole.

Sylus, if I pull on this rope, it means I'm hurtin' so bad that I can't move. If I pull three sharp tugs, you swallow whatever fear you got of bats and crawly things and get in after us.

Sylus nods. He holds the rope with both hands.

It's a mistake to take her in there with you, he says. There ain't no reason to take a girl into a snake hole.

If we was going for an ordinary snake, we wouldn't be here in the first place. Charles wants a giant. He wants the biggest we can get, and this is where she'll be. A snake like that needs two people, Sylus, and you're too big to go through.

What can I do? he says.

Keep that fire going. Don't fall asleep. Sit out here and feed me rope.

Baxter pats him on the shoulder, then nods to Magdalena and ducks into the hole.

The tunnel is a lot tighter now that's he's older and wider, but Baxter can still squeeze through. There are cobwebs, and moss hanging down from the top in thick mats that glow bright green in the beam of the flashlight, which he holds now between his clenched teeth.

Magdalena cannot see beyond him, and chunks of loose rock and mud fall down onto her back and head. Things that feel like cold, wet hair brush up against her face. She can hear him grunting and breathing hard through his nose, and she feels the rope sliding past her, between her knees. They make slow progress. Baxter stops again and again to breathe, taking the flashlight from his mouth, spitting, and clearing debris from the tunnel. He's doubting the wisdom of this now, but there's no way for him to turn around. It's so tight that he'd have to back out all the way and already his knees ache from scraping against the rock.

They reach a point where he must push his shoulders through an opening so tight that he tears his shirt, and the sharp stone scrapes painfully across his skin. He reaches back to touch the wound with his fingers and feels blood. But he pushes through. He wriggles and twists and falls through the opening and sees a bend in the tunnel ahead with steam rising out of it. Then he smells it, an odor in the air that makes his heart beat faster and his hand throb. He can smell the dank musk of the snakes.

He turns to Magdalena to see if she's still there with him, and she is. He pulls a red bandanna from his pocket, wraps it around the head of the flashlight, and ties it off. Then he moves on, the stone walls taking on the look of living flesh in the rose-colored glow of the light. The air is humid and warm, and they can hear the low gurgle of the spring. Baxter peers around the bend into the snake chamber and holds up his hand, signaling for her not to move. Then he disappears into the hole.

She waits there for a long while in the dark. She can hear the spring, but nothing else. She prays to herself and runs her palm back and forth over the rope. At first, the rope inches through her fingers, and then moves in two quick jerks. Then it stops moving altogether. She waits. If something had happened, he'd tug three times, but if he was dead or unconscious she would never know unless she followed the rope to him. She pulls it gently, but there is too much slack in it and she doesn't want to risk disturbing a snake. She feels a quick tug and sees a glimmer of red light, and Baxter appears again from around the bend. He's panting and soaked in sweat, but smiling.

There's a big one, he says. A strange-looking diamondback. Thicker than my arm.

He takes the bag from her and measures it, then he digs into his pocket and finds a length of leather cord that he wraps loosely around his neck.

I know you ain't scared of a snake in a box, or even one in your hand, but there's something different about a whole mess of 'em all in one place.

He reaches into his pocket again and pulls out a small glass vial with a cork stopper which he removes with his teeth.

Snake scent, he says.

He rubs this on the end of the Judas pole and on his hands. He wipes some on Magdalena's clothes.

I think I can get it out of the hole, he says. But you need to be ready with the sack. You can't talk or move until I say so, and you'll need to hold the bag down if it jumps.

I'll do it, she says.

I know you will. You and that boy are made of the same stuff. Let's get in there.

The sound of the hot spring is a low, dull gurgle that makes Magdalena think of the old woman's soup.

They pass through a narrow crevice in the rock that forces them to stand and turn sideways. After a few steps they emerge into the chamber with the hot spring and the snakes. It's a bowl-shaped room cut into the rock by a hundred thousand years of swirling water. Even in the dim glow of the flashlight she can see the dark rings on the walls where the water rose and fell over the eons past. There's a strange quality to the air here, and the room sounds funny. Her ears vibrate and she feels dizzy. She stands behind Baxter, with her hand bunched in his shirt, waiting for her eyes to fully adjust to the darkness and for Baxter to tell her where to stand and what to do.

He pushes her back against the wall and steps to the side. She sees the spring now, and the far side of the chamber, with a low shelf of rock recessed along the wall. Baxter points at the low shelf. At first she sees nothing, just a shadow, but when he raises the light she sees what looks like thick layers of fresh mud. He hands her the flashlight and gestures toward the crevice with the Judas pole and he whispers to her, his mouth so close to her ear that she can feel the warmth of his breath.

Open the bag, he says.

But she does not obey him. She's staring at the crevice now, watching the dark folds of mud move. She's transfixed by a great mass of tangled snakes.

Magdalena, Baxter says, hold the bag open. I see it now. Keep the light up and steady.

He steps over the spring, using the pole to keep his balance. He squats near the crevice, the Judas pole over his knees, and rubs his thumbs over the hooks. Then he drops down onto all fours and begins to crawl. When he's so close that he could reach out and touch a snake, he turns to her and motions with a wave of his hand, directing the flashlight beam with little movements of his index finger and nods of his head.

He signals for her to hold the beam steady. She can see a thick bulge among the other folds in the pile of snakes as Baxter works in the tip of the Judas pole. He slips it in beneath that bulge, slow and easy, as if the tip of the pole were merely the head of another snake. It takes him a long time to place the hook where he wants it, but once it's there he holds it steady and waits for the snakes to settle down. Then he turns to Magdalena and nods. He motions her forward, and she steps right up to the edge of the spring.

With a quick movement of his wrists and arms Baxter spins the pole one half turn, pulls, and then lifts out a snake so large that he needs two hands to hold it. The snake hangs thick and heavy and touches the ground on both sides of the pole. Despite the size of it, it's quick and it slides deftly off the hook onto the floor of the cave. Baxter pins it with the hook about a foot behind its neck—too far down. The snake lashes out. Seven feet of whiplike muscle sweeps Baxter's legs out from under him and he falls to the floor. The Judas pole kicks forward and clatters against the wall. The big snake skims across the spring and brushes past Magdalena's leg as it heads out into the tunnel.

Baxter stands and retrieves the Judas pole and jumps back over the spring.

You all right? he says.

I'm fine.

Good, he says. That's the damnedest thing I ever saw. That's never happened before. Never. And that's the biggest snake I've seen in all my years of crawling on my belly hunting for these animals. He was seven foot and then some. But big don't mean slow. It's too warm in here. I should've known. That snake's all riled up and ready for a fight.

What do we do now, Baxter?

We wait. We let it cool down for a while, let the snake's blood cool. Let it think it's safe. It ain't going anywhere.

What if it comes out the other end?

I don't think it will. The smoke is thick up that way, and it'll want to stay out of that. It will be in the tunnel, where it's hard to work the pole. But if we're lucky, it will be in the bigger chamber just around that first bend there.

What if it's not?

Well, we'll have to see. Like I said, this never happened before.

So they wait. They squat down and turn the light out and wait in the dark. They listen to the spring and the sounds of the water moving along the rock, and Magdalena begins to doze. She teeters and loses her balance, but Baxter keeps her on her feet. They wait for more than an hour before Baxter feels the rope start to move. Sylus is pulling in the slack. This is what he was afraid of—the rope brushing against the resting snake and spooking it again. He turns on the light and takes out his knife and cuts the rope free of his pants. Then he splits the end clean so Sylus will know it was done intentionally. He stands and nods to Magdalena. He puts the light back into his mouth and crawls out of the serpent chamber, with the Judas pole at the ready, and watches the split rope vanish around the bend.

Back in the tunnel the smoke is thicker than it was before and it's harder for them to see. So they keep low, crawling on their bellies in the cool wet muck, until they get into the wider part of the hole, where Baxter hopes to find the big rattler. He scans the walls and crevices with the light, inching forward through the smoky haze, and there it is, curled tight into a hole in the rock and out of the path of the rope. The snake is quiet but alert. He can see its wet tongue flash in the beam of the light, and the red glint in its eyes, the head big as a tomcat's; it has an unusually narrow neck. He could wrap his thumb and finger around that neck if he could get close enough, and as he moves toward it, he sees the familiar pattern of a diamondback there on its dusty scales. But it's a variety of diamondback he's never seen in these parts, too large for these elevations and very old. The tip of the rattle juts out from one of its coils, and there's more than ten rows that he can see. He's downwind of the thing, so it can't scent him, but it knows something is there, moving in the cave. It's cooler here, so there's hope it has slowed down, but he cannot wait any longer. The situation will not improve, it can only get worse. If Sylus comes in after them, or if the snake decides to make a run, they would lose it, or worse, they'd get bit, and a snake this big would carry a lot more poison then its smaller cousins. A bite from this snake would mean death to the most faithful of Jesus-loving sign followers.

He turns to Magdalena and signals for her to open the bag. He fixes his hands upon the Judas pole in the slow and strategic manner of a harpooneer, then lunges at the snake so fast that it can only hiss as he pins it behind its neck with the horseshoe part of the hook. It's jammed fast in the rock and can move nothing but its jaw and tail. It rattles and hisses as Baxter slides his hands down the length of the pole—not for one second letting up on the pressure, and muttering a prayer that he saves for this purpose alone,

> And then shall the Wicked be revealed, whom the Lord
> shall consume with the spirit of his mouth, and destroy
> with the brightness of his coming.

He slides his hands to the base of the hook and steps lightly on the serpent's back. He throws the pole aside, takes the snake by the neck in one hand and by the tail in the other, drops the flashlight from his teeth, and picks the snake up off the ground like Moses bearing the tablets of God.

Get the light, he says. Hold it in the crook of your arm and keep that bag open.

Magdalena does as she is told. She sees that Baxter is using all of his strength to hold the big snake. The veins on his hands are swollen blue and the ones on his neck stick out and throb. He's gritting his teeth as he talks to the snake.

I won't hurt you, old thing, he says. You're gonna be fine. Where you're goin', you'll never hunger and you'll never be cold. You've been delivered, and with the breath of the living spirit, you have been reborn.

He leans in very close to the snake and blows a slow and steady stream of his breath into its face. The snake is confused by this, it opens its mouth but does not hiss, and they can see the twin fangs anchored there in the roof of its jaw.

Magdalena trembles as he lowers the snake into the sack. She can smell it, and its body scrapes her arm. The snake twists, knotting itself into a ball.

Are you ready? Baxter says. It's gonna flop around in there.

She nods, and he lowers the snake to the bottom of the bag. Then he lets go.

The snake squirms and rolls. Magdalena holds the top of the bag in two hands, but Baxter is so quick with the cord she doesn't have to hold it for long. He lashes the top closed and ties it off double-tight. They both step away.

The bag jumps and moves about the floor of the tunnel. Baxter is sweating. He breathes hard and shakes his head from side to side.

You were good, he says. A good handler. I'd take you out anytime.

Magdalena smiles. She's still trembling. Baxter pokes his head down into the tunnel and shouts back at Sylus.

Hey, he says. Sylus, we're okay down here. We got us a snake.

Sylus shouts back, but they can't hear what he says. Magdalena watches the bag. It's big and heavy and the snake is moving inside.

How you gonna get it out? she says.

Gonna go get me that rope and drag it out.

13

A REUNION

They billed him as the boy raised from the dead. They put a picture of a coffin on the handbill with a big snake coiled inside and reared up with its mouth wide open, bolts of lightning shooting out and forming the fiery letters that made up the headline on the leaflet.

BOY RESURRECTED BY GOD

Tobias drafted the wording for the handbill himself and had it passed out at the railroad stations and posted all over town.

Come witness the power of trust and love in Jesus! Witness proof of the Holy Ghost on earth! Feel the everlasting glory of God through acts of faith performed by a holy boy on a holy mountain! The honorable preacher Charles W. Flint and his good son, the serpent boy Jacob Flint, will surpass themselves this Sunday evening at dusk at the top of Slaughter Mountain. Prepare to be reborn.

. . .

The resurrection part bothered Charles, but Tobias reminded him that they could not perceive Jacob's breath that night. He had, as far as they could tell, stopped breathing. They built him a coffin and made preparations to take him home to be buried. In their minds he was dead, so the claim was not a lie. Jacob had survived a terrible snakebite, and now, ten days later, the boy would lead the largest holiness revival in the history of the state of Georgia. He would handle a giant snake, Charles would drink full-strength lye from the jar, and together, the two will cure whatever ailments might come staggering up the aisle.

Tobias measures the boy's inseam and the length of his arm with a knotted string and goes into town to distribute the handbills and order a rush job on a small white suit of clothes. Jacob wants to go with him. He's never been into a big town like Oglethorpe. But Tobias warns he'll draw too much attention and spoil the surprise. Charles agrees. He sees the wisdom of the young preacher, and now recognizes what Tobias has known all along. It is not unknown for a boy to take the pulpit. There have been others, but they were boys who could only handle snakes. There was one child by the name of Richard Beadey who drank strychnine from the glass at the age of eight. But there was never a boy like Jacob Flint, who doesn't just handle snakes, he subdues them. He proved that he could heal, and he could take the poison as well. He performed all the signs as prescribed in the book of Mark, something few old-timers, with decades in the pulpit, could do. This alone will make him a legend. But when they see his crooked head and that big eye, it will prove that it's a man's heart that God seeks to fill, not his hands, his face, or his eyes. When they see Jacob and hear his story, they will be moved. They will never forget him. His words will resonate deeper, because he's humble and homely and speaks directly from the place where innocence and holiness dwells. Though he has yet to find his voice, Jacob has already tapped into his heart, and that is indeed a rare thing.

Charles does not tell Jacob what to say or how to say it. He does not tell him how to write a sermon or research the Bible. He tells him simply to remember.

Just tell them your story, he says. Tell them how you were born.

He makes Jacob tell him the story of his birth in the tree, and when he's done telling it, he makes him tell it again. He tells him to speak as if he was the tree itself, as if he was the rain, to recount the tale from the standpoint of its only witnesses. The thunder, the wind, his own mother. He tells him to remember all the little things she said and felt and saw that night.

He gives Jacob his Bible, the one he carried with him that day on the train, the travel Bible made of pigskin, still bearing the photograph of a young Rebecca as a bookmark, tucked neatly into the pages of Paul's epistle to the Hebrews.

Let the words find you, he tells him. Your job is not to preach, but to tell them what you yourself have learned. If you lead a pure life, if you are true, then they will learn from what that has taught you, and their souls will bend to the light like flowers.

They read aloud together and Jacob marks the passages that move him with pine needles he finds stuck in the window-pane. Then Charles makes him sit in various places around the church, to absorb the very space itself, to view the pulpit from every angle. Charles stands at the pulpit and reads from the Bible in varying tones so that Jacob can hear how the words sound, how they echo and fade depending upon where he sits and how they are read. In this way he teaches him how to talk and how to read, but also the power of silence and the art of the strategic pause. Then he makes Jacob take the pulpit and they see that it's too tall. It has to be adjusted for him, and they cut it down to size.

He has the boy practice with a live serpent. Tobias keeps a big gopher snake for this purpose. It's a long, heavy thing, and it's fast and hard to handle. But Charles shows Jacob the art of soothing it with whispers, how to walk down the aisle with it safely, so it won't lash out and strike a bystander. Jacob holds the big snake, which is not poisonous but not harmless either, and he tries to imagine how it will feel with three hundred people chanting and swaying around him. The sermons are only loosely choreographed despite these preparations. It's the Holy Ghost who truly dictates how things will unfold. Only when the spirit fills their hearts do they dare to handle a deadly reptile or drink poison. But unlike all the other sign followers and holiness practioners, Jacob does not have to call the spirit to him, he does not have to wait, for he is filled with it always. Charles had long suspected that the boy was born with the Holy Ghost in his heart, like John the Baptist who received it in his mother's womb.

Unlike any holiness man that Charles has ever met or heard about, Jacob can perform acts of faith at will, though he doubts the boy knows this. It's better that he believes otherwise, that he needs to pray hard for the spirit to descend upon him. In this way Jacob will stay humble and true to the faith and remain in awe of his gift, treating it with something akin to fear and reverence, as a man respects a loaded gun. Charles never drew attention to his own skills as a sign follower. He never discussed it. Such things are sacred and serve a higher purpose. They are gifts that can easily be taken away. He offers daily thanks for them, but does not celebrate or exaggerate them, and he teaches Jacob to do the same, not by preaching to him but by example. He never tells the boy anything directly, thus encouraging Jacob to rely upon his instincts. He learns by watching, and he has learned much, but there is still much he does not know. Things such as the nature of man, his inherent cruelty and kindness, and the power of fear. The boy knows nothing of the war that just ended in Europe or the bombs dropped on Japan or what they did over there to the Jews. He is too young for such discussions now. But there is one thing he is ready for, the wisdom of snakes.

The relationship between the snake and the one who dares to remove it from its natural place in the world, Charles says, is not one of man over beast, but rather of man availing himself of a sacred resource for the sole purpose of serving God.

Charles holds the gopher snake in his hands. Jacob stares into the serpent's eyes.

This is not only misunderstood by outsiders, Charles says, but by those claiming our faith as their own. There are many people handling snakes without discretion and with complete disregard to its meaning. Folks are being bitten, and many have died. We must never take them for granted. Always assume that each time you hold one will be your last, and that each sermon you give will be your last one on this earth. If you do this, you will not succumb to the weakness or the pride that is man's bane.

Jacob understands this intuitively. He knows weakness, but pride is as foreign to him as hate.

That afternoon it starts to rain. Jacob and Charles sit praying in the church as the drops begin to fall heavy in sweeping waves that sound like fire racing through dry leaves. They stare up at the roof of the church listening to the roar of the deluge as the wind whips great sheets of water across the stained-glass windows. They hear no thunder and see no flash of light, and it's dark outside, too dark to read the tiny print of the Bibles, so Charles lights the lanterns on either side of the pulpit. The walls of the church glow in this wavering light. The rain beats down from above and the trees blow sideways in the wind. Jacob prays with his eyes closed. He smells wood smoke and kerosene.

The rain blows through the pines, and somewhere a shutter bangs against the side of the house. The wind blows and blows. When the lumber Ford pulls up outside, they do not hear it, nor do they hear the boots on the stairs. But there's no mistaking the pounding on the doors, and they both stand to listen. Charles throws back the deadbolt and swings open doors. He is shocked and momentarily confused by the sight of Magdalena draped in Baxter's deerskin coat. Sylus stands behind her, wet and pale. Baxter's standing in the mud at the bottom of the stairs with a big sack at his feet. For a moment, they all just stare at each other as if this meeting between them, in this place, at this time, had been preordained.

Magdalena, get in here, Charles says. He steps aside and takes her over to the warm stove. He pulls the soggy coat off her shoulders.

What in God's name are you doing here, girl? Did Baxter bring you with him?

She shakes her head.

Baxter, Charles says, did this girl stow away in the back of the truck?

Charles looks up at Baxter, but Baxter is not there. Sylus is warming his hands in front of the stove with Jacob beside him, but the church doors are closed with Baxter still outside. He opens one of the doors and peers out at him, just standing there in the rain.

Baxter, he says. What are you doing?

He does not move. His hair is matted down and water drips off his chin. Charles closes the door behind him and stands beneath the overhanging eaves.

Well?

Baxter bends to the ground and lifts the sack that holds the big snake. Charles can tell that it's heavy. He steps out into the rain and puts his hands on either side of the sack, feeling the thick body of the snake inside.

Where'd you find such a massive thing?

You wanted a big snake, Baxter says. And here it is.

Raindrops are running into Baxter's eyes, but he doesn't even blink.

Might be too big, by the feel of him, Charles says. Too big for the boy.

You plannin' on having the boy handle this thing?

You should see him now, Baxter. He could tame a lion if we could find one.

Baxter looks down at the sack and then up at the rain. His shirt is wet through to his skin, but he shows no signs of discomfort. Charles begins to shiver.

You didn't bring me out here to show me a serpent, he says.

I wish I did, Baxter says. I have something else to talk to you about.

Magdalena, Charles says. I should have known she'd do something like this.

No, Baxter says. Don't be sorry about that. I couldn't of got the snake without her. She's as steady and brave as the boy. She's got a good head on her shoulders, and a good heart too. She could help you, Charles, if you gave her half a chance. But that ain't why I brought you out here in the rain.

Baxter puts the snake down in the mud. He puts his hands on Charles' shoulders and looks into his eyes.

The old woman is dead, he says. Most likely by stroke. Magdalena found her lying near the stove with soup still in the pot. She had a smile on her face, Charles. She died happy and she died fast. We buried her up on the little hill where she told us, and it was a nice little service we had for her too.

Charles nods. He simply shakes his head and then he walks out into the road, into the rain. Baxter watches him go until he vanishes into the dark of the storm.

Magdalena tells Jacob all about the Indian cave, describing in vivid detail the pictures on the walls, the pile of bones, and how they stalked and captured the giant snake. She shows him a scrape on her belly where she pushed through the sharp stones.

But her scrape is nothing compared to Jacob's snakebite. He lets her touch it with her fingers. It still feels sore, so he winces, and she reaches out and takes hold of his chin, the way the old woman used to do, to read a face for signs of sickness. Jacob pushes her hands away.

What are you doing?, he says.

I'm looking at your eye.

Well, you can look without touching me, can't you?

It ain't lazy anymore.

What?

Your eye.

What are you talking about? he says.

Well, it don't look the same. You know how it used sorta wander a bit? Now it don't. It looks right at me.

She steps back and looks him up and down. Then she turns to Sylus, who's still shivering near the stove.

Don't it look different, Sylus?

He peers at Jacob and squints.

Step closer, he says. I can't see.

Jacob goes to the stove and Sylus stares into his eyes. He raises an index finger and passes it before the boy's face.

Follow my finger, he says.

Jacob's eyes move in unison, as they follow his finger.

Ain't that something? he says. You see that, Baxter?

Baxter nods, not really looking.

I saw it, he says. Could be the poison or the venom, affecting the nerves.

Sylus shakes his head and stands. I'll be damned if that old woman wasn't right after all, he says. She always said that one day he'd see, and she was right.

Magdalena stiffens. In the excitement of seeing her brother again she forgot about Gertie Bates.

Jacob, she says. There's something you need to know.

What's that? Jacob says.

Magdalena takes his hand. There ain't no way to say it, so I'll just tell you, she says. The old woman has passed on.

Jacob just shakes his head. He stands.

Where's Daddy? he says.

He took a walk, Baxter says.

I should go to him, Jacob says.

Leave him be. Sometimes a man needs to be alone.

Charles walks down the center of the Slaughter Mountain road in the rain. He has no destination in mind other than the dense groves of red spruce growing up the steep grade two miles down where it's peaceful. He's cold, but the rain soothes him. It has now become a heavy mist that doesn't fall so much as it rolls. The mist blows and sticks to the tall blades of grass on the side of the road. It sparkles like tiny beads of glass. It's quiet on the mountain, and this is what he needs now— silence. The old woman told him that all the great tragedies and miracles of his life would happen while he was away from home. And she told him that one day when he got back from one of his many journeys, she'd be gone. He never believed that, mainly because he never believed she would actually die. She was always there, and she always would be there, in the little cabin in the lee of the hill. He can still smell her pipe smoke and see the light burning in the window, and he won- ders now about Rebecca alone there in the house. He'll go into town tomorrow and send word back to let her know that Magdalena is fine.

He follows a rivulet of muddy water that has cut a shallow trench in the middle of the road. The water runs fast here and has washed away the lighter dust, so all that remains is a bed of shiny stones. He kneels at the bank of this tiny stream and picks up a smooth, oval quartz big as a cat's eye and white as a tooth. It feels good in his hand and cool on his lips, and it slides easily onto his tongue, where he lets it rest for a while. The old woman used to call this getting to know a stone. They'd walk along the stream bank when he was a boy, and she'd pick them up sometimes and place them in her mouth and then carry them in her pocket for days before deciding if she'd put them in her potion box with the other stones she'd chosen. She called them power stones. Each one with a soul. She claimed that they'd been carried by ancient people long ago, and that some of them were people, trapped inside the stones.

He closes his eyes and holds the pebble between his gum and his cheek. He hears the wind blowing through the tops of the trees, but he can hear something else too, the sound of an engine, a truck climbing the mountain in low gear. It's Tobias's Chevrolet. He can see the headlights through the mist on a switchback below. He sees the one flickering light on the right side that blinks each time it hits a bump. The truck fishtails and rights itself and climbs steadily up the road. When he sees him, Tobias hits the brakes hard, and the truck skids sideways before it stops. He lets it idle as he rolls down the window and pokes his head out. The two men stare at each other.

Charles? he says. What's wrong?

Charles spits the stone into his open palm and looks at it. Tobias looks at it too. Charles steps over to the truck.

What are you doin' out here? Tobias says. You're wet through.

I'm just taking a walk.

Well, get on in here and I'll take you back up to the house.

I'd rather walk, Tobias.

What is it? You having second thoughts about all this? Because I just got the handbills all done and passed the word all over town.

No, it ain't that. I'm as sure as ever about that.

Well, what is it, then? You look like you just seen the devil himself.

Charles pockets the stone. He wipes his hands on his trousers, but his pants are soaked through and his hands stay wet.

Baxter Dawes showed up while you was gone, he says.

That's good news. Did he bring the serpent?

He brought a serpent all right. A serpent like you ain't never seen in your life.

Big?

Big ain't the word. It's a behemoth.

Well? What is it, then?

My daughter Magdalena snuck into the back and rode down here with them.

The rain begins to fall again, fat drops that splat on the hood of the Chevrolet, which rings like an empty oil drum. Charles watches the steam rise off the grill.

You gonna send her home? Tobias says.

I don't know. I haven't thought about it. Baxter brought some news with him too. Gertie Bates died. I don't know if I told you that she practically raised me herself.

Charles has one hand up on the doorframe of the truck and one hand shielding his eyes from the rain.

Come on in the truck, Charles, Tobias says.

Charles doesn't hear him. He's standing there, blinking in the rain. There are little drops of water stuck to his eyelashes.

I promised to bury her, Tobias. Under a dogwood tree. I told her that I'd do that for her when it came time.

Tobias reaches out and takes hold of his arm.

You'll see her again, Charles. Our time here is short, and you'll see her again. Then you can apologize, and I'm sure she'll understand. Tobias smiles at him. Charles smiles back.

Now come on and get in out of the rain, Tobias says. Come on.

Charles pats him on the shoulder and walks to the other side of the truck. He gets in and sits. He feels the stone in his pocket and wonders if perhaps it contains the soul of an ancient man.

•   •   •

Back inside the church, Baxter Dawes is still in his wet clothes. The bag with the rattlesnake lies on the floor with the coffin, which they had brought in so it wouldn't warp in the rain. Jacob stands at the pulpit as Charles and Tobias come through the door, and Sylus is so happy to see Tobias that he throws his arms around him.

Magdalena avoids Charles all through dinner, which consists of biscuits and deer-meat stew. They eat around the dining table in the big parlor where the Bowsky twins had once entertained the governor. It's a quiet meal, though Sylus tells them all how they first met Tobias the day they jumped off the southbound train. Magdalena keeps her head down the whole time, to avoid Charles' glance. Tobias passes around one of the handbills.

It says that the revival will take place this coming Sunday. The featured orator will be Jacob Flint, with acts of faith and signs following, performed by Tobias Cross and Charles Flint. The proceedings will begin at dusk and end with the departure of the Holy Ghost.

Baxter Dawes does not speak at all. He has a way of biting the inside of his lower lip when he's nervous that makes his jaw tremble, and he's doing that now. Charles knows he's biding his time. Before the evening is out they will have a talk—Baxter was against him taking Jacob out on the road. But first Charles will have to talk with Magdalena, and at the end of dinner he takes her outside.

The rain has stopped and the skies are clearing. They can see the faint twinkle of the first bright stars. They walk away from the house, away from the light, and when their eyes adjust to the darkness, the sky above them blooms.

I had to come, Magdalena says. I know you're mad, but I had a dream, and the old woman told me to listen to my dreams.

I'm not mad, Charles says. She was right. She always said your gift was in your dreams.

Magdalena takes his hand, and they both look up at the sky.

The night before she died, I went down and brought her a spool of green thread and she was fine. She looked the same as she always did.

What was she making? With the thread, I mean?

Just some mending.

My first memory is her sewing something, he says. She was fast and I used to like watching her.

He digs in his pocket and rubs the small white stone with the ball of his thumb.

Was it a nice service you had? he says. Up on the hill?

Yes. We all said something. Baxter read from the Bible and Momma sang. I wrote a poem for her.

That's good. She liked poems. You'll have to read it to me sometime.

I can read it to you now.

No, read it to me up there on the hill near her grave, so I can imagine being there with you all that day.

Okay, Daddy.

They hear a great peal of laughter from inside of the house and they both turn to look. Through the curtains they can see shadows moving and hear the plates clanging together in the washtub.

Don't send me home, Daddy.

Charles turns to her and runs his finger through her hair.

The old woman told me many things, Magdalena. Some I listened to and some I didn't want to hear, but she never lied to me. Everything she ever told me was true, and now that she's gone, it's all coming back. I realize I've been stubborn and ignorant about things. And I've been wrong too. I've been holding you back, both of you.

So I can stay, then? I can help Jacob and you?

Let's just see how things go. First thing is to send for your mother. It ain't right for her to be home all by herself.

Magdalena wraps her arms around his shoulder and kisses his cheek. The breeze picks up, and she takes his hand and pulls him back to the house.

Baxter sits outside watching the sky and the clouds. They're big clouds that blot out large portions of the sky, and they're moving. They drift past the stars like great barges, so slow as to barely be perceived, until there is a break or a hole, and the light of the moon streams through.

Charles comes out to join him after the children have gone to bed. The air smells clean the way it does after a rain. They sit together watching the sky, and for a long while neither man says a word. Somewhere far off they can hear an owl.

A lot has happened since the last we spoke, Charles says. The boy getting bit. Seeing Tobias all grown up and leading this church. And the death of Gertie Bates. I've done a lot of thinking, Baxter. I've thought long and hard. You know there ain't a man in this world I respect more than you, but don't fight me on this. It used to be I didn't think he was ready, but it ain't never been about him being ready, it's about me being ready. And now I am, and you'll be ready too. Give it time and open your mind to it is all I ask. At least stay for the revival. If you want to leave after that, I won't stop you, and I'll not think less of you either.

You're his father, Baxter says. You know what's best.

I've always listened to your advice.

You don't need my advice.

I want it.

Well, you're not gonna get it. Not tonight. There's too much going on in your head, and too much going on in mine.

Charles looks up at the sky and stretches. He bends forward, leans back, and yawns.

I'm going inside, Charles says.

Go on, then. I'm gonna sit here for while and listen to that owl.

14

REVELATIONS

Jacob wakes in the night in sheets that are wet and warm. He sits up in bed and looks around the strange room, confused because there's no oak tree outside the window, and the moon is too bright for this to be his room. Then he remembers where he is and realizes he's pissed the bed. His father snores beside him and the house is quiet. But his ears ring. The latent image of the moon hangs before his eyes.

He removes his wet clothes and pulls on his trousers. He pulls the sheets off the bed, puts his shoes on his bare feet, and tries on the wool shirt that Tobias bought for him in town. It makes him itch, but it fits well and it's warm. He tiptoes to the door. The hinges creak, and he turns to check on his father, who has not moved. He looks up at the painting on the wall to see Jesus hanging from the cross, pale and gaunt beneath the gathering dark. The three Marys weep at the foot of a skull rock formation beside a centurion who is thrusting a golden spear below his ribcage; gash looks like an open mouth. He turns away from the painting and leaves the room. He does not shut the door.

* * *

It is cool on the mountain. The grass around the outside of the church is wet, and it soaks through his shoes. He walks out behind the church, across a flattened-out area where the big canvas revival tent had stood in times past. He enters the woods on the other side of the field and walks through the pines until he finds himself standing on an outcropping of bare stone. From this spot overlooking the valley below, he can see the light on the Oglethorpe water tower. It's a tiny red spark flickering across miles of unsteady air. He thinks of those people sleeping there. He thinks of their dreams and wonders how many will come to see him.

In the sky above him the stars have all shifted. Orion has flipped over on its side since he's seen it last. In the belt of that constellation burns a steady blue star, his star. The star he wishes on. It doesn't speak to him, as he hopes it will, but he can feel it reaching out for him, and the star flickers. Jacob wonders if it might be some sort of code, but he does not understand the language of stars. They don't talk to people like the Bible says. There are no burning seraphim, no four-faced creatures that sparkle like brass, there are no voices in space. Only the ones inside his head, urging him to run away before the dawn comes.

The old woman told him not to listen to those voices. A person's too weak to trust his own head, she told him. When you're in trouble, she said, don't listen to what your mind says. Listen to the faint voices outside of yourself—stones rattling at the bottom of a creek, the rustle of leaves. There's messages out there if you know how to look. There's more meaning in an owl's cry than in a shelf full of Bibles. Watch what the fish are biting, study how a dog sleeps, remember where the dragonflies gather to drink from the mud. This was the last thing she told him before he left.

Listen to what's outside yourself, she said, watch for signs.

The world speaks more clear and more true than your own confused mind, the light on a hawk's wing never lies.

It's strange to think that she is gone, and even stranger that he's not sad. She once told him that he was the reason she had been born.

He turns away from the valley below and walks back to the open space behind the church. There is a field of thick mown grass surrounded by tall trees beyond whose trunks he sees the open sky pocked with flickering stars. Above this field the night sky turns slow on its infinite journey, and the moon hangs watchful among the high boughs of the pines. Though he is not aware of this, he is close to the very spot where his father broke open the African chest the day he was born, and where Sylus Knox and Tobias Cross were both captured by the spirit of God, and where the Cherokee stood against the Creeks and destroyed them body and soul. Of these facts he is not aware, but there is a knowing of a kind that cannot be spoken. There is that palable sense of place and time one feels when the recent events of his life and the things that he's seen and the things that he's heard and felt and thought all seem to conspire with the world itself to create a moment of perfect illumination where there is no beginning and there is no end, and all those human frailties that pull him down and hold him back—doubt and fear, regret and shame—they retreat to the dark place that formed them, so that what remains is a profound feeling of great fortune and communion with the living fabric of the miraculous. Joy. The joy of being alive in this one world and the joy of breathing the air of it, the joy of seeing what light there shines on things and from them, the joy of hearing what the breathed air conveys, the joy of touching the others that live, all these things in one timeless pause, the distinct realization of the hope that all of this living led to this specific moment and will lead again to more of the same, and that only the moments matter and together form the meaning of a life and proof of a loving God.

He realizes that this place must be where he makes his first and perhaps final plea to God. For wisdom and for strength, for courage to face this life, for answers to his burning questions. He will hold the revival here, under the stars, and not within the walls of a church built by man.

The sky outside is starting to glow orange at the horizon as he stands at his father's bedside. Charles sleeps heavily, and Jacob watches him breathe. He counts his exhalations, the rising and falling of his chest. Charles' eyes pop open when the count is at seventy-two.

Jacob, he says. What time is it?

I don't know, Jacob says.

Charles reaches for his watch and squints to see the dial.

Quarter past five.

He shakes the watch, winds it, and presses it to his ear to hear it tick.

I want to have it outside, Jacob says.

Charles sits up and smooths back his hair.

Have what outside? he says.

I want to have it right out there. He points out toward the clearing behind the church.

You mean the revival?

Jacob nods and Charles fumbles for the box of matches beside the candleholder. He knocks it off the table and the matches spill onto the floor. Jacob stoops to collect them.

Light that candle, please, Charles says. He finds his trousers at the foot of the bed and slips them on.

The candle resists the match and will not catch. The match burns down to Jacob's fingers and singes the tip of his thumb. He drops the matchbox and shakes his hand to cool it. Charles lights the candle.

You all right? he says.

It burned me.

Let me see.

It's all right.

Charles looks down at the matches scattered on the floor.

Your shoes are wet, he says.

I was outside walking in the grass. That's when it came to me. I want to have it out there, under the stars.

Charles looks into the boy's eyes as he leans over to tie his shoes.

I think that's a fine idea, but you'll have to talk to Tobias about it.

I was planning on it, but I wanted to talk to you first. He'll ask what you think, and I wanted you to know before he did.

Well, you have my blessing. You know that I'm partial to outdoor revivals.

Jacob watches his father's hands in the candlelight. He can see the little crisscross lines on his skin. He's gripping his knees with his fingers, and the long muscles that run up from his wrists to his elbows throb. The veins on his father's hands are like branches, and in this light his bare arm resembles an uprooted tree.

I'm scared, Daddy, Jacob says.

You'll do fine.

I want to help people.

Well, of course you will, Charles says. That's what you're meant to do.

He can tell by the look in the boy's eyes that he's not convinced.

Jacob, he says, this isn't like fishing. There's no right or wrong way. As long as it comes from your heart, as long as your heart is pure, as long as the spirit is there with you and you feel that joy and pass it on, no man living can tell you what to do. Lord knows I want to, but I can't. Every time I look at you, I have to resist telling you what I think you should know. But there's nothing more personal in this world than a man's covenant with his God. Only He can tell you what to do. . . . But I will tell you something.

He puts on his shirt and looks out toward the window where a low morning fog has turned everything a misty gray.

Son, he says. Don't think about the ultimate purpose of this life. Don't think about the end. Measure your choices by minutes, not years. If there's one thing I learned it's that the answers you desire always come. Always. Faith is not bravery in the face of mortal danger. It is not blind trust in something unseen. It is a belief in God's great promise of an everlasting life of love. But we do have a purpose while we're in this hard world, in these hard times, and that is to help each other to live through them. The strength of this idea doesn't hold a candle to a thousand rattlesnakes or a lake full of lye. You will see and you will feel the great sadness of man's free will, but you will never change it. You cannot heal that. You cannot stop the suffering, but you can help to soothe it, just a little. You can make a big difference in the small things. You can touch a life and change it. Remember, always, that man must choose to come to God. But you can choose to come to man. And that, my son, is everything I know to be true.

Jacob nods. He kneels to pick up the remaining matches on the floor and puts them back in the box. He lays them on the table and he notices Baxter Dawes standing in the doorway.

Good morning, Baxter says. If it's all right with you, Charles, I thought I'd take Jacob out for a little walk.

Good morning, Baxter. It's kind of you to offer, but there's no time for that. There's been a change of plans. We're gonna have this revival outside, and you and Sylus need to go out and get started on building the biggest brush arbor you can.

● ● ●

The light that shines in through the eaves of the portico casts a latticework of shadow on the wall above Rebecca's feet. She watches the shadow rise and skew as the sun dips. Spider's a good dog who does not leave her side for a minute. He scratches at his wound and keeps himself cool in the shade of the old swing.

She waited for Magdalena on the porch all day after Baxter and Sylus left, and when the girl did not return she didn't sleep all night. Every few minutes she imagined the sound of a truck on the road. Before this first night she truly spent alone, she had thought it a blessing to live so far from her nearest neighbor, and miles outside of town. For them, a telephone was still a wonder and to this day she has never used one herself.

On the second night, when Magdalena still did not return, Rebecca knew for certain that she would not. She knew from the beginning that she must have gone with them. The urgency of Charles' request, and the speed at which Baxter rushed to fulfill it, would make him think twice about turning back once they had traveled as far as Georgia, for that was a day's ride away. Baxter would give his life for her children, she knew that, but he had the reckless judgment of an unmarried man. He could not be relied upon to adhere to her notions of safety, nor her standards of discipline, and he would not act in the best interest of prudence when it came to even the most basic elements of risk. He saw parts of himself in both Jacob and Magdalena and justified his indulgence of their whims and their mischief in light of his own wild youth.

So she waited those first two days, calming herself, rehearsing her speech to the girl, and evaluating various options for punishment But after that second night, it was no longer a matter for her to decide. Magdalena would see Charles first. She would soften him, and by the time they saw each other again it would be forgotten, swept away in the great wind of it all—Jacob's miracles, Jacob's dreams, Jacob becoming a man. By the time Magdalena came home, if she came home at all, they would all be strangers to her again.

So it was during that second night that she packed herself

a small bag, with one change of clothes—a church dress and shoes. She baked enough corn bread for three days and cooked a pound of slab bacon. She found some dried apples and a cider jug in the root cellar. She ground coffee beans and boiled eggs. She took a jackknife, four candle stubs, a box of strike-anywhere matches, and a tin cup. She also took the little beaded necklace with the cross she found buried in the Tyborn tree. She had kept it all this time in a brass pillbox beside the bed, never touching it until now. Until it spoke to her. The pillbox caught her eye and the necklace asked to come. For what purpose she did not know, but it helped her then and there was no reason to think it wouldn't help her now. She slept alone in a bed that suddenly felt big, with the dog by her side on the floor, and woke in the hours before dawn, with Spider standing gently licking the residue of bacon grease off her hand.

She leaves a note on the door and lets the goats and the cow and the chickens run free. She wears a heavy wool coat with anchors on the buttons that had once been her father's and she wears Magdalena's work pants and Jacob's socks and finds an old pair of Charles' brogans stained with paint. She takes his hat too, his plowin' hat, he calls it—a black thing of no particular shape with a wide brim all around to keep the sun off his face and neck. She leaves at first light on the third day with the bag slung over her shoulder and the dog loping at her side.

In the blue haze before dawn, she passes the old woman's cabin, quiet and dark now, and she laughs at herself reflected in the windows for the way that she looks—a ghost of the old woman herself. In these worn, bulky clothes, she looks like a small, wandering man. She walks on down the road, a road with no name. It winds down from the Dutch turnpike in eight looping switchbacks and bottoms in a marshy hollow where a log bridge spans a fast-moving creek that feeds the Sequatchie a few miles down. The source of the creek is a spring on the old

Solomon place, so they call it Solomon Creek. It has the best-tasting water in these parts, so this is where she fills her jug and dips her cup. Spider drinks from a pool. He wades out to his withers and sniffs at the air, his head bobbing to catch a scent of things on the other side. He crosses the creek and climbs the opposite bank, but he turns back to wait for Rebecca before moving on. She sits and rubs her ankles. The shoes are too big, they rub at the bone there, and already those two protrusions burn. Spider turns and vanishes into the brush on the other side. Rebecca stands and crosses the bridge, each log wobbling and threatening to overturn. The sun is up and she can see the ground where the tire tracks from Baxter's truck peeled open the mud on the road. This is still private property. The road and the woods around it all belong to the old woman, who left it to Charles when she died. Now it's the Flint Road, she imagines. There's a wooden gate up at the turnpike that's locked with a heavy iron chain. They keep a key hidden in the bushes under a flat river stone.

Rebecca rarely crosses this threshold. She can count on her fingers the times she's been in town since Jacob was born. The job of running the house and the small farm has fallen to her in recent years, and there's always too much work to be done. Even if she wanted to come into town, there would be no time. This is what she tells herself, that she doesn't have the time. But this is only half the truth, the other half having more to do with the whispers and the stares. She is *that* woman. She is the mother of *that* boy. Rooms she enters become quiet rooms. People whisper. People stare. She hasn't been to Shuck's Mercantile in years. He used to have his daughters working there, and when they served her they wouldn't even touch her hand. She heard a woman whisper one time, she called her a witch. Charles has also received a cold reception from his neighbors. They all call him the snake man. Most of the town are Baptists who have their own church. When a few of them came to see Charles preach one time, they returned home to find their barns had been burned down. The Flints are not welcome in Leatherwood. Only Jacob goes into Shuck's now. She considered pulling the children out of school, and would have but for the teacher, Ruthie Bowe, who came all the way out to the house one time just to tell Rebecca that Jacob was a very bright boy and Magdalena could read and write better than most adults. She told her that they both should be kept in school despite the teasing and the taunting and the long, exhausting walk to town. Ruthie Bowe promised to look after them as if they were her own, and she did.

The Dutch turnpike is a county road where the farm trucks come and go with slightly greater frequency than stray dogs; Rebecca is prepared for both. She's never thumbed a ride in her life, but she's picked up riders with Baxter and with Charles, so she knows how it's done. As far as stray dogs go, there are many in these parts, and they're always hungry and they're always mean, but she's not worried. Having Spider along with her is like having a gun, maybe better. She'd rather not shoot a desperate dog nor draw too much attention to herself. Spider's wound is still fresh from his fight with the bear and he limps a bit. His ear is crusted with dried blood, and he holds his head with a tilt that makes him look as if he's gone mad. He's a sweet old dog who loves to be scratched. Once, he was lying beneath her legs under the porch swing when he lunged at a cat and shook it in his jaws, breaking its neck before flinging it over the rail. It was her cat, and a good one too. But it had hissed at her, and she knew he was just being protective. It was Spider who first picked up her scent in the rain that night and found her curled up inside the Tyborn tree. She will always love this dog.

15

THE OLD GLASS WOMAN

He does not know this house, but it calls out to him, it beckons him to come inside, old and broken as it is, speaking from the dark among the hanging willows with the roof beams all buckled, and moss growing thick on the outer walls, and the woods itself reaching out to reclaim the place with green tendrils and sagging vines that seem to be pulling the whole thing back into its living maw.

He crawls in through a shattered window to the smell of wet rot and dusty lace, and somewhere beyond the peeling walls and crumbling lath he can hear the sound of the wind. This is a lonely place, this house in the woods, but Charles Flint is not alone. He feels it and he sees it. The house shows signs of a life lived in fear, with scores of candle stubs arranged on the sill above the wainscoting, and a cob pipe with a warm, smoking bowl sitting on a beat-up little side table near a wingback chair with threadbare arms and a seat cushion stuffed with fresh straw. Beside the pipe is a cup of what appears to be fresh buttermilk, devoid of any mold or scum. And everywhere he looks there are traps. There are traps on the windowsills and on the shelves and on the floor—wire cages of all sizes baited with shiny pork fat and entrails, spring-loaded rattraps with their strike plates sticky with molasses, Indian snares rigged up with twine, and other strange devices fabricated of wires and springs and saw blades and nails. No creature larger than a shrew could move about this room unscathed, yet he somehow manages to pass through, stepping into the few bare places with caution, making his way to the door and opening it, and finding the hall dark and blocked with cobwebs and large pieces of hanging plaster. He sees wallpaper decorated with patterns of diving sparrows, clusters of grapes, and something that looks like golden pinecones. The broken lath snows plaster dust onto his shoulders as he wades through it all, thinking that whoever lives here must have to stoop over or be very small to get through, and he moves with great stealth through this passage narrowed by neglect, passing boarded-up rooms with their doors nailed shut or closed off entirely with planks crudely nailed over them, moving toward a light that is burning at the far end of the hall, where he finds a treacherous staircase with almost no step left intact, a staircase spiraling down into more darkness, down too far for this small house in the wetlands. He goes down and down, slowly, cautiously, descending through a great shaft cut through the earth until he is standing in a room much like the one he came in through, a room with a window and a shiny black sewing machine, and a chair, but with many more traps and elaborate snares set about. The wind blows through stained curtains, where bright yellow sunlight filters through dust-frosted glass, and he thinks, how can there be sun here in this chamber that is surely deep underground? But before he can answer, something comes at him from a dark corner and clasps onto his neck with claw like fingers and the grip of the damned—a demon of savage strength, whose face he cannot recognize until they both spin into the light, and then he sees that it's an old woman, and he's terrified to discover that she's made entirely of glass. He strikes her upon the side of the head, but she's as solid as jade and weighs far more than he does, and they tip over. Suddenly they are falling, crashing through the floors, to even lower regions of this bottomless house where the same themes repeat over and over in the wallpaper—birds on the wing, clusters of fruit, and something like an artichoke set within a crown of laurel and thorns. He falls down through this house laden with gadgets that hang from the walls of the shaft, snares made of wire and coated with dust as thick as fur and greasy to the touch so that he cannot grasp on to anything to break his fall, slide right off his fingers and he falls and falls, spinning with the old glass woman. And then he wakes.

* * *

It's cold in the room, even colder now that he's sleeping on the floor. The windows are fogged over with the warm exhalations from the five sleepers here. The air is dank and smells like the bodies of men. Charles sits up, sweating, his shirt stuck to his back. Sylus is curled under a blanket; his head is covered and his feet are pulled underneath. Baxter is turned up against the wall on the other side, also hidden beneath a blanket. All Charles can see are their bulky outlines. In the dim moonlight they look like hills covered in fresh snow, and he's reminded of that night in the boxcar when he first met Sylus Knox among the bindle stiffs. He can feel his heart thumping, and he's wheezing. He still feels the cold glass fingers of the dream woman pressed into his neck.

He's scared down inside—he feels the fear of the dream in his gut. A large part of the floor is in shadow, and this darkness frightens him. He tells himself that it's only a dream. He sees Jacob in one bed and Magdalena in the other. The two men are mere shadows on the floor. He goes out, through the hall, through the kitchen, out the back door, to seek the counsel of stars.

• • •

There above him the heavens turn. Ten thousand particles of spinning light. The cold darkness of space pulling an old, broken house back into its living maw. And what does the starlight tell him that the dream does not? There is no beginning and there is no end, to the dream and that from which the dream has sprung, so that the falling is a rising and the descent is nostalgic review and the old glass woman is but a form of selfish pride who will not abide him any longer. She will cast him down, and the vanity of it all will consume his very flesh. His faith will fail him. His son will capture the light. There will be naught but darkness to receive the deadly thing, and man will be man again, pageless, wordless, and circumscribed by common fate and the weakness of bone and blood.

Under the light. Under the stars. Under the only thing he sees that he can call by name as God. He makes his confessions to the sea of night with the clear understanding that the trick of time is nothing more than a certain point of view. The great celestial bodies in their three-minute waltz, ever shining, a shower of old sparks that fall like snow upon the quanta. Man, and he among them. Nothing dies. No thing dies. It is but a change in oscillation, a chord change, a new spin. Thus spins Charles W. Flint in the last of his rotations, and his mind travels beneath the stars, for him such a great distance, back to a place in the hills above Leatherwood, when his young brother Garvey was fair to look upon and clear of mind and eye, and they ran through the woods when they were boys in love with each other for being each other, and the trees and the sun conspired to trick them into believing that it would never end so that the days of that summer were each their own full lives complete with births and deaths and sorrow and joy, and the bond of brotherhood was unspoken but fully known to them, as they sat idle in trees and waded knee-deep in creeks on hunts for anything strange and shiny they could pocket and save for contemplation back in the arms of the trees again. Holding in their palms what treasures the world did yield, what things a boy would wonder. You hold onto what you can for as long as you can hold it.

Poor Garvey, he says. He never did believe in dreams.

If only he could sit with him again. If only he had welcomed him back. They will see each other in the land of the old glass woman. They will sit upon the banks of the stream and skip stones. Again.

16

ANY DEADLY THING

Rebecca walks all the way into Leatherwood two steps behind the dust-covered dog. No trucks pass her by, no riders on horseback, and she sees no other walkers on the road. But there are signs of life that she hears beyond it, from the tall grass and through the flanking trees. The banging of a screen door, the beating of a rug, baying hounds, and late-crowing roosters. The squealing of a rusty pump. Her feet are hot and her ankles are raw. She must walk in such a way as to avoid contact with the sides of her oversized shoes. To anyone watching, she would appear to be limping. The red dust kicked up by the dog has settled on her clothing and dried on her face, and she's taken now to shifting the pack from shoulder to shoulder, and sometimes dragging it behind her in the road.

At the edge of town she pauses to wipe the sweat from her face and sip from the jug. Spider stops and turns in the road. He's panting fast and loud. She squats on her heels and calls to him and lets him sip water from her cupped hands. He laps it up and licks her on the mouth. They move on. They walk to the mercantile.

Artimus Shuck is out in front of the store with a broom in his hands. He's smoking a black cigar. He squints and watches as this stranger comes, a dark little man limping behind a lively dog. He leans the broom against the porch rail and takes the bottom part of his shirt between the tips of his fingers, fanning it over his belly. He leans back on the railing with his shirt pulled up to reveal a gut that hangs down over his belt. He blows out a puff of smoke and squints to see who this stranger might be. Business is slow and all he's seen lately are hobos off the train come looking for a free meal.

Upon seeing him, Spider gallops up the road and leaps onto the porch. Shuck reaches down and scratches the dog's hindquarters, all the while peering out at the overdressed stranger. As Rebecca approaches, Shuck realizes the person he's been watching is not a man.

Good morning, Shuck, Rebecca says.

Who the hell are you?

It's Rebecca Flint.

Shuck comes down out of the shade and peers at her with great suspicion.

Woman, what are you doin' out here dressed like that?

Rebecca comes up under the shade of the porch and sits on a crate. She removes Charles' plowing hat and fans her face with it.

I'm going to Georgia, Shuck, she says.

On foot? he says. Nothing ever come from Georgia but refugees, bad farmhands, and other godless.

Art looks out toward the road as a truck rolls by, grinding its gears and kicking up a cloud of dust. It drives right on past.

It's too dangerous for a woman is all I'm saying, he says. Hell, it's too dangerous for a man out there on the road.

I got Spider with me.

Oh, you got Spider, do you? Go on home, Rebecca. I'll get Poppa Hooch to drive you back. He's coming in later for feed, that is, if his car ain't broke down again.

Well, I appreciate your concern, but I'm going down there, even if I do have to walk.

Shuck puffs on his cigar. He scratches Spider on top of the head and looks up at the sky. The clouds are wispy and stretched thin at the horizon. The harvest flies are making a racket in the trees. The day promises to be warm. He looks at Rebecca in her old clothes and shakes his head.

Woman, you look like you been dragged behind a mule.

Why, thank you, Shuck, with that shirt pulled up over your belly, you make for a handsome sight yourself.

Come on in, he says. We'll get you some coffee.

She sits on one of several small barrels that the old regulars use as stools. They're scattered about the checkerboard, reserved for the old men, but it's too early even for those crones. She sips coffee with sugar, while Spider gnaws on a hamhock. The dog's teeth scrape and grind at the bone, and he paws at it as it rolls and clatters all over the wooden floor. His muzzle is covered in sawdust, and Rebecca smiles. She takes off the heavy coat and washes her face while Art Shuck climbs a rickety stepladder to stock a high shelf with shotgun shells.

You think somebody might be going down that way? she says.

Shuck wipes dust off the shelf with a rag he carries in his back pocket.

I don't know of anybody's got business down there.

Maybe Hooch will take me.

He'd take you to California if you paid him enough.

You say he's coming in today?

Shuck backs down the stepladder. He balls up the rag and throws it into the stove.

Any time now, he says. Any time. He sent that girl in here

yesterday askin' if I carried Brock's chicken feed. I didn't know he had any chickens. Probably won 'em in a card game. I don't know, maybe he's eatin 'it. Solly Birch says he's seen him eat dog food from the can. I believe it too. Hard measures for hard times. You got money? He'll take you down there. You buy him some gas and pay him some cash and he'll take you all the way to Timbuktu.

Spider's head pops up from his bone and he jumps to his feet. He lets out a low woof that comes from deep in his throat, and he holds his head erect. They hear nothing. Just the tick, tick, tick, of the harvest flies in the trees. Shuck folds the stepladder and leans it against the wall. Then they hear the muffled slamming of a car door. Spider trots outside to greet Poppa Hooch.

Jacob's alone in the room where the Bowsky brothers slept and prayed and died, and where the wall behind him is now flooded with golden light that transforms the morbid painting of Jesus into something glorious. Magdalena's bed has been turned down, the sheets removed and the blankets taken from the floor. He sees them hanging from a line strung between the kitchen window and a nearby tree. He hears them flapping in the breeze, which bears with it the smell of some variety of smoked meat cooking, and pine resin and naphthalene soap. They let him sleep late. His head feels heavy. He's warm and he does not want to leave the bed.

Outside they're splitting wood. He hears it crack and splinter. He listens to the axe heads bite, he listens to hammers banging in unison and the shouting and laughter of working men. Someone is tearing large strips of heavy canvas and cutting it. Someone else is hacking off the branches of pine saplings and stripping them of bark, planing their ends down to dull points so they will dig into the ground and serve as poles and stakes for the big canvas tent. A truck pulls in and idles, and men laugh as a load of lumber slides and clatters to the ground. He hears them pulling out the long planks they'll fashion into the benches and crude tables that will accommodate what promises to be a huge crowd. Jacob turns his face into the light of the sun and shuts his eyes, but does not fall back to sleep.

The wind blows cool. His hands tremble in the darkness. He feels his heart beat. He kneels between the two beds, below the painted Jesus, where he can just make out the figures on the wall. He hears the slow creaking of the cross as the wood bends under the strain of the weight that it bears in the rising wind of the squall. And the face of Jesus comes to him. It's an image of Christ he created in his mind's eye over the years from things that he's seen and dreamed, an amalgam of tortured faces dominated by the latent image of the one that hangs above him now. A portrait of profound pathos.

And he puts himself in that place, in that time. He sees what Jesus sees. He feels what Jesus feels, a great rising agony, an all-consuming sorrow. Jacob's feet swell, his hands throb, his eyes burn, and a tremor comes upon him, slowly. A profound sadness rises and washes him clean. It rises up from his toes and legs, forcing the air from his lungs so that he starts to gasp and cough. He spits up small gobs of viscous liquid that burn his throat and leave his lips tingling. Blood rushes to his face. His ears swell and particles of colored light dance before his eyes. He feels a warm spot below his belly, an intense heat spreading in concentric waves, filling his gut like some hot corrosive liquid and pulsing outward from the center point below that spot that had once connected him to the womb. The spirit's with him now. His body is no longer his own. He feels a great and indescribable joy, a sensation a thousand times more pleasant than physical love, and though he's only a boy and cannot understand such things, he knows that his is a bliss on a far greater scale than that which is created by the chemistries of man. This is the consummation of the two spirits, man and

God, the dissolution of time, and he trembles all over, with the shiver of truth.

Sylus leans on the handle of a sledgehammer, beyond the church and just at the edge of the clearing where the woods begin to thicken. The big canvas tent has just risen and Baxter is securing a guy rope to the stake Sylus just set. A few yards away, Charles wraps torches with strips of canvas dipped in fuel. He stands near the pulpit, at the wooden podium they pulled up from the church floor and weighted down under the tent with heavy stones. The benches are built and laid out in two rows of twenty each, with an aisle down the center wide enough that four men can walk abreast. They scattered fresh straw over the ground and reefed up the walls of the tent so that air and people can flow in from all directions, and late arrivers can stand on the outside and still see the pulpit. They're ready now. All of the preparations for the revival have been made except one.

Tobias kneels inside the poison chamber. His hands move slowly. He does not want to knock the bottles from their shelves or spill his compound. He shifts his weight to keep his legs from falling asleep as he grinds down the dog button seeds into a fine, crystalline powder, which he pours with great care into a brown glass medicine bottle. The light of a single candle is not suited to apothecary work, and it is hard to tell just how potent a mixture he's concocted. This will be the first time he's ever used this poison, and he's not sure how much a man can take. He looks at the powder, a highly concentrated form of raw strychnine. A deadly thing.

The shadows stretch out on the mountaintop as folks begin to arrive by car and truck. The first few bands of worshippers file in while the sun is yet high and the men are still finishing off the remaining bits of carpentry beneath the tent. These early arrivers have come to claim the good seats up front, leaving

Bibles and hats to mark their places while they picnic in the grass. The sky behind them darkens, and the edges of the clouds begin to glow. More cars pull in, and farm trucks and pickups, all hot and steaming from their climb up the mountain. They're loaded down with more passengers then they are designed to carry and their engines steam and hiss as children pile out, and women in wide-brimmed hats with grand-folks on their arms. All have come to see the boy snake handler preach beneath the stars.

Charles and Tobias change into their revival clothes inside the church while the crowd swells in the field outside. They comb their wet hair back over their heads and put on their best suits. Both men wear black tonight, to provide a sharp contrast with the boy, so that he will stand out, and appear brighter, and holier. Baxter and Sylus wear black too. Magdalena wears a pretty blue church dress Tobias picked up for her in town. She waits at the Bowskys' bedroom door, pressing her ear to it and listening. But she hears nothing from within.

The sky at the horizon is now the color of pumpkin flesh. Above is a band of cobalt, blue as Indian corn. Sylus lights the torches as the crowd draws together beneath the tent. They gather around the pulpit as the fires burn hot and bright. The latecomers stand three deep around the outside, with young ones up on their daddies' shoulders and many of the small boys aloft in surounding trees. The fiddle stops playing and the singing dies down. The only sound left is the sputtering rag torches. Heads all turn to follow Sylus down the aisle. He's holding a single torch close to his face. Tobias Cross and Charles Flint march down the church steps, and the crowd parts for them. A few voices break into song. The singing is contagious. It spreads as they draw near the pulpit but does not grow much louder then a hushed funeral hymn.

On the mountain is the Glory of Jesus,
On the mountain is the Glory of the Lord.
At the river he will be there to greet us,
At the river is the spirit of the Lord.

Tobias takes the pulpit and stands for a moment with his head bowed while the singers repeat the song. Charles stands behind him, his hands clasped around the pigskin Bible. He looks out above the heads of the crowd. The night sky is filled with leopard moths drawn to the flickering light. Tobias raises his arms, stretching them up high, his sleeves sliding down to his elbows. He holds them there above his head and wiggles his fingers. Then he lowers them, pushing his hands down slow, as if he were closing a heavy door. He hushes the crowd this way and bids those who can to sit.

Before we begin tonight, he says, let us all pray for wisdom and understanding, for strength and for peace, so that we may receive the blessing of the Holy Spirit of God. Let us be thankful, and gracious for the opportunity to worship the Lord Jesus, and in such a place as this mountain so near to him.

They bow their heads and close their eyes. For a minute there is no talking, no shuffling. Magdalena opens the church door and makes her way into the crowd. Tobias raises his head and leans in with his fingers wrapped tightly around the edges of the pulpit.

I look out at you tonight, he says, and I can see that there are some among you who were here ten years ago, on a night such as this, when the holy twins, God rest them, brought the dark box and the demon snake to us from the black jungles of Africa. Those of you who remember that night—and I see Hannibal Lee there, and I see Henry Rumm and his good sister Ruth—those of you who were here that night will remember the man who stands beside me now.

He pauses and turns to Charles, who does not acknowledge this introduction.

Most of you were not here. Some of you were not even born. But I know you heard the story of how Charles Flint came and took hold of that flat-headed snake, a full ten foot it was, and mean as the day is long and vile with the blood of Satan in its veins. No one dared take hold of that thing. But he did. He showed us all what faith could do and how love and goodness can give man the power to tame evil. He showed us that a holy man can overcome that which looks impossible if he carries the spirit in his heart. But people, he did not merely handle that snake, he slew it with his hands and reduced its wooden lair to splinters, dispersing the remnants of that heathen enclave to us all, so that we would remember what a man can do if he's got the spirit inside.

Tobias steps back and wipes his face with a handkerchief. Then he turns and whispers something in Charles' ear. They both smile and Tobias turns back to the crowd.

I remember that night like it was last week, he says. I was just a boy who had run off from home to see my first holiness service—not because I believed, mind you, but because I wanted to come see the show, maybe see a person get bit by a snake. Some of you are here tonight for that same reason. Well, I'll tell you now that someone did get bit that night, and it was me. I got bit, I got bit by Jesus. So watch out, you, and you know who you are. Watch out because the venom of the Lord is an airborne thing. No fang need pierce you, no hollow serpent tooth need deliver it, for when the dam that holds the spirit breaks open, the flood of God will wash you clean and leave you baptized with joy.

Again he steps back and wipes his face. Then he reaches down and sips from a clay jug. He looks out over the congregation and nods at them.

I was an unbeliever, he says. I was a truant and a sinner, but I was captured by God that night. I took hold of a snake and my life was changed forever. And I now have the distinct honor and privilege to bring back to the Slaughter Mountain Holiness Church in Jesus' Name the man who changed my life, and with him a very special boy.

Tobias turns to Charles and steps away from the pulpit. Charles steps up to take his place and stares out at the crowd, scanning every face, looking into their eyes. He raises his clenched fists and holds them up high. It is so quiet under the tent that they can hear the moths sizzle in the flames of the torches.

There is a boy, he says. A boy who was born deep in the woods. A boy born within the hollow of a great and terrible tree, during a thunderstorm, where the fire of God was unleashed, striking that tree at the moment of his birth and smiting him, so that he entered this world scarred and malformed. No one gave that boy a chance to survive. But survive he did.

Charles watches the crowd. All eyes are riveted upon him, and he smiles.

Oh, he was a cripple, he says, and a sickly child, and the object of cruelty and scorn. His was a hard life. Yet he is not bitter or hateful, nor does he regret his beginnings. For he is a blessed boy, whom the Lord does favor and protect. God bestowed upon him the gifts of the apostles so that he would spread the good word of Jesus and be an example to us all.

Charles wipes his eyes and loosens his collar. The air beneath the tent is filled with smoke from the torches, and it makes his eyes water.

This boy, he says, who is my son, who is not yet eleven years old, this boy was bitten by a rattlesnake just over a week ago. He was struck and felled by it, and I tell you now, he stood knocking on the Lord's door. So close was he to joining his true Father in heaven that a coffin was built for him, a grave dug, and final blessings bestowed. But in the night he recovered miraculously, and rose as healthy as he ever had been. He was raised up so that he could be here tonight and show you true faith, and true strength, and true humility. He was given new life to give you new hope.

Jacob cannot hear his father's words from inside the Bowskys' darkened bedroom. He cannot hear the praises given him by the congregation. He cannot hear the serpent scratching inside the cedar coffin in the church. The light of the torches does not penetrate his place of meditation. Instead he sees a different fire. He sees a figure crouched inside a flame.

> Understand, O son of man: For at the time of the end shall be the vision.

Outside beneath the tent, the crowd sits silently and waits for a sign. Bibles lie open on people's laps. Lips move without sound. Fingers clasp and unclasp around crucifixes and small painted portraits of Christ. The air is still, and the sooty black smoke from the kerosene torches is dense above them. The two preachers stand together before the crowd, their hands joined, their heads bowed. Beneath the pulpit is a brown glass medicine bottle and a pair of tin cups.

It shall come to pass, Tobias says, that I shall pour out my spirit upon all flesh.

There is a collective affirmation from the crowd, and a cool breeze comes. They can all breathe better as the smoke begins to clear.

Two hands rest upon the casket in the chapel; one man stands at either end, each with his eyes closed. Sylus hears the congregation, and his lips move with them as they sing. Baxter listens to the snake. The serpent is active and nervous. Its head bumps the top of the coffin, and from time to time it rushes to the opposite end of the box in a panicked attempt to flee.

The south windows shimmer in the torchlight that is cast from beneath the tent. The singing grows louder and the two men open their eyes. It becomes more than a chant now, more than a song: it is an incantation. Between each verse the crowd claps their hands. They clap and pause and sing again, and this goes on and on until the words sound like moans and the clapping drowns out the harvest flies. So hypnotic is this rhythm that they do not notice Jacob standing at the open door of the church. He stands there in his white suit with his hands at his sides. Then they turn to Jacob and wait. When Jacob nods, they lift the casket and he leads them out through the door.

Tobias sees the door open, and he quiets the congregation with a sweeping gesture of his hand. All heads turn to watch the coming of the boy. They are all tricked by the darkness, and the genius of the little white suit that glows in the night: Jacob appears to float above the grass. His appearance is startling and they squint to see if he is real. They crane their necks and rub their eyes at this apparition—his warped head, his shambling gait, the way he holds the smaller of his arms, slightly up, slightly bent, his fingers all splayed and crooked as a claw. He looks like someone who died in violence but has risen in a new and glorious form.

Jacob sees nothing but the fires that blaze on the poles. He walks toward the light, passing beneath the canopy. Charles stands at the foot of the pulpit, watching him come down the aisle. Jacob stops and turns to the pallbearers, motioning for them to set the box down. They lower it with care and step back. Charles passes Jacob his Bible as Tobias slides a wooden box up for him to stand upon. He steps up to the pulpit and looks out at the crowd. He can see the whites of their eyes. They're a hardworking lot of farmers, searching for miracles, and there's a yearning here, a weak current of faith, a true desire to believe.

But it's not enough. Jacob feels it, and the big rattlesnake feels it. They share the same insight, Jacob and the serpent. They perceive the world through variants of light and heat, and as Jacob takes a deep breath he can hear it in the coffin, ticking slow and steady as a clock.

You think I'm a child, he says to them. But we are all children in the eyes of the Lord. You can't see it in yourselves. You trust in your eyes, but they're so narrow that light can't even get in.

He pauses and watches them. They are uneasy, and the ones in the back begin to talk among themselves.

Your eyes are deceptive because they see only the shape of men. You think you know what you see? I'll show you that you don't. The Lord made me ugly, and I'm thankful for it. I'm happy this way because I'll never be vain like you. I know how small I am. I know my weaknesses. I know my sins too, and I know yours. I feel them. I see them. Vengeance doesn't serve God and goats don't carry away the sins of man. We are sanctified through the offering of the body of Jesus Christ, not each other.

The onlookers are silent and sit rigid in their seats. This rebuke has washed their faces clean of pity and something in the air has changed. Jacob steps down from the pulpit and all eyes follow him. Magdalena watches him too. As he walks past her, she reaches out and takes his hand. He lifts her from the bench. They walk together to the casket, and he places her hand there on the lid, guiding her palm to the carving of the cross and laying it there. They lean on the casket together, their hands joined. His touch calms her. She can feel his heat and she can feel a heat of her own, starting in the soles of her feet and rising. Baxter and Sylus step away from the coffin, and the snake shuffles inside. Jacob looks up at the people around him.

The essence of the Lord, he says, is the Holy Ghost. The spirit of the living God rises up from the believers. It rises like swamp mist and falls down upon us like fine ash. Those who believe and act in the name of the spirit can invoke him and be protected. From snakes, yes, from poison, and from ourselves.

Jacob steps away from his sister and points out toward the crowd.

The Lord says, I will pour out my spirit upon all flesh, and your sons and your daughters shall prophesy, your old shall dream dreams, your young men shall see visions.

He shuts his eyes tight and shakes his head, as if in great pain. He drops to his knees.

I have seen visions that would make you weep, he says. I have dreamed dreams that would weaken your heart. I have witnessed violence and anger, and have been a victim of it too. You see, I was born in a graveyard without graves, without stones. There were no markers in the place I was born, but there were names and faces, and it is for those men that I pray now. I ask all of you to pray with me. I ask that you take the hand of the person nearest you, and that we form a living chain of prayer.

He takes his father's hand, and Charles takes the hand of Tobias and so the chain forms, with Jacob at the head.

Help us now, Jesus he says. Help us all to see the power of the spirit and the mighty strength that derives from faith. We are weak and let us not forget it. Only Jesus is without sin.

The congregation begins to pray. They take each other's hands and sway, rocking back on their heels with their eyes closed and their heads thrown back, their necks bared up to heaven. They chant, holy, holy, holy. Jacob's body shakes. He passes the Holy Spirit down the line like a flowing current that causes some of them to jerk spasmodically, falling to the ground as if shocked.

Baxter and Sylus lift the casket, raising it above their heads so that it rests on the tips of their fingers. They begin to spin slowly.

Open it, the crowd chants, open the box. Redeem us, they say, show us the light.

They lower the casket and carefully raise the lid. The smell of cedar wafts out, and with it, the smell of the snake. It is not coiled up or cowering in fear, but awake and alert, its body spanning the full length of the box. They all step back but Jacob. They watch for a moment and then encircle the casket, still chanting, still holding hands. At the edge of the clearing Baxter and Sylus stand ready to assist. Somehow Baxter has obtained the Judas pole and like a man-at-arms he holds the primitive halberd at his side. Charles has taken the pulpit now, and Tobias stands by his side. He is reading from the Bible and Tobias is echoing each line, punctuating the more powerful phrases with downward thrusts of his fists. They shout to be heard over the din of the crowd, but Jacob hears not a word. He sees the serpent, he hears its rattle, and he hears the whispering voices of the men who died in the tree where he was born.

He moves closer and stares into the face of the snake, its red tongue like a hot wire dipped in pitch. He reaches for it, and the snake bobs, eluding him. It tries to crawl out of the casket, but Baxter knocks it down with the Judas pole. It crawls back to the other end of the box.

Take him, Baxter says. Take him now.

Jacob does not hear him. He hears instead the voice of his father.

Behold, the fig tree, which thou cursed, is withered away, Charles says.

Baxter rushes to the other end of the casket to keep the snake contained, and Jacob sees Magdalena there, not chanting, nor swaying, but staring into the serpent's eyes, her skin so lurid that her face seems to float, disembodied. She raises her arms and takes the big snake into her hands. She pulls it like a rope. The snake doesn't seem to notice her—it's still staring into Jacob's face. His wound throbs. Magdalena pulls the snake to the other side of the box and the crowd reacts with fascination and fear as she places its neck into Jacob's hands. He takes the snake and closes his eyes. He can feel the power of the thing, surging like water through a hose, and as he lifts it out of the box he hears his father's voice again.

Therefore I say unto you, what things soever ye desire, when ye pray, believe that ye receive them and ye shall have them.

Jacob lifts the serpent from the casket, but it's so heavy that he staggers beneath its weight, though he's using both hands and all his strength. He turns to the pulpit with the serpent hanging between his outstretched arms. Its tail drags in the grass. He lifts it and drapes the thing around his neck. The congregation raises its voice in jubilation and astonishment as he walks to the pulpit, where his father rocks back and forth on the balls of his feet, his arms stretched up so high that his shirt comes out of his pants and sweat drips from his nose and chin.

He that believeth and is baptized shall be saved, Charles says. He that believeth not shall be damned.

He opens his eyes but does not drop his hands. He sees his son there before him, staggering under the weight of the big snake. He looks down at him and smiles. His hands tremble, and his fingers clench and unclench as he turns his face to the sky.

As surely as the moon will rise tonight, he says, so shall the Son rise to affirm the Father.

Jacob stands facing the congregation, his hands fixed round the body of the snake. His head and torso are not bobbing or swaying, but revolving around an invisible axis that begins someplace just below his feet. The snake itself is still and Baxter is watching its eyes for any signs of danger.

The crowd is mostly standing, but there are a devoted few who kneel and bow on the ground before Jacob. They stretch their arms out before them and lie facedown in the straw. Everyone else is moving in a manner that resembles a slow dance, shuffling, rocking, and turning in place.

Tobias steps up to the pulpit and embraces Charles, kissing him on both cheeks. Then he turns to address the crowd. They are joyous and buoyant under the spell of the boy and the snake. They're not just smiling, they're beaming, and he shouts out over them the mantra of his faith.

And these signs shall follow those who believe, he says. They shall take up serpents, yes. In the name of Jesus they shall cast out demons and speak with new tongues and consume deadly things. And they shall not be harmed, for the Holy Ghost will fill up our bodies and become our very blood.

He bends down and vanishes behind the pulpit to fetch something from within. The poison jar. The crowd has grown dead silent with anticipation, and they can hear the pop of the cork and the clink of the glass as the bottleneck meets the rim of a small tin cup.

The snake becomes agitated. Perhaps it's the smell of something on the wind or the sudden silence or the chilling air, but whatever it is, it's nervous, and it shows its displeasure by ticking its tail and coiling round Jacob's arm. Baxter's eyes are on the poison jar as the snake wraps round the boy's neck. He's tiring beneath the great weight of the reptile, and when it shifts its bulk onto his shoulders, he drops to his knees. The snake hisses in protest. Baxter turns and comes toward him as it tightens its grip. Jacob can feel the blood rush to his head. His face begins to swell. Magdalena sees the color of his face change. In this light his flesh looks green. He struggles now to breathe, and neither Charles nor Tobias can see what's going on. They've stepped away from the pulpit, lost now in their own rapturous undertakings. Charles throws his head back and shakes his arms from his shoulders down to his wrists as Tobias extends the cup of strychnine.

The snake tightens itself around Jacob's neck, and he gasps for air. Baxter drops the Judas pole. Magdalena shuts her eyes. Charles takes the cup of strychnine and holds it up in both hands for the crowd to see. Jacob is wheezing now and seeing stars as his father gulps from the cup, consuming the poison in one long swallow. He shakes his head, staggers, and drops the cup into the straw.

Praise Jesus, Tobias says.

The crowd echoes his praise. They surge toward the pulpit as the rattlesnake constricts. Jacob sees only shadows, hears only their muted voices. His vision has blurred. He blinks and sees the torchlight flare up as Baxter takes the snake below the neck, peeling it up an inch, yet unable to break it loose. Its mouth is open wide and its head is twisting, trying to bite. Jacob's eyes roll back and Magdalena shouts his name. Now the crowd begins to gather round the boy, who is kicking his legs, his hands clutching at his throat. Baxter pulls at the snake with his foot planted on Jacob's chest, but he cannot loosen it, and Jacob blacks out and goes limp. Sylus steps in quickly, takes hold of the snake and pulls it, but the rattler turns its head halfway round in one quick grotesque motion to strike him in the shoulder. Sylus smiles. He's got the bone-handled dagger ready and he severs its neck with one clean swipe, then turns to watch its head dangle from his arm, the jaws still pumping venom.

They remove the snake amidst much commotion from the crowd. They can see Jacob is breathing but not yet conscious. The crowd steps back and Sylus takes hold of the snake's head and pulls it out from his skin.

Behind the pulpit, Charles drops to his knees. He looks at Tobias and reaches for him and throws his head backward with such force that he falls over. He lies there for a moment on his back, breathing fast. His head turns involuntarily from one side to the other. The last things he sees on this earth are Tobias Cross's shiny leather shoes.

Then his whole body spasms. He goes rigid, then limp. Rigid, then limp. The congregation has now become aware that something's terribly wrong. A woman calls for cold water. A little girl screams. In the background car doors slam and car engines turn over as people begin to flee. Charles makes a strangled sound and kicks down the pulpit. From his head to his feet he's suddenly stricken with the wild, arching seizures of an electrocuted man. Automobiles are pulling out of the lot with such haste now that there are collisions and the sound of scraping steel. Dust rises in a great choking cloud. The body of Charles Flint bends and twists with sickening speed. His heels smack up against the back of his head. Magdalena wails and rushes to her father, but Tobias holds her back.

No, she says. No, Jesus, no.

Jacob can hear it all as he lies at Baxter's feet. He can hear the sound of his father writhing in the straw—a fast rustling followed by the rhythmic thumps of head and limbs. There is no other sound. They all watch in silence. Sylus extinguishes the torches, barely able to walk, for the venom has sickened him. Charles lies still in the darkness, twisted and covered in dirt and straw. They hear him panting, and Magdalena cries out again.

Daddy, she says, oh, Daddy.

Baxter turns to Tobias, who's been holding onto her.

Take her inside, he says. But nobody moves. Tobias, take her inside.

Tobias pulls the girl away and it's quiet again under the tent. They can smell the torches. The benches are upturned and Bibles are scattered everywhere. Jacob sits up, the headless snake lying by his side. Baxter goes to him and kneels. His eyes tell him everything he needs to know.

There ain't nothing we can do, he says.

The breeze is stiff now. It blows up under the tent from the south, and loose flaps of canvas smack against the bottom of the roof. Jacob doesn't move. Charles starts to shake again, and a shiny liquid, black as oil, issues from his mouth. Baxter covers the boy's eyes with his hand. Jacob smells the snake on his fingers.

17

A MESSENGER

Rebecca Flint kneels and presses her two hands together and she prays right there on Shuck's porch. She asks God to help the old engine turn over just one more time, and when it does, she gasps in astonishment at the speed with which her prayers are answered. First she asked God for a ride, and God brought her Poppa Hooch, and he couldn't have been happier about giving it to her. But the car wouldn't start. They kicked it and rattled wires and rolled it a little ways down the road to pop the clutch. But when she hung that beaded necklace with the crucifix around the rearview mirror, that car fired right up. And nobody took that necklace down. It swings back and forth as they pull out of Shuck's and she watches the sun glint off its tiny black beads

Poppa Hooch smells like a mule put out to die, and the girl, she's almost as bad. She's just come to puberty and Rebecca can smell her too. It's not so awful when she sticks her head out the window but the road's too bumpy for much of that and she envies the dog curled up in the backseat with the fowl. Spider's crammed back there with three filthy chicken cages—

four rust-colored hens and a mean rooster that can poke its head out and peck at things just beyond the slats. And Spider hates chickens. The whole time he's back there she can hear his steady growl.

She's just thankful that it's not her door that's missing. With the road the way it is and the old car lurching from one side to the other she fears that Poppa Hooch will tumble right out into the road. He hasn't stopped talking since they started out, and when he talks, his whole body takes part in the tale. The loose flesh around his neck quivers and his nostrils flare and he gestures wildly with his hands, sometimes letting go of the wheel far too long for her comfort. She keeps her eyes on her side of the road. The girl takes it all in stride. She's heard his stories so many times that she just nods and stares off into a world only she can see. Poppa Hooch doesn't care if anyone's listening or not—he talks like it's a bodily function he can't control.

You should of seen that boy's face, he says. When I laid them cards down he soured over white as milk and nearly choked himself. Couldn't breathe. See, he thought he counted all the jacks but that one, that black one, was a dirty queen, you know how it is with an old deck that's been played too much, sometimes a man's fingers will leave a stain or a smudge or something and there was a spot on that card that made the Q look like a J.

He's got a big grin on his face as he remembers this and he looks over at Rebecca to see if she's listening. This is the good part of the story and he wants to relish it.

He bet big on that hand, he says, too big, and I needed the jack a' clubs, which I prayed for. I prayed for that very card and guess what I drew? You don't have to guess, you know what it was—I had me that straight. Lord, I tell you, sometimes they come and sometimes they don't, and this was as good as it gets. I took a big chance on that hand, and I took it all, including the birds here, which are good layers he tells me. Hell, they were his cards. Anyway, he came up fifty dollars short and all he had was the birds. Says they'll pay me that fifty dollars ten times over in eggs if I feed 'em regular and feed 'em right. They eat Brock's, you know, the special feed? That's why I come into Shuck's and I'll be damned if he don't carry it. That's why I'm headin' downstate myself.

Poppa Hooch is smiling to himself, beaming with that glow a man gets when his luck begins to show itself again after a long spell of misfortune.

It was God sent me that jack and God what put the spot on the queen and brought me into Shuck's for feed where I found you wanting for a ride into Georgia where they carry it. The Lord works in strange and wondrous ways, don't he, Mrs. Flint?

Rebecca sticks her head out the window for a breath of clean, sweet air. She never loved the smell of pine needles so much.

I thought you gave up cards, she says. What happened to the clean life you swore you'd be livin'?

His smile fades and he swallows hard. The girl rolls her eyes. She's sucking on a lemon stick and making loud sucking noises with it.

I done give it up, Mrs. Flint, Poppa Hooch says. I'm clean. But you know how things go. You gotta read the signs. Now, I found me a heads-up dime in the creek and damn if it wasn't minted in the year of my birth. Well, I thought nothin' more about it until I met Henry Foxx sittin' by the side of the road with a flat tire fiddlin' with a deck of cards. I didn't say nuthin'. I never asked for a game. He did, and I thought about that dime, and how Daisy and me is hard up again, and I took it as a sign from the Lord. And a good thing I did, am I right?

He's smiling again and she sees all his yellow teeth, like a knobby ear of corn, and she has to look away. He turns back to the road and grinds the gears and the car lurches. The chicken cages all shift and slide forward and the birds flap their wings. Feathers fly up and blow around the inside of the car like snow. Spider's squashed up against the side window, leaning on the chicken cages, and he just whines. For a few minutes Poppa Hooch remains quiet. Rebecca hears the sucking sounds of the girl working on her candy cane. She's got a chicken feather stuck in her hair. Poppa Hooch has feathers on him too, stuck to the sweat on his big bald head.

No more poker, he says. I swear it. That was the last time. I made a pact with the Lord just before I drew that card. I made promises I aim to keep. One of 'em is this here, drivin' you down to see your boy. But, hell, it's the least I can do anyway after what he done. I owe that boy everything and I won't never turn down a Flint for a favor. It was all part of his scheme, throwin' that dime in the water and that fence post that done blown Henry's tire, then come the smudge on the queen and the jack and the chickens and you sittin' down at Shuck's waiting for a miracle. I'll tell you, it gives me the shivers sometimes.

Rebecca turns away to look out the window. She's smiling, and she doesn't want Poppa Hooch to misinterpret it as a sign of condonement. She believes that God works this way too, that he can grow a special flower just for one set of eyes, that he can make a tree sprout up where it's needed or drop a dime into a creek. Part of faith is believing that small things can have big meanings. A life is like a river: it doesn't flow in a straight line. It flows back sometimes, it eddies and swirls and washes things back for those who need them, and it's best to let the current take you where it will.

The roadside is colored brilliant with wildflowers and the yellow haze of Scotch broom. The smell of flowers comes to her suddenly and she breathes it in deep, masking the odors inside the car. She shuts her eyes and feels the breeze on her face, in her hair. She listens to the engine hum, and for a moment she's alone in a meadow surrounded by tall grasses full of bees. She lets herself drift off to a half-waking nap in that meadow where the sky is dazzling white, and she can see Magdalena and Jacob running through the grass and hear them laughing. But then she hears the hiss of a snake. The old car has been running hot, and she sees smoke coming up from under the hood. She knows that sputtering clunk she hears below her feet is not a good thing. She looks at Poppa Hooch and catches him yawning. He doesn't notice any of the signs the car is clearly giving them. Daisy Jane's got her lemon stick between her teeth, the tip sharp as an ice pick.

The road begins to narrow and steepen. They've left the open ground of the grassy foothills behind and have begun to climb up into the mountains. Poppa Hooch shifts into a lower gear. The car stutters and slows down to a speed just faster than a steady jog. The gears slip and grind. He works the gearshift back and forth, and then the car makes a horrible sound. There's a loud bang from underneath and then a steady rattle, like a screwdriver stuck in the blades of a fan. The car jumps. There's a metallic clatter, and a huge burst of smoke comes up through the dashboard. The back tires freeze up and the car skids to an abrupt halt that sends the top chicken cage up over the seat and onto Rebecca's lap and turns poor Spider upside down on the floorboards beneath the other two birds. They sit there for a minute while the engine hisses and pings, choking on the smell of burning oil. Poppa Hooch tries the ignition and there's no sound at all, just bird chatter and pressurized steam. He drops his head onto the steering wheel.

That's it, he says. She's done.

You said that a hundred times before, Daisy says. When the truck stopped short, the sharp end of lemon stick had pierced her tongue.

She ain't never seized up before, Poppa Hooch says.

Rebecca pushes the chicken cage back up over the seat.

What'll we do?

Get out and take a look, I guess.

Rebecca pops her door open and the dog jumps out before she can get her leg off the running board. They all get out and Daisy Jane goes over to the side of the road, hikes up her skirt and pees. Poppa Hooch cracks the hood, careful not to burn his fingers, and leans over the engine, looking inside with great astonishment. He whistles a long sharp note and shakes his head from side to side. Daisy Jane sits down on a fallen log while Rebecca stacks the chicken cages in the shade of an oak tree where Spider lies panting. The day is as hot as the harvest flies had forecast, with the heat rippling off the dusty road, and Rebecca's overdressed. She takes off the hat and coat. It's too hot to talk but that doesn't stop Poppa Hooch. After he gives them a detailed account of the chain of events that led to the destruction of the engine, he starts talking about the local fauna, the abundance of firewood, and the rising price of chicken feed.

If somebody don't come along soon, we're gonna have to eat these birds, he says.

He starts gathering wood, talking the whole while about anything that comes into his head. He's got a fixed opinion on every man, woman, and child in the town of Leatherwood. For someone who lives as sheltered as he does, he sure knows what's going on.

Rebecca has long stopped listening. She closes her eyes and lets her head droop while Daisy Jane pokes at an anthill with a stick. Poppa Hooch goes off to look for water, and she listens to the snapping of branches as he walks into the woods. For a while she can hear him back there, swearing and coughing sometimes. Then it's quiet again. Birds sing in the trees and bugs click to each other in the grass. She opens her eyes and finds Daisy Jane sleeping on her shoulder. She stares down the mountain. The heat rises and makes the road jitter. The trees on the horizon all seem to sway. The shadows are still short, so it must not be far past noon. She's warm but can't take off any more of her clothing without waking the girl. So she just sits and sweats and listens.

The woods are alive with a thousand tiny things ticking and rustling and rising up out of the grass in spinning flight. Everywhere tiny insects swirl like sparks. She's hot and sleepy and her head bobs. She's thinking about how they're going to get on without a car. This is not the main road. It's a short-cut hacked over the mountain by logging crews. They haven't seen a single car or truck since they turned off the highway. But Charles always says that the Lord will provide, and she believes that. She trusts that idea more than she trusts herself. She's always missed him terribly when he left home, sometimes she missed him when he was there, but now it's worse than it ever was. She's scared for the first time. She never should have stayed away from what he always called the life. But she gave him his space and left him alone while the gulf between them grew and grew and swallowed up the children.

The old woman always told her that one day she'd come into her own. That something would happen to shake her out her sleep of ignorance, as she called it. For, according to Gertie Bates, a woman who does not run her home and run her family is no more than a servant, and a useless one at that. She urged her to get involved with the ministry and travel with Charles, but Rebecca was far too timid to take the pulpit. She feared that joining him would mean involving the children, and she never wanted that life for them, though in her heart she knew they'd find their way into it on their own.

The old woman was right about it all. She should never have stood back and never have let them go. She would walk to Slaughter Mountain if she had to, and never let her family leave her again.

The sun beats down on the road. The air above it shimmers

a full six feet off the ground, and the trees on the roadside blur. She stares at the ones far off where the road dips, at the wavering silhouettes of buckeyes and black oaks. There's one small tree that looks strange—a slow-moving dome-top stump that bobs and oscillates and appears to grow right up from the middle of the road. Rebecca wipes the sweat from her face and shakes her head in confusion, but the figment persists. Closer now. Larger. She can see that it's a man, and she stands and shades her eyes to get a better view of him. Daisy Jane slides off the side of the log.

He's tall and walks straight and proud, wearing a waistcoat and vest with long white sleeves buttoned at the wrists and an old-fashioned necktie. He's got an overcoat slung over his shoulder and a large book in his hand. She would have taken him for a schoolteacher if it wasn't for the hat. He's got a dusty bowler that sits high on his head, which is strange enough, but the hat's got a brightly colored band that catches the sunlight as his head bobs, flashing at her like a signal mirror. He's a black man, a light-skinned fellow with a watch chain hanging from his pocket, and there's something odd about his face. As he comes up the road, Spider stands erect with his ears flat and his tail tucked up under his legs. The man stops. He notices a woman watching him, a white woman, and slowly removes his hat and slaps the dust off his shoulders, never taking his eyes off the dog. Spider hunkers down on his front paws and begins to growl.

Easy, dog, he says. Good afternoon, ma'am.

Good afternoon, Rebecca says.

If you don't mind callin' off your dog. I mean you no harm. I'm passing right on through.

The man talks like he's got a swollen tongue.

He holds up his book to them, making sure they can see the front. It's a big family Bible with shiny gold lettering inlaid on a thick, fancy cover. It's old, and it must weigh fifteen pounds.

Spider, she says. Go lay down.

The dog slinks over to the side of the road, but never takes his eyes off the stranger.

Thank you, he says.

Daisy Jane approaches him and stares. He's a good-looking man with sideburns peppered with gray. His lips are swollen and cut, his jaw's got a puffy look to it, and his face is bruised. Rebecca watches him. He's not shifty. He ran into trouble someplace, but he doesn't look like a hunted man. His hands are too clean and his fingers are about the finest Rebecca's ever seen—long, smooth, with his nails cut nice and not a scab or callus to be found. Daisy Jane peers up at him. She was taught to regard all strangers with suspicion, especially out on the road. Poppa Hooch told her that a colored man walking alone brings nothing but trouble. They are always running off from highway gangs, and he could be a convict or worse. But she's just a girl. She hasn't noticed what Rebecca has seen, his hands.

How come you wasn't on the road when we come by? she says.

The man wipes his forehead with his sleeve. He looks over at the car and then back at the dog.

I heard ya comin', he says. Ducked off in the bushes and hid.

You runnin' from somethin'?

I'm just taking precautions. Had me a run-in with some boys back in Arkville. When I heard your car, I thought it might be them come to finish me off.

Wu'd you do?

Nothing. A black man don't have to do nothing to get himself in trouble in Arkville.

Daisy Jane looks at him, and he smiles. Rebecca notices his teeth. They're long and straight like his fingers, and white as porcelain. The man shakes his head and laughs, looking straight at Daisy Jane.

What're you laughing at? she says.

You know you got candy stuck to yourself?

She looks down and sees the lemon stick stuck to her dress. She peels it off and throws it into the weeds.

It cut me when we stopped, she says. Gave me a bloody tongue.

I bet. I got a little girl just like you, and she knows better than to be eatin' candy in a car. I bet you do too.

Daddy don't care.

He don't, huh? Where is your daddy?

Off in the woods fetchin' water. Should be back soon.

I sure could use some myself if you all don't mind.

Rebecca takes off her coat and lays it on the log. She steps out into the road. Spider stands.

Why don't you sit in the shade a bit? You know anything about motors?

The man steps toward her, and Spider growls.

Easy, boy, Rebecca says. He's all right.

The dog settles, and the man comes over and sits down, showing great relief and satisfaction. He closes his eyes for a moment and then drops his Bible and his coat.

I don't know much about motors or cars. I know a little, and I'll take a look if you think it might help.

Poppa Hooch says she's all done, but another set of eyes couldn't hurt. My name's Rebecca Flint and this is Daisy Jane Horton. Her daddy's Joel Peter, but everyone calls him Poppa Hooch.

Pleased to meet you, the man says. My name is Hosea Daniel Lee.

He stands and walks over to the open hood of the car and peeks inside. Rebecca and Daisy Jane follow.

You goin' to Georgia, Mr. Lee?

You can call me Hosea. I'm going through it, I hope.

He bends over the engine and sniffs, sticking a hand gingerly inside and then pulling it out fast.

You a preacher? Rebecca says.

Used to be. Does it show?

Well, you got that Bible, and the way you're dressed, thought you might be. My husband's a preacher. He's down in Georgia with my son and daughter spreadin' the word of God. That's where I'm goin'.

Not in this car you ain't. Your daddy's right, Daisy Jane. This old girl's found her final resting place. Nice spot for a car to die though, in this little oak grove.

Spider jumps up and barks, and they all hear the sound of something in the woods. Poppa Hooch stumbles out from the bushes panting and holding a jug full of water.

Daddy, Daisy Jane says. Look, a man come. A colored man.

They roast up the mean rooster and eat him for dinner around a glorious oak fire. Spider happily eats the guts. It gets cold up on the mountain at night, but the fire is enough to keep them warm and it gives Hosea the light he needs to read his Bible aloud. He's got a beautiful baritone voice that makes music of the Song of Solomon, a book Charles never read to Rebecca, and now she knows why. It's like a love poem, and it makes her blush. Even Poppa Hooch remains quiet, staring into the coals of the fire.

He closes the book when he's through reading and none of them speak. Daisy Jane is asleep on her father's lap, wrapped in Hosea's coat. It's a clear night, with the stars so thick they almost blur. Rebecca can't find a constellation she recognizes. Hosea feeds the fire with brittle twigs.

It's been a while since I read from Solomon, he says. Used to read it all the time. It's my wife's favorite.

I can see why, Poppa Hooch says. Makes me think of my Diane, Lord bless her.

Hosea opens the book again and looks down on it, thumbing through pages.

Would you like to hear anything else?

Your voice is so soothing, she says. I think it'd put me right to sleep.

I'd take no insult from it.

Well, if you don't mind readin', I don't mind listenin', do you, Hooch?

No, I like it myself, but what I'd like to do first is ask Hosea here if he'd send somebody up from the next town to come get us.

I was planning on staying away from folks. I need to find the railroad. I've not received a good reception in these parts.

Suppose I come with you? Rebecca says.

That's even worse. A white woman traveling with a colored man.

I can look like a man. I fooled Shuck and Hooch here this mornin'. When we get close to a town you can hide and I'll go in myself and ask someone for a ride. I got some money, and Hooch here's got plenty. I'm sure someone'll come up here and get us for twenty dollars.

Hosea kicks at the ground with the toe of his boot. He draws little circles in the dust with the end of a stick.

You folks fed me and quenched my thirst, and you're good company to a man that needs it. I can't say no to you. But I want to stay off the roads. I don't want to talk to nobody. I don't want no trouble. Soon as we find a town, we part company. No offense, but I travel better on my own. You can lead 'em back up here yourself.

I wasn't figuring on comin' back, Rebecca says. Hooch, you're an angel for takin' me this far. But Lord knows you ain't up for this trip on foot. You best get back home. I'll find my way to Slaughter Mountain.

Well, if that's how you feel, Rebecca, I can't argue with facts. My back's killing me and I can't walk too good anymore.

It's for the best, she says. I really think I should go on alone. I got Spider to look after me, and enough money to bargain for another ride.

How long are we gonna be up here? Waitin' I mean?

Two, three days at the most. Give me ten dollars as a down payment on a ride, and I'll pay you back the full twenty when we get home. If you can find someone to take you back to Arkville, you can get a bus.

Suppose they take the ten dollars and never come? What if we're stranded up here?

Don't you worry about that. I'll find a good Christian.

All right, then. Guess I won't be needing that Brock's feed. A dead chicken don't eat. I ain't got a coop anyhow.

Rebecca turns to Hosea. His skin shines in the firelight, and she can see the bruises on his fine cheekbones.

So we leave at first light then?

Before, he says. I want to get a good head start on the heat.

He holds the Bible in his lap, closes his eyes, flips to a random page, and points down at it.

Nehemiah, he says. Chapter eight, verse fourteen. This'll put you right to sleep.

18

THE CHAPEL

It takes a long time to for a strong man to die, even from too much strychnine, and Charles Flint was a strong man. It's not the poison that kills him but the spasms and the seizures, and the exhaustion from the spasms, his muscles flexing and contracting, flexing and contracting, all at once haywire and insane. All Jacob could do was watch. And they couldn't restrain Charles, they couldn't even hold him down. There was no sedative available, and if there was, it would have been impossible to administer for all his thrashing. Sylus had to drag Magdalena inside, while they prayed for just one more miracle. It's hard to beseech the Lord for a dying man when his wailing drowns out the prayers, but no amount of praying was going to save Charles Flint anyway. There was too much poison inside him, and not enough Holy Ghost. Bright light and loud noises trigger the convulsions, and by the time they put out the torches and rid the scene of onlookers, Charles was too close to death for anyone but Jesus himself to save. He took his last gasp with his eyes wide open and his hands stretched up toward the moon.

They had to lock Magdalena in the house to keep her from running out to him. She pounded and pounded on the door so that they could hear it from outside, and she wouldn't calm down until Jacob sat with her. He rocked her, and her whole body shook. It took her a long while to fall asleep, hysterical as she was, but in that time Baxter and Sylus put him in the casket and set it in the chapel to keep it cool.

The Slaughter Mountain chapel is not built to keep out the wind so much as it was built to capture the sun. It was designed as a daytime holy place, constructed in such a way as to gather light. It's drafty and it doesn't hold the heat long after the sun goes down, but the stained-glass windows transform the light into ever-changing spectral configurations as the sun traverses the sky. When he rebuilt this chapel Tobias Cross was not concerned with comfort. He cut his own timber and recruited homespun carpenters from among his flock to build it, and what money he had he spent on fancy stained glass because that is what he saw in his dreams. The Lord told him to build a temple of divine illumination, and that's just what he did. In the morning the pulpit shimmers beneath a slow-moving kaleidoscope of colored reflections. In the afternoon the walls are speckled with blue and gold. In the evenings, they turn red and ocher and they pulse when the clouds blow by. They call it the chapel of glorious light.

But in the nighttime it's a cold place. The walls hum when the wind blows, and the rafters shake, and in the right time of the month at the right time of the year the windows turn the moon shine green as pond moss, and with that same strange glow. Jacob sits alone in this light, watching the casket they put up on sawhorses over the discolored patch of flooring where the pulpit once stood. It is a casket built for a child, too short for a man lying straight out but adequate when the legs are bent and the feet hang out over the edge. Jacob stares at his closed eyes, and the way the light falls on his lids it makes them glow blue from underneath. His face is all sunken and his hair sticks up in clumps. His skin is as spongy and fallow as a mushroom cap.

People are always saying that the dead look so peaceful, so quiet, like they're happy, like they're asleep. But it's not that way at all. There's no confusing the two states, sleep and death, not here, not from what he's seen. This isn't sleep. This isn't rest. He'd never seen his daddy scared of anything, never seen him run, never seen him cry, but to look at him now, with his head arched back and his mouth wide open in the green light of the chapel moon—it's a sight no nightmare can conjure. Such a thing is beyond imagination, beyond even his dreams. He turns away and walks slowly, backward. He walks into the shadows, beyond the moonbeams, where he can see his father lying in the coffin but where his father cannot see him.

Until Cornelius Loop he's only seen the dead in visions. He's seen broken corpses pulled taut by their own weight, or hog-tied, or dismembered, or splayed open with all their shiny magic exposed and ruined. But those were distorted men, transformed into things vaguely human. Far removed and far away, those dark visions, those strangers, would blur and fade like ghosts. In his visions he knew nothing more than what he had seen with his eyes. They had no names, no voices. He never saw them yawn or grin. They came to him dead and left him dead, with only a vague pang of sadness or horror. But never numb. Now, seeing this, the body of a person he knew and loved, makes him sick. It's a different feeling altogether. He's dizzy, he's scared, he's hot in the belly like a gut-shot dog. Inside him now something caustic seeps. He can feel it burn like poison. Things he feels connected to, things he sees from the past, his father's eyes, his father's looks, his father's figures of speech. It's memory, the persistent gnaw of moments lost. Such a cruel gift. That which heals us also tears us apart.

His father, his first memory. His father, the memory giver, the creator of memories. His eyes so clear, the countless aspects of his face, in the morning at prayer, in the evening when he was tired and unshaven, his curved fingers drumming the tabletop, the high white arches of his feet as they dried in the sun, his speaking voice loud in his head now, with echoes of the lost mundane: Good night, Jacob. Wash your hands, always wash your hands, son. Fish keep best in the cool of the shade. Go to sleep now, there's time tomorrow to read that book. Close the light, go to sleep.

The moon makes slow progress toward dawn and heavy clouds pass before it, changing the light inside the chapel so that the stained glass flickers, darkens, then flickers again. It's a continuous flow of mottled darkness and muted light, like shadows on the bottom of a stream. His father ripples beneath this effect. Patterns of light dance and throb across his face. His nose stands out in stark illumination, then his lips, his chin. His teeth flash, and a black line creeps down his jaw along the ridge of the sharp bone. His skin turns blue. Then the clouds all blow away, and the shadows fade. His fingers, his toes, his exposed flesh begins to glow. The wind outside the chapel rises in pitch and he can hear canvas rapping—the loose flaps of the revival tent. Jacob moves closer to his father. He walks slow and counts fourteen steps before his belly rests against the side of the casket. His daddy was the window through which he first saw the world. He taught him the names of the stars and the trees. The words from his mouth filled his head with his first wonders—mountain myths and Bible stories. He learned about the world through his daddy's eyes. A boy learns to look on his own, but it takes a father to teach him how to see, and in the end that's all a man can pass on to a boy, an appreciation for the silence of the woods, for the smooth spots in a stream, for deer and caterpillars and flowers and snakes. This is what his daddy gave him. Not some place in the sky or a name in a book, but a warm spot in his belly that makes him shiver whenever he realizes he's alive and living in this big, beautiful world. The feeling that he calls God.

It's almost dawn in the chapel and colder now, and that's a good thing. Cold air slows decay. Jacob stands looking at the body, not at his father's face now but at his clothes. They're torn and filthy from rolling in the dirt. All the buttons are missing from his shirt, and his underclothes are torn open, revealing his skin. He never realized what a thin man his father was, how bony and pale. He removes his coat and covers him. He grasps the edge of the casket with his fingers and prays. He digs into the wood with his fingernails.

You're with the old woman now, he says.

He reaches over and smooths his father's hair back.

You caught the devil for me, he says. I suppose I should be grateful for that, but I'm not. I would have died for you.

He digs his nails deeper into the side of the casket, prying up tiny splinters of cedar.

Lord, he says, you ask for more than I can give.

The wind blows harder and the trees all shake outside. He can hear the shutters banging on the side of the house.

To the prophets, you sent angels, he says. To those lost in the wilderness, you gave voices, you showed clear signs and delivered strength. Where's my Gabriel? Where are my burning seraphim bearing coals of redemption? If you're going to take my daddy from me, then you ought to give me something back.

The wind blows stronger now and the little door behind the pulpit rattles in its frame. Inside the serpent chamber, the medicine bottles shake on the shelves and he wants to smash them all and kill the snakes, and set the whole chapel on fire just for the sake of the flames themselves. Answers can always be found in fire and there's a mysterious wisdom in flames. Maybe that's where God will show him something. Maybe he needs something as soothing and powerful and mysterious as fire. Maybe he needs the sea. According to Baxter there's only one thing more satisfying than watching a fire burn—the ocean.

I wish you'd of just let me die, he says.

Inside the house it is quiet and cold and just getting light. None of the three men slept much at all. They prayed while Magdalena cried out in her sleep and woke up screaming so bad that Baxter couldn't bear to hear it anymore. He spent the night walking in the woods, scouting a place to dig a grave. Sylus sat at Maggie's bedside smoothing her hair and humming to her so that she could get some rest, but it was he who fell asleep.

Magdalena wakes with the coming light and finds the big man curled up beside her. She rises slow so as not to disturb him and sees that Jacob's bed has not been slept in. She hears the birds outside and sees the glimmer of the sun filtered through the curtains and the trees. She smells coffee, and her belly reacts by making a strange sound. She hasn't eaten since lunch the day before. She gets out of the bed thinking about eggs. She splashes water on her face from the washbasin and drinks a sip from her cupped hands. She runs her fingers through her hair and ties it back and takes off the wrinkled dress, which is stained with dark blood that won't ever wash out. She finds a pair of Jacob's trousers and one of his old shirts. In the corner of the room, behind the washbasin, is the old woman's potion box and the carpetbag with her father's things. Some of his clothes lie crumpled on the floor—his shoes, his trousers, his watch. She holds her breath for a moment, then leaves the room, following the smell of coffee and food.

Tobias sits at the kitchen table with his forehead resting in the palms of his hands. Baxter leans against the wall near the stove, holding a coffee cup close to his mouth, watching the steam rise. Magdalena watches them for a while; they don't notice her standing in the doorway. When she finally speaks, they both jump.

Where's Jacob? she says.

They stare at her, standing there in Jacob's clothes. She looks just like her mother with her hair tied back. Tobias pulls out a chair for her to sit.

He's in the chapel, with your daddy. C'mon and sit. I'll fix you something to eat.

She doesn't move. She cranes her neck up to see out the kitchen window, as if the two of them might be sitting outside having a father-son talk.

In the chapel?

We put him in Jacob's casket and laid him in there. Jacob's been out with him all night.

He's truly dead then, she says.

She looks at Baxter and he nods. He stares down into his cup and blows away the steam. His eyes are black as crow's feathers, with that same oily sheen. Indian eyes, the old woman used to say. Her daddy had the same coal-black eyes. And she has them too.

Momma was scared he'd die out on the road, she says. She'd just holler at him, Don't you die on me, Charles Flint, don't you die out there, and he'd say, Oh, Rebecca, the spirit's just too strong in this man. I can live as long as I want. I can go on till a hundred and ten.

Baxter sips from the cup, swirls it, then lays it down.

I wanna see him, she says.

Magdalena, Tobias says. You need to eat.

I'll eat later.

It's not something I think you should see, he says. It's bad, what that poison does to a man's body. He doesn't look himself.

Seeing him dead won't be worse than seeing him dying.

Go on, then, Tobias says. I'll have something to eat waiting when you get back.

Magdalena breathes deep and closes her eyes. She pushes the chapel doors open and stands at the end of the aisle. It's not as dark inside as she imagined. The sun has come up over the mountain and the chapel walls shimmer with emerald light. Jacob stands with his back to her. She can see the casket, but she can't see what's inside. She steps closer, and now she can see a bare foot dangling out the end of the casket. Jacob turns and squints.

Maggie, he says.

She steps closer to look at the casket and sees her father's face, and everything inside her goes hot. Her head swims. Her knees wobble. He looks like a man who died of pure fright.

Jacob, she says. What are we gonna do?

We're gonna bury him. We're gonna bury him right here on Slaughter Mountain, That's what he'd want.

What about Momma?

He's got to buried somewhere soon.

We should take him home.

No. I see it all now clear as daylight. This is where he's meant to be. He's got to stay on this mountain, and you got to go home.

Where you goin'?

I'm not sure yet. I'm waiting for a sign.

I thought you said you saw it clear as day.

I do. I see the ocean. I was never able to imagine it before. But I see it now. I hear it, and it sounds like a mighty wind.

They slash the guy ropes and pull up all the tent stakes. The tent settles in on itself, gathering round the center pole before teetering, tipping, and floating softly to the ground like a white sheet coming down over a freshly made bed. They heap all the benches in a pile ten feet high and set them ablaze while they gather up the canvas tarp. They work fast, without talking, as the new pine pops and burns. They all gather round the fire, resting, running their dirty fingers through their hair and wiping the sweat from their eyes. It's a clear, beautiful morning and everything but their faces is bright. Sylus squats to stir the coals of the burning pine benches.

Whaddya think? he says.

Baxter turns and looks behind them, at the flattened meadow bisected with tire ruts and drag marks.

We sure won't fool nobody.

What's left?

Baxter pulls a tarp off the bed of his truck. Beneath it lies the serpent box. Inside, the headless body of the big diamond-back. He carries the box over to the fire and drops it onto the flames. They say nothing as it burns.

He turns to Jacob and Magdalena and kneels before them, putting a hand on each of their shoulders.

We got to bury him now. We got to do it quick and secret. No mound, no stones, no marker of any kind. Folks might come up here and ask questions. If anybody asks, just tell them your daddy recovered and walked off into the woods, that it was a miracle from heaven. He went off into the wilderness to be with the Lord.

Jacob stares at him, not blinking. He shows no emotion at all.

Nobody's happy about this, Tobias says. But it can't be helped. We'd all rather he be where he belongs.

This is where he belongs, Jacob says.

There's a place on the side of the mountain about a mile into the woods where there's a stand of shagbark hickory and a meadow not too rocky for digging or too wet for a proper grave.

It's strange for Jacob to see the coffin lying there in the tall grass beside the fresh-dug hole, the coffin that was supposed to be his own. It's bad luck to keep a coffin around, that's what Tobias's daddy said. Build a coffin, dig a grave, fate tempted is fate served.

Sylus and Baxter lower the box, each holding a length of rope cut from the revival tent. Nobody speaks as it goes down into the hole. Tobias asks them all to pray quietly to themselves. Jacob listens to the sounds of the meadow—blue-headed damselflies, mosquitoes big as wasps, click bugs, and harvest flies. He shuts his eyes and listens to the hum of the bugs and the slapping sound of hands swatting them. On the way down he picked up a green hickory nut off the trail, and now he digs at the tough husk with his thumbnail. The breeze comes up and the leaves rustle. The grass hisses, and he can hear pages turning in a book and then a voice. It's Tobias Cross reading Nahum from his father's Bible.

> Though they be quiet, and likewise many, yet thus they
> shall be cast down, when he shall pass through. Though I
> have afflicted thee, I will afflict thee no more.

He bends over, takes a handful of the black earth, and sprinkles it onto the lid of the casket.

Charles Flint, he says. You were a good man, a God-loving man, who sowed the seed of Jesus in all our hearts. You will be sorely missed. Who can say why he has taken thee? Not for sin. These are the hardest lessons, Lord, and now we must listen. But who among us can interpret your will?

He turns from the grave and walks out into the meadow. Baxter steps up and holds Jacob and Magdalena by the shoulders.

Sylus bends over and pulls out the bone-handled dagger that he keeps in his boot and studies it in the sunlight. It's been with him a long time, and was his daddy's knife before him. It's killed many men, cut many throats, but the last human blood to stain its blade was the blood of Charles Flint. He drops the knife into the hole.

They fill the grave. Baxter helps, and so does Maggie. She pushes in dirt with her hands. Jacob walks off into the woods alone, not following the trail but breaking through the tall grass with one hand and holding the other up to his nose, sniffing at his fingers and savoring the pungent odor of hickory nuts.

19

HOSEA

osea wakes beneath a canopy of stars with the moon low on the horizon, pale and chalky like an alabaster eye. He rouses Rebecca with a gentle shake of her shoulder. They don't speak. They gather what little they have to carry and communicate with hand gestures and nods of their heads. Rebecca puts on her trousers and her father's old wool coat and tucks her hair up under her hat. She rubs soot on her face from the fire with the tips of her fingers to complete the disguise.

Hosea Lee is a tall man with a big stride. He sets a pace that even the dog has trouble keeping up with, and he is soon far ahead of them. They walk along the roadside, ever wary of oncoming headlights or anything that sounds mechanical. But they see nothing but bats and hear nothing but birds. All through the dark hours before dawn, there are only the robins and the peeper frogs and the sound of Hosea's voice. He talks to her as he walks along, maintaining his momentum with a constant flow of spoken word that's as rhythmic as a song. He speaks in a hushed tone, not waiting for replies, not looking back at Rebecca, who follows behind him, listening. He seems to address the trees, the stars, and he speaks in a strange manner, not as one person talking to another, but as a man might speak to himself if he was completely alone. And this is what he tells her.

He used to preach to the Indians, as his father did before him, and over the years he managed to visit every reservation between Oklahoma and the Carolina coast. He'd stay in the little native enclaves and camps in the hollows and the hills, spreading the word of God to those who would listen, and he'd sermonize the blacks building the railroads and working in the mining camps, which is where he spent most of his time. But he was always moving, always on the road, traveling from one spot to the next on the back of an old mule named Darney, who he still speaks of with the affection of a man remembering an old family dog. The miners called him Reverend Lee, but the Indians called him Black Daniel, after the story of the youth cast into the lion's den who was saved by the son of fire.

He was a wandering preacher for many years, never taking a wife or loving a woman or even meeting one who struck him in that special way, until a traveling bordello arrived at one of the mining camps. There was a young woman among them who was a wonder and a mystery to behold. At the age of seventeen, she was already the wealthiest of all the whores in the bordello and had a reputation that spread like fire through his camp and all the others, and she had a following that rivaled any preacher or star of stage or pictures. Her name was Tuley, and she had that rare combination of radiant maternal beauty and animal passion that kept men awake at night and fighting in the saloons for weeks after she was gone. She made men remember what men were for. She was a small woman with delicate features, but she had big round hips and a waist so narrow that the inner nature of any man could not help but be stirred up hot and dumb by the mere sight of her bending to wash her feet under a pump—

which she did as frequently as the opportunity allowed. She had fine little hands and beautiful skin that was not quite amber and not quite brown, but some shade in between the two, like those of a dark knot on a fresh pine board. Her eyes were not brown like those of other black women, but golden and glowing—wet and translucent like a honeycomb.

She was a strong and wild lover, well versed in certain lost arts, and she had a way of crying out during the act of love so that everyone could tell where she was exactly and who she was with at any given moment. When she was in camp everyone knew it, and a man could lie back and listen all night as she visited the tents of his friends, counting off each time she earned herself a sawbuck and wondering just what it was she was doing with all that money.

They'd fight over who she liked best and who she claimed to truly love. Some accused her of witchcraft for the way she made them feel—crazy with lust and sick inside, unable to eat, too feeble to work, and unable to tell the difference between the dream and the lie. Every man she was with believed that she truly loved him, and that was her special skill. It wasn't just how she loved a man physically that set her apart as a woman, as a whore. It wasn't just how she used her hands, her mouth, her body to make them forget their miserable lives. It was her way with words and how she used her eyes. She could find the good in any man within minutes; she could find his strength and she could find his weakness. She could make a man feel alive; more than that, she could make him feel like living.

Many of those men would come to Hosea for counsel, he being a preacher and a good listener. And he was moved by what they told him. They were so troubled and torn with guilt and confusion over this woman that he began to wonder what it was about her that made them want to kill each other for her affections and leave their wives. Each confessed to truly loving her, each claimed that she loved him in return, and they all swore she could be changed. Was it permissible to marry such a girl? Could she have babies? Could she be redeemed? Could a woman like Tuley ever be cleansed of sin? And what was it that made a woman do the things she did? It got to where men were shooting at one another for her attention, and one man had been killed in a duel. Tuley herself had been cut open by the dagger of a powder monkey whose proposal of marriage she twice refused. That man blew himself to pieces with his own dynamite. That's when Hosea stepped in.

It got so bad that the foreman asked Hosea to talk to her—for the good of the mining company and for the good of the camp. Hosea understood the necessity of such women in remote places, where large groups of men spend months with nothing but whiskey and cards to pass the time. But Tuley had crossed the line. Hers were more than just business relationships. She got too involved with her customers, and engaged in the most sinister variety of deception by confusing the physical act of love with that other, deeper, and longer-lasting kind. In her mind she loved the men she was with. She had to, for it was the only way she could live such a life. She learned to fall in love quickly, yet could turn off her feelings just as fast, leaving men confounded and sometimes enraged. It had to end. And it fell upon Hosea to help her see the light. He was, after all, one of the only men in camp who had not been one of her customers, and he was a man of God, so he was believed to be immune to her charms. But he was not prepared for her. She was beautiful, this much was true, but he'd seen great beauty close up before and had not been tempted. He'd even seen her, plenty of times, crossing the camp, mostly at night, barefoot and barely dressed.

But what he didn't know was that the closer a man came to her, the more powerful her spell became, so when he came to her tent that first time and walked inside, he could feel her, and he could smell her, and when she turned to him and looked him in the eyes, he shuddered at what he felt. She radiated more than beauty; she radiated a love as pure as Jesus himself. Later he thought about how it must have felt to stare into the eyes of the Lord, how the leper must have felt when he beheld him, how those eyes would have shone through a man and peeled back all the layers of mistrust and pain he'd accumulated throughout his life. That's how Tuley made him feel.

He knocked on her door and she did not reply. But it was open and he knew she was inside. He entered. She stood with her back to him in a cotton dress that was pure white, with a lace back that tied at the nape of her neck. The fabric was sheer, and there was nothing between it and her skin. He could see the outline of her body beneath.

I'd like a word with you, he said.

But she did not turn. She was barefoot, and that's what he fixed upon first. She had the kind of feet you find on a marble statue of a saint, the kind you'd wash and hold every day of your life if you could, with a dark blue vein that ran down from her ankle to a sole white as a soda cracker.

Is that all you'd like from me, she said.

Her dress was held on by a single string that hung from her neck. When she reached back to untie it, he saw her hands. They were small and strong, and he watched how the little muscle bulged and flexed at the crook of her thumb as she squeezed and pulled on the string.

You've become quite a distraction, he said.

A distraction? For who?

You know what I'm talking about.

That's what I'm paid for.

It's more than that. You're leading them on.

They lead themselves on, she said.

You tell them that you love them.

Because it's true, she said. I do.

Come on, now, he said. That's a dangerous game.

She turned to him then, but still did not release the string. She stood there with both hands behind her neck, frozen in the act of untying it. Her eyes were so dark and so big that he could not look away from them.

Every man can be loved, she said. And I can love every man.

Every man, he said.

Yes, she said. Every one. I know that somewhere, sometime a woman had loved him, and that spark, that light, which starts as a heartbeat inside a woman, is what I find. I see it in you, preacher.

She came close to him and put her hands on his shoulders. Her dress fell to the floor. She looked right up into his eyes and smiled.

I can find that spark in any man, she said. That's my gift.

She pushed herself against him and he felt the full length of her. Her knees, her hips, her breasts.

When he starts in breathing heavy, she said. When his hands are on me, on my thighs, on my arms, I feel him, I feel his true heart and soul, and I mean what I tell him. I don't lie. Even if it's for a few minutes, we belong to each other, and I make him feel like the man he is inside.

Hosea did not touch her. She pressed closer and he felt the warmth between her legs on him like a fresh burn. But he did not touch her.

I help them, she said. I heal them, just like a doctor does, but better. So why shouldn't I get paid for it?

He knew he should have never let her get this close. He was trapped now like a bug in a web, and he also knew that to struggle was futile.

That kind of love is a sacred gift, he said. The Lord gave you that to give to one man.

Why would the good Lord only give us something so precious if not to use it? she said.

We all have that gift, he told her. It is precious, and not be fooled with.

You spread love with words and ideas. Isn't what we do the same?

No, it most certainly is not.

What difference does it make how the healing is done? Be they words, gestures, a preacher laying his hands on the sick?

The love you speak of is sacred, between one man and one woman bonded by holy matrimony.

Says who?

Says the word of God.

You mean, says some old book that's supposed to be the word of God.

That old book is the foundation of my faith, and the faith of millions.

That means nothing to me, she said. Who are you to tell me who I can and cannot love? Or how many or how deeply? Who is anybody? Your God lets people kill each other, but he don't let let 'em love each other. What sense is there in that?

That's not true, he said. There's a rule against killing too.

You preachers don't go after murderers, or soldiers, or the Ku Klux Klan.

Some of us do.

I think you got it backwards, she said. You're blind, and you're leading the blind. What this world needs is more of what I'm doing and less of what the rest of y'all is doing. Killing each other. Fighting wars and makin' money off the backs of lesser men. Where is the greater sin?

He pushed her away with such force that she fell to the floor. But she just smiled and opened her legs, and that part of her which worked its magic on so many men before him glistened, and he stared at it and she let him. It looked like the inside of a flower and she made it move, the petals opening slightly and closing again. He turned and fled from the tent.

She was a smart girl, and he was not going to convince her that what she was doing was wrong. And he was bothered by this. The truth was, she made some sense. After he left her that morning he had a difficult time thinking about anything else. Her logic, her body, and the other forces at work, invisible, and sublime. He didn't see her again for a whole week, but he thought about her every minute of every day and he'd make all kinds of excuses just to walk by her tent. At night he dreamed about her. And he wanted her.

She came to him in the night seven days later. They didn't speak a single word, and they didn't have to. Things were said between them that can only be translated by the pads of the fingers, the ridges of the lips, and he knew right then why the miners cut her name into the bark of trees and spent hours chiseling it onto the limestone faces of quarry walls. When she said that she loved him, he knew it was the truth. She wept all through it, and shook in a cold sweat for more than an hour afterward, with her ear to his chest listening to the whoosh of his blood. In that place their breath froze and the stove clicked and the moisture on the window turned to powdered crystal. They laid shuddering together long after the candle flickered out, and she told him things she swore she never told any man. She was born in Mississippi to a riverboat harlot. Her daddy was a gambler and a freemason out of Biloxi who was a steam-shovel operator on the Panama Canal. Her momma baptized her and left her at a convent in a shoebox, she was so small. The convent was the only home she ever knew. When she was fourteen, they sent her off to live with a rich white family, where she was to learn how to make a living as a domestic. She didn't last six months in that place, and ran away the first chance she got. She met a woman who took her in and looked after her as if she were her own. She lived with a dozen other girls, in a city she was sworn never to name. They called the place Madame Genieve's. It was in an old Spanish fort that was the winter home of a famous brothel. In the summertime they packed up like the circus and went out on the road to where men were lonely and worked hard and were sporadically paid large sums of money, which they were apt to spend foolishly on the fleeting pleasures of the mind and the flesh.

That same night, she told him that in a matter of days they were packing up and heading back south for the winter. So he bought all her free time until then, and they spent it alone together in his cabin with the shades drawn. He didn't care what the talk was in the camp, what people said about scandal or sin. He loved her and he convinced himself that she could be changed.

Rebecca listens to this story as they walk along in the dark. As the trees take shape in the graying light, she wonders about this woman, who is the first real whore she'd ever heard of in her life. Hosea's story is at once shameful and compelling—never has anyone spoken so plain to her. Never has she heard a man talk this way about love and sex and the things people do when they burn with passion. And she wants him to go on. She wants to keep hearing his lovely voice tell her what happened to this girl. But he stops talking suddenly, and he holds his hand up in the air, gesturing for her to keep quiet and still. It's dawn. There is but one star visible on the low horizon, and in the distance they hear a motor and see a single, bouncing light.

They step off into the brush on the side of the road. Rebecca holds Spider down and scratches him behind the ears, and they wait. It's a truck, the kind with a long bed where men sit on benches to be taken out to work on a road gang or in the fields. It's got a broken headlight and is moving not much faster than a tractor. As it draws near, she can see that it is filled with men, some standing, some with their legs dangling over the tailgate. Hosea steps out into the road as the truck rolls by and waves at them with both arms over his head. One of them slaps on the roof with the palm of his hand. The truck stops. Hosea motions for Rebecca to wait and walks over to the man leaning out the driver's-side window. After a few minutes he comes back and for the first time since she's met him, he smiles. They have a ride.

The driver's name is Lucius Jones. He's a small man who bounces around on the balls of his feet as he talks to Hosea near the open hood of the truck, where another man is tinkering with something inside the hissing engine. Rebecca stands with Spider off to the side, where several of the workers have disembarked to piss in the weeds. She can't hear what they're saying, but Hosea slips Lucius something that must be money. He motions her to the back of the truck and helps her in, lifts the dog up, and climbs in himself. They sit among the workers, most of them sleeping, all of them black. She wonders if they know she's not a man, but if they do, they don't show it. Spider crouches at her feet. The truck moves on. Hosea tells her that Lucius Jones knew his father, and that after they drop the workers off he's going to take them to a farm where they can get something to eat and ask about help for Poppa Hooch and Daisy Jane. They drive along in silence for a while, listening to the field hands snore and cough. Hosea talks to a man smoking a cigarette who just got out of prison, who tells them that his boss, the owner of the farm, is a fair and honest man who helps people in need.

I thank the Lord for that man, he says. A no-good thief like myself would never find work without a man like Lee Grant. He laughs at himself and flicks the end of his smoke up into air where it gets caught in the wind and tumbles into the road behind the truck in a shower of sparks. They drive on for a while and stop alongside a sugar beet field, where the hands disembark. The truck turns around and heads back in the same direction they came.

They sit facing each other, alone now in the back of the truck, with the dog lying between them. Hosea takes off his hat and runs his fingers over the band.

I spent that whole winter trying to find her, he says. I tracked the brothel down through Georgia, on the back of Darney. I wrote her a letter every day.

But you found her, Rebecca says.

That spring, when the brothel came back north, I met the Cajun woman who ran the place. She called herself Madame Genieve Duçimez. She wouldn't tell me where Tuley was, but then I showed her the letters. A hundred and thirteen letters I wrote, and when Madame Genieve saw that, she told me Tuley was going to have my baby in June.

The truck pulls beneath a sign that reads Grant Orchards, and into a long drive lined by old poplar trees. Beyond them, on either side of the road, are peach trees stretching far off to the horizon. It's a big spread, with a packing facility and a fleet of trucks they use to deliver fruit to markets across the state. Hosea stands and shoulders his bag.

This is where we part company, he says.

Lee Grant is a tall, wiry old fellow who walks with a limp. Rebecca figures that he's well past eighty, but he hops around like he was half that age, working on a truck engine with a young black man named Jimmy. He listens to Hosea tell him about Poppa Hooch and Daisy Jane stranded in the hills. He nods the whole time, chewing on a toothpick. Hosea offers him the ten-dollar bill in his pocket to give Poppa Hooch a ride into town, but the old man scowls and slaps his hand away.

We got a shipment going up over the mountain into Tennessee, the old man says. I'll just have my driver take a detour and pick up your people. You can keep your money. I believe in helping those who need it. My daddy was a hero in the Army of the Confederate States. He taught me that Southern hospitality meant not turning away anybody in need, no matter who he was—a Yankee, a black man, or a convict on the run, it don't matter.

When he learns that Rebecca's heading to Slaughter Mountain, he laughs loud and slaps his knee.

This is your lucky day, he says. I got a truck going to Oglethorpe. You can ride along with Jimmy, if he ever gets it fixed. He sends them inside to see his wife for coffee and eggs.

The old woman's as spry as her husband. The splotches on the backs of her hands belie the fire that still burns inside her heart, for she's still fast in the kitchen and light on her frail, skinny legs. And she can talk. She's full of stories and anecdotes that all connect themselves together in the end, and before long she's giving them advice and calling their children by name and quoting scripture, which she claims heals hearts like a salve.

She reminds Rebecca of Gertie Bates by the way she glares at her and the way she pauses in mid-speech with her hands suspended in the air, with the pads of her fingers moving gently over the pads of her thumbs, like she's trying to feel the texture of her words as they come out. Her name is Margaret Diamond Grant, a fact she repeats every chance she gets.

Nobody ever calls me Di the way I wanted them to when I was a girl, she says. They call me Peggy, not Peg, and Peggy Grant will feed any man no matter where he comes from or what he's done to himself or the world. Feed the hungry, that's my special gift.

She serves them an enormous breakfast and apologizes for its meagerness. After fussing over them at the table, she goes out to check on her washing. Rebecca stares at Hosea, trying to get his attention. But he gazes at the needlepoint samplers on the wall.

Hosea, she says. Why don't you come to Slaughter Mountain to meet Charles, Jacob, and Maggie? I really want you to meet Jacob. He's a blessed boy, touched by God and filled with the Holy Ghost.

Hosea wipes his mouth with a blue-checkered napkin and looks into her dark eyes.

That's kind of you Rebecca, but I've got my own family to find.

Rebecca takes his hand and Hosea shivers at her touch.

I'm gonna tell you a story, she says. A story I never told anybody but Jacob. It's the story of how he was born. You see, my son is a special child, Mr. Lee. He's blessed by God and brimming over with the Holy Ghost, like no child ever was before. He could help you. I don't know how yet, but I know he can.

A person's story becomes true only when it's told. Until that time it's but a dream, with a vague beginning and an abrupt end, joined together by fuzzy pictures that flash instead of flow and with no meaning until it's told and then retold. All these years had gone by, and Rebecca never told hers completely because it was shameful to her. She always blamed herself for what happened and was afraid to hear it spoken. But until Hosea, she also never met anybody who didn't already know it. Most of Leatherwood had heard it from one of the checkerboard crew down at Shuck's. It was never spoken of at home, and she didn't give it much thought during her waking hours. But at night, when she slept, it came back to her, swirling, disjointed, disguised in all sorts of dreams that began innocently then quickly turned into variations of flight, flood, darkness, and fire.

So Hosea becomes her first true witness. She tells him about that night on the mountain, and Jacob's birth in the tree, his deformity, his wisdom, and his gift to speak with eloquence beyond his years—the way the Holy Spirit shines up through him, and his ability to soothe and heal the body and soul of all he meets. She tells him about his visions, how he sees things sent to him by Jesus and the men who died in the tree where he was born.

Hosea has heard some strange stories in his time. A person can't grow up on Indian reservations and spend half his life traveling through mining camps without his share of fanciful tales, but this one strikes him as not only true, but somehow significant, inevitable even, like he's been waiting all his life to hear it told. If it had come from anyone but her, he'd give it no credence at all, but he knows the truth when he hears it spoken. A person can lie about a lot of things, but not about how they see God, and not about such a life as young Jacob Flint's. When he puts it all together in his mind and thinks about how he met her and all the things that had to come together for him to be sitting with her now, he believes it to be a sign.

He is silent, and Rebecca mistakes his reverence for impatience. She apologizes and stares down at her shoes. For a long time they do not speak.

It's been many years since he felt the hand of God reach out to touch him. He forgot what it was like to be filled with light, to be driven toward Him the way this woman and her family seems to be, and the way she talks about their faith makes him feel ashamed. He's forgotten why things happen the way they do, which is not by accident but by his design, and he believes that the good Lord had something in mind for them both when He brought them together that morning on the mountain beside Poppa Hooch's broken-down car. He squeezes her hand and looks into her eyes.

Your boy sounds like he's got true faith, he says, the faith promised us in the Bible. I believe I'll go with you, Rebecca Flint. I've never seen a holiness revival and I sure would like to meet this boy.

Rebecca smiles and blushes at the warm feeling of Hosea's hand. He's got the softest skin she's ever touched.

For a while she stands in the back of the truck with the wind blowing through her hair, her eyes watering. The dog smiles wide, his eyes slits in the wind, his ears pinned flat against his head. Hosea sits with his back to a stack of crates, eating a big, juicy peach, and telling her about the ten years between the time when the first of his children was born and the day Tuley ran off with them all. He had three children by Tuley—Josiah, Micah, and a little girl Jacob's age that they named Pauline. They all lived in the same house his father built with the help of some men from one of the Indian reservations and Darney the mule, who they'd tie to the porch rail, feeding him cookies and pie.

They were the best years he'd ever known, he told her. They were happy times, spent together at the house or in the surrounding woods, but never more than a few miles from those places. It was the first time in both his and Tuley's lives they stayed in one place. All during that time Hosea didn't preach, and didn't even pick up a Bible. He told himself he gave that up for the children, and for her. But he knew it was more than that. He took up farming, and wasn't very good at it, but he managed to feed the family and sell some corn. But they struggled. Tuley had a rough time of it; birthing and raising three children took its toll, but not on her looks. She always kept herself beautiful, sometimes at the expense of the household chores or things for the children that had to be done. She loved them and was as good a mother as she could be, but she was quick-tempered and impatient. She never talked about it, but she was resentful. After she had the children, there was something inside her that changed, and as the children grew that something began to stir.

On a hot spring day, five years ago, she took the children

and disappeared. She simply vanished. He'd been searching for them ever since. It was only two weeks ago that he accidently discovered her location. He was in a pool hall in Memphis when he heard her name spoken by a man who'd seen her in a brothel in Florida. He always knew she'd go back to that brothel, but she had never revealed the location. This was where he was going just before he met Rebecca. He was a few miles outside of Arkville, in a little valley, riding right down the middle of the road on Darney, when a truck came from behind him with its engine cut, quiet as a kite. There must have been a couple of them standing in back with clubs. On the first pass they took out the legs of the mule. On the second, they turned the clubs on him. He must have passed out, but he woke to the sound of the mule. Darney wasn't dead but he was hurt bad, and he brayed like he was being skinned alive.

They left them both there on the side of the road to die. It was bone cold, and wet, and Hosea thanked God that they didn't shoot Darney because that mule was the only thing that kept him alive. He curled up against his belly, and though Darney was unconscious, he was warm and his breathing soothed him and Hosea talked to him all through that bad night. In the morning another truck came down the road. At first he thought it was them, come back to finish him off, but it was a farmer who almost drove right on by. But when he saw the mule, he stopped. First thing that man did was check on the condition of the mule. He didn't look at Hosea. He had a gun in the truck and Hosea begged him to put Darney out of his misery, but he wouldn't shoot the animal. Said it wasn't any of his business. But he loaned Hosea the rifle to do the job himself. It wasn't an easy thing to do. He had a tough time holding the barrel flush to Darney's head because he was shaking so bad and it took three shots to get it done. He had to buy himself a ride to the next town over, which was Dowden, and he was lucky they had a colored doctor in that godforsaken place. After a few days' rest he set out again on foot, and it was only a day later that he came upon Rebecca, Hooch, and Daisy Jane.

Rebecca listens to the sound of the truck as it drives along and gears down for the climb ahead. She looks ahead and sees the driver inside bouncing with the sinkholes and veering around the deeper ruts. Hosea reaches into his rucksack and pulls out a photograph. He examines it briefly and passes it over to her. It's Tuley, an old picture, a stiff-backed portrait done in a studio, worn now and soft as rawhide from the sweat of his hands. But through the creases and the wrinkles she can plainly see something about the woman that lies deeper than the image itself, a burning sort of radiance that seeps out of her large dark eyes, like the eyes of a child, wide, round, holy. She has fine lips, and her hands are folded gracefully over her bare knee. She's never seen a likeness as haunting as this outside a Bible painting, nor eyes so full of something sad and lonely. It strikes her as odd that a woman this beautiful could be so sad. It makes Rebecca feel plain and ugly and old. But Tuley's eyes remind her of Jacob, not in their shape or anything that can be seen or described, but in something that can be felt behind them—a thousand secrets, a defiance struggling back against shame.

The truck stops suddenly in the middle of the road and the driver pokes his head out and says something they can't hear over the sound of the engine. He bangs on the door with the palm of his hand in a clear indication that there's something he wants them to see. He drives on and they both stand. There's a sign on the side of the road, so small and weather-stained that it's hard for them to spot, but there's no mistaking it when they see it. Twenty-two miles to Oglethorpe.

20

LEAVING SLAUGHTER MOUNTAIN

At the top of the mountain, when the sun goes down and the world dims, the edges of all upright things begin to sharpen and glow. In this light even the stones take on significance. Strewn out over the ground, their leeward faces are cast into darkness. Their shadows wobble. Boulders become pale, the pine trunks whiten, and the long, slanting shadow of the boy stretches off like a tire skid and turns cobalt. The sky above him shimmers.

Jacob enters the woods and walks down to the meadow, the old woman's potion box heavy under his arm. When he gets to the spot the sun is gone and the light has changed again. It's no longer gold. Now it's almost green. But that's the meadow playing tricks on him, for the light shines through each glowing blade of grass and makes the whole field ripple with a verdant glow.

He takes measured strides, noting everything he sees, already drawing the map in his head. Forty paces—count twenty twice, and take big, man-sized steps. Left at the deadfall, where the calla lilies grow up from a split trunk, ten more to the chuck-hole warrens, then right, out to the river-stone cairn and right again, one step for each year that his father lived. Thirty-six paces, and there he lies, beneath a granite flat-rock that sparkles like the Milky Way.

Five days now he's been coming here with Magdalena. Every sunset, and again at dawn. But tonight he's come alone. He's got the pigskin Bible tucked into his waist in the small of his back, so that his hands are free to carry the potion box and the madstone. He clutches it so tightly that his fingers throb. He doesn't know why he took it. The madstone has no power to bring back the dead and the potion box contains nothing he can use or understand. But it's old and beautiful, and he thinks that a man should be buried with more than just a nice suit of clothes.

The flat-rock is heavy and makes for a fine tombstone, and it flips over easy enough once he gets his hands under it. The soil below is soft, black, and cool. It feels good between his fingers, and it smells good, like old damp leaves.

He digs down about two and a half feet before the soil gets hard. He won't get much farther with just his hands, so he scouts around for something to dig with, but it's too dark now to find anything other than a sharp stick. He uses this to pick at the earth of the grave. He loosens some more soil, but not much more, and gets down about another foot before abandoning his plan to leave the box directly atop the coffin itself.

Baxter said it might be more than a year before they could get back here to bring him home. So he dug the hole good and deep. But Jacob doesn't think they should take him home at all. It's the kind of spot his father would have chosen for himself if he could. No ornament, no fuss.

He places the old woman's potion box in the grave, but holds onto the madstone. He squeezes it, and prays for strength and clarity, and for his father's soul. The stone fits perfectly in the palm of his hand. It is porous and warm. He shifts it from his right hand to his left, but the sensation of heat does not go away. It's hot now, and it tingles. The old woman claimed it's over a hundred years old. She got it from her daddy, who got it from his, and now he's wondering if this is where its long journey should really end.

You decide, he says. He extends his hand out over the grave and when he opens his fist the stone does not fall. It's stuck to his hand. He shakes it, but it still won't fall.

Thank you, Lord, he says. Now I know.

He covers the potion box with the cool, fragrant earth and fills in the grave. He does this one-handed, with the madstone stuck fast to his palm. He flips the flat-rock over and smoothes the top of the plot with a leafy branch. By now it is full dark. He sits on the flat-rock and listens to the humming mosquitoes. After a while the madstone falls to the ground, leaving a tiny mark on his palm.

He pockets the stone and leaves the meadow by a different trail, circling around the side of the mountain and coming up out of the woods on an old mining road where they had ditched Baxter's truck, now hidden by branches and moss and difficult to see.

He walks in the dark up the mining road and out onto the Slaughter Mountain road, which is covered in a coarse granite powder that crunches beneath his feet like granules of ice. The granite dust feels good beneath his shoes, and he alters his pace, changing the pattern of his stride so that the sound changes. He creates a rhythm with his footsteps that sounds not unlike brushes on drum skins. He keeps this up for a while and then stops altogether, to listen to the silence that should be there but is not. The sound of his footsteps is still there, only distant now, and coming from behind. He turns and squints and sees someone. Two men on the road. He steps back into the brush to watch them.

One is tall and the other is short and between them both is a sleek dog. The tall man is wearing a strange hat. The dog stops, and Jacob realizes that they are downwind. The dog can smell him. It lifts its head and catches his scent. Jacob stiffens, and the dog bays and then breaks into a dead run straight for him. Jacob does not move. He lets the dog get close. It stops, circles, finds the scent again, and whines. It's Spider. He can hardly believe it, but he'd know him anywhere and he steps out into the road, allowing himself to be knocked over and kissed by the dog.

The two men approach him, and the short one takes off his hat so that his hair falls down over his shoulders—and that's when he sees that it's not a man at all, it's his mother, standing there in the dark on the white powder road like an apparition straight out of his dreams. She had been coming to him every night since his father died, appearing in his dreams in all manner of living forms, both natural and bizarre. In one dream, her head was fixed onto the body of a dog. Now, seeing her and seeing Spider conjures this memory and unsettles him, and for a moment he can't tell if he's really awake.

Momma, he says. Momma, is that you?

She comes to him, kneeling to embrace him, kissing him all over and pulling him to her and running her fingers through his hair. But she can tell that something is not right. Jacob does not return the affection. She steps back, struck dumb with the realization that something is terribly wrong. She shakes her head and sways on her feet. She knows. Jacob takes her by the hands.

I'm sorry, Momma, he says. Momma, I'm so sorry.

No, no, no, she says.

He sees panic in her eyes as the rational part of herself slips away and drift off like a puff of smoke. Her eyes close and her hands come up to shield her face, waving, fending him off. She backs away, sliding in the dust.

Don't, she says. Don't you say it.

He died this past Sunday. He's gone, Momma. He's gone.

Rebecca makes a sound that derives from a place so deep inside that it comes out like yelp. It is the sound of a great lost hope. And it is horrible to hear.

It takes them a while to make their way back to the house. Rebecca has a difficult time walking because her knees are weak and she drags her feet. It is an awkward introduction between Hosea and Jacob. They can't shake hands because they're holding Rebecca up and pulling her along. When they crest the top of the mountain, they see the church and the house with all its windows aglow. Rebecca does the best she can to collect herself. She smooths back her hair and wipes her eyes with the backs of her sleeves. It's cold now. She takes a deep breath and exhales a pale blue mist.

Wait, she says. Just wait a minute.

She hears voices coming from inside the house, and laughter. She hears the clinking of dishware, and shadows pass before the windows. She hears Magdalena laughing, and the laughter confuses her. They've had five days to grieve, but for Rebecca, it is not yet real, not yet true, and then she hears Charles' voice from inside the house and she races to the door.

She bursts into the bright kitchen light to find Sylus leaning back on a chair at the table, holding a hand of cards he's just about to lay down. Baxter is there with his cards to his chest. Magdalena stands at the sink washing a dinner plate. Tobias leans on the window frame, just to the right of the door. He's got a small Bible in his hand that he's reading from. It was his voice that Rebecca heard, his shadow she saw in the window. They stop talking when they see her, and they hear her panting as she searches the room for Charles, dressed like a hobo, her face covered in road dust and streaked with tears.

Charles, she says. Charles?

Magdalena drops the plate she's cleaning but it does not break. It rolls across the kitchen floor, wobbling, crossing the length of the room, before teetering and spinning on its rim like a coin. It comes to rest at Rebecca's feet and the room is quiet. She stands in the doorway, scared and confused. Sylus falls backward off his chair.

Momma, Magdalena says. Momma?

Rebecca turns and sees Tobias for the first time, and the way he's standing, with the Bible in his hands and his dark hair slicked back like Charles, makes her head swim, and she stumbles over the fallen plate.

Where is he? she says. Where's Charles?

They look at each other, unsure of what to say or do. They don't know that she's met Jacob outside. Baxter pushes his chair back and stands. He takes Rebecca by the arm. She shakes him off and starts searching the room, stooping to peer under the table. Jacob steps inside then, with Hosea close behind. Rebecca takes no notice of them. She crosses the kitchen and goes out into the hall, calling out for Charles.

Spider comes bounding in behind Jacob, wagging his tail and whining, slipping all over the polished kitchen floor. Baxter grabs the dog by the neck and gives him a good squeeze. Then he notices the tall black man standing in the doorway. In his fine suit of clothes and bowler hat, he strikes an unlikely and alarming visage coming up out of the darkness behind the much smaller boy. Baxter's sure he's seen the man before.

The sudden appearance of Rebecca, dressed in Charles' clothes, and now shouting his name, fills them with a strange sensation. Not like a dream, but a vision. A forgotten vision, whose components, once assembled in proper order, release its participants from the constraints of earth and time so that they seem to float above it momentarily, observing a dreaded event foretold long ago. The dog is barking. The nameless black man removes his hat and steps in through the door. Nobody moves. All is still. The room is somehow brighter, sharper. Sylus sits on the floor where he fell, holding the jack-high flush fanned out in his hand. They can all see his cards. Tobias has the Bible open to Zephaniah. Rebecca is calling for Charles in the back of the house. Not in a panic but calmly and happily as if this was just a child's game. Baxter turns to Jacob.

I told her, Jacob says. She knows.

I better go get her then, Baxter says.

He finds her in the bedroom rifling through Charles' clothes, smelling them and talking to herself. He takes her by the shoulders and shakes her twice, the way he'd shake a child.

Rebecca, he says. He ain't here. He's is dead. Buried. I'll take you there tomorrow. We can go tomorrow, and you can see.

She shakes her head and shuts her eyes.

Listen to me now, we had a big revival last Sunday. Charles drank a glass of strychnine and, I don't know. The spirit wasn't with him, or maybe not with any of us. It was a bad night in a bad place and the poison was extra strong. He suffered. I can't lie to you. It was bad and it took him a long time to die, but he did die, Rebecca, so you go on and cry, get it all out, but you got to stop this. You got the children here to think of.

She opens her mouth but no sound comes out. She shakes her head from side to side and sinks her head into Baxter's chest. He holds her and rocks her there in the dark.

Hosea lays his bag down on the floor and leans over to pick up the fallen plate. Sylus places his poker hand into his shirt pocket, staring long and hard at the stranger.

Who're you, mister? he says.

Hosea places the dinner plate down on the table.

My name is Hosea Daniel Lee, he says. I met Rebecca out on the road when her car broke down. She was traveling with a big bald feller named Poppa Hooch, who had a little girl.

Daisy Jane, Sylus says.

That's right. Dirty little girl, but pretty underneath.

That would be her. How come they ain't with you?

Well, that old car's seen its last trip and they went back home, I hope. We had to leave them up there where the car broke down.

Tobias lays his Bible on the table.

Have a seat, Mr. Lee, he says. I can fix you something to eat if you'd like. How about coffee?

Water would be fine, Hosea says. Thank you.

I'll get you some, Tobias says. He pours a glass from a pitcher and places it on the table in front of him. Hosea drinks the entire glass in one swallow and Tobias refills it. Hosea stares at the glass while they all stare at him. He looks up at Magdalena and smiles at her. She turns away, and smiles shyly back.

You hungry? Tobias says. You must be hungry. I've got a stew on. We all ate.

It's good, Jacob says. I helped make it.

I could eat some, Hosea says. He looks at Jacob. The boy does not look away, and Hosea studies his face and his eyes. He can see Rebecca in the boy, around his mouth and the bridge of his nose. He's got her chin and her lips. But his eyes are all his own—perhaps they come from his father. He, too, sees a little bit of a resemblance to Tuley in the boy's eyes, but there's another resemblance that's even stronger, and it's such an odd comparison, so unexpected that he's struck dumb by the allusion. Jacob's eyes remind him of Darney the mule's.

What's wrong? Jacob says.

Hosea shakes his head.

Are you all right, Mr. Lee?

Yes, he says. I'm fine. It's been a long day and we had a hard ride.

Tobias sets a bowl of stew in front of him.

Eat that and you'll feel better. I'll set you up with a bed, and then you can get some rest.

Suddenly they hear a cry from the back of the house, a short, plaintive wail that makes them shudder. Jacob turns to Magdalena.

It's all right, Maggie, he says. She'll be fine. We just got to give her some time.

Hosea eats two bowls of venison stew with carrots and juniper berries, and fresh biscuits to sop up the sauce. He offers to clean his own plate, but his offer is refused. Magdalena does the washing as Hosea tells them just enough of his and Tuley's story for them to understand that he won't be staying long. When they hear that he was once a preacher, they become interested. The conversation turns to the holiness church and Hosea asks Tobias about his faith.

Why do you do the things you do? he asks him.

Tobias thinks about this for a moment and then tells him the story of Charles Flint and their first time on Slaughter Mountain, figuring that this would be the best way to describe the whys and hows of the holiness church. But he tells it for another reason. He wants Jacob and Magdalena to hear how their father brought hope and goodness into his life and the lives of so many. He wants them to see that his life had a great purpose—to change the lives of others by bringing God and the Holy Spirit to them.

He tells the story of the Bowsky twins, and the big cobra and the day he was himself transformed. Hosea listens, interrupting from time to time to ask questions or tell parts of his own story that happen to coincide. The whole time they are talking, Jacob watches Hosea, the way his father taught him to do when he meets a man for the first time, and it doesn't take him long to decide what kind of man he is. Hosea's quiet, measured way of speaking signifies thoughtfulness and humilty. He doesn't waste his words. He is honest, and it is clear that his faith in God is profound. Like Jacob himself, Hosea seems to live in a perpetual state of confusion and pain. He is a man of questions, and a man who strives to better himself through close examination of his past actions and present thoughts, and also by the lives of others. Hosea Lee's a man who can be trusted and admired.

Baxter comes in looking tired and pale. His shirt is wrinkled and his hair is sticking up. His eyes are red. He goes straight for the stove and pours coffee into the first cup he finds and drains it in one long swallow.

She's asleep now, he says. Jacob, she's in your bed. Poor thing. It's all about time now. There's nothin' we can say—we just have to give her time. I'm thinking about taking her home day after tomorrow. Do you think that's safe, Tobias? It's been five days now.

Tobias shakes his head. He's tired. They all are.

I don't know, he says. It's strange, nobody coming up here all this time.

It worries me, Baxter says.

Well, if you go at night, it should be okay, Tobias says. Leave after dark. I don't figure they'd be settin' roadblocks or anything like that.

If they was to come, they'd have come by now, Baxter says. Don't you think? Either they don't know or they don't want to know.

They know, Sylus says. Re-election is what it is.

Maybe, Tobias says. Dave Brown won by a hair last time and half the town was up here that night. Could be they just want it to blow over.

Could be, Baxter says.

Who's they? Jacob says.

The sheriff, Tobias says. The law. When a man is killed, somebody's got to be accountable, even if it was an accident. But Sheriff Brown needs votes, and he might be thinking that arresting a preacher and a boy might not help his image.

There's another way to look at it, Hosea says. It could be he's waitin' on the state boys to step in. Something like this could get big if the newspapers get hold of it. They might of told him to stay put and watch the roads until they can get a man up here to take charge—a D.A. from Atlanta. That's how they do it. If they're planning on filing charges or anything, it might not be a local thing.

He's got a point, Tobias, Baxter says. They'd send somebody up from Atlanta.

Yeah, but it's been five days.

Five days is a blink of the eye for state goverment, Sylus says. This might go right on up to the governor himself, and that would take time.

Well, let's not get too far ahead of ourselves, Baxter says. We'll leave tomorrow after dark, after Rebecca sees the grave and has a chance to settle down. Jacob, does that sound good to you?

Jacob stands and goes to the window. He can see a good portion of the sky from this side of the house. He can see a sky full of stars and moonlight on the trees, but not the moon itself. The moon is on the other side of the house.

It sounds fine, he says. Momma should be home.

They should all be home, he thinks to himself. But I'm not going back. Not yet.

Out beyond the lights of the house, past the church and its moon shadow, in the flattened spot where the revival tent had stood, the field is frosted over, stiff as straw. Jacob runs his palm over the silver tips of the grass, squatting right where the pulpit had stood, gazing up at a single bright star. But the sky is no longer clear. Heavy clouds pass over, gunpowder gray and tinged with silver, moving slowly across big open patches of sky where moonlight streams down and the stars shine through. The star he's watching does not flicker. It's part of no constellation. But it has, beneath it, a smaller and less steady twin.

One of the big gunpowder clouds passes over these stars, and he counts aloud, until they reappear again. He counts slowly, at a pace that matches the rhythm of his heart. Sixty, one hundred, as many as two hundred beats before the stars reappear. Sometimes the clouds also block out the light of the moon, and the ground becomes suddenly dark. The shapes of the clouds and the shadows of trees move across the grass for a while until the ground is again flooded with light. Then the clouds drift away to other places, to block other boys' moons. Perhaps his daddy was never protected. All these years could have been luck. What if the spirit had never come? If the Holy Ghost was not in his father, then surely it was never inside of him.

A shadow falls over him and he sees someone that he thinks is Sylus, but then he sees the funny round hat, and realizes it's Hosea. The big man squats beside him in the grass and lights a pipe. Jacob can see it glow inside and he smells the cherry whiskey scent of Three Friars tobacco that some of the old men down at Shuck's still smoke.

Sometimes, Hosea says, I'd go out to a little spot I know, up on a hill, not as high as this one, but high enough, so I could see a clear view of the sky and the miracle of stars. And I could feel Him there. I could feel the Lord. I knew He was there, up in the sky, in the treetops, in the clouds, everywhere, and I got the tingle, that shivery feeling that presses up from inside and spreads out like a fever chill.

He puts the tip of his pipe to his lips and puffs at it. He squints at the stars.

I used to get that feeling a lot, he says. At certain times of the day, if the light was just so, or if one of my boys smiled a certain way. And when I read the Bible, too. Lots of times I'd feel like that, once a day at least, I'd feel it. I'd feel the presence of something bigger than all of this, and for most of my life I believed it was the presence of the Lord, I truly did. Now, I don't know. Could be it was just a need, a fear.

He taps the mouthpiece of his pipe against his front teeth and stands. His knees pop and he stretches, raising his arms up toward the moon.

My thinking was that all His creatures, everything that ever lived, was shootin' through me like a bolt out of the sky. So beautiful was that feeling. It was glory. It was truth. I'd choke up and cry from the joy of it, from the joy of living in a pure and perfect moment. And at those times a strange thought would come to me. I'd think that it would really be all right to die—right then I mean, at those instants. I'd just want to die in that state of bliss because of how perfect it was, how real. And I think it was communion. It was a revelation to me that not only are we alive, we are one, the whole earth is a complete and singular thing that's just beginning to become aware of itself. I don't suppose I'm making any sense.

Hosea squats back down in front of Jacob and smiles at him.

It took me a while, he says, to convince myself that what I was feeling was the Holy Ghost come to give me strength, and tellin' me it's all right to live and all right to die. Both. The promise will be fulfilled. In that other life, the next life, it all feels that way, every second of that next life, it's all that good. That feeling never dies. That's heaven, son. That's heaven. That's the light of man.

He sucks on his pipe and stokes the little orange coal. Jacob can see a tiny pearl of moisture at the corner of his eye. He watches it, until it falls.

I still believe that, Jacob, though it's been a long time since I felt it. He's kept it from me, the Lord has. I have transgressed against him, and my punishment has been deprivation. This is what I tell myself. But when I look at you, it comes back a little, that hope. What your momma says is true. You got it in you. You got what I lost. Don't let what happened give you doubt. You have to keep going.

Jacob stands and turns away. He never felt comfortable being the center of attention or talked about in this way. He picks up a stone. It's wet and cool. When he rubs it with his fingers, it grows warm.

I know what you're saying, Mr. Lee, he says, and I thank you for coming out here to talk to me. I know you wanna help. You're a good man, I believe. And I know that feeling you speak of, that chill, that joy. My daddy and Tobias have been chasin' that all their lives, workin' hard for it, prayin' for it, livin' clean and good lives just for that one chance to grab onto it, to hold it for a little while. You know, we call it the anointment, and that's how we do the things we do. But I'll tell you, Mr. Lee, a moment is enough. An instant is all you need. Folks shouldn't be chasin' what they don't wanna catch. I been livin' with that feeling since the day I was born, and you know that strange thought you get, about wanting to die? Well, I gotta fight that feeling every day.

He holds the stone in the palm of his hand. He stares at it and tests its weight. Then he hurls it into the woods and they listen as it crashes down through the trees.

My daddy died in that place you speak of, in such a moment. So I don't fear for him. I don't grieve, not for him. He died in the glory of what he believed was true. And we can't ask for anything better.

Jacob's feet are damp and cold from standing in the wet grass. The sky is now clear. There are no more drifting clouds to obscure it, and the whole time they've been talking he's kept his eye on the bright star above him, and its flickering twin. Hosea studies Jacob's face under that light. The boy's head does have an odd shape to it, and his ears are large. When he turns his head, the light of the moon falls upon him and he sees nothing but blackness in the boy's eyes. But they are not empty, or cold like space or stone. They're deep with the grief of a thousand ages, and pain—like the suffering eyes he once saw in photographs of chained slaves. His eyes, he thinks, have lost their innocence but are still pure. Like the eyes of the sleepless ones, the watchers of days gone by, brave witnesses to no small sin. He cannot look there for long.

Where you going, boy? he says. If it ain't here, then where? Don't you know you're the man now? Back home is your place, back home with your momma. She needs you. You're confused, that's all. But you go on home and you'll see. Listen to me now, 'cause I know. Home. Familiar trees, an old mountain, the walls with the pictures on 'em, and that same old smell of the house. You been gone too long. I know about that. You ain't gonna find what you're looking for out there. It's in here.

He places his palm on Jacob's chest, he pats it and smiles. He feels the boy's heartbeat, and more than that, he feels a heat burning deep inside him. Jacob places his small pale hand over Hosea's large dark one.

It's not about where I'm going, he says. Sometimes, it's just about not standing still. Moving toward something. Flying toward a light, burning your wings. What Momma needs I can't give her. Maybe what she needs is what she's getting right now. The Lord turned us all upside down, and he ain't done with us yet. She's got Maggie anyway, and Sylus and Baxter too. Having me around is just gonna remind her of Daddy. That's what she always said when Daddy was out on the road, that looking at me was as good as starin' straight into his eyes.

He removes his hand from atop Hosea's.

Mr. Lee, I appreciate what you're doin', but I'm not running. I'm going someplace, just like you. You have to go, don't you? It's unfinished business. Your story's not told. Well, that's how it is with me. I'm unclosed. When I go back home it will be for the last time. I don't ever want to leave again. So I have to do this now. It'll fester in me and make me leave one day, and by then it will be too late.

It's cold on the mountain now. Jacob pulls his collar closed.

And I think I should go with you, Mr. Lee, he says. To wherever it is you're going. I see a place in my mind, a place near the ocean, with tall, skinny trees and a stone castle where soldiers once lived, strange soldiers, that wore armor, and iron helmets shaped like spades. The walls of this place are thick, they're made from seashells and rock-hard mud. I see you there, in that place, and I saw you coming up the road too, that day you met my momma. I knew you were coming. I see things like that sometimes.

Hosea stares at the boy. He shakes his head and his eyes open wide. The boy is wise, he thinks, and smart. But he's more than smart. He's got that same mystical sense about him that he's seen in the old women and the Indian snake men he'd meet up in the hills.

You got some kind of intuition, boy, he says. I'll say that for you. You got somethin' in there. Lord, you do. You got a funny way of talking for a boy too.

He taps the bowl of his pipe with his ring finger, loosening the tobacco so it'll burn better. He puts the pipe to his lips and shoots out little puffs of smoke from the side of his mouth.

This whole thing's got me discombobulated, he says. I don't know what to think. Meetin' your momma like I did. The whole way I got up here was something that seems like it was meant to be. Findin' you, and this crazy church. Son, you are God's own mystery, and I confess, I'm at a loss for words. I just don't know what to think. You're just a boy, and I sure as hell can't say you can come with me. That ain't my place. Strange little boy like you, what do you think folks will do when they see us? I'll tell you what they'll do. They're gonna take one look at you and say I stole you outta some asylum, and they're gonna string this nigger up, is what they're gonna do.

Hosea shakes out his pipe by banging the bowl hard against his leg and blowing into it. He runs his pinky around the rim and puts it back into his pocket.

I'll say one thing for you, Hosea says. You got the Lord with you. He's lookin' out over you and showing you things. You were right about that place in your dreams as far as what I know, though I ain't never been there myself yet. Maybe you'd be good luck to me, maybe you'd bring me some of what you got. I don't know what it is, but you burn from within. I used to be like that.

He walks off toward the trees and stops a few yards short of them to look up at the sky. Then he laughs to himself. He laughs hard and long. Then he looks up the sky. He kicks at the grass and looks down at his boots. They're all shiny with dew. He turns and walks back to where Jacob is standing on the flattened grass.

If your momma says it's all right that you come, then you can come. but if she's against it, in any way, if she even so much as suggests that she might rather have you at home, then you ain't coming. Understand? Even if you run off and track me down, I'll just lose you again. Maybe you do see the place I'm goin', but you don't know the name, do you? Hosea smiles.

All I know, Jacob says, is that it's a holy name. A city favored by God.

Boy, your momma was right, Hosea says. You have gifts. You surely do.

Rebecca wakes early and makes them all breakfast. She doesn't cry once and even smiles a few times. She washes and combs her hair and puts on the one dress she brought with her, a white dress with a blue floral print—not at all appropriate for a woman in mourning, but beautiful and vibrant. It's a dress Charles gave her before Jacob was born, and she lights up the room with it on. It makes her feel better by wearing it.

Jacob brings her down to the meadow grave. Magdalena picks a bunch of wildflowers, and they walk together in silence, just the three of them. They leave her alone at the grave site, where she kneels to arrange Maggie's flowers on the stone. They stand off to the side and they hear her talking, but they don't hear the words. She kisses her fingers and lays her hand on the stone. She stands and motions Jacob and Magdalena to the graveside, where they clasp hands and pray. They do not pray for long. Rebecca looks up at the trees and out at the meadow beneath them.

This is the kind of place he wanted to buried, she says.

I know, says Jacob. It's a fine place for him.

But we won't be able to visit him, Magadalena says.

We will, Rebecca says. From time to time. Come on, let's get back.

Rebecca leads them back through the meadow, over the narrow trail to the mountaintop, where Baxter waits for them in front of the church.

When they get back to the church, Baxter takes her aside and explains the plan they made the night before. He tells her about the need for caution, and their conjecture about the sheriff and the D.A. They need to leave fast and, if possible, without being seen. She listens to him and nods, ready to go home, and he promises her that one day they'll return to bring her Charles back.

Jacob finds her packing her bags and takes her by the hand. He leads her out behind the church to the stone outcropping where he had stood with his father the night before the revival. It's a bright day. There's a gleaming river beneath a cloudless sky, and they sit together on a sun-warmed stone.

He takes her hand. I'm not goin' back with you, he says.

I know, she says. I can see it on your face.

I can't go home yet, Momma.

She squeezes his hand and pats his knee.

Don't explain, she says.

It won't be forever. It won't be for long.

You and your daddy are cut from the same cloth, she says. You got your voices to guide you. There's nothin' I can do to stop you from doing anything, and there never was. You're in God's hands. You've always been in God's hands.

You'll be all right, he says. You won't be alone.

He takes her hand and kisses it. He looks her in the eye and then kisses her on the cheek at the corner of her mouth.

I been alone most of my life, Jacob. I don't fear it anymore. The Lord has his reasons for everything.

I'll be goin' with Hosea, wherever that is.

Yes, of course. Hosea's part of something that's yet to unfold.

I asked the Lord for a messenger, Jacob says. Right before you came.

Well, you always seem to get what you ask for.

Momma, I will come home. I'm not goin' out to preach. Ever again.

Your father did what he believed deeply, she says. He did what he felt was right, and I never could compete with that. I'm not bitter. He died the way he told me he would. So it's no surprise to me. I knew it would be this way. Though it was always the snakes I feared most. I don't know why. Maybe because they were alive and I could see the death in them. I never did understand poison—though I suppose they're both the same in the end. A snake's just a poison machine that lives in the ground.

I never thought of that, Jacob says.

Well, don't dwell on it, Jacob. Don't let what happened to your daddy fester inside you. This is a new beginning for you, for all of us. I hope that what you're after out there ain't reasons. If it is, you won't find 'em. People die for reasons we sometimes never see or understand. It's like a ripple in a big pond.

I know it, Momma, he says. I'm not going off to figure out why Daddy's gone. But I do believe he died so that I could go. If I was to go home now, there'd be no meaning to it. Most folks would say he was punished. That he slipped up someplace, or misused the power of the Holy Ghost. But I think it's the opposite. I think he died as a reward for how he served him. Daddy chose how he was gonna go.

Rebecca stands and smooths down her dress. She walks out to the edge of the stone cliff. It's warm in the valley. The air shimmers below, and the river shines like a ribbon of steel.

Well, I can't say I want you to go, but I know you have to and I can't think of a better man than Hosea Lee to go with. He's got his own questions. And I'm afraid he ain't gonna find the answers he wants. But he's a good man. He'll heal somewhere. So will you. Watch out for each other.

They walk together back to the house. There's no breeze and nothing moves at all. The world at the top of Slaughter Mountain is stone still. Jacob can hear the pine cones cracking in the sun, heating up and splitting open. Baxter pulls the truck out of its hiding place and prepares for the ride home, checking the water and the gas and hoses and things. Hosea sits nearby, smoking his pipe. He sees them come and stands. Rebecca puts her hand on his arm but says nothing. She continues on up into the house. Hosea tells Jacob to be ready at sunset, that they will leave with the others, but in the opposite direction, down through the woods to the other side of the mountain where they are less likely to be seen.

21

THE MORTAR AND THE PESTLE

They sit together in the kitchen where it's cool, and they pass around a plate of cold ham, eating with their heads down. They don't eat much. Nobody even touches the spoonbread that Magdalena made, and she clears the table and sets it aside. She's got her father's dark hair but her mother's strong hands—long, thin fingers with the nails all bitten down to the quick. There's a good deal of ham left on the bone, and she cuts that up for later while all the men but Tobias lie down to get some rest before the trip back to Leatherwood. Rebecca remains at the table, making sandwiches with the leftover ham.

Jacob does not sleep. He gets his things together and packs his clothes, then goes outside to the lookout point. He watches the shadows move across the valley floor and counts hawks as he waits for dusk. He asks Jesus to give his mother strength and the Holy Ghost to get them all home. He keeps his eyes closed long after he's done praying and waits for the light to change. The evening wind comes, bringing with it the scent of pine resin and wet leaves.

His body's at rest, but his mind is fully awake. He can smell distant flowers and hear things better than a dog. He takes slow, shallow breaths, and after some time the old pictures come— black faces and gnarled oaks, small, jagged leaves and long, silhouette branches, blood-wet burlap and creosote-dipped ropes. He lets his mind go where it will and he sees the old woman's hands and a ladle full of brown soup. She's opening her mouth and she has the teeth of a young girl, bright white teeth. Her hair is loose and the color of milkweed sap. The sky outside the cabin is clear and silver as a chip of ice. The black faces turn white, the old woman is young, the sky ripens deep orange, and the oaks fade away, replaced in this vision by fiddleheads, young ferns that curl up from fine white sand and grow into giant cycads that bear fruit as big as a man's head. He hears the sound of water crashing down over stones. The sound of rushing water deepens and startles him out of his vision. It is only the evening wind in the trees.

The sun has dipped and the light has changed. The shadows in the valley have grown long. There are voices coming from inside the house. He hears the creaking sound of the truck's hood. When the engine turns over he knows it's time.

They gather at the chapel steps to say their good-byes. He kisses his mother and she smooths back his hair. He hugs Magdalena and shakes Sylus's hand. Baxter gives him a fatherly hug and grips his shoulders firmly.

Remember everything I told you, he says.

I will, Jacob says. I always do.

It's twilight, and the sky is that same silvery color it was in his dream. The big front fender of the Ford truck reflects that color and Jacob fixes on it. The truck backs up with a whine, and turns. A narrow blaze of silver light flashes and runs down the slope of the fender like rainwater, then it's gone. The fender's black again, and the truck rolls away. Spider paces and howls in the cargo bed, his neck out over the tailgate. He's yelping at Jacob as the truck pulls away, and he can see his momma waving through the back window, then Magdalena, also waving and yelling things to him he can no longer hear. They vanish under a canopy of pine boughs, and all he sees are the twin red beads of the tail lamps bouncing off down the darkened road.

Jacob sniffs at the air. The smoke from the tailpipe hangs around them. The cold mountain air keeps it down, keeps it still. He is momentarily engulfed in smoke until Hosea fans it away with a swipe of his hat. Tobias waits by the chapel steps holding Magdalena's spoonbread. There's no wind at all now, so they can hear the truck, far off, and for just a moment they see the sparkle of headlights as it winds its way back around the switchback below. Then it's quiet. Tobias holds the spoonbread out to Hosea, who takes it from him wordlessly. He stows it in his bag. The two men shake hands. Tobias runs his palm over Jacob's head.

Don't give up on on the Lord, he says. He won't ever give up on you.

He gave up on Daddy, Jacob says.

Is that what you believe?

I don't know, Jacob says.

I could say it was his time, Tobias says. I could say that the hour and the manner of our deaths is fixed and inescapable, and that each death serves not the deceased but the living. I could say that because I believe it. But I won't say it. We take a life for what it is. A person is born. And if he's lucky, he lives. If he's lucky, he understands the precious fragility of his life and strives to do something with it. We touch a thousand people, whether we know it or not. Ten thousand. We make a difference, each life does, and he knew it. And he was holy for that. Let not his death take away from this fact. He was alive and he was living. His mere presence made this small world bigger. His death is no more significant than his birth; it is but a moment in a collection of moments. Let us not be diminished by his passing, let us not despair, but celebrate, and allow ourselves to be filled by him, by eveything he was. And if we are all now in possession of some part of him, and we are, then God did not forsake him. He simply divided him among us, where he now lives forever, as a thousand little blessings that will spark and glow in the strangest of moments, when we remember, and will give us his voice, and pieces of his mind and his heart. How is that not a miracle and a blessing? How is it that you can remember such things and believe it is anything but something greater than ourselves reminding us that there is something greater than ourselves?

Jacob reaches out and takes his hand and holds it between his own two. He presses them together. He looks into Tobias's eyes, his tearful blue eyes.

I don't blame you, he says. The poison, the revival. It wasn't your fault. Don't blame yourself.

Good-bye, Jacob Flint. May you return from your journey a better man than I.

They walk together down to the clearing, out behind the chapel, where the revival tent had stood, and cross over to the other side of the mountain. They take the trail leading down to the meadow grave, where the taller pines line the ridge and loom over them with long shadows that stretch out before them like great toppled columns. Tobias walks with them as far as the meadow, and they nod a silent good-bye to each other. He watches them vanish into the cover of the high grass. When he can no longer see them, he walks all the way back up to the chapel and stands in the shifting light below the stained-glass windows where the pulpit had stood. He stands before the serpent chamber.

My Lord, he says. What have I done?

He tilts his head up to the light, to the stained glass. He watches the shadows waver—pockets of hot white amid a honeycomb of gold. Below him is the square hole where the pulpit had stood, but where now he sees the bent nails that were hammered back to render their tips harmless. He looks at the tile at his feet. He looks at the walls. He built this place with his two hands. He cut the wood, most of it, with his two hands, and he hammered many of the nails down through it, with his two hands. With his two hands he captured all the serpents that ever lived in the serpent chamber and constructed their boxes, and he made the wire cage for the rabbits, cutting a hole through the back wall with a saw. The apothecary he did make and assemble, and the poisons he did mix and the mortar and the pestle were extensions of his two hands who were given to him by God to hunt and skin and chip good knives out of stone. How far man has come. Not far enough, despite the Word and iron and clothes. He looks down at his hands. Hands that were gifts simply meant to grab, to hold, to hunt.

I am a killer now.

He sees the blood of Charles Flint on his hands. He sees the serpents and the poisons, from his hands, in his hands.

Keep your hands to yourself, Tobias.

The words of Nettie Cross. The words of mothers, the words of women.

Don't touch that, Tobias. Don't touch that part of yourself. Wash your hands.

Back then, when it was still possible to be cleansed by soap, they were hands, and they held, and they cradled, and they turned strange objects over before his eyes so as to guess at the workings of things—a pocket watch, a carburetor, the marvelous constructs of the paper wasp. When there was no wont and when there was no will his hands were beautiful instruments that delivered to him the world and its wonders. When did they become the deliverers themselves? When he took up that first serpent ten long years ago they became not tool users but tool creators. Charles Flint, who came to him through the woods from a train, dead by his poison, dead by his hands. And the symmetry of this is too perfect to ignore.

He spends the rest of the night cleaning out the poison from the serpent room, heaping it all into a great pile out where the tent had stood, with the empty snake boxes and the empty rabbit cage and the box that held the poison chalice. It all burns with a furious flame that glows at the edges with intense color, a supernatural shade of blue.

The moon is waning, but it's bright enough to see the ground, and they can navigate well. They take the path through the meadow, but they don't stop at the grave. They pass on through to the other side, to a stand of spruce and heavy thickets that aren't as deep or painful as they first appear. They cross into a new kind of terrain where there is no undergrowth, just pine needles and large stones that protrude from the ground.

The trees here are tall and narrow and spaced wide apart, and with the moon low on the horizon, their trunks are half-lit and their shadows cut across the path like railroad ties. They walk all night, stopping only to fill their bottles with fresh water at a little spring that forms a small, deep pool, where they immerse their hands to the wrists and suffer numbing cold.

Hosea doesn't talk or whistle and he's careful not to disturb loose stones or snap twigs. He knows how to walk in the woods. He moves fast but pauses often to observe some mark on the ground, or to wait at the edge of a clearing to watch and listen before crossing out into the light of the moon. He never loses sight of the stars. He navigates by them, and measures their distances with the palms of his outstretched hands. He's good at finding his way where there is no clear trail, and he has an animal's sense about direction and danger. He snakes his way up and around obstacles, seemingly lost, but never at all unsure or confused. Not once are they forced to double back. Even in the darkest parts of the woods he makes steady progress.

Jacob has little problem keeping up the pace, but he can't always see him in the dark. He loses him more often now that the woods are thick. So Hosea ties a white handkerchief around his neck to make himself more visible to the boy. Jacob understands why he dresses all in dark clothing. It's the best way for a black man to travel in these parts. Dark as a panther, quiet as a ghost, and cutting a trail that only a good dog could follow.

They reach a road before dawn and wait in the trees, watching for traffic. They sip the cool water from their bottles. Hosea checks the position of the stars. He gestures off to the right and they slide down the embankment and stand in the middle of what he figures must be old Route Eight. They walk for about an hour on a hard dirt road, rutted by rain and runoff, and come upon some deer feeding at the roadside. Two small does. The breeze is in their faces and the deer don't scent them. They watch them feed for a while. They can hear them pawing at the ground. Hosea raises an imaginary rifle and sights up on the biggest of the two does. She raises her head and faces them, her neck stiff, her ears erect. She knows something is there and stomps her foot. Hosea squeezes off a single shot with a whispered bang, lowers the imaginary gun, and then rubs his belly. They're both hungry.

The deer scatter uphill, making a racket in the dry brush. Hosea finds the trail the deer came out from, and they follow it a half-mile back. It's a narrow, and sometimes treacherous, game trail that is well traveled and worn but never more than a half-foot wide. It's tough going, but worth the effort, for they find an old Indian hunting camp beneath a stone outcropping. It's a huge shelf of granite protruding from the ground, forming a natural shelter in the lee of the hill. The stone roof above the old campfire ring is still black and there's a fine dry spot inside that's safe from wind and rain. It's a good camp that hasn't been used in years. Hosea drops his bag, takes out the pan of spoonbread, and leans back against the stone wall of the shelter. They eat in silence and fall asleep with the sun rising at their backs.

• • •

Hosea talks in his sleep. He calls out for Tuley and mumbles the names of his children. His dreams make him breathe heavy and he sweats. Jacob watches the strange way that his eyes move back and forth beneath his lids as his dreams conjure phantoms of grief and regret. It's hard to see the weak parts of a strong man.

At dusk, they leave the Indian camp and head out again on the deer trail. The wet grass droops over the path and soaks their trousers through to their skin. It's foggy, and a fine mist blows cold on their faces. They go back out onto Route Eight, keeping close to the tree line at the side of the road and watching the horizon for the flicker of headlights. Hosea does not walk as fast as he did the day before, and he no longer looks up at the sky. The fog blots out the stars. He did not sleep well. He staggers in the mist, rubbing the back of his neck and kneading his chin the way a man would when he'd stare into the open hood of a busted car. It's quiet in the fog. Their footsteps echo off the stone embankment on the other side of the road. When Hosea begins talking, it sounds like it's coming from above them, like a voice from the sky.

We're southbound, he says. In case you're wondering. Straight through the state of Georgia. We make for Atlanta, where we'll hop a train to Jacksonville.

Is that where she is?

No. We're going to the oldest city in these United States, where the Spaniards built a garrison a long time ago. That's where she's supposed to be, in a brothel inside that old fort.

Florida, Jacob says. Baxter says that in Florida the ocean's the color of a whiskey flame and warm as soup

He's right about that, Hosea says.

They walk on, crossing a glade covered in soft moss, and there is no sound other then their own breathing. It's cool and wet and hard to see the white handkerchief through the mist. Hosea stops and waits for Jacob to catch up.

The fog lifts before dawn and they find a dry place to sleep beneath an overhang of crumbling shale. They build a fire in this new resting place, the first of their journey, and they use it to heat water for tea. They eat beans from a can, corn fritters, and some dried apricots drizzled with honey. The morning warms. They don't need the fire except to heat the tea, but it's a good thing to have, and they watch it together. It's a pretty little fire, built low and burning hot. The label burns off the bean can and it boils over, hissing in the coals. Hosea spoons the hot beans onto the fritters. This is the last of the food they brought from Slaughter Mountain, but they're close to a town whose lights they saw from the road. Hosea thinks it might be a place called Garberville, but he doesn't know for sure. He has a map that he keeps folded in his Bible, a map so old and torn, and that's been wet so many times, that much of the print has worn away. He opens the Bible and studies the map by the light of the fire, running his fingers over the soft paper and mumbling the names of cities and railroad towns and the distances between them. Jacob can see the silhouette of the Floridia peninsula through the back of the map, a jagged, protruding appendage, like some withered finger pointing south.

Jacob pokes at the fire with a stick and the woodpile collapses. Sparks rise above their heads and are scattered by a gust of wind. Hosea folds the map slow and careful, the way he's done a hundred times before, never once taking his eye off the boy. He places it in his jacket pocket and thumbs the cover of the Bible. He looks off into the trees. It's bright out in the sunlit woods but still dark in their little cave. It's turning into a fine day.

Hosea rubs the bottom of his chin with his fingers, then drops an apricot into his upturned mouth. He looks at the boy. Jacob's deformity is enhanced by shadow and his head is turned in such a way as to cause a dark line to fall along his cheekbone at the outer orbit of the boy's bad eye. That bone, between his eye and his ear, is the culprit. It's sunken, pushed in just enough to destroy the symmetry of an otherwise normal face. The only thing that separates him from other children is really just an inch, maybe two inches, of warped bone. Hosea runs his finger down to a marked passage in his Bible and reads.

These all died in faith. Not having received the promises, but having seen them afar off, and were persuaded of them, and embraced them, and confessed that they were strangers and pilgrims on the earth. For they that say such things declare plainly, that they seek a country.

They watch each other for a moment. Hosea closes the Bible and holds it out over the fire, as if offering it to Jacob, but instead he drops it into the flames, where it upsets the coals and sends sparks and burning ash shooting up into the wind. The swirling red particles race up the shale overhang and fade in the light of the sun.

The Bible smolders and smoke wafts up from beneath its thick hide cover. The pages burn first, curling and crackling like dried leaves, but the cover is thick as a man's belt and takes longer to catch fire. It smells like a burning shoe.

Why'd you do that? Jacob says.

Maybe I'm done with it, Hosea says. Done with it all. Or maybe I wanted to see if you'd pull it out.

The sun has risen and the shadows have slipped away. Jacob's face is bright now, and Hosea can see the good bones, the bones that are not deformed. From this angle, he is perfect.

The town that they see from the road is not Garberville, it's a place called Hadley. They can read the name on the water tower from a mile away. They must have strayed too far east. They might have caught a bus to Atlanta if they'd found Garberville. Now they'll have to take their chances here. They violate their nighttime-only travel rule and go in by sunlight via a series of side roads that cut straight through Atlanta and on down through the Florida swamplands, ending in Ft. Lauderdale, at the sea.

They walk slow, watching the road, squinting at the rusty buildings on the edge of town. At one time there had been industry here. They see abandoned flatbed trucks listing on deflated tires and low shacks with jagged mud-stained windows and peeling tin roofs flapping in the wind. There are iron cranes mounted upon steel towers that swivel slow and squeal in the wind, and a row of armless gas pumps that stand like tombstones over graves of nameless men who toiled here when times were better in days long before Jacob was born.

The wind rises and whistles in the wires. Somewhere a screen door raps against a wall. Jacob wonders where the town has gone. There's nothing living here but paper wasps and feral cats. They walk through this place and round a bend where the road cuts off into a stand of trees. Beyond, there's a collection of clapboard buildings clustered around an old town square consumed now by flowering weeds.

They are road-worn and dusty and they've run out of water. Hosea has money and promises Jacob a hot meal and a night in a bed. But they find no rooms in Hadley. There's no need for hotels in a quarry town, and nobody rents to colored men no matter how much money they can pay. There's a diner on the square with a grocery attached. The windows are dirty and Jacob clears a spot on the glass with his sleeve. He peers inside. It's a whites-only place where large men with dirty faces hunch over their plates, making a racket with their forks and spoons. There's one waitress, and a cook whose tattooed arms he can see through a hole cut into the wall behind the counter. The waitress moves from one end of the counter to the other with a coffeepot in her hand. Some of the men talk to her. She doesn't answer them and she doesn't smile. Jacob goes inside. Hosea squats down and peers in through the spot Jacob cleared on the glass.

There's a cluster of small bells on the back of the door that jingle when it opens, and when it does the heads of the men all turn. The waitress looks up at him and spills coffee on the counter. The men pay Jacob no mind. The waitress puts the pot down and stoops to talk to him. She smiles at him and wipes the hair from his eyes. The cook rings a tiny bell. Jacob turns and points at Hosea outside. She cranes her neck to see out the window and stops smiling.

Who's that out there? she says.

That's Hosea, Jacob says. We're traveling together.

Why don't you sit right up here at the counter? I'll have Henry fix you some eggs.

Can Hosea come in and eat too?

We don't serve niggers, son.

Then where are niggers supposed to eat?

Boy, where you from? They got their own places. He can get himself fed up the road a spell.

She stands looking at him. Some of the other men at the counter have noticed him and are staring.

I suppose a boy like yourself takes a friend where he can find one, she says. I don't blame you. Why don't you sit for a little while? I know you're hungry.

Behind the counter is a display case laden with pies and rolls. Jacob's stomach growls. He looks at the pies. He looks back at the window. Hosea is gone.

I can't, he says.

Will you take a glass a lemonade?

All right.

I had me a little boy about your age, she says, and she pours him a tall glass of the cool drink. The Lord took him from me.

I'm sorry, he says.

I believe that you are, she says. Such a sweet little boy. Where you off to?

We're going to Florida. I'm going to see the ocean for the first time in my life.

Ain't never seen it myself, she says.

Jacob drinks the lemonade in one long swallow and wipes his mouth on his sleeve.

Thank you, ma'am, he says.

Wait, she says. Take this.

She takes a sweet roll from the display case, butters it quickly, and give it to him.

Thank you, he says.

You're welcome. If you come back this way, come on and see me. Ask for Jolene. And here, just in case.

She forces a crumpled dollar bill into Jacob's palm, folds his hand around it, and smiles.

I'll pay you back, he says. And he leaves through the door to the sound of the bells.

There's a shack beneath the water tower with a tin roof and a rusted sign that reads Brimstone Diner; a vestige of when the town was once called Sulfur Springs. Inside there's a group of old black men, who stop talking when they hear the door. Hosea removes his hat and wipes the dust off his coat. The old men stare at the boy. Hosea sits and Jacob takes a low stool opposite him.

The waitress comes over with a pot of coffee and a cup. She's young and smiling like a girl with a secret. She pours Hosea coffee. She's got small, well-shaped fingers, something that Gertie Bates would have noticed. Good for sewing, she'd have said. Her wrists are all bone. Her almond eyes slant down like a cat's, and her skin is dark and smooth. She's not wearing shoes.

They eat in silence and nobody stares. The waitress takes their plates without saying a word. They buy bread from her, smoked meat, cornmeal, and jam, and she wraps everything in waxed paper tied up with a string. She watches them from the awning window as they walk out over the empty lot, Jacob shuffling his feet in the dirt and raising up little plumes of dust.

There's no bus that runs through Hadley, and the trains only stop once a month for the loads of marble that keep getting smaller and smaller. What was once a mile-long vein has all but run out. The station closed when the Hadley Mining Company left town, and the little depot's now boarded up. A family of sparrows has built themselves a nest in the eaves above the ticket window, and somebody made a campfire on the platform that burned a hole clear through to the ground. They walk through the old station and out onto the tracks, leaving Hadley forever. They walk for a long time, looking for a spot where the train might slow—a sharp curve, a steep climb, someplace they can hop on. It's hot, and the tar bleeds up out of the railroad ties and sticks to their shoes. They walk until well after noon and rest in the shade of a coal tipple that's rusted through and leaning dangerously out over the tracks. They sit beneath it and eat. It's warm and quiet. They bunch their coats up behind their heads and cross their hands over their bellies. They shut their eyes and listen to a pair of crows jabbering back and forth to each other. Jacob feels in his trousers for the madstone. It sits in the corner of his pocket near his crotch and he can feel it pressing against his thigh. He feels a slight tingle there where the stone touches him and he shifts it over to the other side. Carrying it is like having the old woman right there with him.

After a while they hear a strange noise that Jacob doesn't recognize. It's a whirring sound, like a wire tossed in the wind. Hosea stands and gathers their things. Jacob sees nothing. He hears a metallic ringing come out of the ground at their feet.

Train coming, Hosea says.

Jacob stands. Hosea goes to the track and kneels. He touches the rail with his hand.

C'mon, he says. He takes hold of Jacob's sleeve and pulls him into the brush.

Can you run? he says

Sure, I can run.

Okay. When I say go, follow me out alongside the train. I'll hop into an open car and pull you in.

They hear the engines and soon see them—twin diesels pulling a good mile of boxcars, stretched out round a long curve in the track, brown, orange, and yellow, like a bright chain of beads. There's a half-dozen tankers and a few blue reefers, and a big flatbed with a folded crane. They keep out of sight. When the engines pass they can see the blackened face of the motor-man. He's smoking a big cigar.

The train rolls by them, moving faster than it looked when they saw it coming around the bend. Jacob counts off thirty cars before they see an open door. Hosea points to it and nods.

Go, he says.

They bolt out from their hiding spot and meet the open boxcar on a dead run. Hosea throws in their bags and swings himself up smooth and easy. He's done this before. Jacob can run fine when the ground is flat, but the gravel and the railroad ties make it hard for him to keep up. Hosea's hand shoots out from the open boxcar, and in a flash, Jacob's lying on his back on the cold iron floor.

They both lie there, breathing hard, and the first thing they notice is a terrible smell. It smells like something dead. Only the one door is open, and it's dark. The car is full of flies. They hear a sound too. It's a gurgling noise, a wet, raspy snort that is not coming from the train but something inside it. They both sit up and let their eyes adjust to the lack of light and before long they can see. On the other side of the boxcar is a man lying in a black puddle.

Don't move, Hosea says. He creeps over to the other side of the boxcar with his legs bent and his arms spread out against the violent motion of the train. He walks slowly. He sees blood on the floor, a great smear of it that runs from the boxcar door to the man lying in the puddle. He kneels above him and the train lurches forward, picking up speed. He does not linger there. He staggers back to where Jacob sits against the wall on the other side of the boxcar.

We gotta get out of here, he says. We gotta get the hell off this train.

He's shaking, soaked in sweat, and there's blood all over his coat.

Is he hurt? Jacob says.

Throat's cut wide open. Almost took his damn head off. I don't wanna be here when they find him. Hell, I don't wanna be here now. Can you jump?

Yes.

C'mon then.

The train is moving fast and the gravel below the boxcar door is a gray blur.

Take my hand, Hosea says. When you hit the ground, roll.

They jump. Jacob tumbles and tumbles and there's a bright flash of light as he smacks his head on a stone. He can't see for a moment, but he can hear the train. He finds himself lying in a thicket of berries. Hosea's sitting near the side of the tracks staring at the blood on the bottom of his shoes.

They wait a full day before the next train comes and they wait on empty bellies because they left the package of bread and meat on the train with the throat-cut man. They go to sleep hungry and wake up tired. When the next train comes along, they don't have the strength to run and they miss the first open boxcar. But the train slows, and they catch another car farther down the line. The car is empty, and compared to the last, it's fresh-smelling and clean. They fall asleep on a cold, hard floor, and Jacob wakes every hour with the sudden fear that they're still in the other boxcar. He keeps thinking he can hear the horrible sound of blood in the lungs.

At daylight the railroad cops drag heavy clubs along the outside of the boxcars and they can hear the sound of men shouting and the heavy doors sliding open as they roust the bindle stiffs and send them on their way. They hop out into the train yard. They're in Atlanta now. There will be food and soft beds on this night.

There's a café near the railroad called Raylene's, a colored place painted pea green inside and out. It's full of transients and porters from the trains. There's no menu, just a specials board written in chalk and framed photographs of famous steam locomotives on the wall. The food is good and nobody pays them any mind or looks twice at Jacob. The fry cook is an amputee whose right arm got in the way of an antitank round in a place called Elsborn Ridge in the Battle of the Bulge. He tells them that the next freight to Jacksonville departs at six o'clock. Jacob leaves him the paper dollar he took from the waitress in Hadley.

They wait where the fry cook told them to wait, in the shade below the water tower. Jacob reads the newspaper aloud. Hosea studies his map and the train comes right on time. It's easy to hop a train when it's still in the yard, so the car's full of men. There's six on their car and they're all drunk and loud. They're all white men. One of them is well-dressed. He sits by himself waving a thin-bladed knife around in the air. He's clean-shaven and wears a fine hat. He's very drunk. He cannot stand or even sit straight. His head bobs. He tells them all parts of the same stories over and over again.

They took my money, he says. Stole my papers, sent a man out to take back my goddamn car. That crooked fellow was just asking for trouble, nobody pulls a pistol on Lawrence Bodeen. Hell, I'm a bona fide war hero. I killed six Krauts for my Bronze Star and I'm a proud brother of the Alabama Klan.

The other men keep their heads down and try to sleep. When the Klansman notices Hosea, he fingers his blade and smiles. It's a fancy Italian knife with a retracting blade that he works with a flick of his thumb. If he could walk he'd be dangerous, but he can't even raise himself up off the floor to piss. Hosea keeps a close eye on him and after a while the man falls asleep. When he begins to snore, Hosea creeps over and removes the knife from his hand and hurls it out the open door of the train.

Would've killed somebody with that thing, he says. Probably already has.

Hosea wakes before dawn to the sound of a thousand iron wheels. Boxcar couplings pull at each other and clank from side to side. He hears chains rattle and the rhythm of squealing springs—a cacophony of wood, steel, and friction and the wheezing of drunken men. He sits up and finds Jacob looking at him, his eyes swollen red.

You didn't sleep, he says.

I couldn't.

How long's it been?

Three nights.

Hosea stretches, goes to the open door, opens his trousers, and pees. He sits back down and opens a packet of salt crackers and a tin of foul-smelling meat spread that they spoon out of the can with a slip of torn cardboard.

St. Augustine is where we're going, he says. We'll be there day after tomorrow, I figure.

The train shudders and slows. The wheels all whine and light floods in through the door as the trees at the side of the track disappear. They're crossing a tall bridge over a large body of water. The train rattles from side to side and cool, damp air rushes in, washing out the funk of men. Hosea smiles.

St. John's River, he says.

Jacob sits at the open door and watches the scenery move by. It's full light now and he can see all the that things that only hours before were just dark shapes in the night. All night long he watched black parallel lines shooting across the gap of the open door. Now he sees that those silver threads that cut across the sky are phone wires, power lines. If he closes one eye and looks at them right, they dip and roll like waves.

They cross the river into the outskirts of a city where there are homes and factories and mammoth structures of latticed iron, water tanks and billboards and all manner of industry. He sees roads and people—a man on a motorcycle, a boy fishing in a pond. Women hang clothes out to dry in the fenced-in yards of buildings made entirely of brick. All night long he'd been staring at the wires and the clouds, and now he can see the land. The air is different here. They're close to the ocean now.

Lawrence Bodeen wakes and staggers over to the door to vomit. He loses his hat. He tries to pee and makes a mess of himself. The train slows. They're coming into the Jacksonville train yard now. Nobody else is awake but Hosea and Jacob. They stare at Lawrence Bodeen.

Holy Christ, he says. He presses his palms to the sides of his head as if he might unscrew it. Holy Christ.

He turns to Jacob. You all got any water?

Jacob shakes his head and points over at Hosea, who offers him what's left in his jar.

Shit, when it gets bad enough that I have to drink nigger water, I'll just shoot myself.

Hosea stands and signals for Jacob to do the same. He walks over to the door where the man is standing. He's a full foot taller than the Klansman and he stands on sturdy legs. The man feels in his pocket for his knife. Hosea smiles.

Lose something?

You son of a bitch.

It's over there. Go on, get it.

Bodeen peers over into the dark corner.

Go on, Hosea says.

Bodeen goes to find his knife, and they jump off the train.

It's warm and humid in Jacksonville. They take off their coats and cut across the train yard to find a road into town. There are plenty of hotels to choose from, colored places too, and they pick out one called the Caroline because the sign says Baths and it's the only one that doesn't have a drunk passed out in the doorway. The room they get is small and stuffy and it smells of disinfectant. There's a Murphy bed in the wall in the same room as a tub with a cockroach sitting in the basin and another on the wall. The bugs don't move, even when they pull up the window shade to let the sunlight in. They just twitch the little hairs on the tops of their heads.

They both take a cool bath and lie out on the bed listening to a gospel show that's playing on a radio across the hall. The bed is old and worn, but it just might be the best Jacob has ever laid in, and on this night he sleeps. He sleeps all that night and when he wakes he doesn't remember the details of his dreams, but he knows he's had them. He can see latent images of faces, feel the sensation of movement and the not-so-vague notion that something bad has happened recently, and close by. The energy of bad dreams lingers in this room like the sulfur smell of a spent match. He looks over at the bathtub and the cockroach is gone. So is Hosea. His bags are all packed and ready to go but he's not in the room. Jacob dresses and runs water for a bath. Hosea comes in with coffee and a loaf of bread, and they eat. Jacob sits in the tub while Hosea reads the paper. Then they switch places. An hour later they're on a bus to St. Augustine.

22

TULEY

The bus runs loud and slow and fumey black smoke seeps up through the floor, causing Jacob's eyes to water. He closes them and sleeps deeply for the first time since he's left Slaughter Mountain. And the dreams come again. They run as fast and wild as the devil's own picture show.

He sees a dark shape in dark water, a large object, heavy, half-floating, half-sinking, a long ridge running down a slick, stippled, whale-backed shape, the wet, veinlike keelson along the hull of a rotten boat—a dory, a dink, blurred through the stagnant gloom of a millpond gone slack, the hull of the boat coated with luminescent green algae and nestled in a bed of flat brown weeds that curl up from the deep bottom like hair on a sunken corpse. The weeds sway in pond water still as resin, dark as wort, and he sees within this bed of water grasses a school of luminescent shapes. White-bellied whisker fish, walleyed and slick, spawned in the dark mud of the bottom, moving upward to the rowboat that slowly rolls over, spilling sheets of silver water and righting itself so that he sees inside where the old woman's potion box lies open on the broken transom. And his dream-self floats out beyond the boat and skims the surface of a lake, his eyes even with the glassy waterline and rising up over the bow of a new vessel entirely, a wooden ketch that cuts the blackness open and peels back sheets of crystal and green foam, gaining speed and pressing on toward the shallows until the boat drives hard onto a submerged stone and tears open so that he hears the sound of buckling teakwood like the muffled thunder of a far-off storm.

The color of the water changes at the depth where the light doesn't shine, and where things that sink disappear and things that rise take form. White becomes yellow, and black becomes gray. Shadows ascend from this place, the silhouette of mandrake roots, with armlike roots and legs stretched thin, writhing now among the opaque corpses of discarded men, whose clothing ripples about their limbs and clings to the swollen places on their bodies where the gut gases are trapped. He does not have to see their faces to know them. They are the men hanged in the Tyborn tree. He passes over them, onto the shore of the lake where a stream runs shallow over moss rocks, where a boy prods a paper boat with a willow branch, and he's flying above the paper boat and following the craft to a low falls where the stream leaves the woods and spills out onto a beach, joining with the sea at a tidal basin, where Spanish men stripped to the waist in white linen trousers fish from the shore and throw their catch to children whose own trousers are rolled to their knees. They bait their hooks with the flesh of ripe peaches, casting them beyond the place where the water swells and crashes, and an old Spaniard shows him how to bait a hook with fruit, speaking to him in a strange but beautiful tongue that he can somehow understand.

Te haré a pescador de hombres.

I will make you a fisher of men.

Then he wakes. The bus shakes from side to side, and he rouses to the sound of his squeaking seat, his head on Hosea's arm.

We're almost there, Hosea says.

Jacob kneels on the seat to see who else is on board the bus, and finds that every seat is taken up by a person with sad, hungry eyes. The people on this bus are more desperate than he. They have their own afflictions. Their eyes droop, their clothing is permanently stained, and they bear the scars of bad decisions and poor timing much prouder than Jacob bears his own. Toothless, armless, bent, crooked, they sit stump-faced and silent, like the victims of a wrecked train. But they are not ashamed and Jacob draws no attention among them. For all they know, he was a dropped child, an inbred, or just another in a long line of badly beaten boys.

The bus trembles and stops. He can hear a sound like a gas valve opened, a long hiss of steam. A man talks through a speaker outside the window, but the words are garbled and he cannot understand. It's raining now. Men turn up the collars of their coats. They all stand in their seats, waiting for the aisle to clear, and he can smell struck matches and fresh-lit cigarettes. They move slow, their shoes beating a hollow rhythm on the rubber-coated deck of the bus. They descend into a depot so crowded that all Jacob can see is the gum-speckled floor. He holds on to Hosea's coat and they file into a public toilet, where they piss into a trough loaded with fresh ice. Men cough and fart and the ice clicks like beads as it melts.

He holds the arm of Hosea's coat beneath the depot awning and watches the rain fall. They wait as buses unload. Hosea looks up at the sky.

Rain comes and goes quick here, he says. Squalls off the sea.

When it clears, they move on. Some folks get into taxi-cabs, others duck into waiting cars. Most just walk away. Hosea moves out into the humid air and heads toward the sea. Jacob follows. They are close to the water now; he can smell it. He can hear waves crashing against a seawall far away, and the sound of shorebirds. He rounds a corner and sees the ocean for the first time.

A rush of cool air washes over him. His skin tingles. The gray-green sea is darker than he imagined, foamy, seething from the passing storm. It breathes and rises, sighs and falls, moving like no river. It roars and hisses and sprays him with a fine cool mist. His ears vibrate, and he is filled with that same feeling he gets when the Holy Ghost comes to him. He trembles with joy.

There's a white beach curving out before him, and those slanted trees without limbs he saw in his dreams. It's all there, just as he saw it, with the sunlight changing as the clouds pass over and everything beyond the beach silver and white and jade green. The undulation of the water makes it sparkle. The heaving swell rises and becomes momentarily blue. Everywhere he looks he sees a palette of shifting color and reflected light. Every cathedral ever built by man was a failure compared to what he now sees before him.

The beach stretches off in a bright curving slash that ends at a walled garrison built upon the rocks a mile away. It has high gray walls of mortar and stone and towers, and cannon jutting from slots cut into the walls where soldiers once stood at arms with pikes. It is an ancient structure that speaks of lost empires and great sieges and lives ruined in the name of God. Parts of the wall have crumbled and fallen into the sea below. It is storm-battered and neglected, and he can't imagine people living in such a cold and broken place as this.

Castillo de San Philippe, Hosea says. Built by the Spanish but occupied by the British and French. It was an armory once, and a prison during the Spanish-American War. This place has stood here for three hundred years.

They walk over the beach and up onto the rocks below the garrison. They cross a wooden drawbridge over a dry moat in order to get inside and knock upon a heavy door of blackened wood. It's just past noon. Nobody is expected this early in the day. There's a peephole cut into the door and after several minutes of knocking it slides open to reveal a large eye. From inside, they hear the voice of a man.

We closed, he says.

I have a friend that lives here, Hosea says.

Everybody has friends here. Come back tonight.

Mister, I walked all the way from Mississippi. I didn't come for that kind of company. You got a girl in there goes by the name of Tuley?

No answer from the eye.

She's got three children, Hosea says. Two boys and a little girl.

Who're you?

Their father.

The peephole shuts with a loud clack. The man throws back a heavy bolt and opens the door. He's a Creole, bigger than Hosea, with dark, shiny skin. He studies Hosea's face and nods.

The little one, he says. She looks just like you, keeps your picture in her room. The boys take after their mother.

Can I see them?

Little one's out and the mother's asleep. Come back at six o'clock.

Where are the boys?

Come back later, the man says.

Hosea watches him. The man's got big hands and big lips and arms strong enough to kill. His eyes are deep set. Animal eyes. Most men would back down from this man. Hosea offers him his hand and they shake.

Hosea Lee, he says.

I am Ephrem. he says. Who is the boy?

His name is Jacob Flint, Hosea says.

He yours too?

No, he's a friend.

Okay, he says. Come back at six o'clock. If you need to rest, go to this place.

The man hands Hosea a card. Tell them you spoke to Ephrem.

He sends them to a place called Belle's Floridian, and Ephrem's name gets them a good meal and a bath. Hosea shaves and Jacob has his hair cut so that it no longer hangs down in his eyes. They take a cabin on the beach and rest in the cleanest beds they've slept in yet. They take their supper in the shade of a mimosa tree, watching the waves. It's quiet here because it's not the season for visitors. Jacob lies in a hammock, kicking his legs slow. The breeze comes off the ocean and rustles the little pink mimosa flowers, the petals soft as hairs blowing down on their heads and in to their laps. They doze here until a far-off bell chimes six. Hosea sets off for the fort alone, into the waning light of the day as Jacob falls into a restless sleep.

He sees through the eyes of his father. He looks down at his hands and sees his father's thumbs, his squashed, moon-shaped nails, wrapped around the body of a fat snake. He stares into the eyes of this reptile, holding him two-fisted by the neck; its white coils bulge, its long belly muscle rolls. Beyond stands a congregation of dark-skinned men. Their shiny black faces are turned up to the light of a rag torch, their flickering eye shine silver as stars and more than familiar. The dead will not go away.

Charles Flint had his own special way of breathing when he handled the snakes. He inhaled through his nose, exhaled through his mouth, and paused in between. He hears this now as his father raises the big serpent above him. The congregation of long-dead men stands, and Jacob sees their unmarred bodies for the first time, their clothing unstained, their limbs unscarred. They're holding their hats in their hands and they have shoes on their feet and from their mouths issue the collective voices of salvation. They hum a low, mournful kind of song that is soothing and soft, the way a momma puts a baby to sleep. They sing with joy and sway slowly with their eyes closed, rocking from side to side and stomping their feet in rhythm to his father's slow breathing, to the hiss of the snake.

The dream changes and he now sees through the eyes of the serpent. He can still hear the men moaning and his father breathing, but he cannot see the same way he saw before. He now has the vision of a snake. He does not see faces, only shadow and light, dark shapes and gray splotches. The torch sputters and he perceives the outline of a man. He senses the warmth of a living body. He perceives hands and fingers and legs and feet. He knows where everything is because the patterns of heat read like a map in his new reptile mind. The burning he feels on his belly are the pads of his father's thumbs, holding him, and he knows he is close to his lips. He can feel the warm breath. His father lowers him into his mouth. Night becomes day. Light floods in, and again he can see through his own human eyes. He sees a flat, muddy river running before him. In the water, his father stands waist deep with his arms stretched wide, waiting to receive men for baptism. They are lined up on the bank of the river, still singing, still stomping their feet. One of the men wades out into the river, and his father takes his head in his hands.

Whom do I take to the water with me? he says. Who comes to the shore for redemption?

Elias Simms, the man says, and he is baptized. His father lays him down beneath the water but does not pull him back up. The man disappears beneath the water, and another man wades out from the bank. His father takes him by the head in the same way and asks again:

Whom do I take to the water? Who comes for redemption?

Percy James, the man says, and he is baptized the same way, sinking below the water and not returning. This goes on and on. The line moves but does not shorten, and many men come, with many names, all of whom he's seen before, scratched on the inside of the hanging tree. William Watts, Jefferson Clay, Horace Biggs. They all vanish in the muddy water and their breath comes up slow as catfish bubbles. He wakes to the sound of faraway bells.

When the church bells ring six o'clock, Tuley sends Pauline down to the beach with her net. She puts out the lamp and listens for the sound of the garrison doors. Then she takes off her clothes and waits for him by the light of a single candle.

When the door opens she knows it is he and she does not turn. She holds her breath and waits. The ceiling is too low for Hosea to stand. He crouches and shuts the door behind him, and the candle flame blows over and makes Tuley's shadow waver and stretch on the curved wall. He watches her, and he is not unmoved. He could very easily forget everything between then and now. She looks fine, beautiful still. In this light there is no distance and there is no time. The room is small, with just enough space for her bed and a chest of drawers with a swivel mirror mounted on top. Her clothing is draped everywhere and cheap jewelry hangs from a peg on the wall. She has a small Victrola inside a wooden box and a heap of records lying on the floor. Tuley runs her hands up from her thighs to her belly and pauses at her breasts. Hosea shakes his head.

I didn't come for you, he says.

She opens her eyes and lets her hands fall. She turns and faces him. He stands in shadow, and she cannot see his face.

I thought you was someone else, she says.

Hosea can see her face now. She's still smoking, and he can tell she's been drinking too. The years of living in the night and sleeping in the day have aged her skin. Her eyes sag, and there's a streak of silver in her hair.

So you found me, she says. Why'd you come?

Don't make like you don't know.

You wanna know why I left?

That don't matter anymore.

I left because I couldn't live in that house. I couldn't live with being judged. So don't say nothin'. Preach to the Indians. Go save a worthy soul.

I never judged you.

I judged myself, you fool. Living with you was a burden I could no longer stand.

You didn't have to take the children. You could've walked away on your own.

She turns away from him and sits down on the bed. She rolls a cigarette and lights it and sucks on it hard.

I never would have made it without them.

I want to see them, he says.

She draws on the cigarette and the room fills with smoke. She won't look at him.

Pauline's down on the beach.

Where are the boys?

They're not here. They left over a year ago. They live some-where over by the river. They come once a month to give me money.

By the river?

In a house, with a man.

What man?

She looks at him now and there's fear in her eyes, and it's not him that she's afraid of.

Tuley, what man?

A man who loans folks money.

How much did he loan you?

More than I can ever pay back.

Where are they?

She stamps out her cigarette and goes to roll another, but her tobacco pouch is near empty.

Goddamn, she says.

Tell me, Hosea says.

A man named Frank Dean runs a place called Gray's. They work for him, and I don't mean sweeping up. That Micah's got a knack for things mechanical. He can open locks and start cars without keys. And Josiah, he's almost as big as you are. They're clever. They got aspirations. They ain't like you, Hosea. Those boys are going places by a different road entirely.

And Pauline?

She's on the beach, like I told you. She likes it down there, catches little fish in a net and draws their pictures in a book. Keeps a jar in her room with crabs and such.

Tuley stands and comes to him. She looks up into his eyes.

You still look good, Hosea. Every time I see you, I just go soft inside.

She puts her arms over his shoulders, but he pushes her away and backs toward the door.

You never did think about nothing but what was right there in front of you, he says. All you are is all you see. You destroyed yourself, and worse yet, you corrupted the boys. You're nothing but a weak little girl, and I can't stand the sight of you. You're gonna die here, Tuley. You're gonna die here alone, and the saddest part is that I don't feel pity. I just don't care at all.

Jacob gets up out of the hammock and sits there for a while, breathing fast. He stands and listens to the ocean and the gulls. Without thinking, he walks to the sea. He climbs into the windswept dunes overlooking the beach. The tide is low and so is the sun. The wet sand below the waterline shines like ice, and in the water, he sees the dark silhouette of a girl. He moves closer to watch her.

The girl is pretty and tall. He's never seen a girl with such fine features, such dark skin. She stands knee-deep in a tidal basin holding a hand net like a shovel, just above the surface, poised there, waiting, peering down into the water, her legs bent, her head cocked to the side. She's still as an egret. The long muscle on the side of her thigh is taut and ready to spring.

From the reeds above the high-water line he watches her fish. Her legs are long and her arms slim but strong. She looks like Hosea. Her profile is the same as his. He knows that it must be his daughter, Pauline. She is graceful and quick with the net. Each lunge is a well-practiced and elegant motion that begins with a tilt of her head, followed by a flash of her arms and a flick of her wrists. The net always comes up sagging with shimmering minnows. She squats in the shallows and inspects her catch, keeping the pocket of the net just below the waterline. She picks out fish she does not want and drops them back into the lagoon. She brings the rest to a bucket waiting on the sand. Then she wades out to a different part of the tidal basin to stalk another school of fish.

He waits for her to come up out of the water with her next haul of fish. He comes down off the dune and walks out to greet her, but he's unsteady in the sand, and he stumbles. He rolls over and over, but gets up quick, spitting out the sand in his mouth. By the way he's dressed, she takes him for a hobo dwarf until she realizes he's just a boy. He falls over again and she runs to help him. Her hands are cool from the water, and he can feel how strong they are as she helps him to his feet. He brushes the sand from his clothes, and she watches him, shading her eyes with her palm.

You all right? She says.

Yeah, I'm all right. I just fell in the sand.

Are you drunk?

No, I just never been on the sand.

Never been on the sand? Where you from?

Tennessee.

You from Tennessee?

I just said I was.

I was born in Tennessee.

She looks at him and reaches out to touch the side of his face. She runs her hand along the crooked bone beneath his bad eye. Jacob flinches.

Were you in an accident? she says.

He rubs the part of his face she had touched. He can still feel her hand there.

No, I was born this way.

Scarred from birth, were you? Look what I have.

She lifts her shirt and there's a puffy slash on her belly just below her navel.

That's where Sanchero took out my spleen. It hurt like crazy.

She kicks at the sand. She has the bucket full of seawater in her hands and Jacob can see the tiny fish within. They're small, silvery things, little matchsticks that flash like mirrors as they swim.

Who are you, boy, and what are you doing down here? You spying on me? Up there in the grass? I seen you up there. You're kinda young to be out on the road by yourself. Your daddy with you?

He looks out over the tidal basin where she was wading before. He can see the waves breaking out on a reef. He hears them crashing.

My daddy's dead, he says. And I wasn't spying, I was just watching.

Ain't that the same?

No, he says. Watching does no harm. I gotta go, he says.

Did my brothers send you down here to keep an eye on me?

I don't know your brothers.

Well, who are you, then?

My name's Jacob Flint. I was just looking at the ocean, that's all.

Well, there it is, she says, and gestures toward the water.

Jacob nods.

Yup. There it is. I gotta be going.

He walks back up to where he was standing before. She waits for him to crest the dune and then goes back and empties the bucket into the tidal basin. She watches the fish swim away and turns to get her net. She looks back to see if the boy is still there, but he's gone. Standing there on top of the dune is a man, in the same spot Jacob had been before. He's a tall black man wearing a funny hat. Hosea walks down to her. When he gets close, she looks into the same eyes from the photograph she keeps in her room.

Daddy? she says.

Jacob watches them from the dunes. They talk for a while and walk off down the beach together. He waits for them to get far enough down the beach so they won't see him come down to the sea.

He stands in the water with his cuffs rolled up, watching the surf crash and the big white birds with the crescent wings wheel and loop above the foam. The seabirds cry out to each other, hundreds of them, sleek and white as moon glow. They swoop in graceful arcs and dip their heads neatly. He's never seen birds so clean and white.

He wades out deeper and feels the pull of the current. Tiny bubbles tickle his legs. Sand rushes beneath his feet and he can feel the power of the ocean, the strength of tides. He wades out to his chest and raises his arms, reaching for the sky. He shuts his eyes and listens to the waves. Light flashes. He can smell and taste the brine. Water swells to his chin and crashes over him. He rolls beneath it, awash in perpetual thunder, swirling like a leaf.

He floats beneath the waves, in a bliss unlike that of the Holy Ghost, unlike that of anything he's felt before. He opens his eyes and watches the blur of surf and sand and a thought comes to him, right there in the midst of the torrent. He recognizes the joy of living. He no longer wishes he had never been born.

They sleep in the fort on blankets spread out on the floor of Pauline's room. It's a vaulted chamber off the main corridor constructed from the same ocean limestone as the battlements that face the sea. Daylight does not reach this place, but the sea breeze blows in through cracks in the walls and makes the oil-lamp flicker. The little flame jumps, and shadows bounce on the walls where condemned men once carved passages of scripture and the names of their sweethearts. When the lamp blows out, the darkness is complete.

Jacob lies awake and listens to the sounds the stone walls carry to him. Hosea sleeps by his side. He hears all kinds of things, not just words. He hears the cries and laughter of women, the groaning of men, glass breaking, pleas for mercy, and other things he can't name. He cannot sleep in so complete a darkness, and the noises continue on through the night.

Much later, when there is quiet within the fort, he can hear the waves crashing on the outer walls, booming like the muffled roar of antique guns. In his mind, he sees a fleet of wooden ships—Spanish caravels, plumes of smoke. Men died here, just like in the tree. He can feel them in the walls. They have stories to tell him. But he will not listen. He will not sleep.

When the sun rises he does not see it come up. Within this place there is no night or day. But he feels it somehow, there is the sensation that outside, beyond the walls, the world has changed. The sea itself tells him that, the pitch of the waves is different, and he can hear the white birds cry. Doors begin to open. Old hinges squeal as men wake to return home and the whores get up to bathe. Then his door opens and somebody comes inside.

He pulls the blanket up over his head and pretends to be asleep. He hears a match strike and sees the faint glow of light.

He peeks out the side of his blanket and sees a woman. He can see her feet and hear her breathing. It's the woman in the picture that Hosea burned along with his Bible. It must be Tuley. He lies very still. She goes back to the door and opens it, and a draft blows in from the corridor. He thinks that she might leave, but she does not, she shuts the door again, very carefully, so as not to make any sound. She turns and he can see her now. From his little cave beneath the blanket he can see her face, and it is true what he had told him, that her eyes are impossible to look away from, that her beauty runs deep from her eyes, that it pours out through those sad, dark places. Her eyes look to him like they were stolen from a picture of Jesus, sorrowful, wise, and filled with tears.

She is barely dressed, and he sees on her parts of a woman he has never seen before. He can also see the black pistol she holds in her trembling fingers. It takes two steady hands to hold a gun that big and she's so scared that the barrel shakes like a dowser's wand. She pulls the hammer back and draws a bead on the sleeping Hosea.

Courage does not think, his daddy told him. Courage acts.

He throws back the blanket and they see each other, in the candle flicker, his big eye, rolling now like it hasn't rolled in such a time, so wild and insane that it makes her shot go wide. It sounds like a lightning strike in the tiny chamber of stone. There's an endless echo and the smell of powder comes home to this place. Pauline shrieks. Tuley cannot turn away from the face of the pale boy and for a moment her lips move, as if to speak, but no words come out. Hosea swipes at her pistol hand and takes her to the ground. The gun clatters on the stone floor and he hears Hosea saying, God, my God.

Pauline crouches in her bed and all Jacob can hear now is the incessant ringing of the gunshot in his ears. The pistol shot went off the curved wall and found his leg. His leg is numb at first and then it feels like it has burst into flames. His hand comes up wet from the place where he feels the fire. His fingers are slick with blood and something else. There is a grittiness to the blood and he becomes terrified at the thought that it could be bone. He can feel the slug in his thigh like a white-hot coal. But then, strangely, he hears drums, pounding, pounding. Fists rapping on the door, a cold draft from the corridor. Many hands lift him and he floats away.

They call the man Sanchero and they say he has very good hands for this kind of thing. He's good at finding fragments of lead and picking out little shards of bone no bigger than a hair. He keeps two fingernails long for this purpose, the one on his pointing finger and the one on his thumb. With his right hand, he can go where the forceps cannot go. He can feel things that are alien to the human body, objects that do not belong. His fingers are very sensitive. And his voice speaks to Jacob as if from a dream.

Steel cannot feel, he says. I will not use the forceps. Do not worry. The eyes of God are in my fingers. I hope that you do not mind if I talk so much because that is how I calm my nerves.

His moustache is long and gray, but he is not old, that's what he tells him. The gray is from the war.

The secret to a man's age lies in his fingers, in the knuckles, and on the back of his hands. The hands cannot lie, he says. I learned that in war. Which war? All of them. Pick a war and I was there. That is how I learned to remove bullets from the bodies of men, by helping surgeons at the front. Perhaps it is not good to tell you this now, but I am not a doctor. I can do many of the things that doctors can do, and I can do them better. I deliver babies sometimes and I tend to the sick, but mostly I am called upon for things such as this.

I undo the damage from the anger, he says. I am not a healer, I am a repairman. I close wounds inflicted by knives and broken glass. I work with needles and sutures, and with my bare hands I stop blood. I am a man who keeps quiet, a man who can be paid. They call me to the brothels and the gambling parlors and the places where men are sometimes killed. But I will not talk about those places, I talk only about wars and the strange and terrible things I've seen people do. I have seen miracles and I have seen many people die, but I have never seen a boy withstand such pain.

He works for a long time on Jacob's leg. The bullet is in a bad place and he must not rush. Pauline sits by Jacob's side, holding his hand, wiping his face with a damp cloth and soothing him with songs. He is in a lot of pain and the whiskey only helps a little. It's Pauline that makes the difference, her voice and her touch, but then it gets bad. His vision blurs. Sanchero's voice warbles and slows. He sees stars and hears the ocean and he prays for his life. He summons the spirit, just like that night in the woods when Poppa Hooch almost died. He drifts in and out of consciousness, and in this state he sees many things.

Sweet flag and the madstone, the wire mesh cover of the serpent box, his daddy's Bible, and the Judas pole. He sees the old woman, he can feel the touch of her hands, and from her bony fingers flows the warm medicine promised by God. He feels Jesus and he hears the voice of the Holy Ghost telling him he will be healed. And he hears his father.

Good night, Jacob. Wash your hands, always wash your hands, son. Fish keep best in the cool of the shade. Go to sleep now, there's time tomorrow to read that book. Close the light, and go to sleep.

Sanchero digs deep with his fingers and finds the splintered slug. He removes it and he removes the strange fragments of pumice he finds in the wound. He stops the bleeding and sews him shut, and not once does Jacob cry out, or even flinch. He has never seen a boy like this, a boy so calm, so still, with a pulse so slow that the blood hardly flows.

When it's over, Sanchero will not speak of it. He usually

likes to brag about his work. But it was not his work that saved this boy.

This boy, he says, he heals himself. He is very lucky. Lucky for the stone he had carried in his pocket. A strange stone. For the bullet was deflected away. Had it struck the big artery there, this boy would have surely died.

Jacob sleeps with Pauline at his bedside. Tuley's locked up in her room. Hosea goes into town to look for his sons and finds them just where Tuley said they would be, at a tavern called Gray's. It's an old structure, long and narrow, built upon pilings out over the river. It sags in the middle and leans toward the water like it might just slide back down and swim away.

The boys are tall but they still look like the boys he remembers. They've got the bodies of men but their faces haven't changed. Beneath their beard stubble, they're still boys. They smoke cigarettes and play cards, and he watches them for a long time, listening to how they talk. They're good-looking and popular and they dress well. Skinny girls hang from their arms. They spend money and they drink and they exercise no discretion with word or action. They do a fine job of playing at being men. They discuss their business in the loud and careless manner of young drunks, and what he hears makes him want to weep. They run liquor and pimp whores. They rob homes and stores. They hurt people who owe them money. He hears them talking about the murder of a man.

It is far worse than he had feared. They are not mere delinquents; they are true criminals. The boys he once led around on the back of a mule, with straw hats on their heads, now wear felt hats and carry guns. He will not look at them anymore. He will not speak to them or stay in this place any longer. He cannot save them. Not now. Jacob must be taken home, and Hosea must consider as fact that he has lost his boys for good.

He approaches them, and he stands at the head of the

table where the taller one, Josiah, is staring intently at his cards. Micah, the youngest, notices him first. He slaps his brother's chest with the back of his hand. The boys look up at their father.

Do you remember the time, Hosea says, when I came into the barn and found you with that cat?

They look at each other. They don't say a word. The small crowd around them goes quiet.

The things that you did and the things that you do, Hosea says. You shame me and you shame yourselves. You were cruel little boys. You learned somehow that pain is a form of power you could use to get what you wanted without having to wait for it. You got that from your mother, and now you're lost, all three of you. I shouldn't blame her. A girl can't raise a man, and I knew what she was. And you became her. But I didn't come here to preach to you. I came over here to tell you that you will discover another form of power much stronger than what you wielded on poor Gip the cat. Do you remember his name? You gave it to him, Micah.

What the fuck you come in here talkin' to me about cats? Micah says. Where have you been, old man? Where were you?

I was out there looking for you, boy. I haven't slept in the same bed twice since the day your momma stole off with you.

Josiah slaps his card down on the table and pushes back his chair. He stands and faces his father.

What?

I don't know what that woman told you, Hosea says. But she took you from me and I've been hunting you.

Your lies stink like the shit you are, Josiah says.

Would you even know a lie if you heard one?

I'm lookin' at one now.

Your momma won't look you in the eye and tell you anything but the truth as I stand here telling it.

What the fuck you want from us? Josiah says. Get out of here before I keep my promise and open you up like I opened Gip.

I'm going, Hosea says. And I'm taking Pauline. If you get in my way I will do what all the laws of God and nature restrict me from doing. I will destroy you, my own flesh. So pull those pistols now if you're going to, draw your pocketknives, boys. I won't roll over on my belly like Gip. I simply came here to see with my own eyes what you have become, and to tell you that I will welcome you back when you've recovered from these delusions. I'll welcome you without judgment and you'll always be my sons.

There is silence in the room, and the other card players are watching the brothers Lee to see what they will do.

Go on then, Josiah says. I'll talk to Tuley. And don't think I can't find you.

You watch her eyes when you ask her, Hosea says.

I know what Tuley can do, Josiah says. And I do know a lie when I hear one, which is why you're walking out of here, old man.

When you're ready, Hosea says, you come find me.

He turns and walks through a quiet crowd of gamblers and whores who do not part for his passing.

When he gets back to the fort, there's nobody working the door. The corridors are empty, the rooms are open, and nobody answers his call. He shouts for Ephrem and all he hears back are the echoes of his calls. He walks through the courtyard, across to the garrison. He opens the door and enters the corridor where he sees Sanchero rushing down the hall. His thoughts race to Jacob.

Is it the boy? Hosea says.

Sanchero shakes his head. The boy is asleep, Sanchero says. The boy is good. But I must tell you something. No, I cannot tell you—you must see for yourself.

They hear commotion coming from Tuley's room, and

Hosea rushes inside to find the tiny chamber filled with people. Ephrem is there, and old Madame Genieve. There are several women in states of undress, and Pauline is sobbing on her knees. It's so crowded in the tiny room that at first he does not notice Tuley floating in the air above them, with a velvet belt tied around her neck and slung through a rusty eye-hook above.

23

LEATHERWOOD

Rebecca sits alone in the Bible room. It's nearly dawn and she hasn't slept since she got the message from Hosea that they're safe and coming home. When the car pulls up in front of the porch steps, it scatters the chickens and raises a dust plume that for a moment obscures the vehicle entirely. It's a black sedan with Georgia plates. Hosea opens the rear door and pulls out a handmade crutch, leaning it up against the side of the car. A girl steps out from the back. She's tall and pretty, and she leans in to help Jacob, who lays his hand on her shoulder while he steadies himself on the crutch.

Rebecca made up a bed for him in the Bible room so that he wouldn't have to climb up and down the stairs. She had Baxter and Sylus take the serpents away in their handmade boxes. They took out all the poisons and the bottle torches, and they took the Bibles that Charles had been collecting all his life. Everything was to be burned.

After they emptied the Bible room they cleaned out the old woman's cabin too, and it was no small job. Gertie Bates kept everything she ever laid her hands on, and there were things in that house that Rebecca could not name. She went through it all and had Sylus pack whatever wasn't moldy or rotten into a big cedar chest for Jacob to go through at some later time. Then they burned the mattress, the curtains, the bedding, and all the old woman's clothes because a hundred years of smoldering herbs, bone soups, burnt shoes, pipe smoke, and tobacco juice could never be washed away. The floor of the cabin was filthy, and the mop water ran down the steps brown and rusty like a waterfall of pekoe tea. It took thirty buckets, hand carried from the spring, before they could even see the wood grain. Sylus whitewashed the exterior walls and fixed all the windows and painted the inside as well. They left the one wall with the bullet holes alone.

Pauline helps Jacob into the house, following Rebecca into the Bible room, where she turns down the bed, removes his shoes, and sends them all into the kitchen with Magdalena, where breakfast is waiting.

She props Jacob up on feather pillows and unwraps his bandage to check the condition of his wound, pressing the skin around it with her thumbs. She squeezes his calf to increase the flow of blood there and Jacob studies her hands. That night on the mountain, she pulled the sweet flag out by the roots with these hands and found shelter in the dark of the rain by feeling her way in the blinding storm, feeling for the hole in which she hid and holding her shins close and almost turning herself inside out to get him born—and then catching him with these hands. He takes them now and looks into her eyes. They're not as dark as his father's, but they seem twice as old.

It's gonna be a cold night, she says. I brought extra blankets down for you. I think Hosea will be all right down in the cabin. That stove gives off a good heat.

Jacob examines the now empty Bible room, which feels light and airy with all the Bibles and the snake boxes gone.

You've done a nice job in here, Jacob says. It's like a regular sunporch now.

I think your father would be pleased, she says.

In the corner, one Bible sits propped open on the portable pulpit. It's the one he carried the day he first met Rebecca, and the only one she kept. She turns back to Jacob and pulls the blanket up under his chin.

Get some rest, she says. There's nothing to worry about anymore because you're home.

There's something strange about the little cabin that soothes Hosea. He has the distinct feeling that he's seen it before, perhaps in his travels, perhaps in his dreams, perhaps in another lifetime altogether. The place feels safe and familiar, like the smell after a heavy rain. The floor creaks and the windows rattle in the wind, and it captures sun, directing the light through a high window whose thick leaded glass casts distorted reflections on the walls and floor, sweeping the room at the speed of time. Pauline takes the bed, and Hosea piles blankets on the floor, but it's so warm that he doesn't need them. The windows fog over, the stove ticks as it cools, and his sleep is filled with the oddest dreams he's ever remembered. He dreams of running dogs, blue serpents, a soldier dying in the grass. He sees babies living in the womb, and fire, and a tree with many arms. He wakes often to the sound of wood under the strain of the wind. There is a soft glow from the open stove, and he can see the sleeping form of Pauline under a single white sheet. On the wall above her, there's a constellation of mysterious holes. He does not sleep well.

Jacob's arms flail out in his sleep. He reaches out with his cupped hands and strokes the air like he's trying to swim. Rebecca touches his head with the tips of her fingers and gently strokes him. He stops flailing but not talking. He rolls over to face the wall, still talking in his sleep.

Daddy, he says. The minnows are here. They all live in the boat.

She pulls the blanket down and checks his leg. The bandage is clean and dry.

It's all right, Jacob, she says. Shush now.

She covers him back up and leaves the Bible room. It's just getting light and the small birds are out chattering. She goes outside into the blue-green light and walks up to the dogwood tree on the rise behind the house, barefoot in her nightdress. She comes up the grassy part of the hill, into the breeze, and she sees something on the ground that makes the hair on her neck stand up and tingle, a long shadow with its arms out like a scarecrow, stretched out on the old woman's grave.

Hosea is startled at the sound of her gasp. He goes straight for the knife in his boot. But he's not wearing his boots and his hand slaps against his bare anklebone.

Woman, he says. Don't do that to a man.

It takes Rebecca a minute to catch her breath.

You don't know what fright is until you see a man lying on a grave in the dark, she says.

Hosea jumps up and smacks his head on one of the low branches of the dogwood tree.

What grave?

The old woman's. You're lying on it. What are you doing up so early, Hosea?

I was just stargazing, he says. I couldn't sleep.

There's another one right beside it, Rebecca says. A soldier's grave. You're standing on him now.

Hosea steps back, still rubbing the bump on his head. Now he's afraid to stand anywhere, and Rebecca smiles at him.

Don't worry, she says. You're all right now. But there's another one here too. A child.

One of yours?

I had me a boy that died three days old. Before Jacob. Before Magdalena.

I'm sorry to hear it.

He was supposed to be Jacob. But Charles didn't want to give that name to a dead son, so we buried him without one. But I gave him one on my own. I called him Asher. Nobody knows that but you.

Hosea looks down at the cabin below them. A light's burning in the window now. Pauline must be awake.

You wouldn't believe my dreams last night, he says.

She smiles, and her eyes drift off toward some private recollection of time spent within the cabin.

Those walls have seen all manner of mystery, she says. That cabin's alive. We scrubbed and scrubbed, but the smell is still there. I expect she's still there too.

Hosea kneels at the baby's grave and brushes away the leaves with his hands. He clears the grave and gathers stones, laying them around the perimeter of the tiny plot so that its boundary is distinct.

Rebecca, he says. I want to tell you that what happened to Jacob was an accident. Tuley, my wife, she was an angry woman, and I came to take the only thing she had in this world. I don't blame her. I expected she'd try something, and I should have been more vigilant. She came in while we were sleeping. It was dark. She had not seen Jacob, hadn't met him, and I guess the sight of him surprised her. She took a shot at me, and the mere presence of that boy saved my life. He lost a lot of blood, but he's got something in him. Strength, and something else. Like you said, that boy is blessed. The doctor who removed the bullet, a man I know and trust, has never seen the likes of it, and he's removed a lot of bullets. We left soon as Jacob could travel. It was just a week after Tuley took her own life. Now all I have left is that girl.

What about your boys?

My sons have chosen a path upon which there is rarely a safe return.

She takes his hand. It's so big that both her hands could fit inside his one.

Why don't you just stay here for a while? she says. There's room enough, and we could put you to work. It might help you figure things out.

I'd like that, thank you. There's something about this place that calms me. Let me talk to Pauline. She likes that boy. They get on well together.

I can see that, she says. We'd sure like to have you, for as long as you'd like. Rebecca kneels over the soldier's grave and pulls out the few weeds that are growing on it.

One of these days we're gonna make some proper head-stones, she says. C'mon, let's get some coffee in you.

They walk back down the hill, and he takes her hand so that she won't slip on the wet grass.

Baxter Dawes did not do what he was told. He didn't burn anything he took out of the Bible room. He hid it all down in the root cellar and brought up from that dank hole what little there was left to eat. There were some jarred apricots and a short crate of stewed pears. He found a hidden case of berry preserves put up by the old woman—black as blindness but sweet enough to win the grand prize at the county fair. But blue ribbons won't feed five hungry people, and they don't have close to enough food stored away for the winter. Last year's root vegetables are long gone, and there's nothing at all in the way of meat. With Charles away, they didn't plant as much as they should have and when they did plant fared poorly, leaving them with little. They'll have to slaughter the chickens just to make September. To get through to the spring, they'll have to trap, hunt, and pray.

Pauline proves to be a big help around the house, and in the kitchen, she can work miracles with just rice and beans. She's good with fine needlework too, and Rebecca thinks they might make some money sewing and mending. It's a blessing to have another girl around the house, and she's never seen Magdalena so happy. The two girls get along like cousins, sometimes sleeping in the same bed or reading to each other aloud from the Bible. Pauline's decided to get her father back in the pulpit, and the two girls have dedicated themselves to that cause. They want to turn the old woman's cabin into a chapel, and Magdalena's been practicing sermons of her own. She wrote one herself that she plans to deliver on the anniversary of her father's death.

Jacob's leg heals, and he moves back up to his own room again. It's much smaller than he remembers, and it feels strange to be in it. He has trouble sleeping the first few nights until he moves his bed so that it now faces the portrait of Jesus that hung above it all his life. He remembers a time when he turned it around to face the wall so that he would not have look into its eyes. But now it's a comfort to him, and the new perspective has a positive effect on his sleep.

It's a bad summer for hunting white-tailed deer. They're all skinny and sick because of the hard winter. Their meat is stringy and bitter. That's what happens when deer are forced to live on tree bark, but meat is meat and they're thankful to have it.

There's an early snow in October that catches them by surprise—a blizzard that comes in by day. It covers all of Jacob's traps and strands Hosea in a deer blind up on the mountain until well after dark. Rebecca worries when he's not back for supper. She can see clear down the hill into the window where the old woman used to stand in years past, but the windows are still dark, and all she can see are the black outlines of the trees and the night beyond them. She waits and watches for Hosea. She reassures Pauline that he'll be home soon and home safe and sends the girls off to bed without truly believing it herself. She considers sending Jacob out to find him, but then she sees a flicker of light in the cabin below, the glow of a lamp. Hosea's shadow passes before the window. He's home, but she knows he must be wet, cold, and hungry.

She brings him fresh coffee and hot soup. He won't stop shivering, and she fills a tub of warm water to soak his legs. His hands are too stiff to build a fire, so she fetches the wood herself and feeds the stove. It's well past midnight as she rolls up the cuffs of his frozen trousers. His feet are pale, his toes shriveled. Another hour out in the woods and he would have lost them. She rubs them gently and kneads his heels. Hosea closes his eyes while she brings back the flow of blood with her fingers. He's wet and exhausted, so she helps him remove his things the way she did so many times for her son and her husband. She has never seen a naked man other than Charles Flint, and she is naive to the power of touch. With the stove door open, the cabin warms quickly and the firelight dances on his skin. The muscles on his legs are firm and large. She shuts her eyes, holds her breath, and lets her hands see parts of him that before this moment she would never have let herself imagine.

Had she known this night was designed for conception she'd have never left the house. Had she known the placement of the stars and the state of the moon, she would have sent Jacob down with the coffee and the soup. But she was not aware of these things. She would never have come to him if the old woman were here to interpret such signs. She did not know that autumn's first snowfall ripens that part of a woman where the lifeseed will catch, or that the wandering spirit of a true love will seek out the first child of spring. All she knows is this: a part of herself that had been long disconnected awakens, and tells her it's time to stop mourning, it's time to move on.

Charles had never made love to her the way Hosea does on this night, and she knows right then that something more will come of their union than simple release, something that will outlive them both. Afterward, she lays her head on his stomach, shuddering as the cabin windows frost over with a thin layer of ice from their breath. Charles had never made her feel so alive or so beautiful. His passions didn't lie in those places. He never held her the way he held the serpents. He never consumed her the way he sipped his poisons. It was true that a part of her had died with him, but a part of her had also escaped.

She walks back to the house barefoot in the gray dark before dawn, stopping along the way to wash between her legs with handfuls of snow scooped up from the ground, hoping to wipe away what she realizes has been done, but knowing too well that it is too deep for snow to reach. Before morning, she conceives their child, and now it makes no difference whether or not she is careful of the signs or considerate of the moon. She can do what she pleases. For the first time in her life she can think of herself.

She urges Pauline to move into Magdalena's room, claiming that it's too cramped for her in the cabin. But they all know the true reason for the arrangement. The house is too old to allow her to pass through it in silence. They can all hear the floors creak late at night as she creeps out to see him. Jacob can see the lights of the cabin from his window, as he's always seen. They burn every night until dawn.

. . .

She's showing by Groundhog Day. She was always thin and carried her babies low, so there is no hiding it. They tell the children before the children can tell for themselves and wonder if it is possible to keep it from the neighbors and the folks in town. They all agree that it cannot be kept secret for long.

One morning in late February, Poppa Hooch brings them a smoked hog, and his truck stalls on the hill between the cabin and the house. It's an old truck and he's lucky to have it, but like his previous vehicle it's prone to trouble and breaks down often. He engages the parking brake and climbs the hill and is greeted by the sight of Rebecca as she emerges from the cabin. She is clearly with child. He nods to her kindly and doesn't say a word. But she sees in his eyes a look that is not just awkwardness or surprise, but fear. In an instant he knows what this will mean. Hosea tows his truck up the hill, and they unload the hog, exchanging pleasantries but not much else. Poppa Hooch pops his clutch on the downslope and drives off without the customary stay for breakfast.

Poppa Hooch is a man who cannot keep his mouth shut, no matter how good his intentions might be. He can't keep a secret for long, and that fact hangs over them all like a sickness for which there's no local cure. When word gets out, life will become difficult for them, perhaps ugly. Folks are already talking about the Negro living in the Flint house. Soon the talk will get worse and soon the talk will end. Then there will be action. It's time they come up with a plan.

By spring, Rebecca is bedridden. She has what the old woman used to call a back baby, the child sitting low with its body pressed painfully against her spine. The old woman used to spend weeks in the homes of women in such a condition, and Jacob remembers running various necessities back and forth to her when he was a small boy. He knows from experience that this is the worst kind of pregnant.

She stays in the Bible room so she doesn't have to walk the stairs and sleeps a lot during the day because that's when the baby sleeps. When it doesn't move, it gives her some reprieve from the pain. They've hung some potted ferns and draped the windows to make it feel more comfortable for her, but they cannot rid the room of the smell of snake. They scrubbed and they scrubbed, but it's still there. Nothing can remove the smell of serpents but fire.

Jacob sits at her bedside often and reads to her, but on this morning she is still asleep and he stares until her eyes flutter open. She smiles when she sees him and asks him to sit.

It's been a long time since we talked, she says. She sounds sleepy, almost drunk.

How ya feelin', Momma?

I feel good today. I might get up and take a walk outside.

She takes his hand and gives it a weak squeeze. She's got that look in her eye she gets sometimes when she knows that there are going to be hard times ahead. A cold, intense stare.

You're gonna have a brother, she says. I'm sure now it's gonna be a boy.

What are we gonna do when they all find out that you're havin' Hosea's baby?

He thinks we should leave Leatherwood. He wants to buy back his farm and have us all go live on it.

Jacob reaches over and feels the top of her head. He feels her ears the way she used to when he was sick, and she feels warm.

I don't know what's happening to me, she says. But for the first time in my life something *is* happening to me. And I like it, I like the feeling of being caught up in something in me. Something that's alive. I don't just mean this child. I love that man, Jacob. I think I did when I first saw him coming up that road.

She takes him by the hand.

Your daddy used to say that the spirit was like a chimney drawing the flame of love up the flue of his heart. I never did understand that. I never felt the spirit the way he did. But I do now, and it was Hosea who gave me that feeling. Pour me a glass of water, would you?

Jacob brings her a glass and holds her head to help her drink. He fluffs the pillows behind her and pulls the blanket up off her legs so her feet can get air. They're swollen and red as a sunburn.

Lord, she says. I sure don't miss being pregnant. This one feels like two babies. I fear it won't go fast or easy. I need you to go get Mary Albert. I'm gonna need somebody with me, and she's the only one knows the old ways.

He rubs the bottoms of her feet. She stretches her toes and closes her eyes.

What am I gonna tell her? he says.

Just tell her I need her and give her this. She reaches for the bedside table and hands Jacob a folded slip of paper. He can see her handwriting on the inside. He takes the note and opens the door that leads out onto the porch. There's a place near the rail where the rainwater gathers off the rooftop, a depression worn away in the wood where his daddy would stand on warm nights and cool mornings, reading from his Bible. It's a good spot to survey the dormant fields rolling off into the far woods and a good part of the road that cuts up through the little valley, the Flint Road, with the rock wall beside it, each stone placed there by his father's hand, each stone dug up and pried loose by him and carried to the roadside.

Momma, he says. I won't leave this place.

She does not open her eyes, and she nods so slightly that he cannot see it.

All right, Jacob, she says. Let me get some rest now. The baby's gonna get up in a little while, and I need all the strength

I can get. Go on and get Mary for me, Jacob. I'll be needing her soon.

Hosea sits in the deer stand, the big one that Jacob built with his father. It has four walls and a roof and room enough for two men sitting back to back. There's a square-shaped hole cut in each of the walls so that a single hunter can stare out one and turn to see out the other, and through which two men can cover a wide range of open land.

He holds a bolt-action, single-barrel shotgun across his knees and a Bible propped open against the barrel of the gun. It's an hour past dawn and the mist still clings to the meadow. He reads to himself and scans the tree line for game.

Jacob knows just how to come up through the meadow unseen. He comes quiet and he comes upwind, the last fifty yards on his hands and knees. When Hosea hears the crackle of dry leaves below the tree, he chambers a slug and raises the gun. He's prepared to blow off the first head that comes up through the hole.

He waits. He can hear the wooden rungs of the ladder creak under the weight of a man, and then he hears a voice, whispering his name. It's Jacob. He lowers the gun, ejects the shell, and exhales.

You gonna get yourself killed sneaking up on me like that.

I'm sorry. I tried to be quiet so I wouldn't spook the deer.

There ain't no deer, Hosea says. Been out here for a week and I haven't seen anything but a few squirrels and some crows. What are you doin' out here? Your momma all right?

She's fine. But she's close enough now to need help.

I know it and I'm worried.

Me too.

We could take her somewhere, Hosea says. We could take her out of here to the big hospital in Chattanooga.

She wouldn't like that. She wants her babies born at the house.

You're on your way to get somebody, aren't you? Hosea says.

Jacob nods.

Be careful, Hosea says. Can you trust her?

She was an apprentice to the old woman.

Hosea turns the gun over in his lap. He blows into the chamber and pockets the shell.

But can we trust her?

We don't have a choice, Jacob says. We don't have too many friends around here.

Leatherwood, Hosea says. I been all over this state and I never heard of it until I met your momma. I want to take her away from here.

This town's like a mean old man, Jacob says. It's shifty, nervous, a quiet kind of crazy. You think he's sleeping, but he's not. Poke him with a stick and he'll shoot you with a gun. You have to take Momma away. Go back to your farm. Spare her the pain of hearin' how they cut you open and hanged you up to bleed out like a hog. Even if they don't come for you, she'll be a prisoner in her own house, and that child will have it worse than I ever did. There's worse things than being deformed. Take her away from here, Hosea. Soon as you can. Not just for her sake, but for yours.

Hosea holds his temples between his fingers and thumbs. The muscles pop out at his jawline and throb.

We might be gone for a long, long time, he says.

If you don't leave, they'll kill you.

Jacob picks up the Bible from the floor. It's one of the old ones from his father's collection, with the title worn away and the binding broken and the smell of leather and dried rosemary. It was printed in Scotland in 1843, and it has a name written inside, a dedication, old words drawn with a quill pen. It's beautiful lettering from a time before the old woman was born.

To James, for comfort and for strength. May you find peace in the new world. God be with you, son.

He hands the book to Hosea, who tucks it into his hunting pack.

You're reading the Bible again, Jacob says.

Pauline's got some notion I might preach at their chapel.

Jacob nods. I'd like to be there. I'll see you back at the house, he says.

He climbs down the ladder and walks off through the meadow. Hosea watches him go, but suddenly the boy stops, frozen in his tracks, and gestures toward the trees before him. There, standing in the shade, is a deer. It's a big animal, nosing the air for a scent and stomping a hoof in nervous anticipation of his crossing. Hosea chambers the slug. Jacob crouches. The sound of the shotgun lingers in his ears long after he leaves the meadow.

Mary Albert is seventy-nine years old. She still plants her own garden and she still walks to Shuck's store once a month for the things that an old woman needs. Sometimes she goes just to let him know she's not dead. This is her second time making the trip this month, but the good thing is that she won't have to walk all the way back home. She's going to the Flint house and Shuck's is on the way. She'd like to get a ride if she could, but the letter was clear about that. She made the boy read it to her twice.

For your secrecy and silence, you will be well paid in cash.

It's a hot June day and the heat brings folks inside close to the lemonade and to where it's dark and cool. It's a Sunday, so the crowd's even bigger than normal. She likes to come on Mondays when there's nobody around. But the letter was clear about that too.

Come quick, and bring the sweet flag, bring everything you can for a woman's pain.

She walks the steps slow, breathing heavy, taking one step at a time. She pauses at the ice barrel and dips her hands into the water. All the regulars are there—the old-timers and some of the younger boys, huddled round the checkerboard drinking Cokes and waiting for noon so they can buy beer. Anybody not in church is here, a variety of men she would rather avoid.

She goes to the medicine counter and fills a sack with necessities—aspirin, witch hazel, quinine, and gauze. The boys pay her no mind. But the old-timers know something's up. When she's in Shuck's buying powders and pills, there's a baby sure to come soon. Leatherwood is a small community and they know every woman of childbearing age within a ten-mile radius. They look at each other and glance at Shuck. He leans on the counter chewing a toothpick, eyeballing the old woman. They don't smile. Poppa Hooch's rumor is confirmed.

Mary Albert pays on credit and doesn't look Shuck in the eye or make any of her usual comments about the weather or the state of the world. Most times he can't get her to shut up. When she leaves, they all watch her. She takes the wrong road home.

There is no moon, and there are no shadows from the oak tree outside his window. The darkness is almost complete, and it fuels Jacob's dreams. He hears the thunder of a thousand horses crossing a wooden bridge—cloven-hoofed creatures, the drumbeat prancing of goats. But these hoofbeats are not what they first seem to be. They are the shoes of men, the sound of boot heels on the porch, in the parlor, in the hall. In the confines of the Bible room a pistol shot cracks like a snapping branch, and there is the noise of confusion, thrashing, scraping, the terror-stricken cry of a young girl. But it's the voices that finally wake him, the oaths of men bring him to his feet, to the top of the stairs, where Magdalena crouches in her nightgown shaking like a poisoned dog.

They drag Hosea through the parlor, with Pauline holding onto his leg. The rug bunches beneath his hips and catches in the entryway, where the men gather and pull him out through the door. They beat him in front of the house, in the dust where the chickens feed, a dozen men or more, their faces masked with white kerchiefs torn from bedsheets so that only their eyes show through. They kick him unconscious, and the blood that leaks out from his head is as dark as wine. It pools in the powder-dry dust, a shiny black meniscus; it looks like they blew away his ear. They drag him off to the waiting trucks, and the dust clings to his wound like fine brown fur.

The men say things he cannot hear. Pauline's mouth is open, and what comes out is more like a song than a scream. Magdalena appears in a pale nightgown, like a blue ghost, crouching beside Pauline and covering her mouth loosely with the palm of her hand. Jacob can say nothing, do nothing, there are too many men with guns. They leave in a wake of whiskey sweat and rage. He has little time to think. He stands on the porch and closes his eyes. He hears a long, low scream, the muffled wail of a Choctaw banshee, a hail of shotgun blasts, hoots, calls, and tires spinning in the dust. Now his momma's out on the rise, stumbling up the hill in her bedclothes, with Mary Albert trailing behind.

Hosea, she says. Hosea, Jesus, no.

Take her back, Jacob says. Get her to bed.

He sees it all unfold in his mind's eye now. They will torture him first, and that will save his life. Their cruelty will provide the necessary delay. There is still time. He takes Magdalena by the arm and pulls her away from Pauline.

Go to Baxter's and tell him what happened. Tell him to go to the old tree on the mountain. The Tyborn tree. My tree. I'll stop them. Tell Momma I'll stop them.

And he runs.

He flies through the world on burning feet, through the

trees, through the woods, shoeless, shirtless. He knows the fast trails and runs like the last wolf and breaks through the brush with a speed and a strength that is not his own. He can feel himself rising, he can feel himself being pushed. There's no fatigue, no pain, he moves quick on the balls of his feet, he's a horse, he's a deer, lithe and nimble. He fends off branches with his hands, he swims through the thickets, climbing the whole way, always climbing, the ground too dark to see, but he knows the way, and the old landmarks float by like puffs of smoke—the boat rock, the bramble tunnel, Moss Creek, the silver meadow, and then the tree. He can see the glow of a fire and he can hear Hosea wail. He stands just beyond them, panting, his ears ringing so loud he can hardly hear. There's yelling, screaming, but beyond that he can hear the voice of God.

He breaks through the circle of men, an angry gathering, high on liquor and the sight of blood. Their faces are covered and dark with soot, but their eyes are white and gleaming. Someone holds a hot knife, the blade glowing orange as if freshly forged. He can smell burning hair and flesh. Hosea is bound naked to the trunk of the old tree, wrapped round and round with bailing wire that cuts into his skin. He's punctured all over with tiny holes, and he's glistening. The air smells like gasoline. It runs down into Hosea's eyes, and he throws back his head, wincing from the burning fuel. He's alive, but a rope swings from a branch overhead where the remnants of other, older ropes still cling. They will hang him soon, or burn him, they've brought plenty of wood, and barbed wire and a steel Texaco can with a jointed spout bent backward like the trunk of an elephant. Jacob cannot waste time with the atrophy of terror. In his mind he hears someone speak.

I heard the voice of the Lord, saying whom shall I send, and who will go for us? Then said I, here I am, send me.

Hosea sees him now—a small boy in the firelight, just beyond the jeering men. Barefoot and shirtless, he's chalky white, pale as a full moon and just as radiant. The fuel that burns his eyes makes the edges of the world blur and wobble, and the boy does not look real. He's a vision, a wish, a spirit summoned from the dark. Hosea reaches out for him, and Jacob holds out his arms, as if to accept his embrace. The men all stop shouting.

The air is filled with voices now, but they are not the voices of living men. They are from other parts of the world. And they join to become one voice, a voice speaking inside himself. It is the tree he hears. The tree is talking.

> Take heed and be quiet; fear not, neither be fainthearted
> for the two tails of these smoking firebrands, for the fierce
> anger they display.

The men are laughing. They are very drunk, and they are laughing at the sight of him. He can hear the fire, the popping of dry wood. Hosea leans forward, straining against the wire. His voice echoes through the woods.

You damn fool. Run, boy, run.

His lips are swollen and his mouth is numb and his words slur and trail off like a man trapped in a mine.

Someone throws a bottle that breaks on his head. A small fissure opens at his scalp and he slumps forward over the wire. Dead or unconscious, Jacob cannot tell. The men go back to the business of their undertaking. One of them cuts the wire with the hot knife and Jacob feels it, he feels how it burns, and again he hears the tree speak.

> For every battle of the warrior is with confused noise, and
> garments rolled in blood, but this shall be with burning
> and fuel of fire.

They lift Hosea and move him beneath the rope. Jacob enters the ring of men and stands in the full light of the bonfire. He raises his arms and they watch him, curious, smiling. They're putting the rope round Hosea's neck and tying his hands.

For unto us a child is born, unto us a son is given, and his name shall be called the Mighty God.

Jacob stands by the fire and begins to spin, slowly. He turns, with arms uplifted, and they watch him with a mixture of amusement and confusion. His head is tilted far back on his neck and his eyes are rolling. He trembles. It's almost imperceptible, but he's shivering all over and clenching his fingers and shifting his jaw from side to side. Those not engaged directly in the act of the lynching step back and become quiet. Jacob is afflicted with tics and spasms, and he speaks with a voice of such authority and conviction that it sobers them all.

Howl, O gate. Cry, O city; thou art dissolved. Woe to the crown of pride, to the drunkards of Leatherwood, whose glorious beauty is a fading flower. Woe to the children, saith the Lord, that take counsel, but not of me, that cover with a covering, but not of my spirit, that they may add sin to sin. Behold, a king shall reign in righteousness and princes shall rule in judgment. Woe to thee that spoilest and thou was not spoiled. For it is the day of the Lord's vengeance, and the cormorant and the bittern shall possess it, the owl also and the raven shall dwell in it: and he shall stretch upon it the line of confusion, and the stones of emptiness. Hast thou not known? Hast thou not heard? The everlasting God fainteth not, neither is weary, he giveth power to the faint and to them that have no might, he increaseth strength.

For a moment, nobody speaks or moves. All that can be heard is the moaning of Hosea and the rushing sound of flame. The men look to each other, and they step closer in, toward Jacob. He crouches on his heels and upends the Texaco can, spilling all the gasoline over himself. The men step back.

> Therefore he hath poured upon him the fury of his anger, and the strength of battle: and it hath set him on fire round about, yet he knew not: and it burned him, yet he laid it not to heart.

Jacob Flint steps into the fire, and is consumed.

EPILOGUE

They named the boy Daniel Jacob Lee, and he resembles nobody living, nor any person in their memory from either side of Hosea or Rebecca's family. Even the photographs of their relatives fail to reveal the source of his features. His eyes are blue as dogbane, his forehead is high, and his skin is pale as bone. He's got Rebecca's lips and Hosea's hands, but that's all they recognize until he starts walking and exploring the world outside the house. They notice that he holds insects carefully in the palms of his hands and touches flowers lightly with the tips of his fingers as if they might break. He holds small creatures and speaks to them softly. He watches everything. He's got Jacob's way of looking at the world. And some say he's got his healing touch.

At seven years old he is a quiet child. He hardly speaks a word at all and does not have that other gift possessed by his half-brother—the gift of articulation. But he can hear just fine, and he writes. He writes things in a book that he will not show to anybody. He writes about his impressions of the world and he writes about his dreams. Some say he's dumb, *off*, tetched, but Rebecca knows better. The boy's not any of those things. He's smarter than them all. He simply chooses not to talk. She knows this by looking in his eyes and watching how he perceives the things that he sees. Daniel's eyes are big and expressive. With eyes like that he doesn't need to speak with his lips. Give him time, she says. He's just waiting for the right thing to say.

When Daniel was born Hosea moved up to the big house, and they turned the old woman's cabin into the pretty little church of Magdalena's dream. They preserved the timbers cut by the old woman's father, and they preserved the bullet holes on the interior wall. Those boards were removed and then placed behind the pulpit, which itself was constructed from the wood of Jacob's old bed. The same picture of Jesus that hung over him as he slept hangs behind the pulpit now, so that when Magdalena stands there to preach to the small congregations, she can summon him, she can feel him inside of her. She hears his voice and she uses it in her sermons to deliver her messages of hope and kindness. Folks say they are the most moving, most beautiful sermons they have ever heard. Not a week goes by that they don't fill the church and stand elbow-to-elbow along the back wall to hear her speak. But it's no longer the holiness way. They are not sign followers anymore. There is no swaying, no jumping, no trances. The sick don't come for healing and there are no poisons and there are no snakes.

Magdalena is the image of her father at the pulpit. Her black eyes burn the way his used to, and she uses her whole body when she delivers her sermons. Her muscles clench and her hands grasp at the empty air, but she does not preach fear.

Faith, she says, comes from no bottle, no box, no jar.

And they believe her. They all believe.

Do not look to things for Jesus, for God, she says. There are miracles in sunlight and blessings in the grass.

Hosea came close to death the night that Jacob died. He lay in a coma for many days, and he missed his son Daniel being born. It was a month before he held him for the first time, and he made a promise on that day, right there, at the very moment he held that boy. He promised himself that he would live every single day, not as if it were his last but as if it were as his first. He now lives his life with the joyful anticipation of a child and through a child's eyes: Daniel's.

He gives the inaugural sermon at the little chapel on the hill but never again takes the pulpit. He's lost the desire to spread the written word of God, but not the love of the Word itself. He teaches Sunday school and spends as much time with Daniel as he can. His son is his life now. His son is the reason for all the things that led to him to Leatherwood and Rebecca Flint. This boy will not get away from him. He will grow strong in heart and radiant in soul. Hosea will make sure of this, because he will give his own heart to the boy and from him he will not hide his soul. He will make sure that he knows Jacob Flint, and Charles Flint, and his half-brothers, and Tuley Jones. And this boy will redeem them all.

Daniel Jacob Lee does not speak much, but he reads. He loves the language of the Bible. He hears it in his mind and he hears it in his dreams. In his dreams he is not quiet. In his dreams he has the strong, soothing voice suited to a son of Hosea Lee. Everything that need be spoken is spoken there, in his dreams. He does not miss the gift of language in the night, in his sleep. In his sleep he is Solomon, he is Jesus, he is Isaiah, he is Joel. They all speak to him kindly, and they fill him with hope that he can change, if not the world, at least a small part of it. And his journey begins in Leatherwood. His voices tell him to go to a place beneath the hill, beneath the house where it is yet dark and cold. You will find your voice there, they say. Those castaways are yours, your pale flesh will glow amber where there is no light.

They have long since abandoned the root cellar. It's covered over now with pepper vines that the boy cuts through easily with a buck knife. He cuts through the thick, tangled vines and pries open the door. The flashlight beam flickers because it's old and he must bang on it frequently to keep it lit. It's icebox cool inside the root cellar and something scurries off in the dark. It smells like mushrooms, wood rot, and the kind of mold that grows in books.

He steps in and trains the flashlight beam along the walls hewn into the dark earth by the hands of Zebediah Bates. The shelves that once held cured meats and thick preserves are sagging now under the weight of books: Bibles. There are hundreds and hundreds of Bibles, some which still sparkle where the light hits the gilt lettering on their spines. They are covered in dust and splotched over with fuzzy green mold. At the back of the cellar, against the wall, lie a stack of boxes too heavy to be jam crates and too ornate to be boxes for food. There are words on the boxes, words he can read once he brushes away the dust.

He that believeth shall be saved. In my name they shall speak with new tongues, They shall take up serpents, they shall heal the sick.

He knows these words, they are from the gospel of Mark, but he does not know why they were carved there in the sides of the boxes, and he does not know what is kept inside. He pulls one down, and finds that it is not empty. Something makes a scratching sound inside and he sees that the top of the box is constructed from wire mesh stapled down over a pair of hinged lids that open up like butterfly wings. The lock has rusted long ago and he breaks it with one sharp tug. He opens the lid and he sees inside a strange pile of bones—hundreds of crescent shapes, like tiny tusks. They are ribs, and what appears to be a skull with large curving fangs.

Snake, he says. And the sound of his own voice surprises him. Snakes, he says again. Bibles and snakes.

And he reaches out with his hand to touch the bones.

ACKNOWLEDGMENTS

A story may begin in the heart of one person, but a novel is written by the grace of many. Beyond the initial spark of inspiration, there are countless moments when the flame falters and the writer fades. That flame can be fanned back to life with sometimes no more than a single word or deed. Writers are not solitary beings. They may work alone, but their strength and motivation is fueled by the faith and encouragement of many others.

The journey of this novel began with a single photographic image that grew into a feeling, that became a story and evolved into a book. I owe a great deal to those who touched this story and helped it to grow. To those people, I wish to express my profound gratitude. You are as much part of this book as I am. Your inspiration, your faith, and your love will never be forgotten.

I wish to thank Jonny Belt, who urged me to stop whining and write, and whose wonderful gift, *Appalachian Portraits*—the haunting photographs of Shelby Lee Adams—provided the initial spark of inspiration for the short story upon which the novel is based. I wish to thank the Writing Salon in San Francisco for providing people like me the chance to start writing in the first place, and to Adrienne Brodeur and *Zoetrope All-Story*, who changed my life by inviting me to Belize, where I learned to be a writer and saw Jacob Flint come alive for the first time, and Terry McMillan, who said one sentence that gave me enough confidence to last a lifetime, and Amy Penticoff, who pushed me to enter the short story in an obscure fiction contest, and Jenine Gordon Bockman and *Literal Latté*, who sponsored that contest and published the original short story. I owe a great debt to Kathy Hepinstall for advice, encouragement, and faith, to Michelle Murphy who taught me to think like, and thus write, more like a poet, to Clark Knowles for love and advice, to *Poets and Writers* magazine for wisdom and recognition, and to Scott Gold for discovering my story through them. I must offer a very special thanks to Lane Zachary for pushing me to turn the story into a novel, and to my good friend Manhal, who runs the Higher Grounds Café where I wrote most of the book in the early morning jazz-fueled magic that was for so long my home. I wish also to recognize the efforts of my agent Laura Strachan, whose faith in this novel, and in me, was undying, Marie Estrada for her insight and guidance, and Rakesh Satyal and all at HarperCollins who believed in this book.

And finally, I wish to give special recognition to a writer who has been my catalyst, my editor, and my mentor. Andrew L. Wilson believed in me, encouraged me, advised me, and guided me like no other human being. Without him, this novel would simply not exist. Every writer deserves such a friend.

Vincent L. Carrella

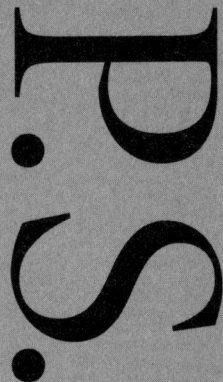

About the author

About the book

Read on

Insights,
Interviews
& More...

A Conversation with Vincent Louis Carrella

Where were you born, Vincent?

I was born in Manhasset, on the north shore of Long Island in New York.

Were you raised there?

I spent the first five years of my life in the town of Massapequa, on the south shore, but I moved to Port Washington, the next town over from Manhasset, and spent the next fifteen years living there. Port Washington is my hometown.

What events from your childhood stand out?

My parents divorced when I was five and that was a bellwether moment for me. I remember my mother in tears, just walking out, taking my brother and me by the hand and leaving. We had to move out of our house and into a small apartment. I was sent to a new school. On my first day I was forced to fight every boy in my class in order to prove myself. I spent the next several years fighting and being picked on. I was small and knew nothing about how to stand up for myself. I quickly learned how to negotiate, and how to run. I was fast and had this almost animal ability to sprint, jump, and disappear into the woods. My father did give me one thing that shaped who I am today: a love of nature and the woods. My mother gave me books and the love of reading. He gave me the woods. There were still areas of undeveloped land near my house where a child could wander alone for hours. I spent much of my early childhood exploring those places. Mostly I'd fish and hunt snakes. I was a huge

© Debra McClinton

fan of reptiles and wanted to be a herpetologist. I collected snakes and kept them in aquariums. My father had a sailboat and my brother and I spent a lot of time on Manhasset Bay fishing, crabbing, and discovering hidden estuaries in rafts and dinghies. That part of my childhood was beautiful. But that was only one part. The rest was terrifying. I was incessantly bullied and spat on and chased by older boys. My mom did an amazing job raising us alone, but we barely made ends meet and life at home was not easy. There were times when the local priest left food on our doorstep.

We weren't close to starving, but the charity was welcome. So I had a childhood that was both magical and scary. But the magic trumps the tragic. My fondest memories are of fishing with my father and brother; swimming; collecting minnows in nets; catching frogs; building rafts and forts in the woods; riding for hours on my bicycle and enjoying that freedom; living in a world of make-believe and taking refuge in what nature there was—and there was plenty— on the gold coast of Long Island. I had a Tom Sawyer childhood. And I read voraciously, which of course was another escape. My mother was a huge reader and our house was filled with books, many of which I can still recall. I can see their spines in my mind's eye—*For Whom the Bell Tolls*, *Portnoy's Complaint*, Anaïs Nin—I was surrounded by books and would hold and leaf through them as a form of comfort, even when they were far above my ability to comprehend. I always found comfort in words.

What was your first great experience as a reader in that house brimming with books?

When I was maybe ten or eleven years old I read a book called *Rifles for Watie*. It was a young adult novel about a boy who runs off to join the Union army during the Civil War. That was the first time I completely empathized with a ▶

> **"There were times when the local priest left food on our doorstep."**

A Conversation with Vincent Louis Carrella
(continued)

fictional character. I could not put that book down. And though it may now be a cliché, *The Catcher in the Rye* really did change me. Maybe changed is not the right word; what it did was basically enter me. I almost felt violated by it— disturbed. I could not believe that a book could do what that book did to me. It was like someone pulled the curtain away, and there stood that little man pretending to be the Great Oz. And this was back before all the hoopla. I had never met anyone who read it and I was not told to read it. It found me. Like all great novels, it found me.

What do your parents do?

My father is a retired New York City cop, and during my childhood that was something that both terrified and fascinated me. My mother works for the New York City Department of Finance. When I was a child she worked for a drug crisis and counseling center. Out of necessity, she'd sometimes take my brother and me to work with her and allow us to commingle with recovering heroin addicts. That, too, had a profound impact on me.

When and how did you first take to writing?

I cannot remember a time when I wasn't writing something.

I had always written stories, journals, and scenarios for paper role-playing games. But I did not begin writing fiction seriously until 1998. I had attempted a few short stories up to that point, but they were failures; they didn't speak to me, they didn't convey anything to me in the way I was used to reading in other's work. At about that time a friend of mine, Jonny Belt, suggested—no urged—that I enroll in a writer's

> 66 I cannot remember a time when I wasn't writing something. 99

4

workshop. I chose one in San Francisco called The Writing Salon. I worked on a story there that I had previously written. It was not well-received, though I got some very nice compliments on the writing itself. That workshop taught me a lot about what a short story should be. I learned a great deal about both the craft and business of writing. Our textbook, Janet Burroway's *Writing Fiction*, really provided one of those Oprah lightbulb moments for me. For the first time I understood that fiction was a process the end result of which should aspire to illuminate. I also learned about John Gardner at that time— *The Art of Fiction* has been the most influential nonfiction book in that it affirmed so many things I felt but never articulated. The whole concept of the fictional dream resonated strongly with me, and everything I subsequently wrote was more powerful as a result. I began to find my tone, my rhythm.

Would you care to relate any unusual or otherwise compelling anecdotes surrounding your early writing years?

I still feel like I'm in my early writing years. I'm a child when it comes to writing, and in so many other ways. I have much, much to learn and am still low on the grade toward peaking. But I remember discovering that mornings were more fruitful for me and that sunlight played a key role in how I performed on any given day. I think the single most important factor for me in becoming a writer was my dear friend Jonny telling me that I should take it seriously.

He believed in me and pushed me in a loving way. So many people played pivotal roles. Little pushes here, little nudges there. There was a writer in that Writing Salon workshop, Amy Penticoff, whom I thought was really good. ▶

> " The single most important factor for me in becoming a writer was my dear friend Jonny telling me that I should take it seriously. "

A Conversation with Vincent Louis Carrella
(continued)

I admired her style. She was always offering me bits of advice, and one day she suggested that I enter one of my stories in a contest. She gave me all the info and pushed me to do it. I was terrified, because that was the first time I had submitted anything. Well, I won the contest. And as a result I got a call from an agent who convinced me to write the novel. Hemingway said that sometimes one writer is born to help another writer write one single sentence—something like that. Well, without Amy I'd have never written *Serpent Box*. I owe her a steak dinner.

Russell Banks dressed window mannequins; Louise Erdrich waved a flag for a road crew; Francine Prose worked in a Bellevue morgue—what jobs did Vincent Louis Carrella have prior to becoming a writer?

Working is one of my great joys, and by working I mean real work—labor, blue-collar work. Because we were poor, I've been working since I was ten: I was a paperboy and a dishwasher; I was a landscaper; I worked at a Carvel ice cream store, a Dairy Barn, and a Swensen's. At one time I wired wing lamps for F-15s. I worked on boats, varnishing, doing maintenance, cleaning teak and brightwork. I cleaned bottoms and hulls. I worked for a yacht club driving a launch. I worked as a mail opener at Publishers Clearing House. I was a busboy and a waiter. I was a set-builder for a New York film studio and a production assistant. I was a telemarketer, a headhunter, and a video store clerk. I swept floors at a supermarket and worked in a greenhouse. I unloaded trucks on the graveyard shift at UPS. I worked for a grounds crew at a Nassau County park and sold custom-designed T-shirts on Grateful Dead tours. All that was before my high-tech career.

> 66 I was a telemarketer, a headhunter and a video store clerk. . . . I . . . sold custom-designed T-shirts on Grateful Dead tours. 99

6

Wife, children, pets?

I have all three. My wife, Beverly, to whom I dedicated the book, was incredibly supportive during the very difficult process of writing and beyond. I have two daughters, a dog, and three cats. I love animals.

Do you hold to a writing routine?

I write in the morning. I like to listen to jazz and sit in a café. There's a place in San Francisco that has everything I need to do my best work—low jazz, great coffee, wonderful light, and no pretense. It's called The Higher Grounds Café. I wrote most of the first draft of *Serpent Box* there over the course of nine months, in longhand, using a PaperMate Uni-Ball Impact 1.0 mm pen. Every day I began by writing a letter to a dear friend of mine, fellow writer Andrew L. Wilson. I got that idea from Steinbeck and it worked wonders for me. Writing a letter loosens me up. I also read poetry before I write. During the writing of *Serpent Box* it was Rumi and Frank Stanford. There are other things. I have a stone I dug off the top of Jack London's grave that I've rubbed smooth as basalt with the back of my thumb. And I have another I found at The Old Manse in Concord, where Nathaniel Hawthorne lived. Writing is a mystical process for me. Lots of people snicker at that. But I strive to channel something from beyond myself, and the way I do that is to try and work myself into a sort of joyous trance.

And then I wait for an image and simply record what I see. I do not plot, I do not outline, I do not think about the work or the story. I put in three to four hours a day and then stop when I'm going good. I don't spend it all in one day. ▶

> 66 Writing is a mystical process for me. Lots of people snicker at that. But I strive to channel something from beyond myself, and the way I do that is to try and work myself into a sort of joyous trance. 99

A Conversation with Vincent Louis Carrella
(*continued*)

I save just a little and then start at that point the following day.

Any other writerly quirks or superstitions?

I don't talk about the work to anyone—perhaps Andrew—and even then it's only briefly. I don't like writing on the computer. I prefer a physical connection to paper. Paper pulls things out of me. I pray; I pray for clarity and strength. I read only great writers and great writing while I am working. Unless it's Cormac McCarthy, I usually read only dead writers. I loathe reading anything by anyone my age or younger while I am writing; it makes me more self-concious than I already am. I also listen to music with moving lyrics. During the writing of *Serpent Box* it was Tom Waits. His sense of words, his rhythms and cadences infected me; they still do. He's a wonderful storyteller who understands the tactile quality of words. He is a great influence. I also try to absorb as much of the natural world as possible: I go to the ocean; I walk in the woods; I touch and talk to trees; I watch animals; if I am lucky, very lucky, I will be found by an owl. Throughout the entire process of writing *Serpent Box* I was watched and guided by a pair of great horned owls. It was uncanny. I had so many strange owl encounters while writing *Serpent Box* that it's beyond coincidence. Of course, the owl is an ancient symbol for Christ. So draw whatever conclusions you'd like.

How do you determine when you're done with a piece? In other words, how do you know?

I never feel done. I don't ever complete anything to my satisfaction. But I try to write in a circle; I try to come back to where I began with some sort of better understanding. There comes a point where that happens and then you know you're close. With *Serpent Box* it was obvious once I knew what Jacob would do. He came to the end of his journey, not just physically, but spiritually. When your main character can go no further, as a writer, you are done.

Do you have any notable vices?

Yes, but no printable ones.

What are your phobias, Vincent?

I'm afraid of trees at night. They're spooky and seem more alive, more menacing. Of course this is silly. It's like Billy Bob Thornton's fear of eighteenth-century European furniture. But I have been struck with cold terror by the sight of certain trees in the dark. I'm also afraid of cockroaches.

How hard was it to land a publisher?

I was lucky enough to have a very good agent before I even completed the book. Lane Zachary, who sold me on the idea of writing the book, took it out and tried to sell it. I think I was rejected nine time before we parted company. After that I had to start from scratch, first finding an agent and then selling the book. During the period between agents I revised the structure in hope of making the book stronger. But Laura Strachan is the one who did all the work to sell it. I just wrote it; she got the deal done. She believed in the book when I was in the depths of despair. She's an angel. I owe both of these women, Lane and Laura, a great debt of gratitude. But in the end the dirty work was done by Laura.

Tell us about the Zoetrope Short Story Writers' Workshop. How did your involvement with the workshop come about? ▶

A Conversation with Vincent Louis Carrella
(continued)

I was involved with an online writer's
workshop through *Zoetrope: All-Story*,
Francis Ford Coppola's short story magazine.
They held a contest where you could win an all-
expenses-paid trip to study writing in Belize and
I submitted a story. I didn't win, but I did get
a call from editor Adrienne Brodeur, who said
she liked my writing and asked if I would be
interested in participating in the workshop as a
paid attendee. The Zoetrope workshop was one
week at Coppola's exclusive retreat on a jaguar
preserve in Belize. How could I say no?

It was the chance of a lifetime, and I felt that
it was somewhat fateful because I love Coppola.
Apocalypse Now was the most influential film of
my childhood. I saw it when I was thirteen and it
had as much impact on me as *The Catcher in the
Rye*—it just rocked my world. So I went. And it
changed my life. I met the most wonderful people
there and learned a great deal. I studied under
Melissa Bank, who was very gracious. The guest
writer was Terry McMillan, and each attendee
was entitled to meet with her for a private one-
on-one. Terry is very honest and holds nothing
back. It's not easy to impress her. But she said
such wonderful things about my writing and
gave me a lot of great advice and encouragement.
She probably didn't realize it, but she bolstered
my confidence and gave me the courage to call
myself a writer, to take it seriously. I made some
great friends in Belize, including novelists Kathy
Hepinstall and Andrew Wilson (both of whom
have been my saviors). Adrienne Brodeur has
been very helpful over the years. I still consider
many of the people I met in Belize family. And
of course I have Coppola himself to thank. One
day I hope to.

*How much of your real world crops up in the
fictional world of* Serpent Box?

> **The Zoetrope workshop was one week at Coppola's exclusive retreat on a jaguar preserve in Belize. How could I say no?**

If by real world you mean me, then I'd say a good deal of it is real and relevant to myself. If you distill the book down to a single question, it is this: Is there a God?

That's the question I was asking myself in 1999 when I began this, and it's the question I dared to try and answer while writing it. Jacob is a boy who doesn't understand who he is or where he fits. I was that boy; I am that boy. At that point in my life I was at a crossroads, just as Jacob is. Which way do I go? Where do I go? What should I do with my life? These are the great questions for everyone. I too was a small, helpless little boy with many disadvantages. I too had a crisis of faith. But of course I am also Charles Flint and Sylus Knox and Daniel Lee. I am the Old Woman. I just kept splitting myself, like an atom, to create all those people, that world.

What prompted you to focus on snake handlers?

This decision was made for me. I didn't make it. Jonny Belt, who I mentioned before, gave me a book of silver gelatin photographs taken by photographer Shelby Lee Adams. These photos portrayed the lives of people living in rural Appalachia. They were haunting and moving. One of them depicted a boy holding a live rattlesnake and a jar of lye. I was struck by it. Several other photos were of various other Holiness People, just staring back at the camera like it was God Himself. I began to wonder: Who are these people? What do they believe? Are they real? I did some research, not to write a book, but simply to know for myself what it was that motivated them to do these things. What I discovered was a lot passion and a lot of faith. I felt pulled in by them. There were so many things going on there that I had often ▶

> 66 If you distill the book down to a single question, it is this: Is there a God? 99

A Conversation with Vincent Louis Carrella
(*continued*)

wondered about and felt strongly about—snakes, God, religion, faith, poverty, outcasts, rural mythology. It was a perfect storm.

Why did you choose a ten-year-old boy to anchor the story?

A lot of my work focuses on that transition from boy to man.

What does it mean to be a man? What is a man? How do you lose innocence? How does a boy know what he knows and learn what he learns? It's such a mysterious and awkward time. It's more than awkward, it's frightening. I think ten is an age where most children are clearly still children, yet they can see through to the other side. They can see the real world yet they don't fully understand it. When you are ten your days of magic and wonder are numbered. You somehow stop believing in naïve things. You begin the process of becoming jaded and cynical. So a ten-year-old is hovering between two worlds and soon has to make choices. Perhaps they have already been made for him. But at ten, everything is still possible. You can really be a major league baseball player or a neurosurgeon if you want to. I hate that we lose that. It saddens me. I wanted to tell this story from the point of view of a person who could be totally objective, yet still bring a certain unique subjectivity to it. Of course I can only say this in hindsight. At the time I didn't think about it. I didn't do character sketches or anything. I simply saw that world through the eyes of that boy. And I think it's because I am still that boy.

> " A lot of my work focuses on that transition from boy to man. "

12

What Is a Serpent Handler?

by Vincent Louis Carrella

THERE IS NO UNIFORM or widely agreed upon description of what a serpent handler is, or should be, even among those who practice what appears to be a bizarre and aberrant rite of Christian faith. Although serpent handlers have much in common with one another, there is nuance to each church's particular interpretation of Biblical scripture and differences between how they worship and live their lives. But the practice *is* real, and serpent handlers are not only real people, they are *sane* people.

To arrive at a manageable description of serpent handlers one must understand how the practice itself evolved from other Fundamentalist Christian movements, and the role of biblical interpretation as the impetus for the ritual.

Generally, a serpent handler is a person who uses poisonous snakes to demonstrate a belief in the physical manifestation of the Holy Spirit as described in the Biblical Book of Acts (Acts 1.5,8) and, more specifically, the words of Jesus to his apostles in the Book of Mark, which are:

> And these signs shall follow them that believe; in my name shall they cast out devils; they shall speak with new tongues; they shall take up serpents; and if they drink any deadly thing, it shall not hurt them; they shall lay hands on the sick, and they shall recover. Mark 16:17–18

For many Christians the Bible is the direct word of God. They believe each passage is literal truth. For such believers, there's no room for ▶

> 66 Serpent handlers are not only real people, they are *sane* people. 99

What Is a Serpent Handler? *(continued)*

interpretation and there's no ambiguity.
Jonah was swallowed by a whale. Moses parted
the Red Sea. Jesus Christ walked on water and
raised the dead. These are not metaphors for
such believers. But in some cases, controversy
over the interpretation of a single word (such
as the word "shall," in "They shall take up
serpents") has fractured churches, leading
to new movements and new ways of
thinking among Fundamentalist Christian
congregations. Such is the case with serpent
handlers who sprang from the Pentecostal
Church in the early part of the twentieth
century.

The belief in Biblical inerrancy, or the
complete accuracy of the Bible, forms the
very basis of Christian Fundamentalism, of
which the Pentecostal Church is the largest
and fastest-growing branch, and from which
arose the practice of serpent handling. But
the handling of serpents is only one aspect
of a rich and complex faith that stems from
a focus on the powers and gifts promised by
Jesus to the most faithful believers, via what
is perhaps the most enigmatic figure in the
Bible—the Holy Spirit. We cannot understand
those who handle serpents without first
attempting to understand that concept,
because serpent handlers believe it is the
Holy Spirit who bestows the gift of protection
to those who handle snakes and drink poison.
But who, or what, is the Holy Spirit, and what
does dancing, singing, and praying while
holding a live wild rattlesnake have to do
with faith in God?

The Old Testament introduces us to a Holy
Spirit, also called the Spirit of God, who bestows
physical power, raptures, or the gift of prophecy
upon individuals who (in some cases) promise
the bestowal of God's spirit to all. The New
Testament tells us that such prophecy is fulfilled

through Jesus, who is the bearer and giver of the Holy Spirit.

From that perspective the Holy Spirit can be seen as a sort of proxy for God, and can be viewed as His physical manifestation on Earth. According to the beliefs of most serpent handlers, the Holy Spirit acts upon man, he literally touches us, and he can bestow upon mortals special gifts (1Cor 12:8–10) or powers, including the gift of prophecy and healing. The Bible tells us that it was the Holy Spirit who made possible the virgin birth of Jesus and who came to him at his baptism. And it was the Holy Spirit who appeared to Mary and the apostles on the day of Pentecost to affirm the resurrection and the faith. This last Biblical event is important to the rationale and motivation of serpent handlers. The Christian Day of Pentecost occurs fifty days after Easter. In the Book of Acts, that first Pentecost marks the beginning of the Christian church and faith. On that first Day of Pentecost (in the New Testament), the Holy Spirit revealed himself as an omnipresent "helper" and "spirit of truth."

For many, the Holy Spirit is not the amorphous, paranormal force that his name implies.

He is a being, a personage, whom most Pentecostals believe is present within all who accept Christ as savior, but who exists in a more powerful form in those who live the most holy of lives. To those people the Holy Spirit may bestow gifts, including the ability to speak (spontaneously and unpredictably) in a language previously unknown to that person and/or previously unknown to any person. This gift of tongues, or speaking in tongues, is viewed as the ultimate blessing and a clear sign that an individual has attained a state of grace and recognition in the eyes of God.

Jesus explicitly mentions this sign in ▶

> **"** For many, the Holy Spirit is not the amorphous, paranormal force that his name implies. **"**

What Is a Serpent Handler? *(continued)*

Mark 16, and the fervent belief in its literal truth gave rise to the practice of handling poisonous snakes as an additional demonstration of devotion, purity, and faith. Since many (if not most) Pentecostals take the Gospels at their word, it was not much of a leap from speaking in tongues and healing the sick to handling snakes. Though the ending of Mark itself has been called into question (there are those who believe that part of it, including Mark 16, is a late edition forgery, and those who argue over the translation of the Greek word for "shall"), serpent-handling Christians adhere to its efficacy and validity.

Snake handling as a form of Fundamentalist Christian dogma has a relatively short and controversial history. It is not now, and never has been, a widely practiced ritual. Serpent handlers are few in number and exist on the fringes of the charismatic Pentecostals—Christians who believe in a very personal and visceral experience of God through the Holy Spirit. They experience God and his miracles literally and physically, and they believe that man can change his very nature toward sin through a spiritual and bodily connection to the Holy Ghost.

A man by the name of George Went Hensley is widely considered to be the father of serpent handling.

Hensley was a Pentecostal who, while preaching at the Dolley Pond Church of God in Grasshopper Valley, Tennessee, is reputed to be the first person to handle live rattlesnakes as a means of demonstrating the veracity of Mark 16. The accounts of the event itself vary, with some claiming 1909 and others 1910 as the date, and seem to have been embellished for dramatic effect. Several descriptions purported that a group of skeptics dumped a crate of live rattlesnakes at the foot of the pulpit during Hensley's sermon and that he reached down

66 A man by the name of George Went Hensley is widely considered to be the father of serpent handling. 99

16

into the pile without skipping a beat, bringing forth an armload of serpents, to demonstrate his belief that the signs mentioned by Jesus in Mark 16 would follow not just the apostles, but all believers within whom the Holy Spirit dwelled.

Though Hensley was most likely the first person to handle serpents in this manner and at this time, he was not the only one. A church in Sand Hill, Alabama, independently began using serpents in a similar manner in 1912. Hensley's church was renamed the Dolley Pond Church of God, *With Signs Following* after the Pentecostal Church of God denounced the practice, which began to spread throughout Appalachia (where it has remained in limited practice to this day). The actual number of people who attend revivals and sermons where serpents arc handled regularly is low, and the number of people who actually do the handling is lower still.

Estimates range that from between two thousand and three thousand people attend such churches, but the actual number is probably lower than that.

The descriptions of serpent handling and tent revivals found in this book are fairly accurate and are based on eyewitness accounts from both observers and participants. It would be superfluous to describe them in detail here. How they use snakes and run their prayer meetings vary from church to church, but this much is accurate and true: the snakes they use are wild and possess venom; they are not manipulated or drugged; they have not been defanged. Many handlers have been bitten, maimed, or killed. Some of these people also drink poisons such as strychnine and lye. Some handle fire, including blowtorches and hot coals, without being harmed. These practices have been witnessed and documented.

These believers, living a clean, simple life

> **❝** The actual number of people who attend revivals and sermons where serpents are handled regularly is low, and the number of people who actually do the handling is lower still. **❞**

What Is a Serpent Handler? *(continued)*

free of sin, attain a state of ecstatic rapture through singing and praying. They claim that the Holy Spirit enters their bodies in this state, providing them with protection from poison consumption and snake venom. They call this union the "Anointment of the Spirit," often described as being marked by an overwhelming sensation of joy. Protection from deadly things can only occur when the participants are in this state, and not all participants in such services attain it. In fact, most do not. Thus these practices are not attempted by all people, all the time.

The impetus for serpent handling, as referenced in the Book of Mark, comes from a passage which deals directly with the faith of the apostles—or the apparent lack thereof. When Jesus was taken from the cross after death he was placed in a tomb that was sealed with a large stone. The tomb was visited three days later by three women. Mary, mother of Jesus, Mary Magdalene, and Salome found that the stone had been rolled aside (a difficult endeavor requiring several men) and the body of Jesus was missing. Jesus then appeared to them on two separate occasions and bade the women to inform his disciples of his imminent return. When they doubted the women, Jesus appeared to the eleven (disciples) and delivered the lines cited from Mark 16 quoted above.

Serpent handlers believe that speaking in new tongues, protection from deadly things, healing the sick, and casting out demons are the signs that follow those who believe in Jesus and who live an exemplary life according to the rules laid out in the Bible. Thus it's more accurate to refer to them as sign followers than serpent handlers, for it is their emphasis on the signs of faith and their interpretation of the word "shall" which delineates them from their Pentecostal counterparts.

66 It's more accurate to refer to them as sign followers than serpent handlers. 99

Serpent handling never spread much farther than Appalachia, and in most states where it has been historically practiced there are laws prohibiting it. Yet it continues. The number of sign followers is infinitesimal compared to the explosion of Pentecostalism worldwide, though both groups believe fervently in the manifestation of the Holy Spirit. The main difference, however, lies in *whom* they believe may be given the powers ascribed to believers in Mark. For sign followers, any man, woman, or child has the potential to transcend his nature and receive the full blessings and powers of the Holy Sprit.

More Information on Snake Handling

Documentaries

THEY SHALL TAKE UP SERPENTS
John E. Schrader and Thomas G. Burton, producers
(Johnson City: Eastern Tennessee State University, 1973)

Thomas Burton's first documentary short on snake handlers, a fifteen-minute overview of the beliefs that prompt snake handlers to worship as they do.

THE JOLO SERPENT-HANDLERS
Karen Kramer, producer and director
(New York: Image Conversions Systems, 1977)

A thorough discussion of the snake handlers of Jolo, West Virginia, Kramer's documentary shows a snake hunt and an attempt to heal with prayers interspersed with interviews with the snake handlers.

CARSON SPRINGS: A DECADE LATER
Thomas G. Burton and Thomas F. Headley, producers (Johnson City: Eastern Tennessee State University, 1983)

Burton and Headley's focus is the consequences of the intense scrutiny on the congregation ten years earlier. Features two extensive interviews with Pastor Alfred Ball and Liston Pack (whose brother's death helped create all the attention in the early 1970s).

HOLY GHOST PEOPLE
Directed by Peter Adair, director and Blair Boyd, producer for Thistle Films (Contemporary Films: distributed by CRM/McGraw-Hill Films, 1984)

A fifty-minute in-depth look at the history of snake handling with extensive footage of interviews with believers and of worship services.

CHURCH VS. STATE: FOLLOWING THE SIGNS; A WAY OF CONFLICT
Thomas G. Burton and Thomas F. Headley, producers (Johnson City: Eastern Tennessee State University, 1986)

Burton and Headley briefly discuss the history of the practice. A detailed discussion of the legal battles and issues surrounding snake handling.

Articles and Links to Web Sites

"Woman Bitten by Snake at Church Dies," Lexington, Kentucky, *Herald-Leader*, November 2006, available at www.rickross.com/reference/snake/snake10.html.

"Snake Handlers Hang on in Appalachian Churches," *National Geographic*, July 2003, available at http://news.nationalgeographic.com/news/2003/04/0407_030407_snakehandlers.html.

"Snake Handlers Holiness Official Web Site," available at http://webspawner.com/users/snakehandlersorg.

"Serpent Handlers aka Snake Handlers and the Signs Following Movement," available at http://religiousmovements.lib.virginia.edu/nrms/Snakes.html.

"Snake Handlers and the Law," available at http://members.tripod.com/Yeltsin/law/law.htm.

"Snake Handling Pentecostal Sects," available at http://www.rickross.com/groups/snake.html.

Bible Gateway, a search engine for the Bible—a helpful tool in finding the passages specifically relevant to snake handling. The Bible Gateway site gives direct access to an online Bible, available at www.biblegateway.com.

More Information on Snake Handling
(continued)

Books

SERPENT-HANDLING BELIEVERS
Thomas G. Burton (Knoxville: University of
Tennessee Press, 1993)

**SALVATION ON SAND MOUNTAIN:
SNAKE-HANDLING AND REDEMPTION
IN SOUTHERN APPALACHIA**
Dennis Covington (New York: Penguin Books,
1995)

THEY SHALL TAKE UP SERPENTS
Weston LaBarre (New York: Schocken Books, 1969)

**THE PERSECUTED PROPHETS: THE STORY
OF THE FRENZIED SERPENT HANDLERS**
Karen W. Carden and Robert W. Pelton
(New York: A. S. Barnes and Co., 1976)

**FAITH, SERPENTS, AND FIRE: IMAGES
OF KENTUCKY HOLINESS BELIEVERS**
Scott W. Schwartz (Jackson: University Press
of Mississippi, 1999)

Don't miss the next
book by your favorite
author. Sign up now for
AuthorTracker by visiting
www.AuthorTracker.com.